DNA
DEMONS N ANGELS

WHAT TO EXPECT WHEN YOU'RE EXPECTING SOMETHING DIFFERENT

KATIE ZABER

ISBN: 9798520255536

Copyright © 2021 Katie Zaber
All rights reserved

Also By Katie Zaber

The Dalya Series

Ashes and Blood

Below Dark Waters

5 Weeks - The Pocono Mountains, Pennsylvania

I can't explain why a Caesar salad with vanilla ice cream—not on the side but on the salad—sounds downright amazing, but it does. The salty, tangy Caesar dressing coating the crunchy croutons and crisp lettuce mixed with sweet soft-serve vanilla ice cream seems like it would taste divine. Without further thinking, I head toward the food court in search of a fast-food establishment that can provide me with the crazy cravings I'm having.

Standing in line, the smell of food is making my head pound and my stomach growl. By the time I make it to the register, my temples are throbbing. I didn't realize I needed to eat so badly.

"Next," says the teenage boy working behind the counter. His orange hair is spiked in the front, but he still has a baby face. "Hi, what would you like to order?"

I give him my order and reach into my purse for my wallet. When I look back up, his face is distorted. Startled, I jump back. His face almost looks censored. Like a beige blur. I blink, hoping that his face is back to normal. It is except for the confused look he's giving me.

"Sorry. I thought I saw something." I really need to eat. I think this headache is turning into a migraine. I swipe my card and grab my tray.

The food before me looks heavenly. The sweet vanilla ice cream and the savory Caesar dressing smells amazing. By the time I find a table, my head is pulsing. In the corner of my eye, I keep seeing blurred faces, but when I look, they are normal. I have only experienced a couple of migraines with auras; usually I see dots or zigzags, not weird faces.

None of this is normal.

The migraine and the mixing of two vastly different food groups and eating them as if they go together like peanut butter and jelly—which makes me dry-heave thinking about *that* combination—isn't normal. But here I am, with a black takeout bowl containing a large Caesar salad and a Styrofoam cup of soft-serve vanilla ice cream. I salivate as I pour the frosty dessert onto the greens. A couple of people even turn to stare. Their eyes bug out as if asking if I'm really going to eat that extra creamy salad, but no one says a word. I giddily combine everything into one big blob and dig in.

The taste combination is euphoric. It needs more dressing and I happily add the spare packet. I dribble it on like it's the last topping on an ice cream sundae. Croutons are the sprinkles, the dressing is chocolate sauce, and the parmesan cheese is candied nuts.

I eat it all. Every last crumb. I scrape the bowl clean, devouring every ounce of dressing, and then sip on the pink lemonade I had bought to quench my thirst, getting rid of the copper taste that has been plaguing me for days. On and off through the last week, it's tasted like I've stuffed a handful of pennies into my mouth. Doctor says it's probably nothing but scheduled me to come in on Tuesday for a routine checkup and lab work.

The stink of spilled drinks, old cooked food, and human funk finds its way to my nose, triggering my stomach, threatening a second tasting. The filth is never purged from this establishment, mostly due to minimum wage cleaners and an idiotic decision. It surprised everyone two years ago when the mall chose to rip out the tile and replace it with carpet—the entire building, even the food court. It's as if they wanted to show off the stains embedded into the fibers after every messy transaction. Across the floor, there are specks of red, brown blotches, black smudges, and cloud-shaped puddles. They are all dry, but remain to haunt the ground. Foul memories plastered onto the carpet like a museum of accidents on permanent display.

I had come to the mall not for food, but for new bras. My current ones are feeling tight and uncomfortable. I woke up this morning and none of them fit. Each one felt like they were suffocating my tender breasts. They are all the same size and I've been a 34B since high school, but I don't know why today, they all felt snug.

Jim laughed while stretched out on the bed after getting out of the shower. The smell of citrus wafted off his damp brown hair. With a loving grin, he said we had both put on winter weight from our holiday takeout feasts. He added that I'd drop the pounds fast since we had started running again, and by summer, when we go to the Bahamas, I will turn heads with my bikini on, then he pulled me onto the bed and gave me a tender kiss.

Picking up my food tray, I walk to the garbage cans and feel my stomach twist from the putrid stench emanating from the bins. I place my tray down and run off without depositing my trash in fear of vomiting. I have to vacate the area before the bile comes up and out. I gag as I force it back down and luckily, I win the battle.

As I walk through the food court, my stomach settles and the euphoric aromas from the dessert counters make me forget I just ate—and almost tasted it twice. When I reach the Sweet Treats counter, I can't take it anymore and buy two sugar cookies, a double chocolate fudge cookie, and a dozen big vanilla bean cupcakes with hundreds of teeny tiny, decadent vanilla Madagascar seeds. Each speck represents a sweet flavor I yearn to enjoy, again and again. I want to buy more, but decide against it since I was just buying bigger bras. Stupid winter weight. Plus, I just made a couple trays of chocolate chip cookies this morning.

Treats and purchase in hand, I make my way to my car, dodging the idiots who don't look behind them while pulling out of their parking spots. There's nothing I'd like to do more than go home, take a bath, put on pajamas, and eat dinner while watching a movie on the couch, but that's not in the cards. The only thing I get to look forward to is eating Jim's delicious pot roast and gravy. His mother is making roasted garlic whipped potatoes, which will go great with the gravy; it's the only thing she can create besides Jim that isn't bitter. She and Jim's grandmother will outright ignore me; they live in misery together now that they are widows. Tonight, Jim's sister and her husband, along with the pack of hyenas they call children, will be joining us too. The things we do for the people we love.

By the time I pull into our driveway, all the cookies are gone and I've been eyeing the two extra cupcakes. I only needed to buy ten for dessert tonight, but I resolve to save them for an after-dinner treat with Jim tomorrow night. I will not eat both in one sitting. At least that's what I keep telling myself as I accidentally stick my finger in the frosting for the second time and lick the confectionary goodness off my pinky. Good thing I made a couple dozen cookies. No one will miss a few measly cookies if I snack on them before dinner.

I push the garage door button and limbo under it. Jim's classic black Mustang sits immaculate, protected from the elements, but that was part of the deal. He gets to park his car inside, but he has to clean my car year round, inside and out, and shovel the sidewalk and driveway when it snows. I still think I got the better end of the bargain.

He treasures that car and spends his weekends fixing it up, carrying on his father's legacy. When he's working on the car, he swears there's a presence, like his father is right alongside him. When he passed from cancer, Jim spent hours just sitting behind the wheel. Sometimes I would sit with him, but most of the time he wanted to be alone, and I gave him that space and time to heal. I married an extremely passionate, sentimental man and I'm happy about it. One of us has to be the loving, emotional type.

Before I can open the door into the kitchen, I can smell the roast cooking. "I'm home! When's dinner? It smells amazing," I say, taking off my shoes and hanging my purse on the rack with my coat.

The six-burner range is busy roasting dinner; it's going to take two-and-a-half hours to cook. When his sister comes in another hour, she will have plenty of room to heat the vegetable sides and whatever her brood of kids will eat this month. I think the boys are getting less picky, since they are growing an inch a day and need a steady supply of calories. The girls refuse anything except mac and cheese or chicken nuggets and fries. Maybe they will be adventurous this month and eat pizza. I think the youngest girl said it was spicy once, referring to the tomato sauce.

I handpick ten perfect cupcakes and arrange them on the center of a serving platter, then take the Ziploc bag of cookies out and plate them around the cupcakes. Before I put the tray in the fridge, I eat two cookies. The other two cupcakes, the ones I keep accidentally sticking my fingers in, I stash in the back of the fridge for tomorrow. Out of sight, out of mind… not really.

"What are you up to?" I yell down the hall, taking one last swipe of frosting before shutting the fridge door. It's too good to resist.

From the lack of noise, it sounds like Jim is in the game room. Most wives who hate sports would never agree to have green yardline carpet in one of the rooms, but that was another compromise. He got to design his fantasy sports room with all of his collectables and signed memorabilia, and I get to have my own quiet reading nook. We did some simple remodeling to soundproof the game room so I can't hear him and his friends shouting at a game when I'm trying to fall asleep.

Jim is a simple man with only a few passions in life: me, his car (which might be number one), sports, and cooking. Watching sports and playing them keeps his glory days alive. He still has an athlete's body, tall with broad shoulders, and he does his best to keep himself in shape by running, doing pull-ups, and his newest exercise: teeter ups, where he hangs upside down and does sit-ups, something I don't think I will ever be able to do.

I crack open the door and find him lounging on the leather couch with his feet up, watching sports stats or something I don't quite understand while thumbing his phone.

"Evie, I didn't hear you come in," he says, getting up to give me a kiss. "How was shopping?"

"A success. Got two new bras; damn, they were expensive. Hope that I won't have to buy any more and can lose this weight soon. They hurt," I say with a little whimper, rubbing my tender titties.

He cups both breasts gently and starts stroking them. "I'm sorry they're sore. After everyone leaves, I'll give them a nice, long massage. You should take a hot shower. Freshen up before the chaos begins. I have dinner prep under control."

"Why am I getting special treatment?" I ask, wrapping my arms around the crook of his neck, ruffling the bottom of his shaggy brown hair.

"Because you look extra cute," he says before sneaking a kiss. "Karen just texted. She said she's running ten minutes late."

"Typical. Your mom and grandma are going to be ten minutes early."

"Typical," he mocks.

I step up onto my toes and narrow my eyes, giving him my *don't piss me off face*, which he ignores and scoops me off my feet and blankets me with kisses as he sits back down on the couch. "Stop. I need to take a shower," I whine, cradled in his arms, but he doesn't stop so I begin to retaliate.

Buzz. Buzz.

We're interrupted by the vibration of Jim's phone. Since it's only an hour before his mother arrives, I can only guess that it's her. Most likely making sure I made something for dessert since that was my job and she always thinks I'm going to fail at it. She doesn't check on anyone else except for me, but at least she's better than Grandma.

"Escape," I proclaim while he's distracted by his phone, crawling off his lap and heading to the door. A shower right now sounds perfect. "What does Mom want?"

"She wants to know if you burnt the cookies," he says while chuckling to himself, knowing how much his mother drives me insane.

"Tell her they look like charcoal and I expect her to eat them all."

He rolls his eyes and types back a nicer response. She knows better than to text me with that passive-aggressive shit, but her son will deal with it.

The shower felt great, but the aroma of the roast is agony. The screaming children outside the bedroom welcoming me made me want to hibernate, even if my stomach is demanding food. It's not that I don't love my nephews and nieces; I love them from a distance, where their sticky fingers can't gunk up my stuff. Two sets of twins and both sets are a boy and girl. The four of them don't look alike, but they all act like rabid monkeys. They are only eleven months apart. We suspect the first pregnancy was planned; the second one, not so much.

"Aunt Evie, Aunt Evie," they cry out as soon as I appear in the hallway with my hands behind my back.

"Hey. How's it hanging, monkeys?"

They puff out their cheeks and scratch their armpits and heads, doing their best impressions, making me laugh. As much as I can't stand children full-time, they bring an occasional smile to my face.

"What's behind your back?" Suzy, the youngest girl, asks.

"What, this? Oh nothing," I say with a sarcastic grin, holding my arms and their surprise where they can't see.

"Let us see!" one of them squeals.

"Is it a present?" another asks.

"Is it for all of us?"

"What is it?"

They all giggle and shout over each other until I can't tell which one is talking. "Alright, alright. Here you go, you crazy apes."

I hand over the wrapped box. Kids like anything covered in cheap paper. They shred the paper in seconds, exposing the silly board game inside. It has a wacky trap and maze on the board and there's clay and color pencils and other fun things involved. I'm sure they'll play with it while they are here and maybe two other times before losing key pieces.

"Thank you, Aunt Evie," they say with gleeful smiles as they rip off the plastic wrap and open the box, sending its contents everywhere. It doesn't matter, as each child grabs a handful and scampers off to the living room to set it up.

"What did you get them?" Karen asks, standing in front of the oven. "You guys shouldn't buy them something every time you see them."

"Ah, it's just a board game to play while they are here. Keep them entertained besides just watching cartoons," I tell my sister-in-law.

I wouldn't say we don't get along. In order to disagree, we would need to talk, and no one in Jim's family really talks to me, not unless it's an emergency. I'd call us acquaintances at best.

"How's work going?" I begin the old routine of small talk with the in-laws.

She reaches into the fridge and grabs two cold beers. "Same old shit, different day," Karen says while popping the caps off. She and Roger both drink piss-poor beer that Jim refuses to buy. He offers them the finer qualities he drinks, but they don't like the strong flavors. They prefer watered-down beer that tastes like dirty water. I reach for the fridge door and grab an open bottle of white wine.

Jim's mother strolls out of the game room. Her white hair is cut shorter than last month; it's barely two inches long. She's still wearing her Sunday church outfit with her matching mother-of-pearl necklace. "Evie, did you gain weight?"

"We just started exercising again. I'll lose it fast."

She sighs. "Drinking already?"

It takes almost everything inside me not to crush the wine glass in my hand. What has it been, five seconds and

I'm already at my breaking point? "Hi, Joan. I figure Karen and I would cheer."

Joan looks at her daughter's beer and shrugs with an *oomph*, making my blood boil. "Well, some people don't get the chance to relax. She's so busy with the kids. It's her only break."

"And I thought we would cheer to that." I turn to Karen and we clink glasses. Karen knows her mother loves to fuck with me. Sometimes she teams up with me when her mother is acting extremely cruel. Sometimes.

Karen winks and says, "Cheers, sister."

Yes, that's what I'm talking about. Go, Karen.

Joan stalks out of the kitchen with a grimace, heading down the hallway to go find Jim and Roger, I'm sure.

"Where's Grandma hiding?"

Karen flips a platinum lock out of her face. "I think she went straight to the recliner; you know her spot."

"Oh good. I get to have a glass of wine before she berates me about the devil."

Karen rolls her eyes. "She's just jealous because your eyes turn that pretty shade of green and everyone in our family has eyes the color of shit."

I can't help but laugh. "I call them brown puppy dog eyes," I retort. "I love Jim's eyes." I sniff the air. It smells like sugar, maple syrup even. I lean over the island. "What are you making?"

"The kids won't eat vegetables unless I make them unhealthy. Maple-glazed carrots and honey sweet potatoes. Don't worry; my mom still made her garlic mash. I also made a side of green beans. I think I might get the boys to eat them since I added almond slices. One of their friends had them during snacktime and they have been on a salty nut kick since. I haven't told them yet that they are healthy."

"The carrots smell good. I might eat some of those tonight."

"Yeah, they are alright. The girls will eat them, but Roger hates the sweet. So I have to make green beans too or else he'll complain. I better bring him his beer. Keep an eye on the food for me?"

"I gotcha," I say and watch the boys wrestle over who cheated during the last round. Thankfully it's not my job to break it up.

"Oh, Trouble still lives here? I thought you had come to your senses and divorced the whore."

"Grandma!" Both Jim and Karen shout at their grandmother, who pretends to suffer from dementia when it covers her ass. She always waits until we are all seated at the dinner table to start her torture. I haven't been able to enjoy a meal with her as company since Jim introduced me to her.

His mother smiles while slicing her meat. "Mother, you shouldn't say such things."

She forgot to add *aloud*, but I know she's thinking it. I shovel food into my mouth instead of talking; that's my plan. Keep eating. If there's food in my mouth, it will make it harder to scream. And as soon as I finish this delicious meal, I get to eat another cupcake and a plate of cookies. At least that's something to look forward to.

"What's a whore?" one of the girls asks.

Grandma opens her mouth to talk but Joan grabs her hand, urging her to stop.

"Don't say that word. Add it to the *no* word list," Karen scolds the kids.

The oldest whispers that he will ask the boys at school. The others giggle. Their mom gives them the look, making them stare down at their dinner plates. The girls have sour expressions, like the food in front of them is poisonous. The boys look like there isn't enough food on the table.

I agree with the boys.

"Your eyes turned green again. The devil's in you, girl. He's wreaking havoc, using you as his weapon."

"Enough, Grandma. So Mom, Roger is looking at getting that promotion."

"Oh really? That's wonderful, dear. He works so hard."

"How can you fools break bread with the devil's puppet? Have you lost your faith? Or can you not see the hellish woman before you? The imp!"

"Okay, Grandma. It's time for you to watch your shows in the other room." Jim pulls his chair out from the table and escorts his grandmother to the game room. I think she does this on purpose so everyone can leave her alone and she can watch her shows in peace.

"Her eyes change; that's how you know. That's how you'll know," Grandma warns the family for the hundredth time about my wicked ways. It is part of the family tradition when we get together on the first Saturday of the month. His mother, Joan, criticizes my baking, Grandma accuses me of Satanic worshiping, and the kids leave behind a snaillike trail of sticky fingerprints. It makes for a miserable Saturday night and a cleaning day on Sunday. It will be over soon, I tell myself and gulp another mouthful of wine.

"Sorry, dear. Some people are just forgetful," his mother says while buttering a roll.

"She thinks I'm the devil's puppet. How the hell did she get that idea? Really, I'd love to know," I mumble.

Joan shrugs and takes a bite of the layered roll. She swallows, taking an extra-long moment before saying, "Some people can just sense evil better than others, I suppose."

6 Weeks - The Pocono Mountains, Pennsylvania

"How many of these do you need?" the pimple-faced teen with yellow and orange hair asks me while snapping her chewing gum, probably wishing she was on her phone.

"All of them," I tell her. The first box of tests must have been defective. Same with the second box. To make sure that I don't need any more after my third trip to the drugstore, I grabbed five more boxes. Just to be sure.

The first time I went to the drugstore this morning, my hair was brushed, my shirt was straight, and I had cared about my appearance. I assume by this point, after having the same woman ring me up three separate times, that I look insane. I imagine my brown hair is now a giant, frizzy mess, and when I last checked, my hazel eyes were completely green with a thin ring of brown.

"Maybe you should go to a clinic and get tested if you want to make sure."

Maybe you should mind your own business, twat. "That will be my next step."

Her blue eyes twitch, like there is something wrong. The color in her face drains. She clutches the counter as if it's keeping her standing upright. I grab my phone. She might be having a seizure or a brain aneurysm; her glassy eyes flutter in their sockets.

"Are you okay?" I ask. "Do you need help? Should I call an ambulance?"

She bares her teeth as her lips snarl like a rabid animal. A distorted voice comes out of her mouth, not what she sounded like moments ago. "You know what you must do. Don't make the wrong choice. It's imperative."

Baffled, it takes me a moment to respond besides blink. "Excuse me?"

"You know what's right and wrong. You know…" the teen says before gagging and coughing, her head in her hands. When she raises her head, the rosy color in her cheeks is back. Her swirling eyes have stopped and look normal. "They also talk, at the clinics. Sometimes it's good to talk," she says. Hacking in between words like she has a tickle in her throat, she pats her chest. "To someone."

My mouth hangs open as I stare at the young woman who just had an entire separate conversation with me. It's then I notice that the cashier's eyes are dilated. I shake my head and put my phone back in my purse. False alarm.

Now, I understand. She must be on some type of drug and it just kicked in. Wow, how professional. She can't be over eighteen, and she has a midday shift while school is in session. Maybe she should rethink her choices and talk to someone about her mistakes and how she's fucked up her own life. "It's always good to vent."

She musters a smile and bags my purchase, giving me a nod. "Try to have a good day."

"You too." I'm polite to her, even if I want to scream at her until my voice breaks.

I climb back into my Civic and chug another bottle of water so as soon as I get home, I can barricade myself in the bathroom and pee some more. It's better than throwing up again.

I can't stop peeing. That's good for all the boxes of pregnancy tests I've bought. All the boxes contain two tests. The instructions are simple and straightforward, but I read them ten times. I check the expiration date, even though I checked it in the store. Then I take a clean cup and pee.

Earlier this morning, I peed directly onto the device, but realized that if I wanted to keep testing, I would need a sample.

Unwrapping the test is easy. Inside, there's a little white piece of plastic. The tip looks like a piece of stiff cotton that sucks up the pee. Then, based on my hormones, it reveals if I'm pregnant in the minuscule result window.

Such a tiny little device. It's so simple, but so life-altering. For some, it brings joy. For others, terror.

So far, the results are eleven yeses, two nos, and one that seems to be broken. It's the two nos that give me some type of hope, if any, that I am not pregnant.

I shouldn't be pregnant. Yes, Jim and I have a very healthy sex life, but he's been snipped and cauterized. I have less than a one percent chance of Jim getting me pregnant. It's almost impossible to get pregnant after a vasectomy. Almost.

If it weren't for the odd symptoms that started, I wouldn't even have thought twice about my period being late. It has an irregular schedule and comes when it wants. Sometimes it's every other month or six weeks, then just to mess with me, it will come every three weeks. There is no rhyme or reason to it; I was told that some women just have a random flow. But the constant throwing up, craving odd food combinations, noticing smells, and my boobs hurting and growing... there are too many telltale signs for me to ignore the insane possibility that I might be pregnant.

The urge to vomit is overwhelming, but that's from anxiety now. Morning sickness has had me glued to the toilet for the last three days.

I stare down at the last test strip that says I'm pregnant. I shake my head, thinking I need more tests. These can't be right. They just can't.

Instead of jumping into my car and hightailing it down to the pharmacy, again, for the fourth time today to get judged by some high teenage cunt, I pick up my phone. "Melisa."

"Hey, girl. What's up? Is something wrong?"

It's hard to talk or put into words what is happening. Every time I open my mouth, nothing comes out. My mouth is dry, but I don't think water will help. How do I even begin to tell her one of my nightmares has become reality?

"Evie, what's wrong?"

"Remember how Jim had a vasectomy three years ago?"

"Yeah... what about it?"

"I think it reversed."

"What? Are you sure? That's nearly impossible!"

I snap a picture of all the pregnancy tests lined up on the bathroom counter and zoom in on a clear *yes*. "Check your messages. I just sent you a picture."

"Oh, damn. Um, have you talked to Jim?"

"No. I'm terrified."

"Now, I'm not going to judge, but honey, did you cheat?"

"No! Never! I love Jim."

"And we can rule out any public toilet seats..."

"Bitch," I mutter.

She chuckles. "Well, then you have nothing to worry about. These things happen and since it reversed, you might be able to sue for big bucks."

Sweat builds on my neck; my stomach does a loop-de-loop as I drag my fingers through my frizzy hair. "Something feels wrong, so wrong."

"Evie, you're pregnant. It's not going to feel right," Melisa says with a laugh. "Girl, you're going to have a little baby. I'm going to be an auntie."

"Ah, don't call yourself that just yet. I don't know. This was never in our plans. We never wanted children. Jim's going to flip. I'm flipping. I can't have a kid, Melisa. I can't."

"Calm down. You aren't having a kid today and if you don't want to, you have that option too. But what you need to do right now is breathe. Drink some water and eat something."

"Morning sickness blows."

"I bet. Have you thought of how you're going to tell Jim?"

"Hide it from him and hope he doesn't notice?"

"Everild."

"Shut up."

"You can do this. He loves you and if his body accidentally rebuilt the tunnel and is pumping little fuckers out, then it's not your fault. It's not his either. If anyone's at fault, it's the doctor who did the sloppy procedure."

"I don't want to go to a hundred doctors' appointments or court. None of this sounds fun."

"There are some good parts to it."

"Name one," I dare her.

"Your hair and nails get real strong and healthy."

"Yeah, you're going to have to do better than that."

"I'll come up with a detailed list later. I wish I could chat and you know I'm a phone call away, but my boss is riding my ass to get this report in. Can we talk after you drop the news? Tell me how it goes?"

"When you say *drop the news*, you make it sound even more dramatic."

She sighs. "Love you, girl. Talk to you later."

"Love ya," I say and hang up and look back at the odd row of white tests arranged like dominos stacked against me, ready to crash down on the countertop with their yeses and plus signs.

Tell Jim. How am I supposed to tell him that our biggest fear, the one thing neither of us wanted, is happening?

Neither of us would make good parents. We'd rather spoil ourselves with vacations and fun gadgets for the house than spend our savings on ungrateful brats. It was a joint decision. Plus, any time we want to remind ourselves of the reason we don't want to be parents, we visit his sister and feel we made the right decision.

God damn it, I don't want to tell him. I fear this conversation more than any other conversation I have ever had. The birds and the bees discussion from my over-sexual, hippie parents who had pictures, made posters, and offered to show me positions—with their clothes on, thankfully—wasn't half as bad as this will be. And to be clear, that conversation left me with some permanent scars.

Ding. Jim texts me.

The instinct to look at my phone when I hear his ringtone is instant. Like Pavlov's dog hearing a dinner bell, salivating at the sound. My response to my phone going off right now, from him, in this moment, makes me pick up my phone and smash it into the wall. The screen cracks, but it still works. It still displays the message. A kind and loving message. A message from a lover and partner.

How are you feeling? I'm thinking roasted chicken, sweet peas, and egg noodles. Are you feeling well enough for dessert? XOXO

I stare at the blank screen, unable to type a single letter. I want to eat everything and throw up on you at the same time, Jim. How does that sound to you? And for dessert, I'll shatter our lives and destroy everything we have worked hard for and built together.

Fuck, it sounds like the perfect night.

DNA – Demons N Angels

※

The rest of the day, I've been rocking back and forth when I can bring myself to sit. If I had black ink on my shoes, the trail all over the house from my pacing would look like a *Family Circus* cartoon. I thought about walking up the walls for a moment, but I instead ventured outside, doing laps around the property.

With my mind racing, I spent the day looking at our house, inspecting every element to see if it is baby safe, asking myself, what does *baby safe* mean? Are the stairs safe for toddlers? There are seventy-two knee-height outlets in the house. That's a lot of plastic covers to buy. The kitchen has rows of cabinets lining the wall and island; we would need at least a dozen safety latches. Probably two dozen to be safe. And ones for each toilet.

The house isn't baby ready and had never planned to be. It would need more time to prepare for such a huge overhaul. I need an overhaul. I'm not prepared. I'm not ready.

I don't want this.

From my serene nook, which has become a tense lookout spot, I watch for Jim's car to pull up. I've researched all the cute ways a mom-to-be tells her partner that they are expecting. Making dinner with baby carrots, mini corncobs, mini meatballs, all the mini baby-sized food you can think of. A t-shirt announcing that we are expecting. Writing a love note with a pregnancy test wrapped inside. If I wanted to wait to tell him, I could order so many different gimmicky novelty items.

But how do you tell your partner if you consider it bad news?

Maybe a card? It would have to be a condolence card, but I don't think Hallmark makes *sorry I'm pregnant* cards. They should start; they would have at least one customer.

I hear his car rumbling down the street before I see it. He slows down, sees me in the window, and smiles. Like a chain reaction, I smile back. I always do when I see him. I watch his car pull into the driveway and into the garage. The motor on the garage door kicks on and I hear a car door open and close.

T-minus two minutes to detonation. He will know the second he sees me that something is wrong. I can't keep a straight face. I can't lie. It might take a minute or two of coaxing to tell him, but it will happen.

Every speech I've rehearsed sounds dumb. Every syllable sounds insincere. Every conversation devolves into a dark, accusatory, finger-pointing argument.

"Honey, how are you feeling?" he asks. The freezer door opens. "I stopped and picked up ice cream, if you're feeling better."

"Um, not better." I walk into the kitchen and watch him put away his thermos and lunch box. "I'm afraid it's worse than just a stomach virus."

He turns around to face me. "What's wrong? Did you see the doctor?"

I try to smile. Maybe if I make it a joke, he won't flip out as much. Comedy normally helps ease the tension. I shrug and say, "It's nothing that nine months won't take care of."

He cocks his head to the side, confused. "What do you mean?"

I take out one of the pregnancy tests and place it on the island counter.

His brown eyes pop out of his head. It takes him a few moments to say anything, even if his mouth keeps opening and closing. "Are you sure you're pregnant? The tests can be false," he mumbles, picking up the white device. His forehead wrinkles as he glares at the test, then at me.

"I'm sure the girl at the pharmacy thinks I'm insane for buying out all the tests this morning."

He squints at the white device. "But I had a vasectomy."

"It's a one-out-of-a-thousand chance but... apparently we are one of those couples."

He blinks his eyes like he's remembering how to use them. "Did you cheat on me?"

"No, never. I promise," I say, walking to him. "This is your stubborn, bratty little bugger." With my hands on my stomach, I ask, "What do we do?"

Jim slumps down on a stool with his mouth hanging open. "Pregnant? I'm, I'm just..."

"Shocked? Freaked out?"

He nods and lets out a tiny laugh, then reaches for me. "We didn't want this."

"Nope. Not at all. But somehow, this little bean formed. It's like a miracle baby that we don't want. What do we do?" I close the gap between us. He uncurls his fingers and places them on my stomach.

"I'm going to be a dad?"

"Yes, if you want to. Melisa said we should probably call the doctor who performed the surgery."

"Oh man, we could sue. This little problem might be a solution to living an easier life. I've read stories of settlements for half a million, even more. We could do so much with that money and set the kid up for life. I guess it wouldn't be that bad, being parents. What do you think? Do you want to? There's always..."

Tears stream down my face. I'm not sure if they are joyful or not. "I don't know. It could work. We could be a happy family. It's terrifying." The thought of having a family that is like the one that raised me only adds to the tears. I will never be like my parents.

He stands up and embraces me tightly. "Don't worry. We'll get through this together. We're going to be parents to one hell of a strong kid! My god," he says, laughing. "The willpower it must have."

I can't help but feel more terrified about having a child with that much raw willpower; the teenage years will not be fun.

"I'll call my doctor in the morning. No wonder your boobs are getting bigger. You also started looking different, but I didn't know what it was. You grow more beautiful every day. And your sense of smell. That should have been the giveaway."

"I think we need to bleach the garbage can. It just doesn't stop reeking."

"I'll do that tonight. Don't worry about it. I'll get all the stinky junk out of the house." He stops in his tracks. "We'll have to renovate the third bedroom. There's a lot of stuff to do."

"I'm only five or six weeks. We don't even know if I'll make it past the first trimester. There's plenty of time." I pause, still unsure. "Are you positive you want to do this?"

He looks me up and down. "I didn't know I wanted this until right now. It's terrifying, unexpected, but this child, it feels right."

I'm glad one of us feels right.

7 Weeks - The Pocono Mountains, Pennsylvania

I hate this pharmacy. I hate how many times I've been to it recently. I hate how convenient it is. I hate the fluorescent lights and lame music. I hate the smell of menthol Bengay and cardstock. And above all, I hate the snarky high-as-a-kite teen who seems to only work when I need something.

"Huh, and I thought you weren't trying to get pregnant," she says as she scans the at-home sperm check kit.

Bitch. I won't respond. I won't open my mouth. If I do, I can't be responsible for the expletive diatribe that will break free.

The night before Jim called his doctor, we spent it in each other's arms, going over everything, even down to names. We felt united in a way that we have never felt before as a couple. Even deeper in love.

That changed after he spoke to his doctor. His asshole doctor planted a seed of suspicion and it has grown over the last few days into a towering beanstalk. All the doctor had to ask was, "Are you sure it's yours?" His friends couldn't have helped, egging him to make sure since the chance wasn't in his favor.

This morning, he gave me the duty of procuring the test today. That's about all he said. Our conversations have become brief and sharp. Sharp enough to pierce both our hearts at any given time. Brief enough to make me question if the conversation is actually over or not, along with our relationship.

I shove my credit card into the chip reader and wait for it to approve the transaction. The register opens with a chime; the cashier closes it with a swing of her hips, rips off the receipt, tosses into the bag, and passes it to me. "Good luck," she says, offering me love and peace when all I want to do is slam her face into the counter.

"Thanks," I somehow mutter and nod while turning away to leave the pharmacy once again, hoping to never return. There must be another local drugstore nearby.

For the last week, Jim hasn't drunk a beer or coffee to prep for the test tonight. It's simple. We will know the results in ten minutes. Even though I know I didn't cheat, I can't help but feel nervous. It's stupid really. I haven't been with another man since meeting Jim, but for some inexplicable reason, I'm edgy. Maybe it's because this shouldn't be happening in the first place and the fact that it is has me freaked out.

After we have dinner tonight, he'll take the test. Suddenly, the thought of food doesn't sound appetizing. He said something about spaghetti and meatballs this morning. I told him I'd pick up the test after I left the office, and then he drove the Mustang to work. I drove myself, something I've been doing since he talked to that damn doctor. It's a lonely commute. I miss my driving companion, my partner.

Fuck. I should have never told him. I should have just taken care of it.

An acute pain hits me in the abdomen for a split second, then dissipates. Sorry, baby. It's nothing personal, but I don't really want you, and I don't think your father does either. We tried to prevent you, but somehow you still wanted to be made. Why? I'm not going to be a good mother and I think about terminating you daily for selfish reasons. What kind of loving mother would do that? Why is your willpower to live this strong?

DNA – Demons N Angels

※

It's weird. I don't remember opening this Pandora's box of nostalgia, hidden in the spare bedroom. Memories are strange. So are pictures. It's weird how a smell, sound, or photograph can trigger a memory. How a simple odor can take you back decades to your childhood. How a picture can bring you to tears. How a certain fruit can make you repulsed for reasons no one can fathom.

"Come on, Bee, eat your blueberries. It is part of your birthday present, your own plot to grow as many berries as you would like," my father said, rolling the plump purple balls in his hands. "Mom will make you a blueberry cake with berry frosting and we'll sing happy birthday. She even got you that number eight candle you wanted."

I wouldn't give my parents the satisfaction of eating a single berry in front of them. I hated their laid-back parenting approach, as if they had all the time in the world to coax me into doing what they said. The amount of times I spat into their faces, hacked a loogie right into their eyes, was countless. And not once did they punish me. Never did they raise a hand when I slapped theirs. Not once did they yell when I purposely poured their precious golden honey all over their marijuana plants and destroyed two expensive products at the same time. No, they didn't believe in punishing children.

"They will make you grow big and strong. Try the strawberries and blackberries. Come on, eat a handful of each," my mother cooed.

Shaded by a willow tree on the large farm that we had occupied for a few years—their cash crop wasn't legal—I sat at the picnic bench, refusing to eat their latest harvest. It's not that I didn't enjoy the berries. I knew they had been organically grown. No pesticides or poisonous gases were used in the growth process. Just fresh cow shit, topsoil, worms, water, and seeds. Worms are important. If your garden doesn't have worms to tunnel, eat, shit, and repeat, nothing will grow. It will be a barren wasteland where you place seeds to die. A seed cemetery, or that's what my parents had told me.

But none of that mattered. It was summer, which meant two things that I hated: festivals and farming.

Thinking back, any child might be excited about going to festivals all summer with their intoxicated parents. As a teenager, I enjoyed it more, but as an eight-year-old kid, I hated it. All I wanted was a brother or sister. A sibling. It didn't matter what kind, but someone else to help share the pain of being *their* child. But my parents said having one child was selfish enough. That having two might result in overpopulating the world. Which would speed up global warming, resulting in less food, epic floods, millions of homeless and starving people, with billions dead. So no second child. It was as if they thought China had the right idea, but they wanted to take it to the next level and force half the population of parents to have girls and the other boys. Make it equal. A man for every woman.

My protests were normally simple and not as damaging as the honey incident, but I did them daily. I think my parents were proud of how stubborn I was. Never bending my will. They knew I loved berries. The second they made a berry patch on their farm for me was the moment I told them they tasted like poop. Maybe they even knew I had sneaked out late at night to my patch and plucked the little treats in secrecy. They must have because of the cameras and guards lumbering about.

But I never ate a berry out of my garden in front of my parents. It wasn't what I wanted from them. Homeschooled and kept on the farm for most of my childhood, with exceptions for festivals—we didn't *do* family. No aunts, uncles, cousins, or grandparents—all I wanted was to be around children my own age. But they told me that was an immature attitude and I should be happy to be given the opportunity to live freely with them and respected as a peer, not treated as a child.

I didn't want respect. I wanted a friend. Not to be alone.

Like I am now, banished to the spare bedroom. The furniture in this outcast room has a very fine layer of dust. There is an armoire that holds old clothes that no longer fit us but are nostalgic. College sweaters with football team emblems, plaid miniskirts, my black combat boots, Jim's ufos, various concert tees; it's like a time capsule from our high school and college days.

Next to the door is a dresser, full of clothes that we still use. Right now, it's filled with winter clothes; I switched everything out when we started to run again. In the middle of the room, in between the two dusty nightstands, is the queen-sized bed from my old apartment that isn't in awful shape, but we bought a king for the master bedroom when we moved into the house. There are filing boxes in the corner filled with photographs, books, records—the last bits of things we never got around to opening when we moved. Bits of paper that don't have any daily significance but contain sentimental value so it's forbidden to throw them away, forgotten until needed.

This is where Jim wants me to sleep for the time being. He said this is where I belong until he knows he can trust me, or if he should. Banished to the storage room that holds all the items we don't use and want out of the way. The forgotten room, where we had placed everything we wanted to forget about. Including the rare photographs from my childhood, all spread out across my bed.

Katie Zaber

My parents didn't believe in pausing the moment to capture it on film very often. Instead, they said I should live in the moment and try to memorize the feeling it gave me. The child pictured in all the photographs doesn't appear happy. In most of the pictures, she's reading a book alone. There's never a smile on her face or on her parents' odd images; they were clearly intoxicated. No friends, no cousins, no neighbors. No one was ever playing with the little girl, swinging on the tire swing all by herself.

She was always alone.

8 Weeks - The Pocono Mountains, Pennsylvania

My baby is the size of a raspberry, or at least that is what I read in my baby book. I downloaded it last night onto my e-reader. Every week it tells me how big it is, what symptoms I could be having, and what is growing. Right now, the baby's eyes are growing retinas. It is forming a nose, lips, and eyelids. The tail had shrunk away and weird limbs in odd spots have sprouted. They say at eight weeks, the baby starts to look less like a reptile baby hybrid and more human, but the pictures still look alien. Like it shouldn't be in me, growing.

I say *my* baby because Jim is now convinced it isn't his, though he said he would wait for the DNA test results before doing anything drastic. But he mentioned the D word after finding out he has virtually no sperm. The test indicated low to zero, but that still means that maybe, just maybe, one or two squeezed through the dismantled tubes and swam to freedom.

I'm officially eight weeks pregnant and can get a genetic DNA pregnancy test. Melisa sits next to me in the doctor's office waiting room. Jim refused to come with me and went to a separate appointment for his cheek swab. When was the last time we were in the same car together? I can't remember.

I'm uncertain if it was because he thought there would be a chance of seeing the little raspberry on a monitor and he didn't want to fall in love with it in case it isn't his, or if he had already decided it isn't and doesn't want any part in this. I don't know. He won't talk to me anymore.

Melisa stares at the redheaded nurse behind the counter and gives her a cute grin, twirling a chocolate curl. She just got out of another six-month relationship and is currently on the rebound, looking for a new girlfriend. In another week or so, she will find one and they will fall in love for the next three to six months before it goes up in flames, sometimes for real. That one woman, Jennifer, another redhead, had set Melisa's condo on fire while Melisa was on a post-breakup four-day cruise. Melisa got the phone call while docked in Aruba that her home was cinders. I had gone over with Jim to inspect it while she figured out a way to get back, but there was nothing salvageable. Everything was burnt or had such bad smoke damage, it could never be used again.

Some of her past lovers have been a little more on the stalky side, really clingy and obsessive. Most never understand our friendship. How we can be so close, finishing each other's sentences like the perfect couple who have been together for years but don't have sex. Some accuse us of being together secretly or say it's not fair to be so connected. That our friendship doesn't have room for her to have a girlfriend, but I think they are all jealous. In the past, when she would introduce a new woman, I'd bring my husband just to make it clear. That usually helps until Melisa and I go off on a tangent about some inside joke and forget about everyone else in the room as we laugh our asses off.

I don't know. Maybe in a different lifetime, it could have been different between us, but I had my college experience and I never felt compelled to do that again. No woman has ever really turned me on. I've only been attracted to men. So, even though anyone seeing Melisa and me out together would assume we are a couple, we will never be. But we will always be closer than sisters. We are soul mates, just not the sexual kind.

"She's sexy. You think she's single? Hmm. On the way out, I'll try to snag her number," Melisa says. A whiff of cocoa butter hits my nostrils as she turns to ask me about the nurse who won't pay any attention to her.

"She's rocking a ring," I say, pointing. Melisa knows she doesn't have a chance with the nurse, but she's trying to distract me from the reason we are here. She's also here to keep me from running out of the doctor's office and driving far away. God, I hate needles. I hate all of this. "I swear, if one more person says something about me giving birth to a Christmas present, I'm going to start swinging."

"Evie, stop it. The nurse doesn't know what's going on with you personally. Some of these women would *love* a Christmas baby to parade around and dress up as a present or ornament or star or any of those weird things modern moms like to do because everything has to be a picture on social media." Melisa rolls her eyes, finished with her mini rant.

I don't want a baby. I've never wanted that kind of responsibility or someone feeling how I felt as a child, a burden. None of this was part of my plan. I just wanted to have fun and live life freely. The thought of planning out a Christmas baby to impress my imaginary friends at the next social lunch-in serving finger sandwiches and tea makes my stomach flip. No, that's not the life I wanted, and it's not the life I'll live. Melisa is the only friend I need and the only one I've ever been able to count on.

We have already discussed the what-ifs, if it isn't Jim's child. How I would move in with her and she would be the best auntie to my little raspberry. I keep telling her it's not possible for me to be pregnant with anyone else's child, but she keeps replying that she isn't judging. I'm uncertain if she believes me or not. But it's nice to know she will never judge me.

Even with her here, I feel alone and outnumbered as I sit and wait for my name to be called so they can take my blood and I can finally prove I haven't cheated. That I'm faithful to my husband. Afterward, he will finally hug me and tell me everything will be all right. Then Melisa will start planning a baby shower for me. She has been pestering me about what kind of theme I want for the shower. Asking how I would decorate the nursery if it's a boy or a girl, but the truth is I can't begin to think about that. Some little part of me is terrified that the baby isn't Jim's, but I also know that it is beyond impossible. The sperm had to come from somewhere and he is the only man I've slept with for the last six years.

"Everild Beeatrix Petersen." A nurse straddling the threshold of the waiting room door calls my name, but I'm too nervous to move.

"Everild," Melisa says with a snicker, knowing I hate my full name. "Come on. I'll come with ya," she says, grabbing my hand so I can't flee. Bitch knows me too well.

"Well, that was easy. Only a little bit of blood drawn—and you'll have the results in three to five days. That's fast. But damn, I wish it was immediate so you and Jim could go back to normal," Melisa says as we walk back to her car, parked two blocks away from the doctor's.

"I just want this over and done with. I want everything the way it was." In my heart, I know it won't ever be the same.

A greasy-haired man with a mangy beard shuffles past. A junkie, from the looks of his face and the track marks on his arms. Big black bags hide under his bloodshot eyes; his skin is jaundiced and covered in welts that resemble pepperoni. The ripped red and brown flannel shirt he has on looks like it hasn't seen a washing machine in months, if ever. I give him a polite smile as we walk by. I always feel bad for those who end up like him. Was it mental illness, lack of support, or desperation that led him here?

The junkie halts. His facial expression is one of recognition, but how would he know me? Damn it. Does he know my parents? His pale gray eyes don't leave my face as he twitches, appearing to be on the verge of a seizure. Suddenly, he releases a wicked laugh that gives me instant goose bumps. Not like an evil villain, but like an insane person ready to kill indiscriminately.

"The devil is alive in you! The devil is alive in you! I see it in your eyes!" He points at me, rambling, obscure words. "Hail, our mother queen! Hail her prince! Rejoice! The end is near!" Then he lets out a sinister laugh that makes my blood run cold.

"Shut the fuck up, you freak!" Melisa screams at the insane man who rocks on his heels with his hands over his head, yelling *hallelujah*.

I run to Melisa's car. She takes a step and then turns around to make sure he isn't about to attack us while she's huffing at him. Every few steps, she checks over her shoulder to make sure he isn't stalking us. The whole time, her right hand is wrapped around her pepper spray. She's got good aim. He still stands in the middle of the sidewalk, arms outstretched, chanting in tongues.

My hands tremble against my stomach as if instinctually protecting my unborn child from the lunatic. I didn't think to place my hands there. Even in the car, driving down the highway, miles away, they are still holding my belly.

I don't know why.

I look into the vanity mirror in the passenger visor—my eyes are bright green, like jade stones. All I can hear is Jim's grandmother's judgmental voice and those eerie words.

Katie Zaber

9 Weeks - The Pocono Mountains, Pennsylvania

"I need you out," he says before he can hang up his cell phone.

The lighting in the kitchen is cheery. A pot of chicken noodle soup simmers on the stove, making the house smell like a home. There's music playing in the background, an upbeat, fast dance song that is the latest club sensation. It doesn't help set the mood. If it were silent and dark, it would be better. I would be able to hear our hearts breaking and our relationship fracturing. Even a passing thunderstorm would help create an accurate vibe. Maybe it would feel more like reality and less like a sick joke.

Bleak hopelessness pounds against my chest. That was the end of this brief conversation. The end of us. Those were the only words he needed to speak. There's no way I can reply.

He looks funny, angrily swiping the touchscreen on his phone to end the call. I wish we had a landline phone that he could slam down in a fit of rage. His fingers twist around the smartphone, turning white at the knuckles; he's probably wishing it was my neck.

I choke. I gag on words to say, but none are adequate. None are sufficient to say how sorry I am. How I myself don't understand. But adding that will only make me look worse. Saying I don't know how this happened will only further exacerbate the situation. Like a murderer who says *I don't know how the knife ended up in my hand while I was patting her on the back* as blood gushes from the wound, down the outreached hand still clenching the blade.

So I nod and text Melisa SOS, come immediately with an empty car.

She knew that there was a chance I would be sending her that horrible message. Did she anticipate it? She keeps saying she won't judge, but it's getting to me that she doesn't believe me. However, how can I expect her to believe something unrealistic? Something that I don't understand. How is he not the father? How?

I know I didn't cheat. I know I would never hurt Jim that way. All I'm left with is crazy ideas of how this happened: I was raped and blocked it out, I'm insane with split personalities, or my favorite, I'm the Virgin Mary reincarnated. They say Jesus will come again. Who better to convert than a sinner who doesn't believe in religion in the slightest?

Still nodding, I watch the three dots appear on the screen. They tell me Melisa is typing a response as I walk down the hallway to the room I've been staying in. My old luggage is in the closet. It will make packing easier if I can get the bulk of it... I can't even finish the thought without gasping. I'm packing my life away.

Our wedding pictures hanging on the walls insult me, scream *whore* at me. I feel like one, but I don't remember committing the crime. I glare at the photo. My dress was elegant but simple, no button, no frills, just a layer of soft white lace over a sheath dress with a small train. I didn't want anything bulky. I wanted to move freely and be comfortable. That was more important to me than fashion. Jim looked so handsome in his black onyx suit and tie. He didn't wear a vest. I wanted him to be comfortable as well. My fingertips graze over our smiles. I thought we would always look that way together. Happy.

What the fuck, baby?

I'm sorry, green olive.

I sigh and continue down the hallway, touching my belly. Don't you know that green olives are disgusting, little one, even more now that I'm pregnant? But don't take offense. Even though you are the size of a vile olive, I don't hate you. I don't know if I ever could, even if part of me wants to blame you for everything and scream at you until my voice goes hoarse. I know that you don't deserve it. I'll call you an innocent bystander. You didn't know what you did to me the moment your life sparked into existence, how you destroyed mine.

I take my dark green luggage out. Jim has the navy blue set. We've used them three times. When going on vacation, we normally pick somewhere tropical. A nice warm, sandy resort. Where were we going this year? Bahamas? I believe the tickets are refundable; I'm always worried something will happen, and this time, it did. Maybe Jim will go all by himself as a bachelor. Won't that be nice?

I open the dresser drawer that has all of my winter clothes, take out a hoodie, roll it into a ball, gag my mouth, and let out a suffocated scream. The lights flicker but stay on. How long was that? A few seconds? A minute? Is it possible to scream for a minute? No, I don't think so. If I could scream for a year, it still wouldn't release the anger, the frustration, the depression, the anguish bubbling up in me.

No running footsteps. He either didn't hear me or doesn't care. Tears pour down my face because I care. I love him. Why is this happening?

I unzip the suitcases on my bed to see how much of my life I can stuff into them. I shake my head—I don't think it will fit. How could it? Clothes will. Yeah, it will be easy enough to sort through what I don't want to wear again or can't. There should be a donation pile. Things a mother would never wear or could. But how am I supposed to cram my life into a couple boxes and bags and be done? How does one do that? Close a chapter on your life that easily. It doesn't compute.

I don't have many things that I can outright call mine. I never had any hobbies besides reading. Really, I don't need to have anything else in my life. My e-reader is always fully charged and ready for a new adventure any time I grow bored with reality. Actual books are too heavy and my reading nook is too small to add enough shelves to include a fraction of my prized stories, even though I have always dreamed of having a personal library with ceiling-to-floor shelves jam-packed with an array of books. Mostly fantasy and sci-fi, but really all elements of fiction, and I have been known to get lost learning about certain eras in history.

But the truth is I don't have many interests. Maybe gardening, but that was to keep our home looking nice. It was more of an adulting thing. Most of the stuff in the home was given to us at *our* shower. We chose to do one together and not make it feminine or lame with all those dumb games, but a big backyard barbeque with lawn games and a local band. A majority of our household appliances came from that day. But none of them feels like mine. I never used the air fryer to cook a meal. I never used the vacuum sealer or mowed the lawn. I used the vacuum and mop, but those are easily replaced, plus Melisa has them already. On top of that, I don't desire any of it. Instead, I feel like I should be punished and everything should be taken away.

I've finished going through the spare bedroom. I'm now sorting a mound of clothes into two piles while sitting in the middle of what was our bed, for the very last time. Clothes that fit me now: sweats, t-shirts, stretchy clothing that will be comfortable for the next couple months until I can no longer fit into them, and clothes that fit normal-size me. The other pile is for outfits I'm not sure I'll wear again.

They say once you have a kid, you never get your shape back. Half the clothes that fit normal-size me, I toss into the donation pile. There's little to no chance once I'm a mother that I'll be wearing any of those outfits. Plus, I will never fit into them again. Skintight shirts and painted-on leggings—they will reveal too much damage from this little wrecking ball.

For the moment, I'm alone in what was our old bedroom. He didn't change or move any of the items around since he kicked me out. I haven't been in this room for weeks, which feels like an eternity. Next year, how will it feel?

If anything, the room looks less used. Only his half of the room has been occupied and the other half, my half, has been left untouched. The sheets on my side aren't wrinkled or appear slept in. Jim always makes the bed, so it's hard to tell unless you study it up close. An inch away, like I am.

I'm trying to remember and engrave everything into memory. Think of every moment we happily spent together in this room. The passion. The playful games we'd lose ourselves in. The time that passed in a blink was so amazing. Blissful.

And now it's gone.

Oh, olive, I could have hidden you and killed you like I've thought of countless times, but somehow I never acted. However, if I did, would I have been able to pretend nothing happened? Would I have been able to lie to Jim for years about the miracle baby that could have been?

There's no way I could have. I can't lie, nor am I good at it. Plus, I can't do that to him.

I love him too much.

"You said you were hungry. Eat at least a couple of bites and then we'll take everything else to go," Melisa says in between bites of her diner hamburger. She hates cheese on burgers, which makes no sense to me. She says good meat doesn't need cheese to cover up its flavor; it should be tasty by itself. I don't think the meat from this diner is exceptional enough not to cover it with gooey cheese.

"I was. I was getting a migraine and needed to eat something."

"Have you told your doctor about them?"

"Yeah, they said my labs are all good. But to monitor and let them know if I get more. I think they are stress headaches. I ate enough for now; my head is feeling better already."

"Alright. You'll eat the rest later. When we get back to my place, I think you should relax. I'll bring the boxes inside real quick. No more lifting or moving for you today."

I nod. She hates it when I don't talk.

"Come on. You got this. We got this. You're not alone. Plus you'll get another DNA test done. There must have been something wrong with the first one. Mistakes happen."

I again nod, but follow it up with a slurp from my salted caramel milkshake. She'll take that as some form of quiet chatter.

"When we get home, you should take a nice long bath and relax. I bought some new foaming bath soaps. I think you'll enjoy them. Supposed to be real good for your skin."

"Organic?"

"Honey and olive oil are the main ingredients, and there were only ten."

I nod.

"I'll heat up your leftover lunch or I have a ton of food in the fridge for dinner. Later this week, we'll go grocery shopping like we used to. Plan the week out. I still have a minifridge if you want to keep that in your room."

I shake my head. "That's not necessary. You have a double-door fridge."

"Just in case if you want it, it's there for you."

"Thank you," I manage to whisper.

"He's a prick, you know that?"

"Don't be mad at Jim. It's not his fault."

"You didn't do anything wrong. Clearly there was something wrong with the DNA test. Unless... you know you can tell me anything and I'll believe anything you say."

"I didn't cheat. This should be Jim's kid."

"Okay, okay. Then the next test will prove it. Babies don't just magically pop in your belly. A man puts them there."

"What about that junkie?"

"What about that crackhead? Don't you tell me you believe in some man's inebriated gibberish. If a homeless man jabbering nonsense convinces you that there is a god, then we got bigger things to worry about."

"It's just so weird. How could they fuck up the test? How is any of this happening? I need logic."

"And some sleep. Your eyes are bloodshot."

"Thanks. I'll make sure to highlight them with some makeup for you later," I snipe back.

"How you plan on doing that? Making those bags blacker?"

"Bitch."

She laughs. "What kind of cake or pie do you want to snack on tonight? A big apple pie or a Snickers cheesecake?"

"Both?" I ask hopeful, tears still in my eyes, even if they stopped falling.

45

She grabs my hand. "Girl, you're lucky I love ya."

10 Weeks - The Pocono Mountains, Pennsylvania

I pull my shawl up, concealing my face as I walk through a town with cobblestone streets and thatched roofs. People in handspun clothing shy away from me as I hurry. Behind me, in the distance, I hear shouting. Some type of angry riot.

The full moon casts shadows on the buildings and streets. The shadows look like they are chasing me. Silhouette creatures with halos and horns follow me.

Shutters close. Doors slam shut.

Something tells me to run. Run down the street! Get out of town! Now!

I try to run, but I'm pregnant. A woman in this condition shouldn't be running. They should be in bed resting. Looking down at my bump, I notice blood splattered on my dress.

How did that happen? It's not mine. I don't feel injured. Just tired. Extremely tired. What happened?

The shouts are getting closer. I turn down a dirt trail and run into the woods. Dogs howl, echoing off the trees. Sweat drips down my face. My chest is on fire. It's hard to catch my breath.

At the end of the trail, there's a cabin. I sprint to it, open the door, and close it. Locking the simple lock, I move a table behind the door. Stepping back, I realize I'm barricading the only door. I'm trapped.

Outside, the mob is getting closer. Their torches brighten the path to the cabin. They will be here in moments. I grab a blanket off the bed and open the back window. Luckily, the window is big enough to climb out.

I run.

There isn't a trail. Branches and thorns rip at my dress. I smell smoke as I struggle up the hill, running deeper into the forest. My heart pounds in my chest. It's getting harder to breathe. A contraction makes me stop and brace myself against a tree. I try to be quiet and muffle my cry. Not now. Please, baby. Don't be born now. You need to wait. The contraction finally stops and I take off into the woods. By the time I reach the hilltop, I'm out of breath, ready to collapse. I turn around and see the cabin on fire.

Men are shouting from every direction in the woods. They must have found my footsteps. Dogs bark, racing up the hill, getting closer and closer.

Frantic, I search for help. I won't be able to outrun them. There's no use. I must hide. I cross a shin-deep stream and see a tree with low branches.

Tired and shaking, I attempt to climb the tree. The dogs splash through the water, snarling, chomping their teeth. I grab a branch and try to pull myself up.

My hands slip. I fall backward. The air explodes out of my chest as I crash onto the ground. Flat on my back, I stare at the night sky, screaming in pain. My thighs are wet.

Then the dogs bite.

I wake up shaking.

That nightmare felt so real. I reach down and feel my stomach. It's still flat. No big baby bump. It was only another crazy dream. I've been having one almost every night.

I roll over and take a deep breath in. The linens smell like clean cotton. It's not the laundry detergent that I normally use. Jim likes the lavender-scented. He said it smells calming, relaxing, makes it easier for him to fall asleep. At night, when I would crawl into bed before him, I'd hug his pillow and breathe in his scent. His pillow and sheets always had a hint of something else added. It had to be his sweat, oil, and dead skin, but it was his own intoxicating odor that would lull me to sleep, not the lavender. I didn't have nightmares then. Weird how the smell of his sweat used to bring me comfort, arousal, and security. Now, all I smell is clean linen. It doesn't help me sleep.

It smells artificial.

The vast bed feels empty, with a space longing for someone to fill it. It's been years since I have slept alone. For the last few weeks, I have been sleeping in the guest bedroom, but it was still at my home. Somewhere familiar.

Melisa's new condominium is nice. It's a two-bedroom, three-bath with a balcony attached to each bedroom and overlooking the woods. There's a two-car garage so I can pull right in and walk into the kitchen without going outside. The driveway is heated, a major bonus.

The bedroom I sleep in is modern, not Melisa's normal style. She claims she is experimenting, but I can change up the room and redecorate whenever I get inspired. It's bland. Sterile. Black-and-white checkered bedsheets on a king-sized bed with a black headboard, and the walls are pristine white. That's the name of the paint. Pristine. Pristine means clean, fresh, untouched, unspoiled. Not me. I'm not pristine. At least, I don't feel like I am.

My stomach flip-flops. It's an odd feeling being hungry, wanting to throw up, and feeling bloated at the same time. I really thought that morning sickness was something that happened in the morning and that the rest of the day, I'd feel seminormal. They should really call it perpetual sickness, relentless nausea, or tenacious tummy turmoil. The heartburn won't stop no matter what I eat. I could eat raw carrots and cauliflower and I'd still have a burning sensation bubbling in my chest and the need to vomit. But no matter what I can keep down, it won't come out. The constipation keeps getting worse every damn day.

"Morning." Melisa knocks on my bedroom door. "I made breakfast. Bacon, eggs, and hash browns. Come on; get out of bed already." Dressed in gym shorts and a tee, her hair is in a messy bun with strands escaping. Her dark brown eyes say *Please don't make me get you out of the bed, because you know I will.*

"Just give me a plate of bacon and maple syrup." I really have a thing for mixing together savory and sweet. Sometimes for lunch, I eat a crunchy peanut butter, crushed potato chip, chopped apple, and marshmallow fluff sandwich. I've been considering adding bacon. It usually makes everything taste better.

Melisa cocks her head to the side. "There's toast and peach jam, plus you need your potatoes, peppers, and onions. You didn't eat any last night. The baby book says—"

"Well, baby says no. It doesn't want any. Seriously, I'm going to overdose on healthy. What if I take the prenatals and eat too many vegetables? Too many vitamins can actually be bad. Could cause kidney problems. People have turned orange after eating too many carrots."

My at-home dietitian gives me a disapproving glare. "You're crazy. Shit like that doesn't happen from a couple servings of assorted veggies and gummy vitamins. You'd need to eat straight-up carrots for a year."

I sigh, knowing I have lost this fight. "One day, Melisa, you're going to find me at a McDonald's, knee-deep in cheeseburger wrappers and cardboard French fry containers, and I will refuse to leave."

She rolls her eyes. "Get out of bed. Start getting ready for your doctor's appointment. It's at noon."

"I don't want to go," I whine.

"Come on. This time, it's going to be a quick blood test. Fast and easy," Melisa says with a wink while pulling the sheets off me and throwing them into a heap at the bottom of the bed. "Get up. The pound of bacon I cooked won't leave the kitchen table. So you better get to it, Everild."

I groan loudly and slowly get out of bed. She had to call me Everild. Damn it, she knows how to get me moving, even if I'm just getting out of bed to yell at her and eat that bacon.

Sitting on the edge of the bed, I stretch. The dresser across from me has a built-in mirror, so every time I get up, my reflection is the first thing I see. I wonder if stress causes my eyes to turn green. I can't remember the last time they were hazel.

I don't want to be a lab rat anymore. Ever since Jim was proclaimed not the father—not once, but twice—the doctors said they found other abnormalities with the baby. They said the baby itself seems healthy, but they want to do some extensive blood work. In one breath, they told me they are certain my husband isn't the father and that my child is different. I asked what was different about my baby, but no one would give me a straight answer. All I know is that it's healthy but different, which isn't comforting.

"How big is the baby now?" Melisa asks, sitting at the walnut live-edge kitchen table. She had already grabbed all the bacon she wanted and put the remains in the middle of the six-foot-long table. She knows whatever is left on the plate becomes mine and I'll fork fight her if needed.

"Baby is now the size of a prune. It's growing bones and teeth."

"Teeth? I thought that didn't happen until later. Oh, you know what might help, prune juice. I'll grab some after the doctor's."

"No, no. That stuff looks nasty. I don't know if I could stomach that. The thought of drinking it…" I dry heave at the thought of drinking something that reminds me of tobacco juice running out of a guard's mouth before they would spit out the wad. Some of the security detail at my parents' farm would chew the black tar-like gum. I don't like gum either.

"Alright, alright, no prune juice. Just a suggestion. It might help unclog you."

"It will come out when it needs to." Or when I burst.

"Any idea what you want for dinner? What kind of meat should I start defrosting?"

I shove a piece of bacon in my mouth, followed by toast with peach jam, completely skipping the hash browns. The next piece of bacon, I dip directly in the jam before devouring it.

"Girl, you have some funky food combinations."

"Oh my god, it's so good. I don't know, maybe burgers? Or chicken. Oh, crispy barbecue chicken with potato salad. And glazed doughnuts."

Her eyes bug out of her head. "I read last night that some women end up with pica, eating dirt, coffee grinds, hair, chalk, sand, and other nasty shit. I guess we're lucky you're eating actual food, even if it's the weirdest combinations I've ever heard of."

I put both hands on the table and give her a serious look. "Dirt? Did you say dirt? I could go for a big bowl of that. Mmm, but make sure to dig up a couple of plump, juicy worms too."

"Oh god, I think I just lost my appetite," Melisa says with her hands over her mouth, feigning gagging.

I eat another piece of bacon and get up to stretch. All my muscles feel tight.

Melisa's mouth drops open. "Dude, have you looked in the mirror?"

"What?" My hair wasn't sticking up comically when I got out of bed or anything like that.

"You got a teeny weeny bump!"

I look down at my belly. "It looks like I just gained weight from the holiday season or ate a buffet. I don't think I'm actually showing."

"You totally are!" She gets up and puts her hands on my belly. "Right here. You can tell with the leggings and tank on. It's not big, but it's there."

I walk to the closet mirror, which is full length, and stare at my morphing body. Turning to the side, I can tell that there's a little something extra there. "Huh. You sure I'm not just bloated? I feel bloated."

"Nope. That's a baby. You are totally having a baby! Auntie Mel. It has such a nice ring to it."

"You're going to spoil it like crazy, aren't you?"

"You know it. After your appointment, let's go walk around a baby store. Get some ideas."

"Maybe. We'll see how this appointment goes. I really don't want to go. I just keep getting these weird, bad feelings about going to the doctor. Like I shouldn't be. I don't know. I think it's stress. I also have to go back to work next week. I'm not looking forward to that."

"You need to get out of the house and do something. It's not healthy for you to be lying around in bed all day. At least work will keep you distracted and active."

Work isn't going to be fun. Jim works on the floor above my office. People will know. People will talk. I hate people. "Yeah, I'm contemplating getting a new job."

"Why? Jim doesn't work in your office. So what if he's on a different floor? You don't have to see him."

"Everybody knows everyone. It's a small building. It's going to be awkward."

"That's the way you have always described that place."

"Maybe I can find something less awkward."

"It will be hard getting a new job before you have a baby. What about health insurance?"

"All I know is that I'm dreading going back. I should look at the help wanted. Maybe I'll be lucky and find something that I can do from home."

"It will be hard switching jobs right now, but you have to do what's best for you overall. And if working there will drive you mad, then we'll make it possible. Somehow."

"Thank you. I don't know what I would do without you."

"You'd be much more miserable," she says with a shrug.

I grab her hand and squeeze it tight.

Melisa gives me a smirk. "Come on, honey. Let's finish breakfast."

The amount of things new parents can buy for their child is overwhelming. Instead of going to check out all the gadgets and gizmos, I stick to the clothing section. I'll slowly get my feet wet with baby things. Who knows; you might not survive the night. I'm still not out of my first trimester. As I'm holding this cute onesie with white frills, almost Victorian-era looking, I can't help but wonder if I will have to return this outfit in another week or two.

"Come on, you have to hope for either a boy or a girl. Stop with the *I just want it healthy* bullshit. Come on. You have to have a preference for one or the other."

I shrug. "No, honestly. It never really crossed my mind. I can think of a hundred reasons why a boy would be more difficult and a hundred reasons why a girl would be a headache. I think I'm screwed either way."

"Always so dramatic," Melisa says, rolling her eyes. "If I ever find my perfect match, I think I'd want boys. Girls are too sassy."

"Boys hump everything and don't stop eating. They go from being walking stomachs to walking dicks."

"You aren't wrong. But I'll teach them right. Show them respect and morals. Girls are evil. They instinctually know how to manipulate from an early age. Always devious; they're the ones to watch out for."

"I know, I'm so evil." I laugh. "Huh."

"What's up?"

"One good thing about Jim and me splitting up is I won't have to hear how I'm the devil from his grandmother anymore. Maybe I'll find a man with a family who likes me. That would be a nice change. Actually have a mother-in-law that I can have a cup of tea with and chat."

"His whole family is whacked, even his sister. As hard as this shit is, you're better without them. Too much negativity in that family for a pessimistic person like you. You need more positive vibes to outweigh your cynical outlook. Nah, you need a nice happy family for this little bugger. What about this onesie? Little froggies on lily pads."

"Everyone wants to sell you something, even if it's their opinion. It's instinct. People suck."

"Do I suck?"

"No. You're a bitch who wants my child to wear frogs. You have such weird taste."

"I got weird taste? You like the plainest but oddest things. That thing in your hands reminds me of an antique baby dress."

"It's so cute, and I like it better than frogs."

"Stop putting down the frogs. You know what? Just because of that, I'm getting this—whatever you pop out—a whole frog section in their closet. Frog nursery theme."

I can't stop laughing. My sides hurt. "Only if it's a tropical rain forest with bright-colored exotic frogs, the kind you lick that make you trip."

"Oh my god, can you imagine."

"Tripping on poisonous dart frogs?" It's seriously hard to breathe. "Where are you planning this imaginary nursery? You only have two bedrooms."

"Rearrange the bedrooms. Remove the dressers and nightstands that aren't being used. It will free up a ton of space. Your room is spacious, once the bulky furniture is out. Put a divider in the room, make a little nursery corner."

I give her a look.

"I've been thinking and planning."

"Scheming."

"That too."

"I think I'm good on buying things today."

"You don't want to buy any of these cute onesies? Start stocking up?"

"I think we should wait until I'm fourteen weeks. Just in case. I don't want to start doing this until I know it's safe. You know? I need to make sure this won't be taken from me too."

"Alright. I gotcha. It was good to get you walking around for a little bit, find out what weird baby-style clothes you want. If it's a boy, you better not dress it up in overalls and a fedora. No bonnets for girls. That shit is eerie and Child of the Cornish."

"No fedoras, I promise."

11 Weeks - The Pocono Mountains, Pennsylvania

I hang up and stare at my phone. With every passing second, it gets heavier until it feels like it will break my arm if I don't let it go. It hits my desk, making a tiny thudding noise, not loud enough to disturb anyone in their cubicles.

A chorionic villus test and a nuchal translucency screening… What are they? The nurse said that they were normal tests. But it doesn't feel normal. Both tests sound invasive. I Google both tests and don't like what I see. Sticking a long needle into my womb? Little strawberry isn't going to like the syringe invading its space.

My stomach grumbles and I can feel thick fluid climbing up my throat, burning each section of my esophagus as it travels up until I think I'm going to vomit, but the slime retreats, receding to fester until lunch.

Yesterday, I had a huge Caesar salad, no vanilla ice cream. Instead, I had a cup of creamy French vanilla yogurt. It still hit all my craving sensations. Today I'm having a crunchy peanut butter sandwich with the works. Potato chips, Granny Smith apple slices, two spoonfuls of marshmallow fluff, and three strips of bacon. Part of me wants to add a light drizzle of chocolate sauce, but I think that would make it more into a dessert instead of lunch.

It's borderline already.

My stomach grumbles again. I can feel a headache starting. I place my hands on my little bump. Strawberry, what's wrong? From what I've seen on the monitors, you are healthy and look exactly how you should. By now, the webbing on your hands and feet should be disappearing, and your limbs should be in their correct spots now. You should look like a mini person, finally. A little me.

But why are the doctors so worried? They say the tests aren't showing any signs of disease, but they keep digging and want more blood. The more tests I get, the more labs they want to run. And I have a feeling that my little strawberry doesn't like needles. Neither do I, but I want to know where you came from and how all this happened, so for now, we're getting all the tests.

The phone rings at the reception desk on the other side of the partition, and it brings me back to work. Back to the hostile office that resents me now. It was peaceful taking two weeks off, delaying their nasty gazes. They all know. Most of the people here have met or know Jim. The office building isn't huge, and the hundred or so people who work in the building know everyone or see each other on a daily basis. So as soon as we stopped driving together, they all knew. And after some time, they all found out who was to blame.

I don't have friends at work. I'm not what you would call a people person. Jim, even though shy, was the talkative one out of the both of us. There are entire days I don't speak to my coworkers. I'm polite, but my job doesn't require me to make pointless banter at the water cooler.

My job only requires a working laptop and could be done anywhere, but the office managers wanted the office to have a full staff for appearances. They like the idea of having everyone together, like a family. They think it unifies the company. It only makes people more distracted, less productive.

What did you do this weekend? What shows have you watched? How old are your kids now? How's your family? What did you eat for dinner?

Those endless questions and mindless dialogue, I avoid. I don't care what they do when they go home, and they really don't care about me, except that I've become the newest source of drama to entertain their boring work lives. None of my coworkers are people I could call in the middle of the night and ask for help; neither do I expect it from them. They aren't friends. They are associates. Nothing more, but I hate being stared at. I hate when people notice me, especially when I'm trying to be invisible.

It wouldn't be so bad if they just sat in their cubicles and minded their own business, but instead they wander around, taking quick, accusing glances at me. Wondering how I could be so cruel to such a nice guy. There's nothing I can say to change their minds. No long speech will make them understand something that I don't.

So I stay quiet in my corner, glaring at the screen saver fireworks display while I scream internally, yearning for an escape. Maybe some fresh air will do us some good. Maybe outside, I'll find a secluded corner to scream in where no one will hear. My computer turns off. The fireworks that were bursting on my screen blink away as I hear something click and grind inside the computer. That didn't sound good. This is not what I needed today. I had to call IT last week because my computer was having issues. They gave me an attitude when I told them I didn't know what happened. Again, I don't know what happened, but there is something wrong with this damn computer.

I'm over this.

Telling no one, I leave my desk. The nosy secretary looks up from her monitor and gives me a snide look. Bitch, don't judge me. You get paid to answer phones and look pretty while filing your nails, moron. I actually saw her once water the fake plastic plants in the lobby. I didn't tell her.

The burst of humid air feels better than the judgmental stares, and instantly my breathing has calmed. I stare out into the parking lot, finding my car and Jim's. He parked his car on the opposite side of the parking lot. It's as far away from my car as he can be. A black sedan catches my eye in the parking lot, only a few spots away from Jim's. It's not like I can identify everyone's car in the building, but I can tell it's out of place.

I head to the manicured garden to find a bench. It's a serene place for employees to escape the white walls suffocating them and enjoy the fresh air and vibrant scenery during their lunch break. It's too early in the morning for anyone to be here now.

This is where Jim caught my attention. Him with a homemade sandwich, me with a broccoli cheddar soup, sipping it from my thermos, my gaze refusing to digress from my e-reader to look in his direction no matter how hard he stared. He had tried to catch my eye, but they were focused on a heroine from another world who was fighting a dragon army. There was no chance I'd stray away from that action during my only break, the time I used to no longer be at work and escape.

He pretended to drop his grapes out of his reusable container and accidentally hit me with one. It was a small red grape, probably the smallest one on the whole vine, but it made me put down my e-reader. He finally caught my eye. His curious smile and lack of charm not only made him more charming in my eyes, it made me see him in a different light. The way as soon as he captured my attention, he could no longer look at me. I realized that he had used all of his courage up with his grape explosion and it left him completely, utterly shy.

It made me swoon.

Since we worked in the same office building and had the same hours, it wasn't long before we were living together. It just made our lives easier. I can honestly say we were officially in love within a month, if not sooner. I just knew he was all I had ever wanted. Quiet nights spent by each other's side, reading while sipping wine. The ability to behave freely with someone who loved me for everything I was, including all the bad and good, completed me. He was perfect for me. We were perfect together. Truly in love. Was June the month we met? It was in the summer. I think it was in June, because we spent the Fourth of July together. His grape explosion happened about a month before we went to his friend's house for the barbeque.

Bing.

I take my phone out of my pocket. Did he know I was reminiscing? Did he hear me thinking about him, or is he looking out the window from the second floor, watching me?

I got a lawyer. I want to keep the house... Are you getting a lawyer?

I look up at the windows. The shades are drawn tight, but there are cracks to spy from. *Nope. No worries, I won't fight. Just send me the paperwork and I'll send it back to your lawyer.*

Three dots appear, then stop. Then appear and then stop again. Did he want me to fight? My head is throbbing.

I'm actually thinking of selling the house and downsizing.

I imagine it would be hard living there. Memories like ghosts, haunting every room. *A fresh start would be good for you.*

If I sell it, I'll give you some money from the sale.

You don't have to. I still feel like I did something wrong and that I don't deserve anything. It's weird to feel guilty but not remember what I did.

What?

I send him a shrug emoji. My stomach makes another crazy noise. I need food.

Are you okay? Are you at work?

I read those words and worry he's on his way to my office to talk in person. I run into the building, fly past the snobby secretary, and head to my desk. As fast as possible, I shove everything into my purse and grab my cooler. I'll deal with my computer tomorrow.

From farther into the office, I hear a shriek. Some type of commotion is coming from the other side of the room. Colleagues stand around in a circle, watching a scene unfold. A man screams and rambles about god and some type of miracle; he sounds like a raving lunatic. People yell at him and tell him to calm down. It sounds like he has had enough of this job. I don't have time to deal with that nonsense, nor do I care. Not when Jim is probably in the elevator on the way down to this floor to talk.

Hurrying out of the office, I sprint for the doors.

"Evie, are you okay?" The secretary stops me. "You look pale."

I turn to talk to her, but her face... it's wrong. The lights in the office are making my head explode. That's why she looks blurry. It has to be. It's because of my headache. I blink a couple of times. On the third blink, she looks normal. "I'm fine. Just a migraine. I've got to go home."

I run out of the building. Once I'm in my car and down the street, stopped at a red light, I text Jim back.

No.

12 Weeks - The Pocono Mountains, Pennsylvania

I'm in another pristine room with sterile lab equipment, but this one reminds me of a horror movie. Set in a mental hospital, deep in the woods, surrounded by overgrown grounds that creep into the structure like ivy, finding cracks to invade. A terrifying place where forgotten mental patients remain, waiting in the shadows to hunt down victims and perform gruesome experiments on them. Get their revenge on the world that left them to rot in a decrepit building, lost in time.

Nurse Freda has crazy eyes. The kind that pop out of her head in a way that makes her look insane. A strained smile doesn't make me feel better as she grits her teeth at me as I cautiously make my way to the table with straps on it. The kind you never want to lie down on in fear they won't let you back up.

"Come on, dear. I don't have all day. Hang your purse here." You get a C- rating for bedside nurse, lady. "Here, change into this gown. You can leave your socks on. Nothing else. I'll check on you in a few minutes."

I nod.

My stomach gurgles anxiously. I try to think this won't be so bad. I've been pricked and prodded since my first doctor's visit and it hasn't stopped. There still has been no news of Down Syndrome, no mutations or missing chromosomes. No reports saying that my baby has Patua Syndrome, so no extra limbs, but still they keep searching for something, like my baby has given them a riddle they can't figure out.

It doesn't comfort me. What do they know that I don't? What do they see as alarming but can't figure out what *it* is?

A large needle sits on a metal tray in a sterilized bag, taunting me. I've never liked needles, and this one looks like it will hurt. Next to it is a smaller needle, I assume, to numb me up before the big one penetrates my skin.

I wish they didn't display the needles; it only makes me more anxious. And today, Melisa is too busy with work to make sure I don't escape my appointment. I'm by myself. It would be so easy to run out of this room and flee into the parking lot, jump into my car, and go.

Running is easy. But where would I go? I have no clue. There's no destination. Just the need. The constant need to leave this town and find a new home.

But it's too late. I'm on the table, stripped down to my socks, with a two-piece paper gown on, waiting to be told what position to lie in. The holsters for my feet aren't up, so that's a plus for the moment.

Freda knocks on the door and comes in after I give her the okay. She looks me over, then goes back to her paperwork, squinting as if what she is reading makes little sense.

"What's it say?"

"Oh, just about what your doctor is looking for and congratulations, a Christmas baby."

I ignore the Christmas comment and give her the sternest look I can muster. "Freda, what are they looking for?"

She gives me a nervous smile. "I honestly don't know. All the codes and initials. I'm just a nurse who helps draw blood and fluids for testing. I know nothing about the test results." She rambles.

"Please tell me. What's wrong with my child? You read something. Tell me," I demand.

"From what I browsed, your child is healthy. No sign of any diseases, but…"

"But what?"

She sighs and applies gel to my abdomen. "They are looking into the child's DNA. That's all. Lay back. You're going to feel a little pinch as I numb the area," she says as she looks on the sonogram to see where my little one is. She marks a spot on my stomach and then cleans the area of the gel using an alcohol wipe while leaving the image on the screen just above the site.

"DNA? Why?"

"To make sure everything is okay and that your baby is as healthy as possible. Ready, here's the pinch."

She takes the smaller of the two needles and delicately jabs it into my skin. Maybe I'll score her a C. I barely felt the needle.

"That needs a few minutes to get numb. I'll be back with the doctor. He'll perform the nuchal translucency screening and then the chorionic villus sample. Do you have questions about the procedures?"

"Not about the procedures."

She nods, then hurries out of the room.

I'm alone.

Well, not quite alone. I have you, little lime, for now. But what secrets are you hiding from the doctors? What trouble are you causing me already? They keep telling me you're healthy, but they keep searching for some answer to a question they won't tell me. Can you please tell me your riddle, little lime? It will be an inside joke between you and me. But please, don't leave me in the dark. Don't let me fall in love with you, only to die. Please don't do that to me. I don't think I could handle it. It's not fair to Mommy. So please, I beg you, please tell me what everyone else is afraid of.

I'll understand. Mommy won't be mad.

Freda knocks but doesn't wait for me to respond to open the door. She walks in, not making eye contact. The doctor follows. He's wearing a trained smile, one that he uses to schmooze his patients. It possibly makes them feel more at ease. Not me.

"Hello, Everild. How are you and your little present doing today?"

I try my hardest to not sound sarcastic when I say, "Great."

"You are aware of the procedure we are doing today and that there is a small chance of complications, but…" He goes through his routine, the same speech he gives to every woman who has sat in this seat, waiting for the same procedure. If I were him, I would have recorded it and played it on a loop for my patients. It's less friendly, but faster. And at least then I would know he doesn't actually care. He only cares that the procedure doesn't go wrong and I don't become a blemish on his career. Protect his title. When he leaves the office to return home, he will forget about me and my child, as he does with every woman. That is all he truly cares about. His words and charisma are fake, but he's an excellent actor. You, sir, get a B rating.

"If you can sign this and date it."

Nurse Freda hands me a clipboard with a consent form listing a bunch of scary words that I don't want to read. I sign.

"Good. Nurse, will you raise the table?" He puts on a fresh pair of gloves, then places a hand on my abdomen. Right where the nurse drew her x. "All numb?"

I nod.

"First, we'll check out this peanut. This should be warm." He takes a bottle of gel and squirts it onto my abdomen. "Nice and warm?"

"Yes." I lie; it's lukewarm at best. At least it's not cold.

"Good. Let's see," he says as he takes the wand and moves it around in the gel. "Mommy, do you want to say hi?"

"Sure, but I don't want to know its sex."

"It's too early to see that. Let's see if we can get a clear picture. Ah, here we go," he says while turning the monitor for me to see.

The baby is so clear now. It's no longer a blob of tissue, but an actual form. It's a little person. I whisper, "Hi, lime."

"Lime?" The doctor turns his head and looks at me like I'm crazy.

"The fruit size. It's in the baby book. Week twelve is lime. I like calling my baby the fruit or vegetable, since I want the sex to be a surprise."

"Huh. Every woman is different."

Now you get a C rating. Keep it up.

"Your baby looks healthy and strong. It's exactly the right size, too. Spot on."

He turns the monitor away and a tear escapes my eye. "I'll see you soon, lime."

The doctor rattles off numbers to the nurse. Every few moments, he presses the wand on my stomach harder and glides it across my skin to get a better image. "Okay, now the not so fun part."

He thinks this is fun? What part of this has been fun for me?

"All numb still?" I watch him touch my stomach, but I don't feel it.

"Yup," I say with a gulp.

He takes a pen and draws a new x just an inch away from the first one. "This shouldn't hurt. It will feel uncomfortable, and please let me know if for any reason you feel more than just pressure."

Sitting on her stool, Freda, the nurse with the lackluster bedside, takes the sonogram wand from the doctor. She still won't look me in the eye, nor is she trying to make any small talk. The look on her face is determined. Determined not to speak a word to me and to get the job done as fast as possible. So does the doctor, but at least he pretends to care.

He studies the screen, gives the nurse a few last-minute instructions, picks up the large needle, and then he squints. "Nurse, did the monitor do anything odd today? The screen, it's all fuzzy. I can't see a clear image."

Nurse Freda shakes her head. "No. This is the first time it's malfunctioned."

The doctor puts down the needle and pushes a couple of buttons on the keyboard. He flips a switch and then flips it back. I get a chill as the gel and rubbing alcohol on my belly cool. This delay has me nervous. How often do their machines break down?

After a few moments, it beeps. "Well, that was weird. But it's working now."

Great, now I feel even more anxious.

The doctor instructs the nurse to move the wand slightly. He picks up the needle, looks at the monitor before quickly darting his eyes to his target. X marks the spot. He gives me a cheap smile. "Now, take a deep breath in. When I say so, slowly exhale. It will help."

He's a liar.

13 Weeks - The Pocono Mountains, Pennsylvania

I stare at the house I used to call home. It's ten minutes after seven. Jim has to be stepping out of the shower and drying off. The man works like a clock. Every morning, every weekday, he follows the same schedule. At least since I have known him.

In my car, I try to smell the cologne I know he is applying right about now. His soaps and shampoos are all earthy smelling. His body wash smells like sage and charcoal. His shampoo and conditioner are a citrus blend. I can picture myself lying on our giant king-size bedspread, teasing him, knowing he won't stop getting ready for work no matter how hard I try. He's punctual. Always has, always will.

The yard is mowed, but my gardens look untouched. I want to tend them, take out the weeds that will strangle the beautiful purple coneflowers. When I had planted them, I thought they were the only thing I might be able to grow. Instinctually, I place my hands on my swelling stomach.

The little bugger is getting bigger. Now when I look into the mirror, I can tell there is a little something extra that doesn't look like I'm just bloated. Fortunately, I can still fit into the same pants, but that won't last for long.

My baby is already the size of a lemon. Its vocal cords are forming, so it can scream at me once it's born. I wonder how much it will cry. How much will it yell at me when I say no? Maybe I don't want my baby to have vocal cords. Maybe I want mine to be the silent type.

The fact that I'd rather build my child to my ideal standards is another perfect reason I shouldn't be a mother.

But I am. Or I will be. It keeps me going and moving somehow, almost like a parasite that has gained full control of my mind. The baby has complete power over me. It tells me when to get up and move or sleep. It demands I eat all the time or puke. It tells me when to go to the bathroom or suffer with constipation. The baby has full command of my body and is controlling my mind. Not me.

Somehow, an internal voice persuaded me into caring for it. Raising it and throwing away the life I had. It rules me. Again, I touch the little bump and know that deep down, I let it.

The downstairs light flashes on and I know Jim is packing his lunch, making his coffee, and listening to the morning news. He should be leaving within the next fifteen to twenty minutes.

I'm not here to stalk him, though it might look that way since I'm parked around the block, watching the house. I have given up on us having any relationship because of this. This circumstance I am in but can't recall how it happened. He hates me. He thinks I destroyed us on purpose. That the vasectomy was his choice, not mine. But we had made that decision together. Though, unlike being pregnant, I couldn't go around and tell everyone *we had a vasectomy*. No one would view it as the same as when a woman says *we're pregnant*. It just doesn't have the same effect. Nevertheless, it is what I had wanted—until now.

He knows I am stopping by today to pick up the last remains of my time spent here with him. We discussed it through text messages after I fled the office and he called Melisa to check on me. That didn't go over well, but she understood why I freaked out. She's more worried than before, acting extra motherly, waiting for another epic breakdown.

Jim said to be here exactly when he left for work, in case I wanted to go through the house on my own and collect anything else he hadn't thought of. But the bulk of what's mine is in the garage.

Knowing I have about five minutes before he leaves, I turn on the car and look in my rearview mirror. A black car with black-tinted windows is parked two blocks down the street.

I continue driving down the street that has been my address for the last three years. We've known each other for six, lived together in my small one-bedroom apartment after dating for a month until we found our home three years ago. When I set eyes on this modern two-story, three-bedroom, three-bath house, I never thought I would permanently leave it.

His car is parked outside where I used to park. He must have moved his car before I got here. I can't imagine he left it outside, exposed to the elements overnight. Like magic, the garage door opens as soon as I pull onto the property; he must have been watching for me. I back the car into the garage for the first time in my life and take in one last deep breath. This will be the first time he sees me with a little baby belly and the last time I assume he will ever see me again.

Without hesitation, the door from the kitchen to the garage opens up and Jim stands on the threshold with his arms crossed. But his face isn't as cold as I had anticipated. Not like it had been the night he told me to leave. His shaggy brown hair is already dry. It normally dries in minutes, but the scent of citrus hangs heavy in the air. His brown eyes take me in, looking at every part of me, just like he did on our wedding day. But he had a smile on his face then. He's dressed in business casual; the pressed button-down shirt and slacks fit his form too well.

"Hi," is all I can whisper, my voice shaky and uneven. Maybe the baby is stealing my voice while it creates its own vocal cords.

"Hi." He stares at me for a moment more and then moves to the boxes neatly set by the door.

I take that as my cue to open the trunk and give him a hand. But before I can pick up a box, he unloads the first one and puts up his hands in protest.

"You shouldn't be doing this. I'll get them all."

"I can lift some. Anything light."

"I packed everything pretty tight. Will Melisa be able to help you carry them? I can stop by after work. Sorry; I hadn't been thinking about what you should and shouldn't do."

I nod. I can barely form words at any kind gesture he gives me, knowing that my miracle child's existence and I have caused him so much pain. "Melisa will be home."

I want to ask him so many questions. Like, has he run out of anything? I used to do all the shopping after we moved in together. How will he find his shampoo and body wash? Does he know how to navigate the grocery store still? Does he need help? Does he know how to do his laundry still? Has he been eating? Is he okay? Does he know how much I still love him?

But I say nothing. Anything I say will only hurt him in another way. Leave him more hurt and abused by me, the one who promised to hold and protect him forever. No words will ever repair our relationship. Nothing will soothe over the pain he is feeling. If I tell him I don't know who the father is, it won't make any of this better. Only worse.

So I close my mouth and try not to cry as he loads five medium-size boxes into my car.

"How is Melisa?" he asks, as if small talk is better than silence.

"She's good. Working, like always."

"Good, good. How are you?" I know that look in his eyes, the tremble in his jaw. There are more questions on his lips, but he doesn't ask. Questions that probably haunt him at night, preventing him from sleeping, causing him to toss and turn, wait on his tongue. They ache to be answered, but he can't bring himself to even utter them. Was it something he did to drive me into another man's arms? Did I always want children, but lied to him? Did I ever love him?

His brown puppy dog eyes are so sad. All I want to do is run to him and comfort him any way possible. But there is no comfort. There are no words I can say to explain this. No amount of apologies or begging to take us back will convince him to raise a child that isn't his. One he never wanted in the first place.

I bite my lips to hold back everything I want to say. Shut my eyes while I sniffle. I hear a box drop rather suddenly into my car, and he takes a few steps closer to me. I can now smell his cologne. It reminds me of Christmas, freshly chopped pine trees. I won't dare open my eyes and see him stare at me pitifully. No, I don't want to see that now.

"Evie."

He says my name and thousands of bolts of electricity flow through me, stinging me, burning me alive. Shocked, I open my eyes to see his. He looks down at my bump and he lifts his hand, about to place it on my belly, but stops halfway through the motion.

"Are you sure it's not mine?"

It's not really even a question, but a lingering sense of hope. Did some part of him, any part of him, actually want to have a child with me?

I shake my head. The word *no* sounds so much harsher.

Any light that shone in his eyes is gone. Extinguished forever. I hope someone puts the light back in them. He deserves that.

"Why didn't you tell me you wanted children? I wouldn't have…"

How can I explain something I don't know myself? What words can I possibly say that will make him believe me? He didn't believe me before. What would change now? Is seeing me like this, with a tiny baby bump, making him second-guess everything?

Instead of responding, I cry.

I cry for all the words I want to say. Because I want him, the only man I have ever loved, to believe them. To believe me. But it's illogical. Nothing about this makes sense and really, you only believe the things you want to, so am I trying so hard to believe I didn't cheat, but did? Am I that delusional?

"Have you spoken to the father? Maybe he could help?"

When he said *father*, I couldn't help but let out a chuckle. The father. If I had any clue who impregnated me, I would have said something.

He doesn't take it as I don't know. He took that as the father wants nothing to do with me or won't help. "I'm sorry, Evie. If it was mine…"

"I know." The words squeak out of my lips somehow as I nod repeatedly.

"I have to go to work. Spend the day going through anything you want. Give me a text if you need any help moving the boxes into Melisa's. Leave your key in the garage."

And with that, our relationship will be completely over, except for the divorce paperwork I know to be expecting. I nod, understanding his instructions—I can't move my mouth anymore.

Jim grabs his lunch box and walks out of the garage. He stops halfway to his car and takes one last look at me. "You know, you really look beautiful pregnant." He smiles and then continues to his car, leaving me with the biggest knife in the heart he could.

As soon as I hear his car turn out of the driveway, I slink down the side of my car and crumble into the fetal position to weep alone.

Katie Zaber

14 Weeks – The Pocono Mountains, Pennsylvania

This time, for the first time, I'm in a fancy doctor's office. No height and weight scale. No sink to wash off your hands. No bin to place used needles. No sheets of wax paper to place over the examination table. No holsters.

There's a pitcher of water on a cart with fruit defusing in it. Lemons and limes. Wasteful plastic throwaway cups sit beside it. A box of assorted cookies and a bowl of apples and oranges are also on the cart. There's a beige sofa to lie down on, with two fluffy white pillows that look like clouds. The couch looks clean and inviting, as if beckoning me to stretch out on its cushions and take a nap on it. Wooden panel walls decorated with awards, diplomas, and certificates cover every square inch of the wall directly behind the desk. There isn't enough surface space for all the frames there, and the overflow starts on the wall to my right. So many plaques, at some point it has to become egotistical.

The office has a homey feel instead of the normal sterile environment I've been experiencing since my first doctor's appointment. This isn't the room where the doctor examines me. This is the room where they tell me the bad news. Grieve with me and give me counsel.

My fingers curl under the blue tank top I have on and press against the little bump. Will you make it past the orange phase? Will you grow any bigger? Or will you become a bittersweet memory?

Vanilla. No. French vanilla coffee, maybe a latte. The soft, sweet aroma makes its way to my nostrils before I can hear kitten heels tapping on the tile floor like a cowbell hanging around her neck, giving everyone a warning of her approach. She stops in the doorway's threshold for a moment to grab the chart attached to the door. "Good morning. How are you feeling today?" Doctor I-have-forgotten-her-name-because-I've-seen-too-many-doctors, walks into her office, closes the door for privacy, and struts to her desk, holding a forbidden cup of decadent caffeinated coffee.

I inhale and savor the flavor lingering in the air. "That caffeine smells good."

"I'm sure it does," she says with a chuckle, sitting behind her desk, eyeing me behind her mug, questioning if I've been sneaking caffeinated beverages, crippling my child even more. She doesn't wear scrubs or any attire that would make me think she is a doctor. If I ran into her at the store dressed as she is in her pinstriped pantsuit, I would think she was an educated business woman. "I have all your test results. Before I continue, would you like to know the sex?"

"No, I want it to be a surprise." Like everything else has been, it seems more fitting. "How bad is it? What disease does it have?"

She bites her lip and tilts her head, placing her mug on the desk. "Not a disease. No. But your child is different."

Okay, I'll reword that. "Is my baby healthy?"

"Not certain. None of the tests results came back as your child having any developmental deformities or any genetic diseases." She pauses. Bites her lip again. How is she a world-renowned specialist? Her unsure posture and lack of confidence only adds to my fears. "Do you know what Parthenogenesis is?"

"What? No."

"It occurs primarily in invertebrates: insects, fish, reptiles, in a few species of birds, sharks. It mainly occurs when there is a lack of males and depletion in the species. However, you, Everild, are the first mammal, the first human, ever to conceive without sperm—at least on record. Your child has no paternal DNA, just yours. Normally, in humans, this would cause a teratoma tumor, but remarkably, a healthy embryo was able to form."

My only response is to blink.

I didn't cheat. I didn't block out some affair or actually hurt Jim. I'm not to blame for any of this—at least not knowingly. I'm not a horrible person. I was true to him.

Tears of joy stream down my face and I quickly wipe them away. "I'm sorry. Um, like asexual reproduction?"

"It is a form of asexual reproduction."

"So is my baby all right?"

"That's hard to say. There has never been an instance recorded of this happening—unless you think the Virgin Mary was factual." She adds a candid laugh. "So it's difficult to say what will happen. At the moment, all the tests have come back clear of any illnesses. If you didn't do paternal testing, we would have never suspected that there was anything different with your baby," she says with a smile.

Her expression drops. All the blood drains from her face as she grows paler and paler until her face is white as milk. Her body shakes, breaking into violent spasms. Before I can open my mouth to cry for help, the doctor unhinges her jaw unnaturally. A deep, echoey voice—not hers—booms out of her mouth.

"Protect the child. Do not allow any more tests. The baby will be born perfect."

Just as fast as the change in her occurred, she reverses back to her normal self. "Ahem." She clears her throat as if she didn't morph before my eyes and is only suffering from a tickle. "Sorry about that." Reaching for her mug, she coughs one more time before guzzling the remains of her coffee. "As I was saying, we won't know until you are further along what problems may arise. As of now, everything looks good, but you may need to terminate in the upcoming weeks. I know it's hard to think about and it's completely up to you; however, you should consider it. The process will be easier on your body to terminate sooner rather than later."

What the fuck just happened? What do I even say to her? She looks like she has no clue she was just possessed for fifteen seconds. I sit and stare at her. So many things just occurred in under a minute. How do I digest what just happened? The homeless man comes to mind, giving me chills.

All I can do is blink as I hug my baby bump. "No."

That's right. No.

No to everything. I'm not killing my only chance to have a miracle child when every test says it's normal. Is it right to destroy something that is healthy against all odds?

Plus, what was that gibberish coming out of her? *Protect the child. Don't allow any more tests. The baby will be born perfect.* What kind of shit was that? It contradicts everything the woman said a moment later.

"I'm sorry, but I'm having this child. I need to go." I won't say home; I don't have one anymore. But maybe, just maybe, if I tell Jim this, he'll take me back.

"Call me if you need anything. And I want to see you in two weeks. We'll draw more blood and order more lab work."

What is in her coffee?

I nod as I hurry out the door, creating as much space as possible between the possessed doctor and my precious, perfect baby.

My hands tremble as I reach for the elevator button. Did that just actually happen? Or am I just going crazy? Alone in the elevator, I tell myself that the doctor couldn't have been possessed. That kind of shit doesn't exist. But how else do I explain what I just saw?

A bell dings as the elevator doors open to the parking garage. I cautiously look around, freaked out and paranoid that someone is going to jump out of the shadows and attack me. I still haven't returned to the first doctor's office where that junkie patrols.

My car is parked three spots away from the elevator. With my keys in hand, gripped so I can jab somebody's eye out, I hurry to my car and check super fast that no one has snuck into my back seat. I unlock it and relock it as soon as I'm safe inside my beat-up Civic.

That's when I let go of the breath that I think I've been holding since I ran out of the doctor's office. I never stopped at any desk or made a follow-up appointment. Something nags at me that I shouldn't go back. That I shouldn't call the office when I get back to Melisa's and schedule my next appointment or go over all the insurance information that I just skipped out on.

I'll decide later. I'm too anxious to think, and I have an annoying forty-minute ride home because of the traffic. It should only take twenty. The traffic jams in this town are unbelievable, but I wouldn't call it a city. Maybe a baby city, but it doesn't have skyscrapers or towers that go up to a hundred floors. Nothing impressive like that, nothing to be proud of or is a national landmark. All it has is bumper-to-bumper, honking and cursing traffic.

After a few rounds of stop and go, before I even make it to the first light, I notice another black sedan. My father's voice tells me to make the next left turn; he is the family getaway driver. He knows how to drive aggressively and fast while evading whoever happened to be tracking down my parents. I think that's why I never liked to watch movies with high-speed car chases; I've been on too many risky drives.

I see an opening in the traffic and the GPS on my cracked phone screen tells me that the alleyway to the left cuts through a couple of blocks and will dump me back on another main route that appears to be moving.

"Hold on, little orange," I whisper aloud. Without hesitation, I cut the wheel and fly across the two lanes of oncoming traffic and make a beeline down the back alley. Anyone watching what I just did would think I got pissed off at the traffic, and I might get more to follow. What I did is technically not illegal, just frowned upon.

Two more cars follow behind me, catching a break in the traffic to make the same suicidal turn I just made. At the next intersection, I make a quick right after coming to a rolling stop and jump onto the main road smoothly, but probably scaring the shit out of the car now behind me.

I watch my six as I pick up speed and blend in with the other cars on the congested three-lane highway, trying to not look suspicious. The two cars that I saw follow me down the alley emerge onto the road. I hold my breath. If a black sedan pulls out of that side street, I know that my crazy suspicions are true. That I am being followed.

When I feel like my lungs are going to explode from the air I've been holding, that's when I see it. The black sedan.

Damn. I'm going to need to check for bugs. Make sure they haven't planted any trackers on me. My mind screams at me to keep driving, don't go back to Melisa's. Don't further involve her. But at this moment in time, I can still play the frustrated driver. I can call and make my next appointment and play along. They seem to just want to monitor me from a distance, which means I have time.

If I learned anything from my parents, it is that having a well-thought-out plan is paramount to surviving, and then fleeing. And if I were to take off right now, in this moment, I would have zero cash—everything I have is in the bank, which means I would need to use my cards or empty my bank account in one quick move, which would alert those who are following me, I'm sure. And I'm not ready. I really don't care about packing anything up at Melisa's; everything is replaceable and mostly clothes. But I have to think this through and also warn Melisa in person or by a note she can destroy.

I look in my rearview mirror and place a hand on my stomach. There is a list of things to do and I can't afford to be impulsive right now. That's how mistakes are made.

Katie Zaber

15 Weeks - The Pocono Mountains, Pennsylvania

I'm sitting in my peeling blue Honda Civic. But it's not on. Not yet.

I haven't been able to put the keys in the ignition. They are on my lap. I was able to get them out of my purse, but I wasn't able to start the car or hit the button to open the garage door. My single suitcase is packed; at least, all the things I'll need are. Everything else, I can store at Melisa's until I decide what I'm doing. I'm not even sure where I'm going. If anyone were to check my luggage, they wouldn't have the first clue as to where I'm headed. Jeans, t-shirts, shorts, long-sleeved shirts, bathing suit, sandals, a coat and scarf—it would confuse anyone.

I smile as I think we would share the same state of mind. A state of confusion.

But that's what I also want for anyone who will question Melisa and the nondetailed note that says I'll call her soon. The less she knows, the better. We didn't have that conversation I've been toying with; however I'm going to assume pear and I aren't safe here anymore. What's worse is that I don't know where we will be safe. But I've emptied my bank accounts and cut up all my plastic cards. I even found the tracker planted on my car. It is on my dashboard at the moment. When I pull onto the highway, I'm tossing it.

The amount of spunk I had ten minutes ago when I called the office and told them I quit has depleted and left me anxious and exhausted. Marybeth talked me in circles for what felt like an eternity, saying I should take a leave of absence until I get everything straightened out, and with a judgmental voice she added that I shouldn't be so hasty with a baby on the way.

Shut up, Marybeth. That's all I said back to her sympathetic, courteous, kind advice. She has a "farts out sunshine and shits roses" personality. Little miss fucking perfect. I yelled *shut the fuck up* repeatedly at her until she hung up the phone on me. Good. I'm never going back. I couldn't stand working there anymore after Jim and I broke up.

I signed the court papers yesterday. They are in the mail now. Within a week, our divorce will be final. Our life together will be annulled. And he will be safe from whoever is after us.

I thought long and hard about going back to him, telling him I'm a freak of nature and my body decided I was going to have a baby whether we liked it or not. That it was my miracle baby, and how could I say no? But he never wanted a baby. He never wanted children. How could I force this on him? How could I pressure him to take us back when it's not the life he wanted? Besides that fact, the people who are following me are most likely dangerous and might want to keep me locked up in a lab somewhere. He would go insane if anything like that happened and would try to rescue me, killing himself.

I can't do any of this to him. I still love him. It's better if he's mad at me. At least he'll live and maybe, just maybe, one day feel happy again.

Plus, on top of everything else, there's the whole creepy people thing that keeps happening. It would completely freak out Jim, who was an altar boy. I'm freaked out and I don't believe a word they said. If it was just the junkie, I wouldn't have given it a second thought, but the doctor? What was that about? And a few weeks ago, I thought the clerk at the pharmacy was on drugs, but maybe not. Why do they keep talking about my unborn baby? The punk teenager said I know what to do, what is right. The junkie proclaimed it's the Antichrist and that I'm the queen of Hell. The doctor warned me against any more doctors and tests, saying my child will be perfect. I can't make sense out of their gibberish, nor do I believe in anything they said. Religion is hocus pocus funded by a greedy clergy. Even so, it's frightening to have had both experiences, both pertaining to the same thing. My baby.

Baby, why are you here? Are you here to destroy my life? Take away everything I love? Everything I have worked hard for? Or are you trying to replace them? What's your goal, tiny evil one? Is it to create chaos and destruction? Is it your plan to bring Hell onto Earth, my sweet pear?

I still haven't started the engine. Across my cracked phone screen are reports of three missed calls and two new text messages. The other women in the office must have just heard the news and want the details from me. Coworkers who have never called or texted me before act like we're friends, just to get the gossip. They only want to feed off my drama like scandal vampires, sucking the world dry because their lives are too mundane.

I don't want to be part of it anymore. They won't be mainstreaming my drama into their veins to distract them from their meaningless lives. They will have to find a new dealer. In a fit of rage, I take the sim card out of my phone and break it in half before smashing the remains of my phone into my dashboard.

There should be music playing. That would set the mood. I should turn on an encouraging soundtrack to start this road trip without a destination. But my old base model sedan doesn't have a working radio. Normally I would play it off my iPhone, but well... I bought a burner phone that is literally just a phone. The only person who has the number now is Melisa, and she won't give it to anyone.

So I don't get music. I don't get the extra encouragement I need.

The car magically starts—well, I put the keys into the ignition—but it feels magical. Within minutes, I'm on Route 80 and I toss the tracker while in the middle lane, with a truck directly behind me. I watch the device fly in the wind and land on the truck's grill. Hopefully, it still works and will stay there for a couple of hours, giving me time to gain some distance. The worst-case scenario is it's broken.

I could take this interstate clear across the country to sunny California if I wanted. I'll drive this shitty car as far as it takes me. The road is my home now, and it's funny how happy I am. A manic laugh leaves my lips as I drive faster. But the car barely has any power at all. Really, it's a device to travel from point A to point B. Nothing else. No bells or whistles. The speedometer says I'm going fast, but somehow I don't think it is fast enough. I have lollygagged around for too long. I should have been speeding down the road hours ago. Days ago. Weeks ago.

Suddenly, I feel late. As if I should have left sooner. The only problem is, I don't know what I am late for. Am I late for life? Was I ignoring fate for the last few weeks, pretending my heart and soul wasn't longing for a new home?

Screw it. I don't need a radio. With the windows down, the air swooshes in and around the car like lyrics. The other cars on the highway make enough noise to become my melody. Fuck record labels and everyone and their rules. I have my own music. It's a chorus of wind whipping hair into my face, screeching tires, and engines roaring. A real life soundtrack. Not some made-up story with a tune produced to make the masses think it's their song.

No. This is my song.

Katie Zaber

Middle of Nowhere, Nebraska

The old dusty road was hard to find. So was the unmarked driveway leading off it. I passed by it twice. There is no mailbox. No marker or identification that there's a farm or home in the woods. Before I left, I wrote down the directions to their new farm. I had never gone and wasn't sure if I would end up here. But figured it would be handy to have the directions, just in case.

I texted Melisa once I found a motel and tried to calm her nerves, but somehow I don't think it did. She's called and left seven messages since. She found my note and knows I took off. She knows me, so she also expected it, but she keeps saying to come back when I'm ready.

It's only been two nights of motel sleeping, so I'm not desperate. I really don't know what brought me here. Or why I bothered to come.

I left these people, years ago, and vowed that I would never go back to them. Truthfully, I'm not coming here to stay and will never, under any circumstances, raise my child here, but I think I might be overdue for a visit and an update.

For the past two days, I've been checking to make sure no black sedans were following me. After the first two hours on Route 80, I think I lost them. Weaving in and out of traffic, pulling off at random exits and jumping back on, double backing. Plus, with the tracker either destroyed or attached to that truck, I lost them fast. All the tricks my father taught me at a tender age that I would have never guessed that I would need to use in the future.

Yesterday was when I decided to come here.

After ten minutes of driving down the dirt road and seeing multiple cameras in the trees, I find a gate. It's not a really impressive gate. If I had a fancy pickup truck, I could no doubt ram it, but I'm more than positive it's going to open.

"Name," the speaker crackles at me.

"Everild. Everild Smith."

Silence. A few moments later, the gate swings open.

I continue for another five minutes before I see RVs, large tents, sheds, and a log cabin. Everything except the house looks newish. The house looks well over a hundred years old and in need of repair. This might be the largest farm they have ever bought. The property at least seems more expansive than the last one. Fields of tidy marijuana crops in neat rows surround the property. Lookout towers loom over the crop, scattered throughout the plot.

Two people burst through the front door. Both of their bodies are refusing to look a day older since the last time I saw them, which was at least five years ago. They never made it to my wedding. Which, I guess, doesn't even matter now.

"Bee! My little Bee!" my father and mother exclaim in unison.

I still haven't gotten out of my car. The urge to drive away and back toward civilization is hard to fight. Without realizing it, I end up taking the keys out of the ignition, but I still haven't left the car by the time my parents are standing outside it.

"Bee, what a surprise! You should have called. I would have made a special dinner." My mother's mouth drops. She sees my hands resting on my stomach. "Is that? You're pregnant. Come inside. Let's have some herbal tea."

Both of their eyes shift to the passenger seat, expecting Jim to be there. They gratefully say nothing yet. Maybe they are just waiting to get inside, away from the security and their families. At least now, the farm has evidence of more children, with a playground and swing set. I wish I'd had one when I was a kid.

I follow them back inside the cabin, which I realize quickly is probably an old hunting lodge, based on all the taxidermy animals. Mounted heads collecting dust litter the walls haphazardly. No rhyme or reason for the placement, but as if whoever was decorating wanted to squeeze as many as possible into every space available. The wooden walls and wooden furniture are all the same shade of black cherry oak, making the main room darker than it needs to be. The living room, dining area, and kitchen are part of the main room. Upstairs, there are three other rooms with their doors closed.

"Come sit down. Put your feet up on this stool. Are they getting swollen yet? My feet were plum-purple from the day I found out I was pregnant with you," my mother says as she points to a classic rocking chair with simple padding. Then she rushes over to grab a nearby stool.

"My feet aren't bad. My sides are killing me though," I tell her while she's acting motherly. It won't last long.

Meanwhile, my father stands in the corner of the room. His smile reaches from one ear to the other as his eyes glisten, looking me over. I'll never admit it, but in his eyes, I have always been a daddy's girl. Always running to him when I was in trouble, hurt, or upset. My mom tried, but we are both stubborn and usually ended up butting heads within fifteen minutes of talking. But my father knows how to handle our stubborn nature. Somehow, he understands us even if my mother and I don't understand each other. At least there has been some love. That's a building block of a semi-healthy family, right?

"What kind of tea would you like? Hot, cold, citrus, berry? I have every kind."

"Your mom collects tea for a hobby these days," my father says with a wink, teasing my mother in the kitchen.

"It's a healthy hobby. You know how I love a good cup of tea in the afternoon."

Seeing them playfully bicker only makes my heart ache for Jim. One thing I can always say about my parents is that they actually love each other. I have never heard them fight, nor have they excused themselves to argue privately. They have always been lovebirds. Babying each other, making sure each other's needs have been fulfilled. If they were to get a divorce, it would mean the end of the world. "I'll take a cup of berry with honey, please."

"So how are you?" My mother asks after the kettle screeches and she pours three mugs of tea.

"I'm good. Tired, achy, hungry all the time. But overall good."

"And how's Jim?" she asks.

"He's good. We are no longer together." It hurts to say the word divorce out loud.

"I'm sorry, dear, that it didn't work out between you two," she says.

"Me too. But it wasn't meant to be." I won't cry in front of them. I've done enough of that in private already.

"Where are you living now, Bee?" my father asks while following my mother, holding a plate of Danish pastries. Cheese and fruit-filled.

"With Melisa. She has a nice two-bedroom condo. It's spacious. There will be enough room for the three of us."

"And how is she doing?" my mother asks.

"Well. Busy working and cooking for me. Thought I would give her a break and take a little road trip."

"Well, I'm glad you stopped here. We've missed you, Bee," my father says with a loving smile. If it weren't for the heartwarming homecoming, I wouldn't feel so relaxed. But I know it won't last long. The tension will slowly creep into the room.

"Do you think you'll be staying long? If you're here for just a couple days, I can set you up in one of the guest rooms." She motions to the second floor. "If longer, there's a yurt with indoor plumbing you can stay at—giving you more privacy. Perhaps a place closer to town."

There's Mom already kicking me out of her house before I'm even in it for more than ten minutes—a new record. Ever since I moved out, my mother has hinted that she never wants me to move back in, claiming privacy or there isn't enough space for me. If I was ever in financial trouble and needed a place to stay, I would never turn to them. My warm welcome is over and I'm remembering all the reasons I left.

"After tea, I want to take you on a tour, Bee," Dad says.

"Sounds good. I need to stretch my legs. When did you hire so much help? I don't think I've ever seen so many trailers and kids on any farm you guys have operated."

My mother sits back in her chair, getting into her defensive position. "Well, we aren't young anymore and the times are changing. Plus, we have always been known as some of the best growers around. We are actually pretty prestigious in the growing community, so they flock to us, wanting to learn from the pros," my mother says. From her facial expression, she's getting ready to throw a verbal punch. "But it's not like you would know. Placing us in the same category as criminals, killers. You've always looked down on us, thought less of us because of our chosen profession." She shrugs. "Nowadays, it's practically legal."

I sit back in my chair and bite my lip. "That didn't matter to me. I just didn't want to be alone. I wasn't allowed to go to school. I had no friends, no cousins, no neighborhood children. I was isolated as a child and I begged for change. That's why I resented you. And now, the first thing I see when I pull up is exactly that. So yeah, it stings to know you will do it for other people, but you wouldn't for me. You didn't allow me to be a kid."

"We thought that giving you respect would be—"

"I needed parents as a child and other kids to play with. Respect comes with age, and a five-year-old doesn't want to be considered an adult. I wanted a normal childhood, something you never wanted to give me."

My mom rolls her eyes and cocks her head to the side. "When I had you, no one gave me a book—"

"But when your daughter is begging, pleading to go to school so she can make friends and you ignore her pleas, you have to realize how bad you fucked up."

"One day, you'll understand the choices we were forced to make. It's not easy being a parent," Mom retorts.

I laugh. "You raised me on an illegal pot farm with armed men patrolling the fields and were high all the time. I was isolated from other kids. You did everything wrong."

Mom lets out a snort. "And you'll do things right?"

"At least better than you."

Dad gives me a sympathetic smile. "Bee, we tried. Hindsight is twenty-twenty; I wish we had done things better. Given you a better life—"

"Oh, Keith, that's right. Take our child's side. You always do."

Wow. That might be the first nasty thing my mother has ever said to my father, at least that I know of.

"Well, Shelly, she's right. We fucked up. We should have given her a better life somehow. But we didn't try. We did wrong. At least we can admit it."

"I will never say I did wrong. I did what I felt was right, and I always will. My mind may change with the times, but I will always choose what I feel is right. And at that time, I thought raising Bee as we did was the best for her. She's a functioning adult. At least she's not some crackhead turning tricks for blow."

I sit back and watch my parents, who have never argued once in front of me, curse at each other over me. My father truly looks heartbroken and remorseful, as if this was a long overdue conversation that's been nagging at him for years. My mother looks resentful that this conversation is even taking place. The fury behind her eyes is something I've never seen before, and unleashed toward my father is something I never thought would happen.

"Bee," my father says, taking a step toward me, "I'm sorry. At least I can admit how we raised you wasn't right, even if your mom is too stubborn."

My mother glares at my father, and for once in my life, I feel like they are normal, dysfunctional parents. With a smile on my face, I stand and hug my father, feeling the smoldering heat radiate off my mother. "You wanted to give me a tour, Dad? Let's go?" I loop my arm in his and we leave my mother alone.

Katie Zaber

16 Weeks - Blue Star Memorial Highway, Nebraska

The '50s era rest-stop diner is deserted except for the couple truckers who sit at the bar countertop, separated with at least a stool between each other. None of them know each other, and they don't appear to want to. There isn't a hostess or anyone to show me to a table, even though the sign says *wait to be seated*. It doesn't seem like anyone is going to come out to seat me. With my head pulsating and my stomach eating itself, I take a menu and sit down.

Ravenously, I look over the simple diner menu. I almost stopped two hours ago, but I decided I would push on since the last restaurant looked dingy. For some reason, I thought I would come across a better establishment; I just wish that it wasn't two hours later.

The He-Man breakfast catches my eye, consisting of a short stack of pancakes, hash browns, two links of sausage, four pieces of bacon, and a slice of ham. But my stomach gurgles, confirming that baby needs more food. So I decide to order an extra side of bacon and French toast. What the hell, a cup of fresh fruit, too.

That should stop Melisa's nagging voice in my head, reminding me to eat something healthy.

After waiting for five minutes, a middle-aged server strolls out of the kitchen in an old-fashioned gray and white waitress dress with a faded yellow apron. She spots me sitting alone beside the window and stops to grab a glass and a pitcher of ice water, bringing both to the table. Most of her ruby red lipstick is on her lips, but there's a good portion on her teeth. Her retro green eyeglasses connect to a pearl chain looping around her neck. Her expression is tired and worn, as if she started working her shift twenty years ago and never clocked out. The dimples around her lips and the crow's feet around her eyes grow as she gives me a warm but practiced smile. An odor of cigarettes with a slight hint of alcohol wafts off her breath, masked by bitter coffee.

"Hiya darling. What can I get ya?"

Her accent is Southern. I can't place exactly from where, but she's a long way from home.

So am I.

"Morning. Could I get the He-Man Breakfast, an extra side of bacon, a short stack of French toast, and a cup of fresh fruit? Could I get all the meats crispy?" I ask.

"Certainly, dear. Any coffee?"

"Ah, decaf tea please." I place a hand on my swollen belly.

"No caffeine for you and that little babe." She winks and walks away to bring my order to the cook, placing the ticket on the revolving ticket table. Then she goes to help the three other men, refreshing their coffees and clearing their plates.

I take a couple sips of water and zone out. My head is throbbing. Since I sat down, not a single car has gone by the lonely stretch of road. Route 83 runs through a rural part of Nebraska, where I honest to God believe there are more cows than people. I drove by signs that would name the tiny, nonexistent towns and under the name, it would say the population. Most were lower than a thousand. After I visited my parents in Nebraska and swore never to do that again, I jumped onto Route 83, the Blue Star Memorial Highway. There has never been an actual destination in mind, just the need to go.

She startles me when she comes back to the table with a tray carrying a mug of hot water, various tea bags, a lemon, and a small silver pitcher of milk. I go to give her my thanks, but her face—it looks like a twisted Picasso painting. All her features, everything from the neck up, run together in a blended mess. Her green glasses, ruby lips, and leathery tan skin combine into a contorted facial expression.

I reel away from her.

The bell on the diner's door jingles and a man in a pressed suit walks in. I look back at the waitress. The lipstick is back on her teeth and lips. Her glasses are over her eyes. Everything is where it should be on her face.

She raises her eyebrow. "You okay, dear?"

"Yeah, I just have a headache. I need to eat." I take another sip of water.

"Your food will be ready soon," she says, disappearing into the kitchen.

The man, who just walked in, looks completely out of place with his finely dressed black business suit but no tie, and black Italian leather shoes. With slicked-back black hair, midnight-blue eyes, and a smile that could charm anyone, he makes it hard not to ogle. Where did he come from? I thought I looked out of place in this empty diner, but he looks like he came directly from Manhattan. He scans the restaurant starting from his left, which is completely empty, looks at the countertop area with the three men, and then to his right, spotting me. He gives me a smile before taking a seat at a table next to my booth.

I look outside to see what fancy sports car he drove here or if there is a black-tinted sedan, but find nothing. There are just the three tanker trucks and my beat-up blue Civic. How did he get here? Did someone drop him off? He doesn't look like a government official or cop; he doesn't carry that swagger. Shoulders relaxed, jacket unbuttoned, top button of his shirt undone, he looks like he's out for a stroll and grabbing a cup of coffee at his local diner.

It's odd to see him on this lonely stretch of road. When I saw the abandoned Blue Memorial Highway, I thought that it would be a good place to check if someone had started following me again. They would have no place to hide. Before I left my parents, I had asked my father to search my car for any other tracking devices I may have missed. He raised an eyebrow but didn't ask questions and reported my car was free of them. The only thing he asked before I left was if I was in any trouble. With a wink, I told him I wasn't a troublemaker. He relaxed slightly, and he gave me a second extra-long hug, but that was it.

Turning my head to face him again, I catch tall, dark, and handsome staring at me, not in a creepy fashion, but rather watching me with those dark blue eyes. Suddenly, he gets up and closes the gap between him and my table.

"Since we are both here alone, would you mind some company while we eat?"

I can't think of a reason not to sit and chitchat while eating. My head is starting to feel better. I guess all I needed was some water. He doesn't look like a creep, but a stable, educated man in his midthirties. I haven't gotten any vibes from him that make me feel uncomfortable, so I shrug and nod.

"Wonderful," he says with his eyes aglow. I swear there's even a twinkle in them. "My name is Lucas Star. What is yours?"

"Evie." I don't give him my last name.

"Do you live in one of the small villages around here?"

"Nope, passing through. You?"

"Traveling for work."

"What do you do?"

He pauses and tilts his head slightly, his smile growing even more, if that's even possible. "Hospitalities."

"Like hotels?" I ask.

"Yes. I'm a hotel consultant. I usually stay at a hotel for a couple of weeks before traveling to the next. So, what brings you to the middle of nowhere?"

"Road trip."

Just then, the waitress notices the addition at my table and comes over with her worn-out grin.

"Hiya, handsome. Why, you look super snazzy. What can I get ya?"

"Hello, Sally," he says after looking at her nametag. "I'd love a cup of black coffee and an omelet with cheddar cheese, onions, and peppers, with a side of hash browns and bacon."

"Coming up," Sally says, returning behind the counter to get his coffee.

"So, Eve, where did your road trip start?"

"Pennsylvania, near the Poconos."

"That's a beautiful area."

"Yeah, it *was* nice."

"Are you meeting up with your husband at the end of your trip?"

I want to ask him why he's asking me so many questions but decide he is trying to converse with me. His eyes look down at my hand. I'm still wearing my engagement ring and wedding band. I somehow forgot to take them off. They have been a part of me for years and in the past, when I went to clean them, I felt naked without them. But they will fetch a nice amount of money. Jim always bought me the best jewelry. "No. We are separated."

"I'm sorry to hear that. That is a shame."

"Yeah."

"I don't want to pry, but you seem rather lost," Lucas Star says.

The words escape me. Of course I'm lost. I've lost everything for this miracle child, and I don't even know what I'll ever gain from having it.

"Isn't everyone?" I say with a chuckle, trying not to think about everything.

"Some more than others."

The waitress reappears with a tray of food, most of it mine, and his coffee. She loads the table with plates of hot, delicious breakfast of goodness. I'm starving. I hadn't eaten since yesterday afternoon. Without replying to his last comment, I dig in to the French toast, slathering syrup all over it and the pancakes. After a couple bites of pancakes, I dip my bacon into the maple syrup. The combination of salty pork and sweet maple syrup tastes euphoric.

Lucas cuts up his omelet and butters a piece of toast, digging into his much smaller feast. He takes a glance at my feast, struggling not to look surprised at all the food.

"I'm pregnant and always hungry. Everything I eat goes straight to the baby."

"Congratulations. I didn't mean to offend. It's not often that a petite woman out-eats me. I was honestly wondering where you were going to put all of that food."

"Right here," I say, pointing to my stomach before a belch erupts from my lips. I must look like a pig.

Lucas laughs, then lets out his own burp. "I'm glad we can be ourselves. It's refreshing."

For the first time in weeks, I laugh and smile and possibly relax a little. "It is."

In fifteen minutes, all the plates on the table are cleared. Not a crumb left. Finished with my meal, I take out my wallet to pull out my cash.

"I got this. My treat. Thanks for the company, Eve—I hope you don't mind me calling you that. It feels more fitting," Lucas says, adding a wink.

"Eve is fine, but are you sure? I ate a ton, enough for two." I literally ate every piece of food the waitress brought, scraping my plates clean.

"Absolutely," he says, laughing, pulling out two fifty-dollar bills and putting them under his empty coffee mug, at least quadruple the actual bill.

"Thank you."

"Well, Eve, take care of yourself and that precious child you carry. You know all children are precious?"

I look down at my round stomach and place a hand on my child. "Most are," I say as a joke.

He stops smiling and leans across the table for my hand next to my mug. His midnight blue eyes grow. "They are all precious and should be treated so." He takes out his wallet again and goes to hand me a fist full of hundreds.

"Oh no," I say, refusing to take the money but really wanting to take it. Hell, his suit cost more than the cash he is offering me, and I bet he has a closet full of them.

"I insist. Take care of that child and yourself. Take it." He hands me a minimal business card along with close to a thousand dollars.

"Is this a trick?"

"No, Eve. I want to help you."

Katie Zaber

17 Weeks - Badlands National Park, South Dakota

My baby can hear me. It knows the sound of my voice and might even find it soothing, though I haven't said much in the last two weeks. Since I have left Melisa's, the only people I have had a conversation with are Lucas and my parents, besides brief sentences spoken with restaurant and motel staff. I should give Melisa a call.

But I think my large onion—that's what the baby book says—needs to hear my voice or at least get used to it.

So I sing to the onion growing inside me, nothing special, just a song from the radio while staring at the ceiling, which also happens to be a mirror at this cheap floozy motel I found. The bed was clean, which was all I could really hope for. The mirror is weird and makes me want to smash it. I thought of taking a blanket and attempting to cover it, but I have nothing to stick the blanket to and don't want to make holes in the ceiling. I tried to request a different room, but apparently all thirty-eight rooms at this fleabag motel have mirrored ceilings. *It's what they're known for,* added the snarky pimple-covered front deskman, sitting behind his plexiglass fortress of protection against the lowlifes who frequent this sleazy motel.

I toss the idea around about going to the restaurant that borders the parking lot of the motel. Some type of diner; they all look the same after a while. When I try to think of what kind of food onion wants, nothing comes to mind.

No cravings. No appetite. Just loneliness. Me and my onion.

Oh, little onion, what a troublemaker you are already, making your momma tear up.

Why won't you tell me what you want to eat?

Little onion, what happened? Are you all right?

Stop sleeping and tell me what to feed you, because I don't really want to feed myself. But I will feed you, little onion. I will try to keep you alive.

My stomach grumbles, but I still have no appetite. On the corner of the motel dresser, there's a card. I can't for the life of me remember taking it out of my purse and putting it there, but I have pregnancy brain—or at least I can use that as an excuse. I get off the bed and hold the shiny business card in my hand. The only information on the white glossy cardboard paper is his name and phone number in raised black ink. No address or company name. No border or logo. Just the bare minimum contact information.

There was no reason for Lucas to be nice to me. Pay for my meal and hand me a fistful of cash. No one does that without any reason. What was the reason? Was he just being nice? Where did he come from?

He seemed like he wanted me to call him, or at least that was the impression I'm stuck with, and I can't think of a reason not to. I checked my car as soon as I left the diner and found no more additional trackers. I'm almost certain he works for hotels and not some laboratory, waiting and watching. I grab my cheap, prepaid flip phone and leave the room.

Outside on the second-floor balcony, the sun dips below the horizon, turning the sky shades of orange and neon pink. The air feels stale. I can never remember feeling so hot in all my life, but apparently this little one is a fiery ball of life. The parking lot below is empty except for the handful of rusty pickup trucks scattered about. There has been no sign of a black sedan, so at least that's a relief. One less problem to worry about.

A little girl stands outside her room, two doors down, completely alone with her back to me. Gauging by her height beside the balcony railing, I'd say she's young. No older than seven, and skinny. Too skinny. In her hands is a dirty, ripped doll. It reminds me of Raggedy Ann. The blonde girl with greasy, matted hair happily hums a song. Her pink shirt is stained and her pants are soiled. The girl could use a meal and a parent. I'll order takeout and share with her. Who knows when she ate last or when she'll eat again?

"Hi. What's your name?" I ask the child.

Slowly, her head turns around at an unnatural angle, twisting her neck, wrinkling her skin. The crunch of her bones grinding against each other makes my stomach flip and forget about food, making me step back. It sounds like someone is grinding their boot into gravel. Her back is still toward me, along with her face. No one can survive their head twisting around without snapping their spine, but somehow she's still standing. Clicking and popping sounds come from her neck as she lifts her chin, showing me green frost-covered eyes. "I shall silence it. We shall banish it. Kill it and make it no more," she says in an eerie voice that doesn't come from a kid. "Kill it! Kill it! Kill it!" she shrills.

I almost drop my phone as I jump backward, pushing up against my door. Startled by the possessed child, I can barely think straight as my body trembles. I'm scared out of my mind. The motel keys jingle in my hands as I try to unlock the door, but I'm not turning my back on the pint-size terror, afraid she'll leap at me.

Suddenly, the kid's eyes return to normal as she turns her head to look back at her doll, returning to a normal child, bones popping back into place, skin smoothing out. She turns her whole body around, revealing a child—not a demon playing with her doll. "Hi. I'm playing with Mary until my mom says I can come back in." She lowers her head. "She has a man friend over."

Okay, maybe all the weird things that have been happening aren't just coincidences. For someone who is a nonbeliever, I'm starting to think there just might be something cosmic at play—and I'm terrified that I'm just a pawn in some bigger plan that my insignificant mind can't begin to comprehend. Am I destined to be a surrogate mother and nothing more in life? Odd occurrences, like this kid's neck snapping and reverting back to normal, can never happen without a godly intervention. Really, that might be the only explanation at this moment that makes any sense. Otherwise, my life has just become a legit horror movie.

"Mary," I choke out. "That's a pretty name."

"Yeah, like the Virgin Mary. She watches over me."

"And all the angels," I blurt, thinking about celestial beings.

"No, just her." She says it as a matter of fact and then moves her doll along the balcony railing.

"And what's your name?"

"Logan."

"That's a beautiful name."

"It's not," the girl says, her green eyes attached to her doll's movements. "I was supposed to be a boy."

"It is a very pretty girl's name. It's unique, like you."

She doesn't respond, but continues to play with her doll in silence, no longer paying any attention to me. I place my hands on my stomach and vow never to raise my child like this. To give mine a better life. Somehow. Some way.

I leave the kid and go back to my room to order takeout, making sure I get a grilled cheese and fries for Logan to eat by herself. I'll feed her, but I won't go near the possessed child again.

On the table is a menu for the diner bordering the parking lot. Nothing fancy on it. All simple fare. Run-of-the-mill breakfast platters, lunchtime sandwiches, and the normal truck-stop dinners. I put Lucas's card back in my wallet, deciding after that conversation with Logan that I really don't want to talk to anyone else. What if I call him and midconversation, he rambles on how I'm the queen of Hell and my child will be its prince?

No, for the moment I'm going to continue coveting our last conversation, which brings a mix of lust and guilt. At night, he creeps into my dreams, his dark blue eyes hungry with want, searching my body before he crosses the room with a half smile on his handsome face. I run my fingers through his solid black hair and pull him close to me so I can feel his bare chest against mine. Smooth hands wrap around my hips, slowly sliding my underwear off, teasing me. I take off his boxer shorts and push him onto the bed. Straddling him, I moan with ecstasy as he rocks under me and that's always when I wake up, mid-orgasm, with my hand between my legs. I'm soaking wet, needing to finish. And while I'm awake, vibrating my fingers, I return to my dream and fantasize about Lucas.

The realization hits me. I no longer dream of Jim.

I look down at the faded menu and know exactly what I want. Something different.

Katie Zaber

18 Weeks - Casper, Wyoming

Baby, are you bored with me yet?

Today, my e-reader says you've mastered yawning and that I could start feeling you hiccup. Please don't hiccup inside me. That sounds weird, and Mommy doesn't like it when she hiccups. Can you be considerate and not do that in me? Or is that too much to ask, cucumber?

Late at night, when I have nothing to hold except you, I picture you curling your tiny fingers around my pinky. They should be perfectly developed now, including your unique fingerprint, which will attach itself to you forever. You have that now, but not a name. Nor a known sex, but we aren't normal and I don't want us to be lab rats, so we'll just have to wait until birth to find out.

I can't help but wonder, what are you? Are you a tough little boy or studious scholar? A dainty little girl or a fierce female? What will you look like? Is it possible for you to even be a boy, since from what I've read, you're basically going to be a clone of me? So chances are you're a little girl. Will you look like me when I was a child? Straight brown hair, freckles, hazel eyes that change color, depending on my mood. When you're up to mischief, will your eyes turn forest green? When you're sad, will they be mud puddle brown?

What personality will you have, or will I be in charge of molding it? Please don't be like me. Don't have my temper or mindset. I'm not a good role model. I'll have to find you someone else to look up to.

Please, I beg you, be better than me.

And don't be something cursed or wicked. I need to keep believing you are perfect and not someone destined to bring Hell on Earth. We have to believe those obscure ideas in order for them to be true… right? Plus, I'm pretty sure you're a girl. So I think we are safe. Or that's at least what I'm going to continue to believe. The other thought leads down a dark rabbit hole of insanity that will eventually end with me in a padded room, without you. So, I will not go down that road. The only thing I'm certain of is that we need each other. And I'll do anything to keep us together, including pretending to be sane when I know I'm slowly losing my grasp on reality.

The plain business card has somehow found its way into my hands, again. Raised black ink typed on white cardstock paper.

Lucas was the first and only conversation I didn't steer away from, with the exception of my parents, which felt more like I had to. It was an awkward visit, but somehow an eye-opener and something I needed to do. For the first time in my life, I actually feel closer to my father. Closer than I ever have before, but at the same time more distant from my mother. But there has always been distance with her. The stranger question is, what makes me so attracted to Lucas? Why do I feel the need to call him so badly? What do I need to say to him?

The blistering summer sun is melting me in a motel parking lot that is shared with another diner. Two weeks and I barely have any of the money Lucas gave me. Between the bottomless pit that is my stomach and the need to stretch out and sleep in a bed with cucumber doubling in size, the thousand went fast. Now all that's left is sixty-two dollars and some odd change.

I should count it.

The cash I had taken out of my bank account has dwindled to virtually nothing. Meaning, I have a decision to make with the cash I have left. Either rent a room or eat at the restaurant and camp out in my car in the hot Wyoming sun and end my little run away.

I can make an easy phone call to Melisa. She would wire me money in a second and jump on the next flight to Casper to fetch me back to her house, but I don't want that. My parents would offer me a tent or yurt at their farm. But with how fragile I feel, I don't think I could survive another visit with my mom right now.

How many times now have I picked up a random working pay phone outside of a gas station and called Jim, merely to hear his voice? Just to hear the first breath expel from his lungs as he says *hello*. So many times, I wanted to tell him I'm sorry again in case he didn't hear me or thought it was just something I said, that there were no emotions behind my words, but there were. I'm sure by now, Melisa has gotten in touch with him and told him I disappeared. But I hope she didn't. He doesn't deserve this shit. The way he smiled as he got into his car, the last time I saw him, it broke me further. We had plans. A life we were building.

And in a moment, it was gone. Like none of it ever existed. The farther I drive, the more it feels like the home we had made is a memory from some distant life that wasn't mine. As if it were a story I read and confused with reality.

So no. I won't contact anyone from my past life. That life vanished when I made my decision. At least not now. Maybe later. When I'm ready.

The phone crackles as it rings. When the fear of him picking up the line comes to a point that I can no longer stomach, I hang up as he answers. I sit there, petrified, unsure of what to do.

The phone on my lap rings. I sit there, looking at the electronic device. Is it a trap? Should I answer? I know the number on it.

It's the one I just dialed. An unknown number not programmed into my phone. He's calling back again.

Fuck. I pick up the phone. "Hello."

"Eve, is that you? I was hoping you would call. How are you?"

"I've been better. How are you? Where are you traveling today?"

"Right now, I'm standing on the balcony of my hotel room outside of Denver, Colorado. It's actually really pretty here. The temperature is comfortable; flowers are blooming."

"That sounds nice."

"What are you up to? Where are you now?"

"South of Casper, Wyoming."

"You're not too far. I'm just a few hours south. Are you headed this way?"

I stifle a laugh. "Sure."

"Great. I'd love to meet up and get lunch or dinner—my treat."

"That sounds wonderful. What's the address?" I ask as my stomach rumbles.

I don't have a GPS or a smartphone. The directions Lucas gave me are simple: Turn off ramp blah blah, make your first right, and continue for ten miles. The old-school directions most people don't give anymore. He said I should arrive at the hotel by six o'clock, and he was right.

My car sits in the shadow of a sprawling Swiss Chalet that I would guess costs upward of a grand a night. Private large balconies, filled with wooden patio chairs, extend off every room. I avoid the eight-car-wide covered valet. My car looks out of place in this parking lot. All the cars parked are brand new or rentals. Mine is literally the only one I see that's over five years old.

Why did I come here? Was it to be embarrassed? Of course he was going to stay at a fancy hotel. Why would he be working for a motel chain?

Driving through the parking lot, contemplating if I should speed toward the exit, I find him sitting on a rocking chair and reading a newspaper in a courtyard, waiting for me. Dressed in tan slacks and a silver relaxed-collar t-shirt with the first button open. There is no escape. He stands, smiling and waving before brushing back his thick black hair.

I could pretend not to see him, but he would just call my phone. Plus, I'm starving and I coasted in on fumes. How can I escape? And really, with his luscious black hair, sharp cheekbones, and sexy smile, do I want to leave? No.

I surrender and park the car begrudgingly and hungrily—a dangerous combination. Lucas said on the phone that he made us a dinner reservation at six-thirty, so I'd like to hurry inside and freshen up before stuffing my face, something I haven't done since lunchtime yesterday. My headache is becoming a migraine and I really want to eat before I get any more weird auras.

Quickly, before he gets to the car, I fix my disheveled hair and look in the mirror. The black bags under my eyes get bigger every day. It looks like I haven't slept in months, which is pretty accurate. There's no amount of makeup that would conceal the dark pillows under my eyes. But I can remove the yellow eye crust stuck in my bottom eyelash. Now that I feel shy and even more self-conscious, he strolls up with his gorgeous midnight blue eyes and a grin that makes me feel giddy, among other things. He puts a hand on the door handle, opening the door for me.

"Eve, it's so nice to see you. You look excellent," he says, helping me out of the car, and then gives me an air kiss and a polite hug. "You should have used the valet. How many bags do you have?"

"Thank you. I only have one."

"I'll take it for you," he says, opening the back seat and grabbing my sole piece of luggage. He grabs the handle graciously, then escorts me to the entrance of the log-cabin-styled hotel. It is rustic charm elevated to a sophisticated level that I have never experienced.

Inside, my eyes widen at the grand entrance's ceiling, two floors tall, with a fireplace just as big. Ten desks with associates wait to help guests check in. There are multiple concierge desks, staffed with men and women waiting to plan day trips for anyone who will shovel out thousands of dollars on what they market as a once-in-a-lifetime excursion. To the right is the wraparound wooden bar and to the left is one of the prestigious restaurants on the property.

He walks me past the desk, down the hallway, and to the elevator, one hand rolling my luggage, the other looped around my arm. "I'll get you your own room after dinner. You can stay as long as you like, and feel free to use all the hotel's services. They owe me," he says with a wink.

"What did you do for them?"

"Helped them understand their clientele's needs."

"Hmm, thank you, but I really can't accept a room. That's a ton of money. I'm happy to eat a fancy dinner and sleep on the couch."

"It will be compensated. You don't need to worry about it." We get off the elevator onto a floor with a long hallway and five rooms spread out. He opens the door at the end of the hallway.

My mouth drops. "Yeah, that four-piece sectional is big enough for me and another person. I think I'm good for the night."

He clicks his tongue. "But a woman in your condition should be treated like a queen and lie on that size bed or bigger. Fine. I'll take the couch; you can take the bedroom. If you insist on sharing a room."

"I just don't want to be a bother. You've been so nice... why?"

"Everyone should be treated kindly. You looked so small and alone in that diner. And I'm always traveling alone. When I saw you, I thought it might be nice to be alone together."

I try not to blush and roll my eyes at his pickup line, but give him a smile before entering the bathroom to clean myself up. When I went on this excursion, I didn't plan on going anywhere nice. The only outfit that is semi-appropriate for a fancy dinner reservation is a faded black spandex dress. I take a towel and wash my face and do a quick once over my body since I don't think I have time to take a shower. I brush my hair so it's not a frizzy mess and pick out fresh black panties and a bra that barely fits me. I pull the dress over my head, tugging it down over my stomach and hips, yanking at it until it's at least midway up my thigh. It doesn't look horribly stretched out, but it's definitely not fashionable and there's no way I can bend over. But I have a feeling that even if the hostess turns her nose at me, Lucas will make it right. Somehow.

I step out of the bathroom and I'm greeted with a whistle.

"Wow, Eve. You look amazing."

I huff. "I didn't do anything except make myself look like a black sausage. Didn't even put on makeup."

"You don't need makeup. You should never cover up your natural beauty."

Is he really this into me? How? I give him a suspicious smile. "Thank you."

"Come. I'm hungry and dinner is about to begin." He goes for the door like a gentleman, leading me out of the room.

Arm in arm, we stroll through the lobby to the hostess podium. She smiles at Lucas. Her eyes pass over me disapprovingly. Inspecting her nails, acting as if she just found something under them that's more interesting than the conversation we're about to have, she says, "A table for two will be thirty minutes."

"I have a reservation for the chef's table. Star."

"Oh, yes." Her tone changes tune, suddenly aware that she is being rude to the wrong person. "Mr. Star, please follow me." The young blonde steps into the swanky but dark lodge-style restaurant. Chandeliers with at least fifty lights do little to brighten the expansive room and ceiling, creating a romantic atmosphere. She keeps walking until we are ten feet away from the kitchen and sets drink menus on the table tucked into an alcove, separated from the main restaurant but with a view of the kitchen madness. "Here's your private table. Chef Lorenzo has been working hard on his menu for you tonight. There will be five courses and he will come out to present each one. There are no allergies, right?" She looks at both of us.

"Nope, I'm good. Just can't eat anything raw," I tell her.

Lucas shakes his head.

"Perfect. Enjoy."

I watch the young, attractive hostess walk away, then look back at Lucas. His eyes aren't on her sexy ass, but are staring at me. "Lucas, a five-course private dining experience, at a chef's table? Seriously?"

"I wanted to impress you."

"Two burgers, fries, and an extra large milkshake would have done it. This... I've never experienced anything like this before. Is this your normal?"

"Well, I have to try and approve everything the property has to offer," he says with a mischievous grin.

"Lucky you... does that include massages?" I ask as a joke.

"Of course," he says, not skipping a beat.

"You have the best job I've ever heard of. Is it hard?"

"Not really. It's all about understanding desires. How to package and deliver them to guests."

Damn, I wonder if he can guess my desires and deliver. I'm positive he could.

The chef introduces himself and places our first course on the table, a double boiler with hot, oozy cheese. Swiss cheese and herbs, and I believe I even smell a hint of earthy hops coming from the fondue pot. Six skewers rest on two identical plates along with bread, apples, pears, mushrooms, carrots, peppers, cauliflower, and broccoli. I can hear Melisa nagging at me to dig in and eat all of my veggies. Chef Lorenzo's Italian accent is thick and I can barely understand a word he says, so I nod and look at the food hungrily, not wanting to be impolite and start eating in front of him. Or is he waiting for us to try it?

Lucas thanks him and tears a piece of bread in half and dips it into the steaming cheese. He motions for me to follow, and I don't hesitate to skewer the broccoli and cauliflower. Only when the both of us are chewing and moaning in delight does Chef Lorenzo leave the table.

With all of my six skewers in the cheese, I realize that I have forgotten the handsome man sitting across from me because of the food; I look up to see him only fixing his third skewer. Great. This is the second time I've gorged myself in front of him. Half my pumpernickel and honey wheat bread are already gone too.

"Sorry. I haven't eaten all day and if no one was watching, I'd lick this cheese pot clean."

He laughs and takes a sip of wine that is supposed to pair well with the cheese. Some twenty-year-old white wine that smells dry. "If you like this, wait until the entrée. His veal Zuricher Geschnetzeltes is incredible."

"A veal what?"

"It's sautéed veal in a creamy mushroom Chardonnay sauce. Tender, juicy meat smothered in decadent wine gravy; it's really divine. He usually has some type of potato dish alongside it."

"I've never had veal before, but it sounds delicious."

"It is," he says with a smile that melts me to my core, giving me chills.

The sweet and savory flavor of the granny smith apple and gooey Swiss cheese might be my new craving. I wonder if just a piece of sliced Swiss cheese wrapped around an apple would satisfy. I take another bite and decide no, it wouldn't.

The only complaint I have about dinner was that each course was too small. Granted, the plates were crafted and the cooks arranged each component just so, but within three to five bites, I cleaned my plate. The roasted artichoke soup was gone in six spoonfuls and the cup wiped clean with a fluffy roll. I could see the bottom of the plate under the sparse salad that had more candied nuts than leaves. When I saw the tiny portion of veal, I almost cried and ate it in four bites, but it was heavenly. Dessert was a sliver of blueberry cheesecake and a quarter portion of a raspberry tart loaded with fresh whipped cream.

The food was outstanding and I don't think I've ever eaten a meal that took so much preparation and planning, but for as much work as the chefs put into it and how much it cost, I should be full and bursting at the seams. Instead, I'm thinking of ice cream, brownies, and waffles with a mountain of whipped cream.

Lucas keeps asking me if I would like my own suite, and I keep telling him not to waste the money on me. That the couch is fine and his huge suite can fit at least four more grown adults if needed. He shakes his head and makes a *tsk* noise each time, but he stops bothering me once I get out of the shower.

For the first time in months, I feel refreshed. In my last clean t-shirt and stretchy shorts, I curl up on the couch under a light blanket and flip through the OnDemand channels in search of a movie for us to watch. I need to do laundry tomorrow. I'm sure there are washers and dryers somewhere on this property. Maybe I can even drop off my stinking pile of filth and pick it up all clean and folded.

"Hmm, decisions, decisions. You said we can order anything? There are a ton of movies I've never seen."

"What do you normally watch?" he asks, coming out of the bedroom freshly showered and wearing a white t-shirt and black gym shorts, looking how I dreamed.

TV? What's TV?

When was the last time I watched TV? While on the road, I hardly watched anything on the sticky, expensive, mostly porn channels available in the motel rooms. Half the time, I reread books I've had for years on my e-reader. I think I watched some garbage shows with Melisa when I had stayed with her. She loves reality junk. Jim used to watch black and white classic movies and old Westerns when there was a lull in sports, while I read. Ninety percent of the time, ESPN was on and showing a game of some type; he wasn't picky. Basketball, baseball, football, soccer, lacrosse, surfing; literally any physical competition was entertainment for him. For the life of me, I can't recall the last movie or prime time show that I watched. "Let's watch a stand-up. There has to be a good comedian on here."

"Stand-ups are good. Just as long as it isn't that guy with the puppets," he says, cringing.

"Agreed."

We decide on a comedian and settle onto the extra comfy couch that even has a huge ottoman for our feet. His arm isn't touching me. We aren't snuggling. But the gap between our shoulders is miniscule and our legs are inches apart. About five minutes into the show, my stomach rumbles loudly, gurgling for more food. I look at the clock; it's only been an hour since we've gotten back to his room.

Lucas turns his head and looks down at my bump. "Are you hungry? We can order some room service."

I give him a bashful smile. "If you're offering…"

"What are you in the mood for?"

"Dessert."

"I could go for that," he says, licking his lips, looking at me.

I can't say what excites me more, dessert or him. "Ice cream sundaes and waffles and brownies. Oh, and extra chocolate syrup and a mountain of whipped cream."

"A mountain of whipped cream?"

"If possible," I say innocently.

He reaches for the phone and puts in our order, asking for two vanilla sundaes with the works, along with extra sides of whipped cream and chocolate sauce, a tray of brownies and cookies, and two Belgian waffles. When he gets off the phone, the impulse to lunge at him and thank him for ordering our treat is hard to fight. Instead, I smile at him.

He licks his lips. "I haven't had a sundae in years."

"Mmm, with chocolate sauce and whipped cream. I hope sprinkles too. I'm dipping the waffle, brownies, and cookies into my sundae. I can't wait." I'm so excited. Excited and horny. Yeah, I'm horny. It's been months since I've been this close to any man. I can't help but squirm a little, and I can't help notice him noticing me. But really, I'm not sure what I'm craving more, food or sex.

"Excited?" he asks, teasing, sitting down in his spot, but closer this time so our shoulders are touching.

"Very," comes out more of a growl.

He rests his hand on his leg; his pinky finger touches my bare thigh. The want is intense. But I swallow it down and hit play on the TV.

Every time there's a joke, we laugh, rubbing our shoulders together. Then the comedian tells a big punch line, making me fall over on my side with laughter. I cry out, holding my belly, afraid that all the diaphragm movement will disturb the baby, "Oh my god, he's too much. I can't breathe!"

Lucas laughs, holding his stomach. His cheeks are turning red. He's got a huge smile and twinkling eyes. They captivate me. I'm still on my side, out of breath, lying on the couch, when he reaches for me, placing a hand on my face.

Knock, knock. "Room service."

My face lights up at the thought of ice cream. His thumb grazes my cheekbone as he gets up to answer the door. Introducing himself, he learns the worker's name, Kevin, and welcomes him into his suite. The worker rolls a large gilded cart into the living room and then takes off the lids, displaying the feast before me. My heart leaps at the sight of food for the second time today. I don't even realize

I'm standing, hovering over the ice cream sundaes before the young man has even stepped away. Lucas hands the guy a twenty before closing the door behind him and joining me in the smorgasbord.

Halfway through a waffle, two brownies, four sugar cookies, and four out of the six scoops of a vanilla ice cream sundae is when I notice that I'm covered in chocolate sauce. It's on my face and has dripped all over my last clean t-shirt. "Wow, I'm a pig. Shit, this was my last clean shirt."

"It looks good on you," He says with a coy smile. "You have a little something here." He reaches for a dollop of whipped cream on my nose, swiping his finger down the arch, wiping the tip of my nose clean. His jaw muscles unhinge as he parts his lips and licks the cream off his fingertip. My body tenses as I'm mesmerized by his movements, envious of his finger getting all the attention.

Then his eyes focus on my lips. "And a little something here."

He leans forward; I sit, ready for a kiss as he drags his tongue over my lips, softly and slowly. A sensation begins in my chest, traveling across my breasts and downward, giving me goose bumps. Shifting my hips, I open my eyes when he pulls back. There's no point in fighting the urge to rip his clothes off and have him strip me of mine. With my stomach satisfied, I'm filled with a hunger that craves satisfaction. No, demands it. I cup his cheek with one hand and run the other through his damp hair.

His dark blue eyes brighten. I feel like the nerd in high school who snagged the attention of the heartthrob jock. I'm excited and shy, mixed with nervousness—I haven't slept with anyone since Jim. I'm officially five months pregnant this week and couldn't feel more awkward. Having this baby bump isn't something I'm used to. Having sex with a baby bump is something I've never done. Suddenly I'm worried, as a flash of questions and concerns flood my mind. Will anything we do hurt the baby? Is it possible that being too rough will hurt little cucumber? I know it's impossible for his dick to poke the baby, but the thought still enters my mind.

He looks down at my bulging belly and caresses it. "We don't have to if you aren't ready. You just look so gorgeous. Majestic, even."

"I'm the queen of dessert," I joke, feeling the heat in my cheeks as they flush under his gaze.

"You are a queen. Queen mother," he says, then plants a soft kiss on my stomach, above my belly button. "No title is more meaningful and honored than mother."

My nipples harden until I can feel them poking through my shirt. The need to have him, to feel his skin against mine, to moan in ecstasy, to feel loved, if only for a moment, overrides all other emotions. Licking my lips, I taste chocolate. I must look ridiculous, horny and panicked while trying to pose seductively with a swollen tummy as beads of sweat drip down the questioning look on my face, mixing with the splatters of chocolate sauce.

But he smiles at me. In an instant, all my fears, all my worries melt away before his lips even touch me.

Katie Zaber

19 Weeks - Denver, Colorado

With soft Egyptian sheets smothering my body, a stack of feathery pillows cradles my head. The hum of an air conditioner blasts frigid air into the steamy hotel room. My nipples are rock hard from the cool air, but my legs are warm, entwined with his. Black, luscious hair sits perfect on his head. Even after my fingers have run through it countless times, his hair remains picturesque. He looks ready for his close-up after a heated sex scene. Midnight blue eyes open and find me ogling him. A smile creeps across his face as he stretches his arms and chest. This is where I want to be.

"Good morning," Lucas says so casually. As if this isn't the first time we've woken up together. Well, it isn't, but oddly it feels more familiar than that. He rolls over onto his side, cups my cheek with his hand as he gives me a soft kiss, and then gently brushes his fingertips over my ever-expanding belly. "How did you and your little one sleep?"

"Wonderful. I only got up twice from leg cramps and to pee. So, overall, a good night. Better than the night before. I still feel bad I woke you up three times."

He kisses my forehead. "Don't worry about it. You can't help it. I just wish there was something I could do to help."

"You've done so much. Between buying me a new wardrobe and luggage... You're amazing."

"Being able to grow a baby, now that's amazing," he says.

I roll my eyes at him. Scooting out from under Lucas' hand, I shake out my leg cramps and get out of the mahogany four-poster bed. I can feel his gaze lingering on me as I leave the room. Then I hear moans, a shuffle of sheets, and then him getting off the bed to stretch.

The bathroom is swank. There are his and her private toilets with a bidet, a two-person Jacuzzi tub, a humongous walk-in shower with three shower heads, and double sinks. We can be in the bathroom at the same time and not know. It's that spacious. And there's a second full guest bathroom off the living room too.

I've honeymooned in the Caribbean with Jim and island hopped, vacationing at different all-inclusive resorts, but none of the hotel rooms I had stayed in are as fancy as this one. If this room were in any of those hotels, I'm sure it would be the presidential suite.

Every day since I've arrived has been a dream I'm afraid I'll wake up from. Spa days filled with pampering, shopping, spending thousands of dollars on clothes that fit my swelling body. At first I didn't ask for anything, even refused, but he wouldn't take no for an answer. So I gave in.

Five indulgent days. I keep wondering when he will say our time is up. That his work at this hotel is done, and it's time for *him* to go back home to his model wife and mansion, but he hasn't. He doesn't awkwardly look at his phone either, like he's hiding it from me. Nor has he hinted that he wants me gone, but has insisted that I stay.

And really, with limited options, I will not end what this is. Whatever this is.

I wipe, flush, wash, and walk back over to Lucas, who is now sitting up, flipping through the channels to find the news. Sliding back into bed, I snuggle up next to him as he puts his arm around me. With my head on his chest, I close my eyes again and try to decide what I want to order for breakfast from room service. We could go down to that one restaurant for breakfast, but my back is sore and all I want to do is lie in bed or on that comfy couch.

I think mango went through a growth spurt or something because all of my clothes no longer fit and I started seeing stretch marks. My body feels like it's being rearranged. Fat moving and growing in places where there wasn't any. I don't want to even know what my ass looks like. The container of cocoa butter comes everywhere I go. All day, I reapply it and still my skin constantly feels dry and itchy. I've upped the amount of water I've been drinking too, which I think has only resulted in me peeing more.

Baby, I'm trying to take care of you. But I don't know how long this is going to last. I'd do anything to convince Lucas to fall in love with me and take care of me for the rest of our lives, but a man who can have anything at any time with a simple nod is bound to become bored with me. At least I'll have a nice parting gift: suitcases to pack up all my pregnant designer clothes.

"So what's the plan today?" I ask, afraid of the answer.

He's looking at his phone—from the looks of it, an email. "Breakfast, room service, okay? I have to send some emails, do some work."

"Breakfast in bed sounds perfect."

"Afterward, maybe we'll go down to the outlets."

"Again? What else is there to buy?"

"My schedule has been rearranged. And I didn't buy you any beach attire."

"Beach? What do you mean?"

He looks up, giving me a hopeful smile. "If you want to come, my next hotel visit is in the Florida Keys."

My first impulse is to ask when we are leaving, but I stop, coming to my senses, ending this brief interlude. "I can't."

He looks hurt, offended. "If it's the flight, I'm sure you can still fly. You're only five months—"

"It's not that. I can't fly. Not because of the baby, but… it's actually better if I left today before this becomes something."

"What? Why?"

I'm already off the bed and heading to the closet that has all of my new clothes. "Because it's safer that way."

He rushes over to me and places a hand on my shoulder. "Is someone after you? Is that why you've been driving around, on the run? You can tell me. I'll protect you."

"I'm not sure anyone can. I'm not even sure who is after me." My hands wrap around my middle. "Ever since I've been pregnant… there have been black government cars following me. I think I lost them a couple of weeks ago and I check the car for trackers. I don't know what's going on, but I think they want me and my baby. And I won't let them take us!"

His arms engulf me in a big hug as tears pour down my face. How long have I kept this secret inside? I only told Melisa the weird test results and how I'm giving birth to a clone. I didn't tell her about my stalkers. If she knew people were after me, she would flip the fuck out and try to kill them.

He brushes my hair. "Shh. It's alright. Everything will be okay, I promise. They won't take you or your baby away. I won't let that happen. You hear me," he says with a deep, dark voice that sounds extremely threatening, not to me but to anyone who would hurt me.

I step away from him. "Why? Do you really like me that much that you would jeopardize your life for a… fling? A one-night stand? Am I really worth it?"

"Yes, Eve, you are. And I didn't think this was a fling."

"We barely know each other," I say while wiping away tears with my hand.

He runs into the bathroom and grabs a box of tissues. "I know that I'm falling for you. It's been short, but I enjoy your company. It's been a long time since I've wanted someone's constant companionship. I don't know what it is about you, but I'm drawn to you and desire to know why," he says, giving me a handful of tissues.

I dry up some tears and blow my nose. "Really? With me pregnant? You want to date a pregnant woman? Do you even want children?"

"I like kids. But I really like you. That includes everything about you. As for kids—" He clicks his tongue before sighing. "My father abandoned me as a child. Everything I remember about him is painful, and I never met my mother. I was never adopted. I don't know if I would make a good father. Family has always been a bitter memory for me. But for the first time in a long time, the thought entered my mind."

"Shit. I'm sorry. My childhood wasn't perfect and some could argue that I should have been adopted or placed in foster care, but I had parents. I don't even know how to relate. I'm sorry; I'm just anxious and emotional. Nothing in my life has gone according to plan since becoming pregnant. This baby was never supposed to happen. It's a legit miracle. I think that's why the black cars are after me. They want to study its DNA and mine. I just want to be left alone and live a normal life. I just want to be in control and I haven't been for months. I'm spiraling."

"Don't apologize. You didn't know about my... lack of family," he says with a shrug. "Did they say what was wrong with the child's DNA?"

I laugh. "Long story short, I'm growing a healthy little clone."

He tilts his head. "Huh. And I thought I heard of everything."

I roll my eyes. "So now you know why I can't fly. I don't want my name coming up on any flight list."

He gives me a sly grin. "That's why we'll fly private. I should email my accountant; he should be able to get you a new identity."

A new identity.

It's not that I haven't thought of getting a new identity. My problem was that I didn't know where to start. I could have asked my parents, but really, when I thought about it, I'd rather not have them involved. It's weird that I want to protect them after all the bullshit they put me through, but I can say I'm a better person for not dragging them into this mess.

As for Lucas, he's volunteering and from the looks of it, has the money to back up everything he is saying. My parents are hippies and don't have a savings account.

"Wow, um, thank you?"

"You don't have to thank me," he says while stroking my hair. "I'll take care of everything. There's no need to worry," he says with a flicker in his eyes that begs me to trust him.

Against everything I know and have experienced, against my better judgment and the voice screaming inside my head, I do.

"I have to say, even though it's a hunk of junk, I'm going to miss my car. It was the first one I bought brand new," I tell Lucas, reminiscing about the day I stepped onto the lot, by myself, after weeks of research, comparing other makes and models before deciding to buy this car. The salesperson watched me step on the lot, thinking I'd be easy prey. I wasn't falling for any of those shady sales tactics.

Driving off the lot, blasting music with the windows rolled down, made me feel proud. It didn't matter that it wasn't a sports model or had power windows or anything like that. What mattered was that it was mine and after all my hard work and saving, I was able to buy something, make an adult purchase on my own. It was the first time I had ever felt like a true adult.

I contacted Melisa and told her I needed the title to my car. That was a fun conversation. She didn't like that I was going to sell my car at all and when I told her I didn't need it, she thought it was a suicide cry, but after some arguing and convincing, she mailed the title overnight, especially after I gave her the name and address of the rich hotel I'm staying at. When she looked it up, it probably calmed her nerves, but also made her want to ask a hundred questions. Before I hung up, I promised to call more often and keep her posted.

I didn't tell her about Lucas. Part of me was nervous to say it out loud, that we are… something. The fact that I couldn't name what we are made me freeze when I thought about telling her. Even the titles *boyfriend* and *girlfriend* sounds like teenage slang. So I'm uncertain how to define us. If asked, I can say I'm in a relationship, but that sounds cold. However, calling us *partners* implies that we've been together for a while. And the fact that I'm overthinking what we should call ourselves only solidifies how nervous I am, but at the same time, happy to start a brand new chapter in my life.

"And now it will belong to someone who needs it," he says with a grin.

We're waiting outside the hotel in the courtyard Lucas was sitting in when I drove the shambling car into the parking lot. Within hours of putting the car up for sale on a local social media site, we had three offers. The thought of agents knocking on some poor person's door looking for me crossed my mind; however, Lucas said not to worry and the most they could do after a legal sale was ask them if they have seen me or know my whereabouts. Since we won't tell them anything, all it will do is lead them to a dead end if they decide to continue pursuing me. This car sale will be the last thing Everild Smith does. After the paperwork is done and signed, my new identity will be Eve Burns.

I have no idea how Lucas's accountant pulled those strings, but I now have a new identity. A new persona. A fresh start, which is something everyone needs and deserves. So instead of going with the one who offered the most, I decided to respond to the mother whose profile implied that she was a single mother of three. After a few minutes of social snooping, it became clear that she was struggling and in desperate need of a car.

Sipping on pink lemonade while snacking on an oversized pretzel, dunking it into blissful beer cheese, I recline in a garden chair in the courtyard just next to the lobby and entrance.

"I think that's her." Lucas points to a brunette with three children who all look under the age of ten, stepping out of a car at the drop-off by the valet. Their taxi pulls away, leaving the woman and children. Lucas waves to her and calls out, "Sharron?"

She lifts her head and says something to her children. They nod and hold hands as they walk across the parking lot and into the courtyard.

"Hi. You must be Lucas and Eve."

Their clothes look faded and are definitely secondhand, being too big or too small on them, but they look healthy and loved. The kids stare at my plate. One of them even licks their lips. "Hi," I say. "Are you guys hungry? This pretzel is way too big for me to eat by myself."

All three heads swivel toward their mother, asking permission. She nods. "Say thank you."

They say thank you and slowly approach the feast on the table.

That's when Lucas flags down our server. "Excuse me. Could we please have four more lemonades and a large order of cheese fries with bacon? And some extra plates." He turns to the mother and asks her, "Is there anything else you would like? Our treat."

The mother looks confused. "No, you don't have to. We just came to look at the car. I can't afford anything off the menu here."

"Eve gets hungry all the time and needs constant snacking. It would be rude for us to eat in front of you after inviting you here. It's only polite to share."

She smiles while shaking her head. "Fries, pretzels, and lemonades are a treat enough. Thank you."

Lucas turns back to the waiter. "That will be all for now. Thank you, Mike."

No matter where we are, Lucas always finds out the name of every person who helps him or speaks to him, and he never forgets their name or to address them by it.

Thirty minutes after the kids tell us about their school and Sharron tells us how she works two jobs but always has time to check their homework, we head over to my piece of crap car. I feel guilty selling her this car, which will most likely break down on her in a year. What will she do then? How will she provide for her kids?

"So this is it. It's an excellent car for the amount of miles on it." Lucas opens the driver's side door so she can sit down and inspect the inside of the vehicle.

"Looks clean. You kept good care of it," she says as she runs her hands over the seats. "Mind if I take it for a quick spin to see how it drives?"

"Of course. I'll take the ride with you while Eve stays with the kids. She can walk them over to the park over there."

The children have been eyeing the brightly painted playground ever since they arrived. It can't be over two years old and seems in great condition, along with everything else at this deluxe hotel.

"Sasha, turn on your emergency phone. I'll be back in ten. Don't cause any mischief and watch after your brother and sister."

The oldest, who isn't quite a preteen yet, takes a prepaid simple phone out of her pocket. It can literally only be used to make emergency calls. "Yes, Momma."

Since they now have permission to go run around, they waste no time crossing the parking lot.

"Hold hands in a parking lot! You are too short and they won't see you!" She shakes her head as I catch up to them. I have a lot to learn and remember. This is my first time around kids since I saw Jim's nieces and nephews.

The youngest makes a beeline for the swings, while the middle child climbs up the jungle bars. I find the nearest bench and settle into a comfortable position. Sharron's oldest daughter doesn't join her siblings. Instead, she sits down next to me and watches them.

"You should go have fun. Run around," I tell the child.

"Nah. That's for kids."

"Sweetheart, you are a kid. Act like it while you can."

She shrugs, never taking her eyes off her brother and sister.

"I bet you they would love for their big sister to play with them. If I could run right now, I'd be playing tag."

A small grin slowly appears on her face before she shakes her head. Each sway shrinks her smile until it's gone. "If I get hurt, no one will be able to help Mom."

"Your brother and sister are old enough to help take care of you. How badly do you think you'll get hurt?"

"I saw a kid break their arm at the park. I even saw the bone sticking out. I would rather sit and watch."

Poor kid. I wonder how old she was when she saw that happen. Sounds like the incident traumatized her. Since I won't force her to do something she doesn't want to, I switch topics and ask her about her favorite subject in school, which turns out to be art. We talk about painting and molding clay and how fun it is to create pretty things.

Before I know it, Lucas and Sharron join us.

"So how did you like it?"

"It runs great. I opened the hood and saw nothing alarming. Online, you said you were asking for two grand?"

"Actually," Lucas butts in, "the price has changed."

I tilt my head.

The woman's face pales. "I can't afford more. Come on, kids."

Lucas shakes his head. "A dollar."

"What?" the woman asks, sounding perplexed.

"Legally, we must sell it to you—paperwork and whatnot. We don't need this car and honestly, without taking it to an auto mechanic, we have no idea what problems are under the hood. I can't sell it in good faith to you for the price listed and have the guilt that it might break on you at any point. So for a dollar, you'll get the title and will be able to save money for when it does regrettably break down."

Some part of me was hoping to keep that money for a rainy day fund, in case Lucas and I don't work out. Lucas made this decision without us discussing it; however, I feel great about it. After seeing how generous he is to a complete stranger who desperately needs help and not just a pregnant woman alone in a diner, I can't help but find myself falling in love with him.

The mother turns to me. "Are you sure? I never heard of anything like this. Is this a scam of some sort?"

"No. Everyone deserves kindness, and I think you are due for some," I tell the trembling woman who is clearly overwhelmed with emotions, remembering what Lucas told me.

Tears stream from her eyes. Her mouth hangs open, but she can't speak. The oldest daughter walks up to her mother and gives her a napkin, which makes Sharron laugh and bend over to hug her daughter. "See, honey, you work hard and be a good person, good things will happen. You gotta keep believin'."

"In humanity," Lucas adds.

The mother looks up with glossy eyes and says, "Yes, that too."

20 Weeks - Florida Keys, Florida

"How are you able to read while driving? It makes me feel sick. I can barely read my messages," Lucas says, shaking his head at me as our car pulls away from the chalet-style hotel en route to the airport. He keeps promising, saying that we won't have to go through any security, but I'm still scared.

"I'm used to it. My parents drove around a lot and if I can read with the way my father drove... this is easy."

I'm nervous. No amount of reassuring will calm my nerves, even though Lucas has tried over the last few days to get me to relax, saying he will take care of any authorities and I have nothing to worry about. But I'm terrified when we pull up to the plane that the first airline official who greets us is going to ask for our driver's licenses and something will be wrong with my freshly printed one. It has to be normal protocol, even though I'm uncertain because I've never had the luxury of flying on a private jet. Focusing on my baby book and learning about this week is at least distracting me, a little bit; at least it's keeping me from tucking and rolling out of the car. "Did you know if I were to go to the doctor right now, I'd find out what I'm having?"

"Really? How?"

"Sonogram or blood work. I would have testosterone in my blood, meaning boy, and if it's not shy and exposes itself on an ultrasound..." But there's no way I'm going back to be poked and prodded and tested on repeatedly. Baby doesn't want to be a test subject in or out of the womb and if I see any doctor, I'm afraid they will discover I'm not Ms.

Burns and never let us go. "But I think I want my little sweet potato to stay a surprise. Anyway, the odds are it's a girl because of... well... everything."

"Huh." He slides an arm around me and snuggles me closer. "Sorry you can't have a normal pregnancy. Those people should never have come after you. If they continue to pursue you, I will have them taken care of," he says casually in the back of a car that has a sleek, soundproof barrier dividing us from the driver, unlike the cheap plexiglass found in taxis with smudge prints of various body parts and coated in those fluids, but I'm still certain the driver can hear every word and is contemplating reporting us.

I don't respond and sit, shocked that he thinks he can flash his cash and the people who have been following me will stop. Or is he implying he will have them killed? With my mouth open, I grasp my belly. Lucas kisses me on the cheek reassuringly before going back to checking his emails, completely calm. Not a bit worried the driver overheard our conversation or that I'm about to be taken away to be experimented on. He's completely at ease, which helps my nerves, and oddly, his temperament makes me trust him more. The sensation Lucas gives me is hard to fight, especially when I see him shrug at the thought of destroying the people tormenting me, like it would be easy and not something to waste time worrying about. How can he be that sure of himself? How can he possibly think he's powerful enough to take on a part of the government or whoever is after me and succeed, let alone live?

The thought that he is some type of spy has crossed my mind numerous times, but I don't think any organization would support a frivolous shopping spree worth thousands. And he doesn't seem like a bureaucrat; he's too carefree.

Plus, there's the whole tropical trip he's taking me on, his next job. But what if he's not taking me there?

Anxious, I decide to steer the conversation away from those thoughts. Outside the window, I see signs for the airport. "What would you want?"

"Hmm?" He looks confused.

"A boy or a girl?" I reiterate.

"Oh, both? A boy to carry on my name and a girl to spoil."

"Just two?"

He shrugs. "How many do you want?"

"I don't know. It used to be none. I guess I would want at least two. That way, little sweet potato has company. It was lonely being a single child."

"Two is a good number," he says, giving my hand a squeeze. Looking out the window, he points at a parked jet. "I think that's our ride."

The car stops by a moveable staircase that leads to a small, shiny jet. For the first time in my life, I'm afraid of flying. I've never flown in such a small plane. Freaking fantastic. I'll have to add that to all the other fears bouncing around in my head.

I won't open my car door. It may look like I'm some snob waiting for my driver to open it as if such tasks are beneath me, but that's not it. I'm terrified to leave the safety of the car and flaunt myself in front of anyone who keeps a record of people traveling.

Lucas doesn't move either. Maybe he is waiting for me to take the first steps. Maybe this is a complete setup and I'm not going to a tropical paradise but to a secret laboratory. Now I really can't move as I stare in dismay out the window, watching the driver place his hand on the door handle and pull. It takes everything for me not to pull back and lock us in.

"Ready?" Lucas asks.

I turn and give him a horrified look.

He cups both of my cheeks, bringing me inches from his face, and looks me directly in the eyes. "It's okay, I promise. I will not let anything happen to you or your baby. I swear it on my soul."

I've heard people say they swear on their life, but never on their soul. I've never met someone so sure. All I can do is nod as I clutch my purse and slowly step out of the car, eyeing everyone around me, looking for agents posing as airline crew. None of them are even looking at us as they prepare the jet for takeoff, inspecting the outside of it and loading it up with our luggage, which was just taken out of the trunk. I'm nervous to the point of trembling but Lucas loops his arm through mine and leads me up the stairs, past all the workers, and sits me down on a tan leather reclining chair.

The cabin is beautiful, with four reclining chairs that look like they can recline flat like beds and a sofa couch that folds out into an expensive futon mattress. Toward the cockpit, there's a bathroom and on the wall next to it is a large projector screen. Under it are different remotes and game controllers to consoles I have never seen. On the opposite wall, there's a minibar with a moderate-sized fridge and a hallway leading to a back room.

This is insane.

A woman steps onto the plane. Her hair is in a tight bun and she is dressed in a black pencil skirt with a white blouse and black business jacket over it. "Ah, miss?" Lucas calls to her. "I'm sorry; what is your name?"

"Hello; welcome. My name is Cleo. I apologize for not greeting you sooner. We were slightly behind schedule, but should still take off as scheduled. Is there anything I can get you? Water, juice, soda, wine? We also have a limited pantry. After takeoff, I'll give you a list of what is available. The fridge is fully stocked and you may help yourself to it at any point."

"Hello, Cleo. Nice to meet you. May we please have some sparkling water and may I have a glass of your best red wine?"

"Yes, of course. I'll get that for you in just a moment. I'll also prepare a snack for you, as well," Cleo says before turning her attention to me. "Don't worry, dear. These pilots are very experienced. You're in excellent hands," she says before going down the hallway.

I must look petrified.

The pilots must have gone into the cockpit before we boarded. Instead of talking over the speakers, they come out and introduce themselves in person. They give us the pilot speech, telling us the flight duration should be three hours and forty-three minutes, before taking their seats. No one else bothers us. No one asks us for a license, passport, or tickets. I think we're safe, little sweet potato.

"See? Nothing to fear," Lucas says with a smug grin.

"I'm still nervous for when we land, but I think you are right. This might be the best way to fly, even though I have never flown in something so small, so that only adds to my nerves."

He places one hand on my mine and one on my belly and stares hard with his midnight sky eyes. They look like they captured twinkling stars. "No. More. Worries. It's time you enjoyed your life and for you to be treated like the queen you are. I'll make sure of it."

I kiss his lips softly, then pull away, leaning my head against his to whisper, "Thank you."

A bell dings as the captain lights up the seat belt sign. Sitting side by side in the recliners, we fasten our seat belts. Engines turn on, making the whole aircraft rumble. As the sound builds, so does the momentum, pushing me back into the seat. I swear I can almost feel little sweet potato shift inside my belly as the wheels leave the ground.

How different would my life be if I had met Lucas years ago, before Jim? Would we have enjoyed spending our days traveling the world and our nights sipping expensive bottles of wine? That's one thing I honestly can't wait to do. Have a glass again. I've tasted a mouthful of what Lucas was sipping on, but I won't indulge any more than that. Only a couple more months until you are born, and then I can drink guilt free. But will Lucas and I still be together? What are we? Neither of us has given *us* a title, but those feelings I get when he's stealing a look at me... he makes me swoon.

Once we've reached our altitude height, Cleo serves us our water, his wine, and a charcuterie board with meats, cheeses, crackers, and an assortment of fruit. I wish all flights had meals like this. Everything is fresh, making me rethink airplane food.

Lucas takes out his laptop. "Want to see what the island looks like?"

"What do you mean island?"

"It's a private island with thirty bungalows, accommodating sixty people—and no children allowed. It has two restaurants, four pools—everyone gets their own private hot tub, infinity pool, and their own private cove. They have a state-of-the-art spa and a ton of water activities."

"What? For real?"

He nods with a mischievous grin.

"This is unreal." I stare at the screen and can't believe that we are headed to such a tropical paradise and that it is considered work for him. Pictures scroll by on the screen as he gives me a sneak peek at a place I would have never imagined going. Hell, I had envisioned a trap and a laboratory at the end of this flight. I was so wrong. "How much does it cost a night to stay there?"

He shrugs. "I don't know. I never see a bill; I only give them one."

The *no children allowed* sounds like a dream. No matter where I've vacationed in the past, there's always a couple who thinks they should bring their children to a not-so-family-friendly resort, ruining the vacation of everyone else who was unlucky to book their trip for the same week. Some people spend years saving for those kinds of trips to only have screaming kids running around the beach, throwing sand, and crying. It's not fair.

I'll be respectful to those who don't have kids. Don't worry, sweet potato. Mommy still loves you, even if she goes away for the weekend to an adult-only resort. Sometimes, moms need a break. You'll understand someday.

We land at a tiny airport in Key West. The plane lets us off right on the tarmac. Lucas loops his arm through mine as we climb down the stairs. A soft wind carries the heavy scent of saltwater and coconut sunblock. There are no clouds in the sky, just the brilliant sun and endless pale blue. Palm trees and other exotic Caribbean flora line the runway, giving tourists a first glance at the vivid vegetation.

Cleo walks behind us, pulling our luggage. Mine is a brand new forest green hard shell rolling case—three times larger than the one I had before—and his is the same design and size, but in black. Never had I thought I would ever have enough clothes to pack a suitcase this size for a one-week stay. And all the clothes in it are mine. The flight attendant greets the driver halfway to the car and gives him both handles; Lucas already tipped everyone on board a hundred-dollar bill each. We walk to our limo; its back door is open and the air conditioner is blasting.

Thank god. I'm not that big yet, but I always feel like I'm overheating. The hot flashes are for real. In the car, I cool down and lean into Lucas. He doesn't seem to mind that I like to cuddle; it has to be the hormones. After twenty minutes of driving on a long bridge highway that connects the islands, we pull up to a dock and follow our driver and our luggage onto a private yacht that will ferry us over to our exclusive hotel. The entire time, I keep pinching myself because this, this just can't be real.

The clear teal ocean is calm, making for an enjoyable boat ride. The Keys have thousands of islands scattered about, some that are habitable and others that seem to be a tangled mess of mangroves. The wildlife is abundant. White, long-legged herons skim shallow tide pools for fish that I can clearly see from the boat. Captain Ed, who Lucas remembered from his past trip, points out different animals, mostly different birds, as we cruise along the channels.

Our boat approaches an island with a long dock and bungalows peeking out from the indigenous trees. Two men wait on the dock, dressed in island attire that somehow comes off as business casual.

"Welcome! Welcome to Palm Resort. Lucas, it's so good to see you again. And who is this lovely lady?" the hotel worker asks, taking my hand, helping me off the boat.

Once I step foot on the dock, he kisses my hand. I've seen that happen in the movies, but I've never experienced someone actually kissing my hand as a form of greeting. Weird. "Hi, my name is Eve."

"Pleasure to meet you, Eve. My name is Ricardo. I am the owner of this paradise. If there is anything I can do to make your stay more enjoyable, please contact me personally."

"Thank you, Ricardo."

"Lucas, your partner is enchanting, you sly fox."

"I'm very lucky," Lucas says, looping an arm through mine with a smirk on his face.

"Just the two suitcases?" Ricardo asks, as if he were expecting more.

"Yes, just those two."

"Wonderful. Manuel, please bring their luggage to their suite."

"Right away." The man standing behind Ricardo takes our luggage and loads it up onto an electric cart.

"Shall we go for a brief tour of the property before heading to your bungalow?" Ricardo asks, flashing a charming smile that looks overpracticed. Botox must be used frequently.

After driving for fifteen minutes, we pull up to an enormous suite with a wraparound porch. The thatched roof and the mahogany wooden structure look authentic. Tropical flowers line the path to the steps. The front of the porch has two rocking chairs and a table; however, the circular back deck is almost as big as the suite. The entire back of the deck has a cloth curtain enclosing the space, giving couples privacy from others staying at the resort while still getting full sun exposure, perfect for naked sunbathing. The curtain stands about ten feet high and billows gently in the breeze. Two dark brown wicker loungers and a matching full-sized futon with a clamshell shade line the one side of the deck. The other side has a four-person hot tub and a small rectangle infinity pool at the edge of the deck. I bet if I sit in the pool, it will line up with the horizon and create the illusion that I'm in the ocean.

Twenty feet from the deck's last step is our own private stretch of beach. There's a small firepit with two more loungers and tables. Hanging from a tree is a double wide hammock. Crystal blue water laps gently against the sand.

Holding back tears as I get emotional for no reason again, I follow Lucas and Ricardo inside the suite. Large wooden fans move the air gently above our heads. This is a house, not a vacation suite. A beautifully carved mahogany dinner table that's big enough for six people utilizes the space across from the kitchen, which kitchen is built for a chef with an eight-burner stove, three separate ovens, two fridges, two different sinks—I honestly feel lost just standing in the kitchen, and I haven't even ventured into the second living room yet.

The owner pulls Lucas aside for a moment, I assume discussing business of some sort. Teal waves crash against the sandy beach. The view is really spectacular. All of my cares, all of my troubles, seem to disappear as I stare out into the clear blue sea.

Fuck it.

My sandals are off and I'm making a beeline to the ocean. Halfway to the water, I realize I'm still wearing my sundress and decide, screw it, that's what laundry service is for. Cool, crystal-clear blue water cools my swollen, burning feet. I didn't think my feet would swell yet, but they feel like balloons today. Must be from all the sitting. Mom said she suffered from swollen feet. Maybe it's genetics.

For the first time, it feels like I've swallowed butterflies and they are pounding against my stomach. Is that you, sweet potato? The fluttering of wings continues. I place a hand on the spot. My hand doesn't feel the movement, but it's below it. As fast as it started, it stops, leaving me breathless. Was that the baby's first kicks? I think so. But I'm not sure how they are supposed to feel, although that fury of flaps was something I've never felt before.

Crunching footsteps in the sand tell me someone is coming. I turn to find Lucas barefoot and changed into a buttoned casual shirt with beige shorts. "Sorry. If we want pleasure, dear, I must work... a little," he says with a grin, coming up behind me, wrapping an arm around my waist. "The water feels amazing."

"How is this your job? How do I get this kind of job?" I ask, astonished.

"The opportunity fell into my lap, so to speak. It's a long story. I'm not sure how you would go about getting this job."

"Wait, so the jet we flew here on. Do you own it?"

"No, no. But I could own one. Maybe I'll buy us one."

I feel my eyes bug out. My mouth hangs open. Did he just say he'll buy *us* one? How far into the future is he thinking, and does he really want me to be a part of it? Because I could really get used to this lifestyle and I still won't bring myself to think that L word... but I am falling harder for him every day. "Lucas, you surprise me every day."

"It's good to keep you on your toes. I hope happy."

"I couldn't be happier. I just keep thinking it's a dream."

"My queen," he says, turning me to face him. "You are my dream."

"I'm your queen?"

"Yes, if you let me be your king," he says, his mouth hovering over mine, teasing me with a kiss.

"Yes," I whisper.

My virgin piña colada is almost empty. I'm making a slurping sound as I scrape my reusable metal straw against the bottom of the glass. The resort has a strict no plastic rule that

I absolutely love. It keeps the beaches clean and protects the abundant wildlife. Before I can ask, another drink is already on its way.

Butler service is amazing. I don't know why I have never spoiled myself like this while on vacation. Maybe it's because it costs thousands of dollars a day, which seems like nothing to Lucas. Money has no value to him. He also doesn't seem worried that I currently have no income, nor has he suggested careers or anything like that. It would be heaven if I didn't have to work and got to travel to amazing places while raising a kid with him.

I bite my lip, put down my glass, and walk into the cool ocean water, only footsteps away. Whole shells and broken pieces swirl across the seafloor. We went snorkeling yesterday. I was timid since I am pregnant, but he said there would be an instructor with us and that I would love the experience. And I did. A loggerhead turtle even swam by. He was so majestic and beautiful as he gracefully glided past us. It was a precious moment, a one-in-a-million chance, swimming with a wild sea turtle. The day was perfect and Lucas, of course, arranged for us to have dinner on the boat after snorkeling. He rented out a yacht so we could rinse off and change into something more comfortable for dinner. The entire experience must have cost upward of twenty grand and he didn't bat an eye.

I've never been a gold digger, but if these feelings we have for one another are real, and he's rich, then I think I just won the lottery. And maybe, just maybe, this is meant to be.

Maybe Lucas is meant to be your father, sweet potato, if he really wants to be. "You know, I could get used to this."

"Is that so?" Lucas asks, stretched out on the hammock.

"Where does your next job take us?"

"A magical surprise."

"More magical than this?" How can he possibly top this?

"A different type of magic."

"If it's anything like this, it will be a fantasy come true."

I hear Lucas get off the hammock as I splash through the knee-deep water. "Claudia, Mark, that will be all for now. We'll call if we need any more service today." I hear the sand grind under his feet. "Have I told you how beautiful you are?"

I turn halfway to him. "What are you doing with your phone?"

"Taking a picture of you. Stay just like that."

I blush while holding my belly. It looks so weird when I put on a bikini, but also kind of cute. "Stop," I say feeling my face blush, but then panic. "You can't put these online," I say, afraid of someone tracking us down.

"I don't have any accounts. I don't like to share," he says with a wink. "You're gorgeous," he says, still snapping pictures and approaching me with a sly grin. "Let me," he whispers into my ear, the heat of his breath melting my center.

I don't know what he wants to do, but I nod. His hand goes to the back of my neck and unties my bikini top so it hangs down my front, the whole time snapping pictures. Then he undoes the back strap, letting it flop into the water. With his head against my neck, he takes a deep breath in, breathing me in. His free hand finds a breast to caress, dragging his thumb over my nipple.

My eyes close as I purr. "Put the phone down. How many pictures are you taking?"

He tenses against my back, tickling the nape of my neck with his lips. His hand slides down and over my stomach, slipping his fingers between the bikini bottom and my skin.

The entire time, he's snapping photos and I think a couple of selfies.

"Lucas, right here?"

"No one can see us," he whispers into my ear. "And if they do, does it really matter?"

Fuck it. I step out of the bathing suit floating around my shins. I'm completely naked. His free hand, not the one controlling the camera, is still between my legs. A throaty groan escapes my lips. All I want is him right now. His stroking intensifies, becoming a vibration as his fingers move faster and faster. The warmth on my neck only melts me more as his tongue flicks my earlobe. My back arches. I need him now.

He lets go and steps back, his midnight eyes twinkling, staring at me with a hunger that demand to be fed. I turn to find out where he is going, hoping he's leading me to a bed or hammock, anything, even a blanket on the sand.

"You look so sexy like that," he says, looking through his phone. I think he's recording now.

"Like this?" I tease back, biting my lower lip, one hand on my breast, the other between my thighs. I think this is what he wants right now. And it's super kinky.

He watches me, licking his lips. After thirty seconds of me humming, he throws his phone onto the beach and kicks off his trunks. Slowly walking toward me, the sun glares behind him, making his glistening skin golden. I can't help but stare at his chiseled chest and follow the V shape of abs to the bottom, ending right above his throbbing erection. He looks like a horny god, knowledgeable at making me chant his name until I'm breathless. The two of us can form a new religion on bent knees right here.

On the tips of my toes in anticipation as he approaches, just the sight of him makes me ache in a way I have never felt before. My hands are still busy while I enjoy the view.

He looks envious, stalking over to me, looking famished. His gaze sends chills throughout my body. Circling around me, he pushes my hands aside, taking over for them, almost mad that they were doing his job.

I lean into him, feel his dick brush against my ass; my fingers grip my belly. I nuzzle my head into his shoulder as I let out an eager groan, anticipating him plunging into me.

He slides in easily, causing me to bend slightly and moan. I can't move my head too far. His teeth hold my earlobe firmly, flicking it with his tongue. His arms brace me with each thrusting motion. Cries of ecstasy erupt from my mouth. Every time the tip threatens to slide out but slips back in, I say his name louder and louder, no longer caring who hears my bliss or his moans.

My mind goes blank. Every thought, worry, concern fades away as a euphoric explosion ripples through my body. In his arms, I feel weightless. Thrilled. Satisfied. Happy.

He releases my ear. I purr. Still inside me, I can feel him shrinking as our juices run down my legs. The heat of his breath lingers against my skin as my body feels heavy, wanting his arms to engulf me while I nap. He takes in a deep breath and moves his hands from my breast to on top of my hands, still resting on my belly. "You are my wildest fantasy, my queen."

I crumble in my king's embrace.

Katie Zaber

21 Weeks - Orlando, Florida

I can't open my eyes.

I tried to sleep on the flight in the comfy leather reclining seats that support all the right spots, but was woken up an hour later, which only made me cranky and even more disoriented. Damn, a cup of strong tea would taste so good right now and jolt me awake. Even a sip might give me a decent dose of energy; it's been months since I've had a cup of caffeine.

I yawn and stretch, blinking my eyes open. Banana is making swooshing movements in an attempt to wake me and it's starting to help. Thanks, baby.

Outside the window, palm trees and other tropical plants line the highway. I notice colorful 3D billboards advertising different theme parks.

"Huh? So, that's where are we going," I say to Lucas from the back seat of a luxury limo. Even the cup holders are fancy, with built-in warming and chilling settings. Strip bars of LED lights cycle through ten different colors, illuminating the limo in shades of green, blue, red, and yellow.

"Surprised?"

Signs with a large blue hat and stars, beside all the main characters and princesses, line either side of the highway. "Yeah, this is the last place I thought you'd take me."

"It's the happiest, most magical place on Earth. Wait, have you never been?" Lucas asks, completely puzzled.

"No, my parents don't believe in spending money on big corporations."

"They're that strict?" he asks.

"No. The opposite. They are weed growers. I grew up on a pot farm and was homeschooled. My parents hate big business and corporations though."

"Marijuana is a huge business."

"Try explaining that to them. They are backwoods hippies who hide from the government." As I say those words, I realize I'm also hiding. Will I eventually live in the middle of the woods as well?

"You're full of surprises. I would have never imagined you grew up like that. You seem like the type that has never tried it."

"Only a couple times when I was a teen. Growing up, it was my parents' number one priority. It made me hate the stuff. My life has more important priorities," I choke. "I had more important priorities." My arms wrap around my stomach. No, baby. I don't have any regrets about you. I just wish things were different. "Everything I had worked for disappeared in less than a month. Everything I had known. Everything I had built vanished so fast. How did I end up here?" I ask with tears trickling down my cheeks.

"Through hard choices and decisions you didn't want to make. You haven't told me what happened with your ex, nor do I want you to tell me if you're not ready, but I am here for you."

I stare at a light changing bar. It fades from shades of green into light blues. "It's simple. He had a vasectomy years ago. When I told him I was pregnant, he questioned who the father was. We did a DNA test and found out it wasn't his."

"Did you ever tell him the baby only has your DNA?"

"No. He never wanted children. I couldn't force it on him."

"You still love him?"

My chest tightens. Lucas doesn't look upset or envious, only sympathetic and understanding. "He was my first love. I think part of me will always love what we had, but it's over. Until a few months ago, I had never pictured myself without him, until you. Are we a… thing?"

"I hope we are a couple. That's how I see us."

"Like boyfriend and girlfriend?" I can't help but frown. "But you know nothing about me except I'm poor. Homeless. Carless. I live out of a suitcase. My parents are pot farmers. My child is a clone of me… that's about it. And I know nothing about you except that you were orphaned at a young age."

"Hmm. I'm carless. I live out of a suitcase and I was an orphan. Although I'm not poor, I don't have a home per se. My Manhattan apartment is merely a fancy storage unit that I might stay at a week or two out of a year. There isn't too much more to know about me."

"What was it like being an orphan?"

"A revolving door. I had a couple of good foster parents, but it always changed." He pauses. "It's probably the reason I like to travel so much. Anytime I anchor myself to any location, it just doesn't feel right."

I reach for his hand and hold it. "Lucas, at some point, I'm going to need to be stationary. At least for a couple months, but I agree, this lifestyle is much better than having a house to take care of."

"So it's settled. After this trip, we'll start looking into a place. We'll head to New York first. I have some business to conduct there. Plus, you can check out my apartment, see if you like it and the area. If not, we can always look at other places. A place that will feel like home. That makes us officially a couple. So stop overthinking it and enjoy."

I nod. "But Lucas, you realize I have nothing to my name. No money. Nothing. Literally nothing."

He cocks his head. "You just got a new name. It will take time to build it. All you need to worry about is being a good mother, unless you want to do more or have a career. However, if you stay with me, you'll never need to work again."

"For real? You don't care if I work or not?"

"Why would I?"

"It's not fair if you're the only one working. Makes me feel like a gold digger."

"Are you with me for my money?"

"No."

"Then you're not a gold digger."

"Don't you feel used?"

He places a hand on my leg. "I think I get the better deal," he says while his fingers crawl up my upper thigh. "There's something about you I just can't ignore." He spreads my thighs apart with a mischievous grin. "Something I want. Something that makes me… incredibly happy." His hand disappears under my skirt and I brace myself. "I want to make you feel as elated as I do."

"Lucas, the driver."

"Don't worry, my queen. He can't see. Tinted window and soundproof."

"Why do you call me your queen?"

Flashing me a mischievous grin, he says, "Because you are the only woman I'll get down on my knees for."

He demonstrates and kneels before me, spreading my legs open with his hands. Hot breath heats my inner thighs as he moves up them, both warming and teasing. Under my skirt, his fingers have curled around my thong, pulling it into position for his teeth to drag it down my legs, leaving it draped around my ankles.

"But aren't we near the hotel?"

He pokes his head up above the window and says, "At least twenty minutes. I'll have you saying my name in five."

It happens within three.

I really hope the back of the limo is soundproof. Honestly, with the way he had me panting, yelling his name at the end—I swear sometimes he has two tongues—I'm sure the driver knew what we were up to.

Snuggling next to Lucas, feeling euphoric, we turn down a road with manicured landscaping so precise, they must measure each blade of grass. A beautiful Spanish hotel looms ahead with luscious gardens encircling the property. The limo pulls under an awning. Two doormen wait, ready to open the limo doors and usher us into the air-conditioned lobby. Polished marble floors stretch in every direction. Whimsical chandeliers hang from the ceiling, looking like fireworks exploding near the crown molding. Marble pillars strewn about the lobby only add to the grandeur.

On one side of the lobby there is a Theme Park Planning Center; the workers' nametags at the desk say *cast members*. Everyone else has the name of the hotel printed above their name. "Lucas, are we still on the theme park's property?"

"Yes and no. It's not owned by them; however, they work in tandem at the hotel," Lucas says as he walks over to the front desk. "Good morning, Maria. I'm checking in under the name Star. I believe you also have something for me from your boss."

"Good morning, Mr. Star. I'm so happy you'll be staying with us. Here are your room keys, passes, and the portfolio, from the big guys," she says with a wink, handing over room keys, two park passes, and a black leather portfolio. "If there is anything I can do to make your stay more magical, please ask."

"Thank you, Maria. Have a magical day," Lucas says with a wink, grinning like a kid.

A bellhop in a pressed uniform named Tony waits by the elevator with our luggage. We follow him into the elevator. He pushes the button for the sixteenth floor and also swipes a card before the elevator moves.

Tony smiles. "You need to use your private keycard for the elevator. The top floor is off limits to our other guests." Off the elevator, this floor only has five rooms; he leads us to the very last one at the end of the hallway. "Here is your room," the young man says while unlocking our door. He brings our luggage into the center of the sprawling living room, complete with two gas fireplaces on either side and two separate large seating areas that can fit at least a dozen people. "Would you like me to bring your suitcases into your walk-in closet?" he asks.

"That would be wonderful. Thank you, Tony," Lucas says as he puts down all the things the receptionist just gave him, plus a hundred-dollar bill in the middle of the dining table.

On the table is also an oversized welcome basket. Two Champagne bottles, a box of chocolates, some other fancy brand snacks, bathrobes, slippers, and other goodies cascade out of the basket and onto the table in a such a way that it must have taken some time to arrange it just so. Everything in the room is placed in a way that it looks perfect. I find more hidden ears in the décor, only subtle hints that tell you are still on the property.

This has to be some type of presidential suite or something like that. I just passed by a half bath and I'm staring at an eight-person, long, solid wood dining table. "How many people can this suite accommodate?"

"Two. There's only a king-size bed. Come, check out the view." Lucas opens the French doors to the balcony.

In the distance is the famous castle and farther away, I see the top of the big ball. Other hotels and buildings are tucked in between the trees so they don't obscure the sight line of the castle. The rest of the view is a luscious forest surrounded by a tranquil lake. On the balcony, there's another large table with seats, an outdoor sectional, and plenty of chairs. We could host a party here and have enough space for thirty people.

"Wow, this is spectacular."

"It's a magnificent view of the fireworks."

"Really? Tonight?"

He nods.

"I can't wait. This, this is beautiful."

"I'm glad you like it."

"I do." I can't help myself and yawn. "But I'm still really tired. I'd love to take a nap before going out for lunch."

"Go rest, my queen. It will give me time to do some work before we have fun."

"Ahem," Tony clears his throat, trying to get our attention. "Is there anything else I can help you with?" he asks, sticking his head through the doorway.

"That will be all, Tony. There's money on the table for you. Have a great day."

"Wow. Thank you, sir! Have a wonderful, magical day." The bellhop leaves the suite, looking ten times happier than when we arrived.

Outside the window, in the courtyard below, nuns wearing gray tunics and habits scrub clothes and sheets in large wooden tubs next to a well. Others hang the wet laundry on clothing lines to dry. A couple of children sing and play, teasing each other, running around the women working.

I place a hand on my large belly and walk down the stone hallway. In the small chapel, the choir is singing songs in Latin. Down the stairs and into the hot kitchen, I find women busy making dinner. Fresh baked bread steams on the counter. A large, bubbling pot hangs over the fireplace. It smells like beef stew. Nuns busy themselves, preparing dinner for everyone who lives here. They smile politely as I make way through, heading to the door leading outside. There are lemon trees to the right. I find a shady spot and breathe in the citrus aroma.

This place feels safe. Almost like home.

Suddenly, I'm sitting down at a long table with thirty other women. Candles flicker around the room. The hearth in the center gives the room a cheery glow. An older woman at the head of the table says a prayer before we all eat supper. Everyone passes bowls of food to each other and digs in. Nuns laugh, share stories, and smile while eating. There are large jugs of wine on the table. And these women know how to drink it.

One nun picks up a three-stringed instrument with a tear-shaped body. Another plays a recorder or flute. Before I know it, the nuns are dancing and singing to the music, having a blast. I can't stop laughing as I join them, dancing until I feel exhausted.

It's dark. Lying in bed, I hear my door open. Footsteps creep across my room. I sit up. I don't see anyone. No one at all. But my door is open.

I get out of bed to shut it and look around the modestly-sized room. I swore I heard footsteps, but it's just me in the room. I lie back down on my side and bring my blanket up to my chest. I take a deep breath and close my eyes.

From under the bed, a hand grabs my arm. I roll over as a knife plunges upward through the straw-stuffed mattress, narrowly missing my chest. If I had stayed on my other side... I sit up and scream, prying the hand off my arm, digging my nails into my attacker's flesh.

A shriek comes from under my bed as a nun slides out from under it. The knife is stuck in the mattress, not in her hand. She stares at me with frosty gray eyes. Dozens of footsteps run, echoing outside my room. Help will be here in seconds.

The crazed woman says something I don't understand. She tilts her head back and cackles. Then, without warning, she lunges at me. I shift to the side and hit her as hard as I can, slamming my fist into her cheekbone. She falls backward on the bed, impaling herself on the knife. Her gray tunic darkens as blood seeps out of her back. Her eyes stare at the ceiling, laughing and speaking in a language I can't understand. Blood drips from the corner of her mouth. She giggles until she gargles, becoming silent and still.

My bedroom door opens. The nuns scream.

I scream.

"What's the matter? What's wrong?" someone asks. It takes a moment to realize it is Lucas. "Are you okay? Was it a nightmare?"

"Yes, I'm sorry. It was so lifelike," I say, sitting up, leaning against the headboard. My hair feels damp from sweat. I need a shower.

"The way you screamed, I thought someone was attacking you. You scared me."

"I'm sorry," I say, reaching out for his hand. "Did you get any work done?"

"Yes. How about you freshen up and we go explore?"

"That sounds good, as long as that includes food. Banana and I are getting hungry." My stomach is growling loudly.

"So am I. What are you in the mood for?"

"I don't know. Can we be tourists and find something fun and themed?"

"Hmm. Why don't we eat around the world? "

"What?"

"In the one park, they have a section that takes you around the world. We can have a bite of everything."

"Really?" I think of all the different foods that there might be. "I'm sure I'll find something there."

"Why don't you get ready while I make the driving arrangements," he says in a way that makes me think he's up to something.

From the bathroom, I can overhear part of the conversation. He said something about tonight, but couldn't make out exactly what he said. Something about fireworks. I'm sure whatever he's planning will be epic. That seems to be his style.

"Hurry," Lucas says as he darts to the elevator at our hotel. "I think we are just in time."

"You rushed me through my tacos and still haven't told me what you have planned."

Though, I think I have a pretty good idea. When he said we could eat around the world, he wasn't joking. The day started out with fish and chips and shepherd's pie. The mashed potato crust on the pie was perfect. After we walked around for a few hours, working up our appetite, we split a greasy turkey leg. While we were finishing up our tacos, Lucas kept checking his watch, urging me to hurry. At first I protested and said that I wanted to grab some type of dessert, but he gave me a smile and said I wouldn't need it.

"Seriously, what are you up to?"

"You'll see in a moment," he says as the elevator doors open to our floor. He is practically skipping to our hotel room. He opens the door and moves to the side for me to walk through.

A hotel staff member wearing black pants and a white polo waits by the balcony. "Mr. Star, Ms. Burns, you're here just in time. My name is Christy. Come this way."

I cock my head to the side, wondering what Christy has been doing in our room. I see roses that weren't here before on the dining room table. There is candlelight flickering in the bedroom. We follow her onto the balcony. "Here are your seats. Can I interest you in Champagne or wine? How about a cup of tea, coffee, or juice?"

"I'll take a glass of Champagne, Christy. Can you pour her a baby size Champagne, for a toast? And you can bring the bottle and leave it with us. That will be all for the evening. I left a tip in the envelope on the table."

"Thank you for your generosity," Christy says. "I'll be right back. The buffet is open right over there." She points to a long table I didn't notice.

"A buffet?" I give Lucas a questioning look. "We just ate."

"Now my queen, it's time for dessert."

Christy steps inside while I digest the news that I get my own dessert buffet.

"I need to check this out." I hurry to my personal six-foot-long table covered with decadent treats. Cannoli dipped in chocolate, an assortment of mini cupcakes, mini cakes, mini fruit pastries, bonbons, an ice cream bar, warmed bread pudding with vanilla icing, chocolate mousse with fresh whipped cream and sliced strawberries, a chocolate fountain with every type of food I can possibly think to dip and more—literally every dessert I could dream of and ones I didn't even know existed fill every square inch of the table in an elaborate display.

I turn around and stare at Lucas sipping on Champagne, flashing me a shit-eating grin. At this moment, I could pounce on him. How did I end up so lucky after losing everything? Is this what it's supposed to be like? Completely magical?

"Grab a couple of plates and sit down. The fireworks are going to begin in a few minutes," he calls from our very own candlelit table.

"Don't you want anything? My god, chocolate cream pie!" I squeal.

"No, I'm sure you'll grab enough for us to share."

"Who says I'm sharing? I'm devouring!" I gorge and gather at the same time. This crazy buffet of treats is all for us. Two people!

"Eve, hurry, darling."

"I'm right here. And I got a plate for you, too. Just for you."

"How kind of you to share."

"We aren't sharing. You got your own plate."

He laughs, almost spitting out his drink. "You're feisty tonight."

"Yes, sir. Extra. It might have to do with my personal dessert buffet under the fireworks."

"So you like it."

I cock my head back. "Like it? I've never experienced anything like this! It's a dream come true."

He says nothing but smiles at me intently. I can't help but glow. Music begins to play from hidden speakers, signaling the beginning of the show. Moments later, the first rocket launches into the air, showering the sky with blues, greens, and reds. One after another, they shoot into the sky. The colorful bursts this close captivate me. I lose track of time, nibbling on my dessert and watching the explosions.

"I have something else for you," he says, taking my attention away from the brilliant show.

"What? This is already amazing. How do you plan to top it?"

He takes out of his pocket a golden chain. At the end of it is a heart-shaped locket. The heart has a ribbon of diamonds zigzagging across the front of it. The chain is soft, and the locket feels like I could crush it in my hands. The gold has a buttery-like hue to it I have never seen before. It has to be twenty-four karat gold.

"Lucas," I somehow whisper.

"Open it up."

Inside is a picture of us and a blank spot on the other. The picture was taken days ago while fooling around on our private beach.

"Eve, I'm not a fan of weddings. But, if you'll have me, I promise to take care of you and your little one, as my own. If you'll allow, I'd like to be considered its father and your partner."

How long have I known him? Less than a month. Millions of people make similar spontaneous choices, sometimes over the course of a weekend. What other choice do I have? If I turn him down, he leaves me penniless—basically how he met me. I say yes, and this magic, it doesn't stop. It keeps going. And I want it to. No part of me wants this to end. I want him. So even though saying yes to him, this early in our relationship, without any idea of who he is, goes against every gut instinct any educated person can have, I say, "Yes."

I climb onto his lap, brush back my hair, and hold out the necklace for him to put on me.

He takes the locket and drapes it around me, tenderly kissing my neck. I lean back against his chest. His arms wrap around as he plants another kiss on my neck. And then another. Inching his way up to my earlobe. One of his hands moves down my side, making its way under my dress, the other gently strokes my aching breasts.

He purrs into my ear, "Lean back. Enjoy the show."

A soft moan escapes my mouth.

And I do. Lying on him, I watch the grand finale of fireworks explode in the sky as I relish my own internal eruption.

22 Weeks - New York City, New York

It's massive, but looks old and cold. The stone is gray and almost sad looking. On the top of its towers, I half-expect to see macabre gargoyles keeping watch. Tall scaffoldings create a maze of dangerous travel, high above the heads of those entering the old building. The outside doesn't have the grandeur I had imagined when thinking of the great St. Patrick's Cathedral. But as soon as I cross the threshold, I understand some of the hype. Polished floors, smooth, glistening walls, and a ceiling so high above, it makes me tilt my head back just to see where it ends. The ceiling intimidates, making me feel small and especially impoverished compared to the church's wealth, even when wearing designer clothes that cost upward of a grand.

Candles and donation boxes flank the entrance. People sit there, solemnly praying for their loved ones. They shove dollar bills into the boxes, take a burnt stick, and find a candle. Some look panicked, searching for an unlit candle. If they can't light their own, will their prayers be answered, or will they go unheard like mine? When I had tried to pray, I never lit a candle. Maybe that was the reason my prayers went unanswered as a child.

I stopped believing in Santa at the age of eight when I realized God wasn't real. The Easter Bunny was shot and skinned when I was six—my parents made rabbit stew out of him for Easter dinner, thinking it would be a more practical use of the meat instead of having it as a pet. And don't get me started on the Tooth Fairy. I know she doesn't leave propaganda on how sugar rots your teeth and how the candy companies created Halloween with the help of dentists so they could have swimming pools filled with cash. At least that was the claim made by the strangely colored, homemade pamphlet that I found under my pillow in exchange for my first front tooth. I didn't leave any more teeth after that.

Before the rows of pews begin, bowls of dirty water sit on top of pedestals for believers to dip their grimy fingers into and make the sign of the cross on their forehead or their whole bodies, forehead, shoulders, and heart. How long has the stagnant water been sitting here inside the church? What diseases does it carry and spread? The gold bowls even have little bits of dust, maybe skin floating along the bottom, and short pieces of curly hair. It's hard not to gag as I watch the elderly dunk their fingers in.

Inside, there's a single large scaffolding going up to the second floor. It's the only one within the building and it looks so out of place. How I feel.

A man with tight, curly red hair and a five-o'clock shadow, who is dressed like a priest but without the collar, paces back and forth, looking aggravated while having a hushed feud with a clergy member. The redhead keeps pointing at some documents and it appears the clergy doesn't agree or care, infuriating the man further.

I avoid their argument and look at the sculptures at the ends of the pews, probably saints. Alcoves line the walls with hassocks to kneel at or have their own private section of pews, reminding me of mini chapels. Each one commemorates a saint; at least, I think. I haven't stopped long enough to read the information. I only pause long enough to admire the artwork.

My parents didn't believe in what they couldn't see. I raised myself to rely on science to explain the unknown. But now, at this moment, with all the crazy things people have said to me over the last few months, I'm unsure. Angels and demons, are they real? Is any of this real?

My entire life, I fantasized that a stranger would find me and say, *Magic is real. Every monster and creature you have heard of exists, and this is Mandor, a dragon to ride away on,* but no one said those things and my fantasies never came true. And really, in reality, if a person claiming they were a wizard or dragon tamer actually crossed my path, would I believe them?

When I was a child, I remember late one night—it might have been early in the morning—I was watching infomercial TV. I discovered a channel where all the people chanted together. The man in black, the priest, had said that God would answer all their prayers because they were believers. I thought, *That's easy. Is that really all I need to do?* At the time, I believed in Santa and he always brought me a single present, so if I believed in God, would He answer my prayers?

Dressed in overalls and a flannel, with the forty bucks I stole from my mom—it wasn't like she would miss it or realize I took it—I raced across the fields, past the twitchy security guards who waved good morning to me as I ran by into the woods, taking the trail into town. In retrospect, stealing money to buy a Bible wouldn't help my soul get into Heaven, but I was seven and desperate for my prayers to be answered.

Not far from my parents' farm was a little old church that could barely hold a congregation of fifty people, but the tiny town didn't even have enough people to fill the church halfway on Sundays. There were only a few young families who attended. The majority walked with a cane and had either hearing difficulties or a hunched back.

In the back parking lot, behind the church, there was a trailer with a little gift shop that was open on Sunday mornings after church. The trail I took ended right behind it. The trailer wasn't big and showed signs of being refurbished from a home into a shop. I opened the door, startling the wrinkly woman behind the counter, who may or may not have been asleep.

"Good morning," I whispered as I stared at all the figurines, all the saints and key figures in Christianity, shrouded in gold and silver, emanating faultlessness. Next to them was an assortment of pretty beaded necklaces with crosses on them. I couldn't stop my childish fingers from reaching out and touching the pretty beads in different, vivid colors. My favorite was the black iridescent necklace.

"You don't wear those, dear. They are called rosary beads."

"What do you do with them?" I asked her.

She tilted her head and asked, "Where are your parents?"

"I'm interested in praying. Can you help me?" I asked.

"Sure. Have you ever read the Bible?"

I shook my head.

"Can you read?"

"Yes. I read every day."

"Wonderful. I have the perfect Bible for you." The retired shopkeeper got up from her stool and slowly made her way to what I'd call the children's section. "Here we are. Your first Bible. Do you like to color?"

I nodded as I took the cheerful Bible from her. The cover had a collage of pictures on it, including a man with a wooden staff herding animals onto a ship and a mother, father, and baby sitting on a pile of straw in a shed.

"Here is a Bible you can color and read. Have you ever heard of saints?"

I shook my head.

"They are people you can pray to that will help deliver your message to God if he is too busy at the moment."

"Really?" I asked. If they could help me when God was busy, I'd pray to all of them.

"Yes. They all listen, but when you say their special prayers, your voice becomes louder."

I pictured prayers floating above the clouds, surrounding saints like a flock of seagulls, shouting over each other in order to be heard. "Which one is closer to God?" I asked, not wanting to waste time praying to some nobody saint that barely conversed with God.

The old lady laughed. "They all are. It's about choosing one that you feel close to. Come this way. Do you like nature and animals?"

I nodded.

"Here are a couple of saints who also like animals." She handed me a stack of cards that were postcard-sized, with pictures of saints on the front and information about them on the back.

We made our way back to the counter, and I stopped by the pretty rosary beads. "What do you do with them if you don't wear them?"

"You count the beads and use them to hold your place while praying. Which one is your favorite?"

I pointed at the black shiny one that reminded me of an oil spill on a parking lot. They always looked beautiful, displaying the rainbow in a black puddle. I had never seen jewelry like it before.

"Oh, that is beautiful, isn't it?"

I nodded and handed the woman both twenties. I asked hopefully, "Is this enough for everything, including the rosary?"

The woman flipped over the plastic box that came with the rosary beads and peeled off the sticker. "It is now."

She put all of my forbidden knowledge into a bag and I ran back home to stash everything under my bed. My parents usually slept in on the weekends and I was hoping my mom hadn't woken up yet. But when I got home, she was bumping into stuff in the kitchen, making coffee with Baileys while yelling my name and to wake up.

That night, when my parents passed out from smoking blunts, I took out my flashlight and began with the prayer cards. I started with Blessed Kateri, Lilly of the Mohawks, who from what I heard in recent news, is now a saint. She was my favorite out of all the saints on the prayer cards. The poor girl had to run away from home because of her beliefs. She died in her young midtwenties, but from what I read, most saints died around that age.

It was the running away part that drew me to her. How she fled her home and family so she could live the way she wanted. When I read that, part of me believed God helped her. He showed her how to be free from her horrible situation. I recited the prayer, praying to become more like her, saying how much I loved Jesus. I said the rosary before falling asleep. That became my new nightly routine, learning about saints and what they fought for. Most of them were men, but there were a few courageous women.

For months I did this, going to the holy trailer shop, buying new prayer cards and information on different saints and reading about them all night until I fell asleep. The shopkeeper even ordered an assortment of saint cards so I had a never-ending supply of new ones to read.

I wasted so much of my parents' money at that little shop. The night my parents' farm was raided, my Bible bag was left behind, but I was overjoyed. I thought my parents would go to jail and I would go to a better home. But that never happened. The stoners were better prepared than I had ever thought. Or maybe they knew their time was limited because they had an escape plan.

My dad carried me through an underground tunnel, his head barely clearing the dirt ceiling. Mom ran ahead of us with two large book bags. Waiting for us outside the tunnel was an escape car. Inside the car were suitcases, black garbage bags filled in haste, and other plastic containers. Some had money in them. Others were stuffed with clothes, sheets, paperwork—a sedan packed with the articles of our life. Fragments of who we were. Like a time capsule, the car drove us away from that farm and town, and that moment in time was officially over.

I really thought at first that God had answered my prayers, but nothing changed. They bought a new farm and restarted their business with a different name and hired a new set of security. That's when I stopped believing and praying and looked elsewhere for help. I created my own escape plan like my heroine, Kateri. She didn't need some man sitting on a cloud to guide her; she always had the strength, just not the confidence.

Now I question the truth behind poor Saint Kateri. Her history was a lot more bloody than the kid-friendly stories I had read. Pressured into marriage, running away to live with the Jesuit priests so she didn't have to wed, living a life of sacrifice because she thought that it would bring her to heaven—her life had been a living hell. All she wanted was salvation, and those priests promised her that through acts of penance. Sleeping on a bed of thorns, burning herself, eating just a couple seeds a day, or making her food taste foul, she would even punish herself for crimes others committed in hope it would save her corrupt soul, so she would finally feel peace, even if it was after death.

I walk around aimlessly for an hour and find a seat in a pew tucked away in a small, extravagant alcove with no one around. All the gold doesn't impress me, but more or less enrages me that the church is so greedy. If it really wanted to help the less fortunate, why did it waste money on making such gaudy decorations? Shouldn't the church be humble? Sell all of its valuables and give their money to the starving? That's what they are supposed to do, but power always corrupts and the church is as corrupt as any government, maybe worse, from what history has proven.

A tall man looking like he wandered into the church by accident approaches me. He's wearing hippie sandals, khaki pants, and a black t-shirt with a picture of the Virgin Mary holding baby Jesus saying, *Abstinence was only 99% effective.* Someone should tell the lost hippie where the music festival is and lead him there. His eyes are glassy and I'm suddenly worried about why the dazed idiot is staring and walking toward me.

"Hi. Can I help you?"

The man's eyes are frosted over. I can't tell what color they are. He keeps coming closer. I slide down the pew in the opposite direction, trying to maintain distance.

"What do you want?" I ask the drugged man, raising my voice.

He opens his mouth and an unnatural voice booms from his lips. "The child must die! Others have failed, but it ends now!"

"Stay away from me!" I scream, running away through the maze of pews that are now empty. The church had a few people praying; where did they go? I look behind me. He is less than fifteen feet behind me. I can barely run. The man doesn't even need to jog. Walking fast, he's almost caught up to me. "Help! Help me! Someone please!"

"No one can help you. No one will come to your aid. You, the queen of all that's wicked, and your evil creation will end now."

"Stay away from me!" It's odd what goes through your mind when in a life-threatening situation. In this moment, I realize I should have organized my purse better. I should have had a designated pocket for my phone for emergencies when I need to grab it fast and not have to dig through a bottomless pit. Also, I should carry a knife or pepper spray.

"Help!"

"You cannot prevent the inevitable! If you assist me, I will make sure your child's soul is spared!"

He's seven feet away. I hurl my purse, my feeble attempt to hurt him. He swats it away like an annoying fly.

"Help! Someone! Please!"

Is this really how I'm going to die? In a church at the hands of a lunatic? One more step and he'll be able to reach out and grab me. I'm sorry, bell pepper. I tried. I tried to keep you safe. I tried to be a good mother. I'm sorry I let you down. I'm sorry I'm not strong enough or fast enough. You deserved better.

The redheaded man dressed like a priest shouts in Latin, darting around the corner, charging toward the hippie. Screaming, spitting Latin verses, he raises his fist and cracks the man's jaw with a nasty right hook. The possessed man doesn't flinch, but he covers his ears as if the Latin words are burning his eardrums.

"No, you don't understand! Stop!" cries the hippie in a crackling voice.

Still the redhead chants louder and louder, drowning out the pleas from my attacker. The hippie falls to his knees, looking weaker and weaker. He looks in my direction and points a finger at me and says, "I'll be back to…"

Then the man's eyes roll backward and he falls onto his back, guided by my rescuer. Once the crazy man is lying flat on the ground, looking like he's asleep, the redhead gets up and turns around, inspecting me for injuries. "Are you okay? Did he hurt you?"

"No, but what the hell was that? Who are you?"

"My name is Ken. Are you sure you're alright? Do you need an ambulance?"

"I'm fine. I just want to know what's happening. What was that? Who is he?"

The man on the ground stirs, making me jump backward, almost falling if it weren't for Ken's fast-moving arms.

"He can't hurt you anymore. He was possessed," he says, looking around the cathedral like he's trying to find a ghost floating above us. "I've never seen a possession take place on holy grounds. Has this ever happened to you before?"

"What? Are you telling me he was actually possessed? Like by a demon?"

"Yes, well, as far as I can tell. I've never seen an angelic possession where the angel was trying to hurt a person. When an angel possesses someone, they perform acts that seem like everyday miracles. Demons are the only ones who attack and kill, but they normally can't stand on sacred ground."

My brain is having a difficult time understanding the words he is saying. They are words. I know all their definitions, but strung together in those sentences, they become illogical. "What? Angels and demons can possess people? And let me guess, you can exorcise those entities?"

"Yes," he says with a straight face.

I scoff at him, unsure how to reply. Am I going crazy, or does this make sense? Do I need to be semi-crazy in order to understand?

The man on the floor groans. "Where am I? Tara? Where's Tara?"

Ken runs over to him, helping him to his feet. "You're in St. Patrick's Cathedral. Looks like someone spiked your drink. Where were you partying? I'll get a taxi for you."

"St. Patrick's? How did I get here? I hope Tara is alright." He reaches into his pockets. "Where's my phone and my wallet? Shit. She's going to kill me."

"Don't worry. I'll pay your fare," Ken says, walking the man toward the entrance.

I walk over to my purse contents, which are scattered across the floor. Literally everything except my phone is on the ground. The new American Express card that Lucas gave me, with my new name on it, is on the ground. It must have slipped out of my wallet when I flung my purse. My phone has four missed calls from Lucas. His meeting must have ended early. I send him a text saying I'll call him in a few minutes.

"Sorry. I wanted to get that man out of here. He didn't know he threatened or attempted to attack you. The less he knows, the better. Most people can't handle this sort of information."

"Like having possessed people scream and threaten you?"

"Yeah, things like that. What did he say when he wasn't himself? Did he mention a name?" he asks while picking up a pocket calendar and some notes that were stuffed inside it, handing them to me.

"No, no name. Just that he was sent to kill me and my child since others failed. He said if I cooperated, he would spare my baby's soul."

"No demon can spare a soul."

"That's if we even have them."

He cocks his head to the side. "Have what?"

"Souls," I say, rolling my eyes.

"You don't believe?"

"No." I rake my hands through my hair. "I don't know."

Ken nods and ushers me to a pew to sit down. "You said he mentioned others failed. Have you been around other possessions?"

I laugh. "I don't know what to call the strange events, but yeah, weird things have been happening."

"Like what? You can trust me. I used to be a priest."

"Used to?"

"Excommunicated for some of my ideologies. I don't agree with the church on everything, so we broke up," he says.

He doesn't look like a pedophile, so I don't think it was anything like that, but I'm curious why they would kick out a young priest. Ken can't be much older than me. "I'm sorry. What didn't you agree about?"

"Many things. But that's another story for another time. What strange things have happened to you?"

"Well, a store clerk told me to make the right choice and a junkie screamed about the Antichrist and told me I'm the queen of Hell." I roll my eyes. "Then a couple weeks later, my doctor had a seizure midsentence and told me in a disembodied voice to stop seeing doctors and to not perform any more lab tests on the baby and it will be born perfect." Ken reaches into his pocket and takes out a small notebook and pen, writing down my story. "Then there was a kid who, I'm not sure what I saw, but her head twisted almost all the way around and then went back to normal. She also threatened to kill us, silence us."

"When did this all start?"

"A couple months ago. It happens randomly."

"Has anything like this happened before you were pregnant?"

I can't help but chuckle, thinking about Jim's grandmother. "No. Not unless you count a crazy old lady's ramblings."

"I think we'll consider her senile, for now. If you want, I'll do some digging in the archives and see if there are any other similar instances. See if there's any information that will help. Would you like a blessing? It might keep the demons at bay until I've done some research."

"But you're not a priest. Is that allowed?"

"I know the prayers and what's in my heart. God knows too."

"It can't hurt," I say with a shrug.

He recites a prayer and does the sign of the cross. Bell pepper starts kicking up a storm, being a little acrobat. We exchange phone numbers and he walks with me down the front steps.

"Thank you. I don't know if I said that before. If you hadn't been there…"

"I was in the right place at the right time. Glad to help you… I'm sorry I didn't catch your name."

"Sorry; I'm still kind of jumbled. My name's Eve."

"Nice to meet you, Eve," he says, shaking my hand. "Give me a call if you need help or if anything else happens. I'll let you know when I find something. I still have connections in the Vatican. They should be able to discover something useful."

"Do you really think people are becoming possessed around me?" I ask, still confused, but at least this time there was a witness besides Melisa.

"Yes."

"How do you know?"

"The first possession I witnessed was when I was five and my older brother was being tormented. Since then, I've traveled the world, learning and saving as many people as possible. The things I've seen would make you a believer or would drive you insane. Maybe both."

"Is your brother okay?"

"The priest tried his hardest, but the demon was too powerful."

I stop in the middle of the steps. "You mean the demon…"

"It killed my brother. Made him snap his own neck. The demon was in control of his body, but I believe my brother was a riding passenger, sort of to speak. It's my mission to prevent things like that from happening."

My mouth hangs open and I hug my belly. "I'm so sorry."

He nods. "Stay safe. Call me if you experience anything abnormal."

"I will. Thank you, Ken."

He hails me a taxi, opens the door, and says, "Be careful who you tell. Stay safe, Eve."

I think how dangerous his line of work must be. He punched that guy and looked like he expected a big fight, even though the possessed didn't fight back. His nose is definitely crooked like it has been broken before, but I wouldn't say that it makes him ugly. For an ex-priest, he's rather handsome. I tell the cab driver the address to Lucas's penthouse suite and then call Lucas.

"Hi. Is everything okay? What's wrong?" I ask him after he picks up on the first ring.

"Nothing's wrong. I was worried. I came back to the penthouse and you were gone. I thought I'd take you out for an early dinner. There's a restaurant I'd love for you to try. How's our little bell pepper been feeling today?"

The words *bell pepper* make me swoon. He really is in this for the long haul. When I talk about how big you are, little one, he is actually listening. He really cares about us, about you. How did we end up this lucky? "Fine. We are both fine. Don't worry; we are on the way back."

"Eve? Is everything all right? You sound upset. Where are you?" Lucas asks.

"We're okay. I went to St. Patrick's Cathedral."

"Why? I didn't think you were the religious type."

"I'm not, but I wanted to check out the building. Get out and do something touristy while you were working."

"I'm sorry you went alone. I'll take you out tonight and do something touristy; your pick."

"Oh, Lucas, I don't know what I would do without you. I've missed you all day."

"Come home, my queen. I have two touristy restaurants in mind. You can freshen up and look over the menus and decide where pepper wants to dine."

He said *home* and *pepper* again. Without a thought, the words come out. Maybe it's brought on by the stress of experiencing a traumatic event. Even though neither of us has said it to each other yet, the words echo in the back of my mind every moment that I'm with Lucas.

I can't help but utter those three words. "I love you."

Katie Zaber

23 Weeks - New York, New York

"You know, you make this place feel like home," Lucas says while stirring his bitter black coffee without sugar. The expensive European coffee smells stronger, like espresso mixed with crack. The smell of it wakes me up; a single sip might give someone a heart attack.

Separating us is the square kitchen island made of stainless steel. It's completely clear of clutter and the metal looks recently polished. Shiny enough to reflect the Edison light bulbs dangling on wires from pipes welded together into an industrial chandelier. Black drawers with steel handles line the top part of the island. There are no cabinets. Instead, pots and pans that look unused are stored underneath on an open rack. All the appliances are stainless steel, too. The whole kitchen and apartment is a shade of gray with accents of black. It's dark and dreary.

When I first walked into his penthouse, its sheer size blew me away, but I was unimpressed with the aesthetics. The place has a gloomy atmosphere. It had to change.

"Really? Are you sure I haven't modified your apartment too much? I don't want to cramp your somber style."

He laughs. "You've brought light and color into a dull apartment. You haven't changed it too much. The rugs add a cozy touch."

We bought a couple of different brightly colored accent rugs so we aren't walking around on cold tile that resembles concrete. "Right? I honestly hate cold tile floors."

"Agreed. I should have put more thought into this purchase. I never realized that everything in the apartment is a shade of gray. It looks like a black and white film with a few random specks of color. I wouldn't mind adding more."

"We could get some artwork to cover the walls. The furniture is brand new so I wouldn't replace that, but maybe some new colorful pillows and blankets will break up the ashy color scheme."

Lucas gives me a genuine smile, not one of his mischievous grins or I'm-up-to-something smirks. "Are you happy here?"

"What do you mean?"

"Can you picture us raising a family here?"

The kettle whistles and I pour the hot water over a decaf tea bag. While I dunk the tea bag and swirl it, I consider how much I hate the noisy streets. I want my kid to have space to play and not breathe in exhaust fumes on the way to an overcrowded park. "New York City is fun, and this apartment is stunning, even if it is impersonal, but I want a yard with a huge swing set and space for grapefruit to grow and explore."

"Do you have any idea where you would like to live?"

I had loved the Poconos. It was close to a few major cities, the Jersey Shore, mountains, lakes—the area really had access to a ton of places, but there is no way I can move back there and chance running into anyone I had known. I really don't want to live in the middle of the woods near my parents; that's too far away from civilization for me, plus they would drive me insane. "Suburbs somewhere close to everything. Do you have any ideas?"

He shrugs. "Where have you felt the happiest?"

I roll my eyes. "Well, it's not like we can live at a theme park," I say, joking, even though that was the happiest I've been in a long time. I loved the Florida Keys, but I can't eat fish every day, though island life is tempting.

"We can't?" he asks with a mischievous grin.

"Lucas? What are you thinking?"

He comes around the kitchen island and plants a kiss on my forehead. "Don't worry, my queen. I have some work to do."

I roll my eyes. It won't be long until I find out what he's planning. He loves planning surprises, but usually the surprise is planned in the morning and happens in the evening. Within a day or two at most, I should know what he's scheming.

Grapefruit, what was that? That kick felt so weird. You're wiggling up a storm in there and getting stronger every day.

That reminds me I'm getting hungry. I had oatmeal earlier, but I want something else. A cream cheese Danish with strawberry jelly sounds amazing. What do you think, little one? Should I ask Daddy to get us some treats? He'll probably say I need to get up and stretch my legs and how we should go for a family walk. It feels good to call him your daddy and refer to us as a family. It feels right.

I decide to go out to the balcony and recline on the most luxurious outdoor patio set I have ever sat on and enjoy my tea hundreds of feet up above the noisy streets below. Up here, it's actually quite peaceful. Down there, isn't. It's a chaotic mess, but high above the chaos is serenity. Like Heaven above Hell. Overlooking the city of ants makes me strangely feel like a god looking over their creation.

Ken hasn't called and I don't have any weird events to report, so my phone has been quiet except for Melisa, who I'm talking to daily again. She also knows about Lucas, but I'm stingy with the details. The only thing she knows for sure is that I'm happy, even though she has said she wants to see that for herself. I haven't told Melisa or Lucas about what happened in the church or about Ken and his odd job. As much as I want to tell Lucas and be truthful, I don't want him to think I'm crazy. Melisa already does, but she doesn't judge. I just think that kind of conversation is better done face-to-face. It will be more believable when she can see the horror in my eyes, and I'm not a fan of video chat.

"Eve, pack your bags for two nights. We are being picked up in an hour," Lucas calls out from his study.

"What? What about breakfast?"

He comes out from the study before I can get myself off the patio lounge. "I want to check something out that I think you might be interested in," he says with a scheming smile. "We'll grab breakfast on the way."

"What are you up to?" I ask as I get to my feet and give him a kiss.

He spins me around so I face the New York City skyline. His hands settle under my belly button, cradling us. I lean into him.

"Hmm, it's a surprise. You'll see if you like it when we get there," he says while gently massaging my belly. His hand moves lower.

A small moan escapes my lips as I grind into him. "I thought you said we leave in an hour."

"We can be a few minutes late. You're just too beautiful to not want," he says before nibbling my earlobe, making my legs weak.

Now I'm standing before a mansion somewhere in the USA. I'm unsure exactly where. However, the three-hour flight and the landscape are a dead giveaway.

"It's on the market."

"Seriously?"

"Yes. The community is called Magic Gardens."

I roll my eyes at that name. Now I've heard of everything. "How close are we to the theme parks?"

"A few miles. We should be able to watch the fireworks from the backyard."

"This house is too big!" The Spanish-styled house before me must be at least four bedrooms with a huge two, no, a three-car garage.

"I thought it wasn't too big, but not small for a house. Four bedrooms, five baths. I also want to check out the six-bedroom unit down the street. There are more available too. Different styles and designs. Ready for buyers—if you like it here. But we will also keep the Manhattan penthouse. Stay there for work. Come here to enjoy life. A second home."

"A second home? Why do we need two?" I'm dumbfounded. Never have I thought I'd be rich enough to own a second home.

The real estate agent comes out of the mini mansion, a folder in her one hand and two water bottles in the other. "Hello! Welcome! Welcome! You must be Lucas and Eve. Oh, it's so nice to meet you. Come this way, out of the heat." She ushers us through the huge double doorway entry and into the great room. "So what do you think? Is this along the lines of what you're interested in?"

"It's huge, but the dark wood makes it feel small to me," I say as I gravitate toward the pool and summer kitchen. "It will only be the three of us. So besides two bedrooms and an office, I just don't see the need for so much space, but it is beautiful."

"I need an office. What if Melisa comes to visit after you have the baby? Your parents?" Lucas asks, which is surprising.

"Alright, I'm fine with four bedrooms, but I don't want something monstrous. I'm not going to have the energy to clean."

Lucas gives me a questioning look. "We're hiring a maid. You won't be cleaning."

Wow. He doesn't expect me to clean the million-dollar home he wants to buy. I need to have a serious conversation with him about how much he makes. I give him a coy smile. "As long as I'm not cleaning, it's all up to you."

"No, no, no. This is for you. You get to pick. I get to see you smile."

After touring six different luxurious mansions that are completely furnished, we eliminate the ones not baby safe and narrow it down to four. There are two different styles of ranches I like, one with Caribbean charm that feels relaxing and calm. It has three bedrooms and four bathrooms with a detached guest suite. The other is a Spanish cottage. It's alright, but the bedrooms are smaller than the Caribbean-styled home and it costs more. Lucas rolled his eyes when I made that point.

Both have a fantastic, low maintenance but resort-like yard. The backyards, also known as the pool and spa areas, are amazing and unique to each house. Down the street from both houses are parks for children. The views are nice and I can imagine raising a kid in either home.

The other two are the ones Lucas is more inclined to buy. The French six-bedroom mansion with the most expensive finishes and crown molding I have ever seen really make him excited. It is over the top. Not a place for a sticky-fingered toddler. The second one is a sleek modern style five-bedroom. The whole front of the house looks like one large glass pane, but you can't see inside. I don't feel comfortable living in a fishbowl.

I hate to say it, but out of the two he likes, I'd rather the six-bedroom mansion than the glass house. However, I'm still not done arguing my opinion. And I can really picture us happy in the Caribbean cottage with its island aesthetic. The pool area was the nicest and the guest suite is really appealing, especially if my parents ever come to visit, even though I doubt they will.

Never did I think a couple of months ago that I would be in a gated community, looking at houses with the most amazing man ever. How did I get so lucky? Is this real?

"Well, that completes the tour today. Do you have any more questions? Are you interested in any of them?" our real estate agent asks.

"Do all the houses come furnished? They aren't just being staged?" I ask, never having anything like that happen before. When I moved into my first apartment, there was a rickety kitchen table, but I think the previous tenant left it there and the owner of the complex didn't want to toss it out. The home Jim and I bought was completely empty when we went on the house tour.

"Yes, our designers thought of everything. This comes exactly how you see it." She gives me another rehearsed smile.

"Thank you for all your help today. Maybe give us a few moments to discuss in private," Lucas suggests to the overbearing agent.

She nods. "Of course. I'll wait on the patio."

From the oversized great room in the five-bedroom mansion, we both watch her close the door behind her. The ceiling has glitter on it and the chandeliers look like fireworks. At night, it must look magical.

"You don't like this one," Lucas says, giving me a side grin. "Why not? It has everything and all the space we could ever need."

"It's a fishbowl and too big. I know you said we'd hire cleaners, but it's still massive. I don't see the need to have this many rooms. Even if I invite Melisa and possibly my parents down at the same time, all we would need at most would be a four-bedroom. I don't know. I like cozy and small. The Caribbean charmer. That house was comfortable. I could see us being a family there. It felt like home the moment I walked through the doors."

He closes the distance between us and places his hands on my shoulders. "Let's make your vision a reality."

"Really? It's not too small for you or not fancy enough?" I tease, waving my hands in the air.

"No, it's fancy. It's not large, but to be honest, I've never looked for a home before. I guess this is a little ridiculous for the three of us. And you think you'll be happy here? You can always change your mind…"

"This neighborhood is perfect for our little one. Filled with magic and safety. Though, I never thought I would ever say I would willingly move to Florida, but I guess this area isn't like the rest of Florida. I'd still like to go to the local stores and see where I'd be grocery shopping."

He cocks his head. It's in that moment I realize that we've never been to a grocery store together. We've never bickered over what vegetables or cuts of meat to buy or whose turn it is to cook. When we arrived at his penthouse for the first time, it was already stocked by a personal shopper hired years ago. Whenever Lucas is on his way home, he sends his shopper an email. That way, there is always something in the apartment when he first walks in. They also spruce up the place, making sure it's clean of dust.

Lucas's mouth hangs open for a second before he says, "We'll order groceries. I can't imagine you wanting to go grocery shopping seven months pregnant or with a newborn."

"Lucas, have you ever gone inside a grocery store?"

He shrugs. "Never had the need. I've always eaten out or could order whatever I wanted."

"Wow. Never?"

"Nope. I've been to convenience stores to grab a drink or snack. That's about it."

"What about in college?"

"I ate out. I never cooked a meal."

"I'm shocked. I don't think I've ever met anyone who hasn't been to the produce section."

"There are many other things I'd rather do with my time than shop for broccoli. But if you want to go grocery shopping, we can. However, I'd recommend getting a personal shopper. It makes life simpler."

"It would be nice for when the baby comes. One less thing to worry about."

"Exactly." He gives me a kiss on the head and then motions to the agent, who is pretending to be on her phone. "We've decided. The island-style house. She loves it."

"Wonderful. I'll draw up the papers. When would you like to move in?" she asks.

"Tomorrow," is all Lucas says.

The poor woman's face drains. "I don't know if that is possible. There are procedures and steps. It might take a week, possibly two, before inspection."

"I'll have my accountant sort everything out with you. I've already sent him your information. He'll be calling you shortly."

"But, but..." she keeps stuttering. I'm sure she has dealt with high-end buyers, those who are purchasing their third or fourth vacation home, but I doubt she has ever dealt with anyone like Lucas Star.

Katie Zaber

24 Weeks - Orlando, Florida

Music blasts out of the new entertainment system. The tiny speakers hidden around the house are powerful. They aren't bulky like the speakers Jim had mounted on either side of the television in the game room. Those made the house vibrate. These speakers are built into the walls and are completely flush with them. It's a sleek, modern design. Rectangular shapes made of white, hard, shiny plastic smaller than my hand are the only visible parts. The rest is embedded in the walls. If I crank the volume, the walls might shake everything off them.

It's all controlled by an app on my brand new smartphone and tablet. I finally caved and got a new phone with a new number. Switching my number again wasn't hard; I can literally count on one hand all the people I had to notify.

It's been lonely the last two nights without Lucas, even though we video chatted until I fell asleep. I didn't realize how much I would miss him. We've spent the last six weeks together, almost inseparable. Maybe that's why I feel like we've been together forever. It's hard to remember before Lucas, when I was with Jim. Either I'm over that relationship or it was truly never meant to be.

Don't worry. Daddy will come back this afternoon and then we're going shopping for all the different things we need in the house. We need dinnerware, silverware, pots and pans, kitchen accessories, bedding, and a bunch of personal items. The house came with sheets freshly put on the bed and a few plates and cups, but only the basic for a family if they came down on a vacation for the first time. We might even look at some cribs today.

The generic ringtone on my phone is ringing. It's not Lucas's or Melisa's unique songs. I haven't had single telemarketer call since I've gotten this phone. There's only one other person who might call. I turn down the music so it's just background noise.

It's Ken.

Since we bought the house, I have been preoccupied with online window shopping and planning out the nursery. Nothing crazy has happened, and I honestly thought I would not hear back from the ex-priest. It crossed my mind that he was also a crazy man who happened to interfere and save me from another, more insane, lunatic.

After the fourth ring, I pick it up. "Hello?"

"Eve, how are you?"

"I'm great. How are you?"

"Same. Has anything odd happened?"

"No. Everything has been good."

"Good. I've talked to my resources and I'd like to get more information from you. Are you nearby?"

"No, we just bought a second home in Florida. I'm down here getting it organized."

"Florida? When are you planning on coming back to the city?"

"Probably within the next week or two."

"The sooner, the better."

"What's wrong? What did you find out?"

"I don't want to go into details on the phone... Just be careful and call me as soon as you're back in the city. If you can't fly, I can come down there."

"I should be back soon—the next time my boyfriend goes to the city for work. But please tell me something."

"I'll explain when I see you in person. Stay safe," he says and then hangs up.

My finger hovers over his number, deciding whether to call him back and demand that he tell me something. How paranoid can he be that he won't give me a hint at all? Or is it that bad and I should be jumping on the next flight to New York to find out how to help us? I want people to stop threatening you, pomegranate. I want to protect you, but I'm also terrified of what he will say when I see him.

Before I can hit redial, Lucas sends me a text, asking if I'm ready to go shopping.

I text him *yes* and realize that the music stopped while I was talking to Ken. I open the app and from what it says, the music is still playing. I open and close the app. It says it's still working, even though the music won't play from the speakers. Lucas is going to have to look at it. He's better at technology than I am. I hope I didn't already break our new sound system. It would be my luck. I'm sure the IT guys at my old job are happy I'm gone.

I try to forget about Ken and what weird religious information he was able to find, and focus on happier thoughts. Such as making a list of things we must buy today and things I want to check out later.

"Do you really think we need a twelve-piece place setting? It's going to be years before pomegranate eats off them," I ask Lucas as I load up the dishwasher for its maiden wash. It took me five minutes of reading the manual to figure how to select a normal wash cycle. I'm not going to fuss with all the other buttons. Maybe one day I'll read the rest of the instructions.

"Why not? By then, we can buy a new set."

I roll my eyes at Lucas. He's so wasteful, but I think from the way he was brought up that splurging is a coping mechanism. Really, I can't say anything. It's his money, and he has an endless supply of it.

When he says shopping spree, he means it. I think we got most of the household items taken care of in one swoop. There are a couple things that I'm sure we forgot, like salt and pepper grinders and a citrus juicer, besides items we can buy at the grocery store. He insisted we purchase an air fryer since it's the latest rage, and bought the one the size of a toaster oven with five racks. The massive machine was seven hundred and fifty dollars by itself. The silverware and kitchen knives together cost over thirty-five hundred. By the time we left the high-end boutique, we had spent close to seven grand and Lucas didn't bat an eye. Instead, he said it was cheaper than expected.

My response was shaking my head and rolling my eyes at his insane spending habits. But if he has the money, might as well spend it.

"I'm too tired to cook after sorting all this stuff. What are you in the mood to eat?"

"You don't have to cook if you don't want to. Ever. If you want, we can even hire our own personal chef."

I think about the allure of having a personal chef, but then remember they are in your home often and I'd rather have a maid twice a month. Fewer people in my home equals more privacy, and I value that above everything. "No. Tomorrow I'm going to start cooking. We have to start. I know we aren't eating fast food, but all that takeout has to be unhealthy."

"With every meal, I eat a decent side of vegetables. You're the one who skips them."

Even Lucas is on my case about how much I avoid all the healthy food. I should never have him and Melisa in the same room. "Yeah, but they aren't cooked the way I want to eat them. Plus, it will be fun. And you'll get to use all these expensive gadgets."

He makes a clicking noise with his tongue. "If you say so. I've never cooked before and don't know where to start. It would be all up to you."

"I haven't cooked in years; we'll learn together. Cook side by side."

"Sounds like we are going to burn a lot of food and then order takeout," he says with a smirk.

"At least we will have worked for it."

Lucas laughs and gives me a kiss. "You. You are something else."

"Plus, pomegranate won't have your refined palate. We've got to be able to feed it kid food when it's done breastfeeding. We should practice."

"We have plenty of time to learn how to burn and eventually cook meals. Tonight we'll get something different. Tomorrow we'll go… grocery shopping," he says, cringing while staring at his phone, mumbling something about eating local.

When you buy groceries for the first time in a new house, it's always expensive, at least a couple hundred to stock the pantry, spices, oils, and basics, besides expensive items like meat. I'm guessing we'll spend five hundred without trying and still need to buy more. I sigh, waiting for him to name a type of food he wants for dinner, from some far corner of the world I have never heard of before.

"Looks like a good deal. Pizza, hot wings, mozzarella sticks, potato skins, and cannoli for twenty-nine ninety-nine," he says with a smug look.

"A deal? I've never heard you utter any of those words."

"Even I get in the mood for a greasy extra cheese pizza. What? You don't approve of a fried feast before we cook bland, extra-crispy home-cooked meals."

"You love to surprise me and drive me crazy, don't you?"

"Do you want to add bacon to the pizza?" he asks.

I can't help myself and kiss him.

"Do we need one or two carts?" Lucas asks as we get out of the shiny black Cadillac Escalade.

I refused to be chauffeured to the local grocery store and told him no more private drivers unless it's a date night and I can drink or if we're in the city. So logically he rented a luxury car. Part of me is happy that it wasn't a Mustang convertible; the other part thinks he would consider that car cheap. In the next week or two, we'll go car shopping, but right now it's not my main priority. Plus, the rental is nice and it gives me time to compare cars, even though I'm sure Lucas is going to buy the safest, most expensive SUV for us. It felt weird to get into the front seat of the car after weeks of traveling in the back. I even asked Lucas if he had his driver's license since he doesn't own a car, which made him laugh, but he didn't answer my question. Thankfully, the grocery store is a five-minute drive.

"Two carts. We can race each other," I tease as we walk into the mega grocery store packed with people.

Lucas stops and stares at all the people mingling about. "This is a grocery store? Strange. And you enjoy such activities?"

"I wouldn't go as far as saying I enjoy grocery shopping, but it gets me out of the house and gives me something to do each week."

"You can always go to school or find a career worth your time. This seems…"

"It's not beneath me to pick out food. And it isn't for you either."

He gives me a baffled look. "I only meant that there are only so many hours in the day. Why fill it with mundane tasks?"

"Because until I met you, I couldn't afford to pay someone else to do those things. It feels strange to have someone chauffeur me and purchase my daily needs. I'm not used to being a snob," I say, rolling my eyes.

He clicks his tongue. "Do you get any gratification from this?"

"I like to pick out different things. Try different snacks and see what's new. Though getting a job might be nice or going back to school for something other than liberal arts."

"Liberal arts? Did you study anything in particular?"

"I was interested in everything that didn't involve math."

"So no business classes? Should we get bread? That seems like an ordinary household item."

"No, no business classes. We don't need to buy bread. You bought me a state-of-the-art bread maker; I'm going to make a fresh-baked loaf when we get home."

"What do we need to make bread?"

"Not that many ingredients, and they are all on the list. Come on; I don't want to spend all day here."

We have spent all day at the grocery store.

Taking Lucas was a mistake. He's like a child wanting to explore every aisle, touching and picking up every item and asking a slew of questions. I know he's never gone grocery shopping, but it's insane to find out how much he has never tried. He must have been hungry his whole childhood. When we went down the snack aisle, he wanted to sample every lunch box treat he never had. By the time we got to the checkout line, his cart had all the paper products and cleaning supplies, plus twenty different confectionary and novelty ice cream treats. My cart has all the spices, pasta, cans, flour, sugar, tea, coffee, dairy, and frozen. We spent over three hundred and I'm sure we forgot a ton of stuff.

As soon as we step outside, Lucas rips open a box of funfetti muffins. I look into the parking lot crowded with oversized vehicles and get nervous. "Lucas, be a dear and drive the car up."

"What's wrong? Are you feeling okay?"

"My feet are sore and the car looks really far away from here."

He gives me a questioning glare and stares at the parking lot, slowly looking around before turning back to me. "When we get home, you should soak your feet in the tub. I'll be right back."

"Thank you," I say, blowing him a kiss, still watching the other large SUVs and cargo vans for any suspicious behavior, ready to ram my cart into an abductor, giving me a few extra seconds to run five feet back into the safety of the store.

I hate being paranoid.

25 Weeks - New York, New York

"So you want a detailed account of every instance?" I ask Ken. He still wears a black button-down shirt, albeit missing the white collar, tucked into dark blue jeans.

Since Ken's cryptic phone call, I've been more on edge, afraid, even. As soon as Lucas said he was heading back into the city, I told him I'd like to tag along. I need to know what's happening, and if Ken has any news, it might put my mind at ease. Might. Or whatever information he is about to give will send me into a padded room. When the plane touched down, I sent Ken a text and we agreed to meet up at a local hipster café.

So far, I've woofed down two scones and a breakfast sandwich. And that was before Ken arrived. He came forty minutes late. It's been close to an hour since I ate and I'm tempted to go up and get a chocolate chip muffin. But I'll stop. It might be too much sugar, even though I really want one.

The redhead with the unkempt beard sitting across from me looks like a priest. When he stands, everyone can tell for sure that he isn't. Almost like a magic trick. Priest. Normal man. Priest. Normal man. He does this trick every time he gets up for more coffee or sugar. He keeps adding more sugar but doesn't add a drop of cream. It must be out of pure politeness that he isn't adding anything out of a flask. I'd bet there's a plain silver flask in his pocket. He looks like a disheveled alcoholic who thinks he's out to save the world.

"My Vatican contact wants more details. But he's worried. He wasn't able to find any records of a demon possession in a church. There are accounts of bringing possessed individuals into churches to exorcise them, but half of them died as soon as their bodies touched consecrated ground."

"What happened to the other half?"

"Most went insane. A small portion was healed. But none of those possessed by an evil entity could withstand being in a sacred place without displaying some amount of pain."

"And the guy who attacked me..."

"Everything was odd. He wasn't afflicted. Normally when I start an exorcism, the demon in control of the person becomes violent. They try to kill me rather than go back to Hell."

"Seriously?" I ask a little too loudly for coffee shop chat. A couple of heads turn my way and continue to stare, probably because I look horrified. "Sorry."

"I've been in a couple of fights. But I'm undefeated," Ken says with a wink.

"Has it come close?" I ask.

"More than twice."

I take a sip of my herbal berry tea and try my best to speak in a whisper. "Is it always a different demon, or do the same ones keep escaping?"

He leans back into the chair and takes a swig of coffee. "There are some tougher, smarter demons bent on wreaking havoc with a grand scheme, and there are normal ones who were lucky enough to break out with no plans and just want to inflict as much chaos and pain as possible. Either way, people like me send them back where they belong."

"How many are there?"

"Demons? Countless. There's always more."

"No, I meant people who fight against them."

"Not enough," he says with a grim expression. No despair. "There have been more cases lately. There's no shortage of work for my comrades and me around the world. A lot of child possessions lately. Tons in the city. Enough that I have been trying to get the freaking archbishop to help, but he refuses, saying that there's no such thing as possessions. He claims that it's some type of neurological phenomenon that doctors haven't identified," he says with a sneer.

"He doesn't believe?"

"He chooses not to. All the evidence is in front of his eyes. He even looks at it but shrugs, calling it bullshit. And with this current uptick, I'm exorcising one to two people a day. Most are kids."

"Why kids?"

"Easiest to trick and manipulate, scare. Demons prey upon the weak. They are easier to control."

"So the church is aware of possessions, but some don't believe?"

"Yup," he says with extra emphasis on the p, making a popping noise. "It's a joke. Depending on who leads the church, that's who decides if the church believes possessions are real. One pope believes in possessions, funds and builds a school for people with my abilities. The next pope demolishes the school and turns it into a park, declaring exorcisms an excommunicable offense."

I gasp. "How can they just pick what to believe?"

"Humans always do. It's in our nature. We pick out the details we want to believe and ignore everything else that terrifies us, pretending it doesn't exist. At least, the cowards do."

"What abilities? Do you mean you were born differently?" I have so many questions that it's hard to just ask one. But my head is starting to hurt. Maybe I need to drink more water. Though, I could eat.

"I'm not here to talk about myself. There's no helping me or my cause. But I can help you."

"Why can't I help you?"

"You just can't. There are things you can change and things you can't. I don't want to make your head explode with all the problems I face daily, all the evil that lurks in the darkness. Take my word on it. Let's focus on your problem. I don't want anyone possessed attacking you and your child."

"What about all the children? All the recent cases?"

"I still take them, but I always help the most vulnerable, and currently your child is the weakest. I don't mean to alarm you; it's just the way I operate. I have a soft spot for kids and babies."

"I'm sure your brother is proud of the work you do."

He looks down at his empty coffee cup. He's drunk at least four. "I see him in every child healed." He narrows his eyes for a second and lets out a long breath. "But back to your case. Explain every event, in detail, that has happened between you and anyone who you suspect may have been possessed."

"Before or after I became pregnant? Because my ex's grandmother swore I was the devil incarnate for years," I say while stroking my belly. Eggplant's kicks are getting stronger every day. Yeah, I think I am going to get that muffin. Or maybe a fruit cup. That might be healthier.

Ken cracks a smile. "Sounds like she really liked you."

I shrug. "At least she'll die happy, knowing her grandson is free from my demonic grip," I say before confessing everything to the ex-priest. But first I buy a fruit cup and a chocolate chip muffin. I have a lot to confess.

Orlando, Florida

In the airport, it's hard to hear anything over the hundreds of conversations and relentless announcements with chimes; it's driving me insane. Plus, I have a stowaway that won't stop kicking. I swear eggplant is having a dance competition or is a future martial arts master, using my internal organs as target practice. That last one hurt. And now I have to pee again. I peed three times before we left the house.

Airport bathrooms are nasty. I really don't want to use it. Especially after I've watched at least a hundred women enter and exit since we arrived ten minutes ago. But I'm going to have to do something because this is becoming an emergency. Even if Melisa is the next person to come down the escalator, the moment she hugs me, I'm going to explode like a water balloon.

"I have to go," I whisper to Lucas, who's looking exceptionally handsome holding a sign with Melisa's name on it and a large square box wrapped in periwinkle blue wrapping paper with a sweet pink bow on top. I have no idea what it is. Earlier when I caught him with the gift, he told me with a sneaky smile that it's a present for both of us girls.

"Again? Eggplant, stop kicking Mommy's bladder," he says while bending down close to my stomach. It's cute how he talks to the baby all the time. He gives my belly a rub before standing. "Eve, you better hurry before she comes down the stairs."

I roll my eyes and head to the bathroom. Luckily, with the constant flow of traffic, there's a stall open; unfortunately it's the second to last one in the aisle. I've made it this far. I can make it to the seat. At least I keep telling myself that. I used to laugh at pregnant women when they'd waddle-run; now I know why.

With my blue summer dress bunched up around my waist and my ass on the cold toilet seat, I get a chill, intense enough to give me goosebumps. That's when I notice the only sound is the echo of the stream pouring out of me.

I flush and go to wash my hands. Outside the stall, the airport bathroom attendant hums "Oh Susannah" with her back toward me, washing a sink. The bathroom amplifies her voice, making it sound strange. While washing my hands, I look at her.

She isn't cleaning the sink. No. She's draining the blood out of her wrists, pumping and squeezing it out of her.

"Oh my god!"

I begin to run for help but a cackle interrupts her humming, making me stop and face her. On second thought, maybe this is something Ken deals with.

"Oh Evie, don't you cry for me. I come from the abyss with an incredible dream," she sings in an enthusiastic manner as the streams of blood slow. Her face continues to pale, matching her frosty eyes. Her hands hover over the sink drain, making grasping motions like she's trying to siphon the last drop of blood out since it's down to a dribble.

"Who are you? What are you?" I ask what I think might be a possessed person, since no one in their right mind would empty their wrists while singing a children's song.

The demon keeps humming and forcing all the blood out of the body it's using. How long can it stay in a dead person's skin? The possessed shakes its wrists, splattering the last of the blood into the sink. Not a single drop comes out of her slit wrists. The poor woman has been completely drained.

"Who are you? What do you want?"

"Oh Evie, don't you cry for me. I come from the abyss with the most incredible dream." The animated corpse finishes its song.

"Answer me!"

All it does is cackle in a way that makes me want to get out of the bathroom now, even if I want answers. I back out of the bathroom, keeping an eye on her.

That's when I notice no one has entered or exited since I've come in. Do normal people sense the evil and flee the area like rats fleeing a sinking ship? What's wrong with me?

A security guard paces back and forth by the entrance. Maybe she senses the wrong sensation in the vicinity but can't place it or figure out where it's coming from.

"Miss, I need help," I call to her.

She turns, eyes darting, sweat building on her brow, hand hovering over her taser gun.

"A woman slit her wrists. She needs medical assistance."

Her eyes bug out as she repeats what I just said into her walkie-talkie and runs into the bathroom. A few steps away, I hear a yell and muffled laughter. Poor possessed woman. Poor traumatized security guard. I'll call Ken and tell him later. I don't think there is anything he can do now.

"There you are—what's wrong?" Lucas asks as he runs to close the gap between us. He touches my stomach and places an arm on my back. "What happened? Eve? Are you okay?"

"I'm okay," I choke out. "A woman broke down in the bathroom. She cut her wrists. There was so much blood." I cover my mouth and gag.

Lucas wraps his arms around me as tight as he can without crushing me or eggplant while looking in the direction I just came from, watching medical workers run toward the bathroom. A shrill comes from the bathroom.

Please, God, send the demon back to where it belongs.

I get chills again. Did I just pray?

"I'm sorry you had to see that. Hopefully she gets the help she needs. Come; Melisa should be here any second. The luggage carousel just started." Lucas drags me away since I'm still too shocked to think.

A joyful cry pulls me out of my thoughts and back to the busy terminal, and suddenly I see Melisa getting off the escalator. "Evie! Oh, my god! Look at you!" She gets closer and notices my mixed expression. "What's wrong? What happened?"

"A woman in the bathroom slit her wrists. It happened while I was peeing."

"God damn. That sucks. Hope she got some help. But enough of that depressing stuff. I'm here!"

I nod and attempt to muster a smile. As much as I've been wanting to see Melisa, what just happened has me freaked out. Feeling a thousand things at once, I wrap my arms around her and whisper, "I've missed you."

"Girl, you are the one who took off on me! Don't you ever do that again." She adds a whack to my shoulder to drive home the point. "You had me worried sick."

"I'm sorry. I promise I won't do that again."

She cocks her head to the side and says, "Sure." She turns and stares at Lucas. "And who's this tall, dark, and handsome man?" she asks while crossing her arms. I already warned him.

I make introductions while Melisa glares at Lucas.

Melisa unfolds her arms. "Well, I guess I'm going to learn about you in person because she didn't tell me squat."

"You're here for the next two weeks. I'm sure at some point, we'll get to know each other. This is for you. Let me grab your luggage."

"A gentleman," she says, adding emphasis to *man*. As soon as Lucas turns to lead us out of the airport, she takes my arm and whispers, "He's hotter than Jim. Damn, girl. And he looks loaded."

"Yeah, he's amazing."

"You are completely googly eyed. You're in love with him, aren't you?" Her mouth drops open. "Is he the father?"

"No, that's still me, cloning myself, but he wants to be."

"Oh love, you have so much to fill me in on."

Lucas waits by the rental Escalade, acting like our personal driver, closing the doors after we get in.

"So what did you get me?" Melisa asks Lucas as we pull out of the airport parking lot.

"It's not just a present for you. It's a present for the both of you."

"Ooh, wrapped in baby blue with a girly pink bow." She snaps her head toward me. "Are you having twins? One of each?"

"Oh god, I hope not," I say with a laugh.

She gives me a crooked smile. "Alright, let's see what your prince charming got for us. You better help me. This box is huge, but not heavy…"

She takes off the bow first, and then we each grab a side of wrapping paper to tear off. Underneath is a plain cardboard box. I expected something fancier from him, which only makes me smile more. He's full of surprises.

After lifting the flaps of the box, she pulls out a gorgeous silver journal, two fancy pens in their own personal cases, two plush bathrobes—one extra large—two sets of slippers, and an oversized envelope. She holds up the envelope. "I wonder what's in here." She opens the flap and takes out a printed card along with a white plastic gift card. "Welcome, Melisa. Eve has missed you more than she can put into words. So I thought it would be nice for the two of you to have some overdue friend time and relax at a spa in Palm Beach. First you'll take a private jet—a what? I know you just bought me round trip first-class tickets, but a private jet?"

"Keep reading," he says with a mischievous look.

Melisa stares at him with her mouth open. She gives her head a couple of shakes before continuing to read. "Your flight should only be a half hour, and you will have a private car waiting to drive you straight to the spa. Eat, shop, relax—get every spa treatment you desire, and savor your time together. There is no price tag on this trip. Just enjoy." Melisa sits back with an astonished look on her face. "Is this for real? So, is this a one-day trip?"

"Nope. Spend as long as you want down there—well, until you need to go back to work," he says, grinning ear to ear as he pulls off the airport road and onto a private section of tarmac.

"Lucas, I didn't pack a bag."

"I did. I hid it in the trunk while you were peeing for the third time," he says.

He stops the car close to a private jet. A flight attendant with a practiced smile stands at the bottom of the stairs leading up to the jet.

Melisa gets out of the car and stands slack-jawed. "Is this for real?"

"Yup," I say with a smirk, strolling onto the plane. "Get used to it. This is the only way he travels."

Her legs eventually start moving and she walks up the stairs, Lucas behind her. I settle into an oversized leather recliner and watch Melisa take in the grandeur. I must have had the same expression weeks ago. Not that I'm not still blown away by the glamour, but I am getting used to Lucas spoiling me.

"Take care of our little eggplant," he coos. Once I'm settled into my seat, he leans down to give me a kiss goodbye while giving my stomach a rub. "Remember to spoil yourselves and fill out that journal."

"What's the journal for?" I ask.

"Baby planning. I thought you would like the opportunity to do that with your friend. Maybe plan a baby shower or something along those lines. Whatever you want; sky's the limit;" he says, giving me one last kiss on the forehead.

"You think of everything and spoil me too much."

"I try. Enjoy yourselves. I'm flying back to New York for the next few days. Stay at the resort as long as you wish."

"How did I get so lucky?" I ask him.

"Ahem, how did you get so lucky? How am I so lucky to be sitting here with you love birds?" Melisa teases.

I shake my head at her and laugh. Melisa has never been one for romance.

"Stay safe." And with that, Lucas exits the jet. The cabin door closes behind him as the flight attendants ready the plane for takeoff.

※

"I need to tell you something... But you have to promise me you won't call me crazy," I say to Melisa as we lounge with our feet in our private plunge pool. It's late, maybe eleven. The stars are all out, blinking on and off. Check-in was a breeze and of course we are staying in the ritzy suite that most people will never see.

"You can always talk to me. What's up?"

"You know how the doctors were saying I basically made a clone of myself?"

She shrugs. "I've always known you were a freak of nature."

"Do you remember that junkie? That guy who freaked out at us on the way to your car after my first doctor's appointment?"

"Yeah, what about that crackhead?"

"He hasn't been the only person to act that way around me."

She tilts her head and puts down her glass of deep red wine. "What do you mean?"

"My doctor, right before I left, said some legit crazy shit. Also the clerk at the pharmacy I bought the pregnancy tests from. Both of them became possessed in front of my eyes. The doctor's voice changed midconversation, and she told me to stop seeing doctors and not to get any more tests. That my baby would be born perfect. The clerk told me to make the right choice."

"Honey, you were really stressed out then. Are you sure you're not remembering it differently?"

I shake my head. "Then there was this weird incident with this little girl at this motel whose head did a one eighty and spoke... not in a child's voice. It said it wanted to kill it. Kill my baby. Silence us. Then, when I went to the city with Lucas, I stopped by St. Patrick's Cathedral. This guy charged after me, screaming that if I let him kill us, he would spare my child's soul. A priest started chanting until the possessed man passed out and then suddenly, he was back to normal. At the airport, the woman who killed herself said she came from the abyss with a dream. Melisa, some small part of me is terrified I'm going to give birth to..." I shrug. "Since I conceived without a donor."

"You are not giving birth to the Antichrist. That's fucking insane." She smiles and chuckles. "Honey, every mother is terrified and at some point thinks they gave birth to a demon. You're looking for signs when all of those weird events were just freaky coincidences. Nothing more.

You don't even believe in God or the devil; how can you think for one minute you can actually give birth to something immortal?"

"I don't know. If it was just the junkie, I wouldn't think twice about it, but all the others? I can't stop thinking about it in the back of my head. I feel like I'm going crazy. I haven't told Lucas. I'm fine with telling you because you already think I'm nuts. I don't want him to leave us. I can picture him being a really wonderful dad."

"Really? He's dad material?"

"I think so. He didn't have one growing up, but he seems really into it. He even goes along with calling the baby whatever size fruit or vegetable it is every week. He's sweet, protective, funny, and quirky in his own ways. He's not bad to look at either."

"He's a model and you know it. Way out of your mousy librarian league. As long as he treats you right. The fact he's crazy rich is a major bonus too. How d'you meet Mr. Right when all I get is insane sexy women who threaten to burn my house down? It's unfair."

"It's still early in the relationship. I might still surprise him."

She laughs and takes a sip of wine. "But really, you trust him? Do you think he's good? You don't get any weird vibes or red flags?"

"Nope. He's been my prince, my king, coming to my rescue."

"Girl, if you say so. As long as he treats you good. I want the best for you. Oh, Evie, I've missed you. You're sounding more like yourself. Like the Evie I know and love. I'm so glad to see that light back in you. It's good to see you happy."

"It's weird feeling happy after everything that happened with Jim. It's like it happened for a reason. For the first time in my life, I think I believe in destiny."

26 Weeks - Palm Beach, Florida

"But he said we could stay as long as we wanted. I don't want to leave! My god, my back hasn't been knot free since I was a kid!" Melisa begs from the other side of the breakfast table in the swanky restaurant. A large chandelier hangs high above our heads, surrounded by a beautiful fresco depicting what I can only describe as hidden gardens. Outside the stunning wall-to-ceiling windows is a tropical oasis. Hunched palm trees break up the horizon, separating the clear blue sky from the crystalline blue ocean. And the food—don't get me started on how much I've eaten over the last week—has been scrumptious.

Today is the eighth day of our vacation. We plan to check out tomorrow and go back to Orlando to spend some time at my new house before she flies home after her two-week vacation, but saying we're going to leave this heavenly resort and actually forcing ourselves is a different story. Even I don't want to leave this place. To be honest, the resort in the Florida Keys with my own private cove was better, but I love the spa. All the pampering we have received: back, legs, arms, shoulders, neck, and head massages. I didn't know there was such a thing as a scalp massage, but damn, it's amazing. Melisa got to appreciate all the hot tubs, saunas, and any pools hotter than ninety-eight degrees that I couldn't go in because I don't want to boil baby in the womb. But there were plenty of other things for me to indulge in. Besides, I'd rather cool off than roast. Making myself sweat just doesn't seem like a pleasant experience, but Melisa likes to and doesn't get to enjoy these experiences often.

I still can't get over myself in a bathing suit. My belly button is morphing from an innie to an outie. The only part of my body that has improved has been my hair. Florida's humidity has made it frizzy; however, it has grown at least five inches since I became pregnant and is silky soft besides somehow straighter.

"Tomorrow our private jet is bringing us back to Orlando and you are going to see my new house. Plus, don't you have to catch up on work?" I ask as I eat my last piece of bacon, instantly wanting more. Also, a waffle with whipped cream. The guy at the waffle bar is making them fresh. I wonder if he'll add some pieces of bacon to the batter for me. Oh, that would taste amazing.

"Eh, I can do most of it from a laptop. Maybe a video conference or two will hold my bosses off a little longer. Evie, what are you hungrily thinking about? You have that glazed-over look in your eyes you get when thinking of Caesar salads and ice cream."

"Vanilla ice cream. And they go together perfectly. Now if you'll excuse me, I need to pester a certain waffle maker."

She sits back and gives me a full-hearted laugh. Damn, I've missed her. Which only makes me think of Jim and how I should also miss him, but don't, and that only makes me feel guilty. Anytime Melisa brings him up, I steer the conversation in another direction. It's over and done with. I've moved on. I can only hope he has too. But the thought of someone sleeping where I had makes me angry—besides an onslaught of other intense feelings that I'm not ready to face. Not yet. I might need a drink or two in order to, and I'm not allowed that until you vacate, my little acorn squash.

After I talk the waffle maker into adding more and more bacon until it is half bacon, half batter, I stroll back to my table, giddy with my perfectly golden waffle. Melisa stares at me as I pour a quarter bottle of syrup on top of a heaping scoop of freshly whipped cream.

"That can't be healthy, but damn, it looks good. I'm getting a bite of that."

"No, get your own," I say as I swat her fork away from my plate playfully, but then let her have a single bite.

"You got some weird craving combinations, but they taste good. After breakfast, do you want to go for a swim? Maybe snorkel?"

"Sounds good. Take our golf cart and go for a swim. And then we'll go for a snorkel excursion. Sorry your manatee dive was a letdown. Maybe we'll get lucky with some pretty fishes."

"I just want to enjoy as much of this as I can while I can," Melisa says, sneaking her fork back onto my plate for another bite. This time, I don't put up a fight and let her think she was stealthy. It will taste better with her little victory.

The last week has rejuvenated and revitalized me in ways I didn't know I required. I didn't realize how much I needed to see Melisa and spend time with her, having fun, being ourselves without a care in the world. It's been refreshing.

One day after another shopping spree at an outlet mall near the spa, Melisa stopped in her tracks and said that we should go on a baby shopping day—since I would never, ever want my mom at my baby shower and Lucas has no family, so the party would be rather small, just the three of us. An intimate shopping spree would probably be better and much more fun. No stupid or disgusting games like *guess what candy is melted into the diaper* or anything like that, which, if you ask me, is painful and I would never want to make anyone I care for suffer through games like that.

I love the way Melisa thinks. Plus, I can pick out exactly what I want and need. What will Lucas think? I hope he wasn't thinking I'd know people to invite to shower me with gifts. I have no one except Melisa for that. No coworkers or neighbors. No one. I have no one except Melisa and Lucas, which is comforting and also terrifying.

Sometimes I get scared that I'm going to wake up and find out he doesn't love me. That he tricked me to be cruel, or that he pitied me. But then I see the way he looks at me and know that it isn't possible. That Lucas could never be that malicious. But now and then, the thought creeps into my mind and makes me feel ill. I don't want to wake up from this dream that has become my reality.

"Are you coming in? Girl, this is our last day here. You better get your ass in the water," Melisa calls from where the waves crest, lapping gently against her.

"Yeah, I think baby is getting hot. I'm definitely sweating." I put down my tablet, take one last sip of my virgin piña colada. The ocean is footsteps away from my shaded, cushioned lounger. Five steps and I am ankle-deep in the cool water.

"So many women would kill for your pregnant body. You're only baby. There isn't an ounce of fat on you. How do you do it?"

"Eat everything I want and more?" I say, adding a shrug.

"Girl, you are lucky. So, he called a few weeks ago. He misses you," Melisa says, making me stop my approach.

Second thought: I might just run away from her and head back to the hotel room, but I'm halfway in and the water feels so nice. Even if the conversation has turned sour, I think I'll just stay underwater the whole time. I sink into the water, staying under for a couple of seconds. When I breach, she's standing with her arms crossed.

"Evie, he asks about you."

"And?"

"It's clear the man still loves you. He's just hurt. Maybe you should tell him about your test results."

"No. Don't talk about it. Don't say anything to him on the phone or tell him where I live. Nothing. Never. Not even in person. I think there are people who would love to keep us under a microscope, locked up somewhere, studying little acorn squash and me. Please don't tell anyone. And don't involve Jim."

"I won't. I promise. I'd never hurt you, love. But if you told him, I think he'd take you back. Not saying that Lucas isn't great and all, but is it real? Like what you had with Jim? Or are you a gold digger now—I'm sorry I have to ask. Private jet and all."

I roll my eyes at her. "I think it's love. I'm scared, but it also feels like something that I'm supposed to do. Like it's destiny, or something weird like that. Like this was all supposed to happen and Lucas and I are meant to be together. Fate. I don't know how else to describe it. The more I think about it, the more I don't think Jim and I were meant to be. A part of me loved him, but it didn't feel like this. Or maybe at one point it did and I just forgot, but either way, I am truly happy. This is right."

She gives me a sideways glance and grills me for a full minute before she shrugs and says, "That's all I want. Your happiness. If you think the price is right, then I'm glad you found it."

Katie Zaber

Orlando, Florida

"You live here? Right here?" Melisa points in the direction I've watched fireworks light up the sky. Everyone in the neighborhood gets to enjoy the nightly spectacle. "Really?"

I laugh at her and thank the driver as he opens my door and scoots around the car to the trunk to retrieve our luggage. Lucas's return flight from New York got delayed by an hour for bad weather, so we just missed each other at the airport. But he'll be home soon. After he freshens up, he wants to take us ladies out to dinner and hear about our girls' trip.

"Close your mouth; it's hanging wide open."

"I just can't believe you, out of all people, would choose a house here. You've never been here before."

"Lucas took me after our stay at the Florida Keys. He set up a romantic dessert buffet on our balcony while the fireworks were going off. It was magical. That's when he gave me my locket."

"He won you over with chocolate and cake. That sneaky devil," she says with a wink. "No wonder you fell for him."

I click the garage door. Inside is vacant with the exception of a black golf cart that wasn't here last week. It has four black leather sport seats and a half-size trunk. Above the trunk are slots to hold golf bags. Next to the steering wheel is an iPad on a stand connected to the dashboard, and there're speakers in the roof. I open what I think is the glove box, looking for a manual or some information, and discover a mini fridge. "Dude, we are taking my new wheels for a spin."

"You have a luxury golf cart? Is that even necessary?"

I say with the most snobby accent I can muster, "When you like the finer things in life…" I burst out laughing and leave the golf cart to inspect in greater detail later. Right now, suddenly, I have to pee like nothing else matters in the world. It had to be the laughing. "It wasn't here when we left. It must be a new toy. He mentioned something about golfing together. Plus, everyone who lives in this community has one."

"Damn," Melisa says with a whistle as she follows me into the kitchen and into the open living room. She spins around in a circle, mouth dropping even more when she sees the pool and hot tub. "What the… what did you say he does?"

I run down the hallway and hike up my dress, just making it to the bathroom. "Something in hospitality, hotels." I wipe and flush, then wash my hands with my foamy, non-scented soap. I find Melisa reclining on the sofa, scrolling through her phone, and realize she could probably use this time before dinner to catch up on work. "You can either stay in the main house or you can use the guest house. Both areas have a desk and you'll be the first one to sleep in either bed."

"Hold up. You have a guest house. That"—she points across the yard to the cute little studio house—"is your guest house? Damn!"

"He wanted a six-bedroom mansion; this one has three with the detached suite. I complained that I didn't want to be a new mom and clean an enormous house, but he said that's what a house cleaning service is for."

"Shut up. Now you're just rubbing it in."

"Wait until you see my walk-in closet. It even has a couch in it."

"You have a couch in your closet? That's not where they belong! Is there a runway too?"

"No, but there are a ton of mirrors and a platform to stand on so I can see my back."

My best friend stares at me, speechless. All she can do is shake her head.

An hour later, we hear a car pull up and a door open and close. Seconds later, the garage door opens and Lucas steps into the kitchen, pulling behind him a small rolling suitcase in one hand and carrying a large bouquet of roses in the other. Not normal roses, either. Roses unlike I've ever seen: Golden yellow centers with burgundy tips on long dark green stems wrapped in clear plastic garnished with a silver bow.

"Lucas, where did you get those? They are beautiful!" I put down my tablet and walk from the living room, where Melisa is clicking away on her laptop and I was reading about another world filled with strange beings, and rush into the kitchen to greet the man I'm falling for. Falling hard. This has been the longest we've been apart since we've been together, and until this moment when he came home to me, I didn't realize how much I truly missed him.

"I know an exotic florist that grows some of the most striking flowers. When I saw he had these roses available, I knew I had to get them for you." He gives me a kiss on the cheek and touches my belly. "And how are you today, little acorn squash? Baby just kicked. I missed you too." He bends down and kisses where he felt the kick. "Let me take a quick shower while you lovely ladies decide what you would like for dinner. We'll go out somewhere nice."

"Hmm, I think I want pasta," I reply, rubbing my belly. "Mmm, maybe Alfredo. Some type of creamy cheese sauce."

"Of course you do." He gives me one last kiss before heading to the master suite.

Melisa takes a sip from her dark red wine. It is too dry for me. "Pasta? I'm down with that."

I smell my roses, which are already in a crystal vase. All I have to do is take off the plastic and set them on the living room coffee table. I rub my temples; I can feel a headache starting. "I'm getting hungry."

"Me too. Hope he takes a fast shower."

"He'll be out in ten. We should go get ready."

"Like doll up?" Melisa asks.

"Every restaurant I have ever gone to with Lucas has a dress code, and I'm sure he wants to treat us tonight since this will be your first meal with him."

"He's treated me for the last week. He could feed me dog food for dinner and I'd still thank him," Melisa says, walking to the back slider door that leads to her private suite.

I laugh at her and decide that I haven't seen Lucas in what feels like forever, and I could use a quick shower.

27 Weeks - Orlando, Florida

One sign that I'm getting older is that the grocery store plays the music I either listen to or was the greatest hits of my teen years. They are targeting me, my demographic. People my age are now spending their time buying food for their growing families. That is what we are supposed to do at this point in our lives. It's the normal thing to do. The way every ordinary person progresses, matures.

It's still weird to think I was part of the minority who didn't want children. A person who would have preferred a selfish life of luxury instead of fulfilling my life's purpose for existence. How did I change so fast? Or is this who I always was but I didn't realize it? Was I always meant to be a mother but Jim wasn't meant to be a father? Is that why this happened?

Boring days like today give me too much time to think. Days when I have nothing to do but I feel the need to move. I don't know why, but I need to expel excess energy. My legs think they can run marathons, but they haven't spoken to the rest of my body, which doesn't want to move.

Since my legs needed to move, I put on my back brace and went grocery shopping. It's too early in the day to know what my little cabbage will want for dinner, but I figured I'd browse and buy whatever looks yummy. The last few nights, I've done a pretty good job cooking. Nothing fancy, but home-cooked meals. They have been edible. I'm not a master chef and I won't fool myself with any notions that my culinary skills are amazing—they aren't—but we won't die from my cooking, and that's what matters.

Besides, cooking has given me something to do. Buying the food and cooking it is the only thing I really do besides read and walk. And with Lucas not in the house, it gets really boring. It's not that Lucas hasn't invited me to go on the current trip, but it was some ski resort where it had already started snowing and I didn't want to slide around all uncoordinated and fall. Plus, I realized I didn't own a winter coat anymore and would need one big enough to fit cabbage too, which isn't something I need next year after I lose the baby weight. And honestly, as much as traveling to luxurious hotels is fun, it's tiring and right now all I want to do is explore locally and take naps in between.

The air is cool and moist; it must have rained while I was in the store. The rental has water spots on the body and windshield; however, most are already evaporating under the Florida sun. My phone rings. Lucas must be eating lunch. With my hands full of grocery bags, I hurry to unload them so I can call him back. I miss him too much. I can't wait to see him tomorrow.

Behind me, I hear screeching tires. Then brakes squeal to a halt on the wet pavement. Before I can turn my head to look, two sets of hands grab me.

Groceries go flying as I scream for help. I twist to grab hold of someone and try to fight back. It's useless, as hands come from every direction. A dark canvas hood covers my head. I hear a snap and clatter as the gold chain holding my locket breaks. Arms force me into a vehicle, no matter which direction I swing. Someone inside grabs me, pulling me in. People climb over me. A door slides shut and the locks click.

What was that, five seconds?

They work fast together, one zip tying my legs, the other my arms, keeping me from kicking and punching. Then they search my body, which is a waste of time. My phone and everything is in my purse, in the grocery store parking lot. It sounds like there are four men in the van altogether: a driver, a navigator, and the two goons who grabbed me.

It's funny. I haven't thought that I should continue screaming or what words I should scream, but the tirade coming out of my mouth is endless and relentless, just like the tears pouring down my face.

They found us.

"If you don't shut up, I'll gag you, bitch!" one of the assholes says.

"Don't hurt her! They said not a scratch!" another yells.

"Quiet," demands a female voice. It comes from the back of the van and hasn't said a word until now.

None of the men say anything else. She must be the boss.

I get no visual hints from the hood over my head. Instead, I sit back and listen to every sound. Someone is chewing gum or tobacco. I smell cherry mint. I assume the woman is filing a nail. Another raps his fingers against his leg.

After what I guess is fifteen minutes of driving, we pull over. From all the turns and nearby highways, plus proximity, I think I know where they are taking me. If so, it will be impossible for Lucas to find me.

"Get her out and gently get her seated and buckled. We take off immediately," the woman commands.

Someone cuts my feet restraints as hands escort me out of the van and lead me up a set of stairs. Engines turn on with a rumble. Beeps come from slow-moving vehicles. Gritty noises come from tires rolling down the road. I know this place. I've been here recently.

I'm getting onto a private plane. But I suspect it's not fancy and there won't be any in-flight meal. None of the accommodations I've been used to. I might be able to use the bathroom.

There's no way to contact Lucas, nor do I want him involved in this situation, whatever this is. Clearly this was a planned operation and these people are professional kidnappers. Or is it adultnappers? Either way, I don't want him hurt, too.

Little cabbage is kicking me nonstop. Baby is doing cartwheels, handstands, punching, and kicking, trying to fight for us. Sorry, baby. I thought we were safe. I thought it was going to be okay. I thought that since I had a new identity, my old one would be forgotten.

But Mommy was wrong. So wrong. I will get you out. You will escape whatever is about to happen. I will free you from this. I promise. You won't suffer from my mistakes.

"Get her ready for takeoff," a man says, hiding whiskey with mouthwash.

The cabin smells fresh, like chemical fresh. Almost like bleach. Like someone sanitized the space of any incriminating evidence. That's what this plane is, a device to erase people out of existence. Make them disappear.

Someone pushes me into a seat and straps a seat belt across my lap. My hands are still zip tied. I think about kicking, but I won't get far. I need to be smart. I need a plan. What we need is help. But help isn't coming. So we need to be smart and right now, attempting to fight my way out of this will end in failure. They'll just knock me out and drug me before I land a kick.

What will Melisa and Lucas, think? There will probably be some story about how a pregnant woman was abducted, suspected killed, and the baby stolen. If there is even a news story.

※

The plane lands. Hands grab me and put me in a wheelchair, strapping down my feet and waist, but not too tight around my belly. The pricks are careful about you, cabbage. They free my arms momentarily, only to restrain them with the wheelchair's tighter, more secure bonds.

Cabbage's kicks are unyielding, how I should be. Part of me wants to rip out throats, but the other half knows we won't survive. And my goal is to get us out of here alive, especially you. So I'll play nice for now. Kill later.

They roll me into a building and through a busy corridor. I can hear paper shuffling, people talking, giving each other assignments, even water cooler talk. I hear someone ask if they watched the latest episode of... Damn. I didn't catch the name of the show.

If they all had the same accent, it would be easy to pinpoint where I am, but they are all different. French, British, Boston, Southern, Midwestern... I have no idea where we are or how long the flight was.

There's a lot of boots on the ground, stomping. I'd guess that means there are a lot of soldiers or guards. The other sounds make me think of an office. A medical office, but not quite. It lacks the friendly receptionist and nonstop ringing phones. I hear a glass shatter and a woman scream.

No, not a scream. An eerie shrill-becoming-manic laughter. My wheeler jerks the chair to a stop. This doesn't seem part of the plan.

"Oh no, what have you fools done? It will be so much fun to watch! How will you be punished? What will serve as a justifiable torment?" the crazed woman laughs in a not-so-human voice.

Good. I hope everyone around me goes nuts and kills each other while we are locked safely inside our prison cell. But then, how do we get out?

"Take her away!" another woman shouts.

"Where?" a man asks.

"Put her with the wall crawlers!"

Wall crawlers? What the fuck.

Voices continue to shout frantic orders about containing the poor, possessed woman who is currently describing in vivid detail how they are all going to die. Hung by their intestines, shoving a pen in one ear and out the other, a broom crammed so far up their asses it will come out their mouths: those kinds of deaths, with extra-gory descriptions thrown in.

I think I hear someone retching.

"Why are you stopped? Get her to her room!" the same woman orders.

My wheelchair starts to roll again, this time in a more urgent manner. The commotion fades away. After a few moments, we come to a stop. A door clicks open and I'm pushed over the threshold along with two sets of boots and maybe a pair of flats. I hear delicate footsteps, so I'm assuming a woman, or at the very least a petite male.

"Remove the hood. And her restraints," says the same woman who ordered the possessed staff member to be caged with the wall crawlers.

At first, the room is too bright and I need to close my eyes against the brilliant fluorescent bulbs that are blinding me. While I adjust, my hands and feet are released. I rub my arms where they were cut into, and I blink.

I don't recognize her. She doesn't have a lab coat on but an office-appropriate floral skater dress. It's actually really cute, if I liked to wear bright orange and magenta flowers. Melisa would like her style. Her blonde hair ends at the top of her shoulders and her wispy paperclip-thin eyeglasses almost blend in, if it weren't for the glare of the lenses. Her appearance doesn't appear sinister, but when I look into her eyes, I can tell she's empty inside.

The armed escorts point their guns at me, but the woman waves them away. "I don't think there will be any need for that, will there?" she asks me like a mother who already reprimanded her kid before arriving at the party.

I stare.

With all of my internal focus, I try drilling holes into her lifeless eyes.

"Good. Now, I'll give you time to relax after your stressful journey. My name is Crystal. This is where you will be spending most of your time. You can request movies, TV shows, books, games, even snacks. If you crave something, just let us know."

Even her smile is empty. I wouldn't even call it practiced. It's beyond that. She's a complete sham.

"You have your own private bathroom with a huge spa tub for long baths. You also have access to a garden. Think of it as your own private resort." She forgot to add *until we kill you*. She pauses like she expects me to ask for the brochure to this mad laboratory retreat. "Do you have any questions?"

I wait and stare. Stare hard at her, try to make her feel uncomfortable, but she doesn't react. She has the same amount of emotion, life in her, as a robot. "None that you would answer."

"Good. You're smart enough to know not to ask stupid questions. I don't have to explain your situation. I hate meaningless banter. If you're truly smart, you will take my advice: behave. Keep your head down and listen. Let us study your miracle and we'll let you leave. We want to study you. Learn from you. Really, that isn't such an awful thing, now is it?"

I think she has a touch of country in her voice. She sounds like she's a Southern belle trying her darnedest to hide it. Is that where I am, or is that where she is from?

"You know, you could have asked instead of going through all the dramatics."

"And you would have said yes?"

"We won't know since you took my choice away."

"Well, you have new choices now."

"Hmm," I say and nod, realizing I don't even have a window. Not even a fake simulated one. "How many women are there like me here?"

"You, dear Everild," she says, but I refuse to correct her. People who respect me call me Eve or Evie. She doesn't respect me. "Are the only unique woman in your situation here. You are very interesting. Take it as a compliment."

I should say something snappy, something witty. All I can think of is one thing. A fact. An event that hasn't happened yet, but it will. "I will kill you."

She smiles like a predator; her neck twists like a bird stalking its prey. "I'm so very glad to meet you, Everild. I think we are going to be very good friends."

"Lucas?" He looks so sexy wearing only black silky boxer briefs. I'm in a bedroom I've never seen. The bedsheets are black, the headboard looks like a sharp, jagged pumice rock. Everything in this room is black and dismal, including the look on his face. His midnight blue eyes don't shine like the night sky. He has never been anxious, upset, or worried. "Lucas, what's wrong?"

"Eve! Where are you?"

"I'm here," I tell him and go to embrace him.

But he doesn't move. "Where are you? Were you taken? Tell me you were taken. Tell me you didn't leave."

This is a dream. He can't talk to me. Not like this. "I'm here. Wherever this is," I say, looking around, realizing I've never been in this room. "Where am I?"

"This space is very private. I don't allow anyone in here."

"Then why am I here?"

"You're not anyone. You're the mother of my child, and I need to find you. Where are you? Were. You. Taken."

"Lucas, this is my dream. I need it to be good. My reality is… I don't want to wake up. I'm so scared." I close my eyes and gulp.

Footsteps hurry across the floor, and I can feel the warmth and satiny feel of his skin as he wraps himself around me. "I'm sorry. I'm so sorry I'm not there to kill them. When I find you and you are safe, I will take my time killing them, gleefully," he whispers into my ear. He rocks me in his arms gently while stroking my hair, then pulls away. "Eve, my queen, you need to tell me where you are. Have you seen anything that can lead me to you?"

"They'll kill you. I can't have them kill you too." I sob and fold in on myself.

Lucas braces me and leads me to the bed. I lie down on my side and curl into a ball, weeping. His body presses against my back and he drapes an arm over me, holding me tight. In his arms, I feel safe.

This is where I want to stay, forever. In his arms. Please let me stay asleep. Please God, don't let me wake up. *Please*, I pray.

Katie Zaber

Next Day - Somewhere Locked Up In a Mad Scientist Laboratory

Bang, Bang!

One second I'm embraced by his warm, familiar body, both of us resting, cuddling in each other's arms, the next I'm back in this mommy-to-be prison. There is no way to know what time it is. Should I yell I need my beauty sleep and that baby wants another two hours of undisturbed rest... Would they let me? Or would I just piss my capturers off first thing in the morning?

Before I can decide, the door clicks open. The lights flicker on and two guards stomp into the room, followed by a nurse with a wheelchair. I blink in a dazed response and start stretching my sore and tight body. I roll onto my other side and attempt to sit up, but I'm so exhausted that I end up falling back down onto the bed. Propping myself up on my elbows, I begin to get up. The nurse sees me struggling and comes to help me up, pushing the wheelchair to the side of the bed.

She gives me a hand, but doesn't open her mouth. She has to be my age, maybe a little younger. How much will this eat at her conscience? I hope it consumes her.

"Where are you taking me?"

"Full examination. Lab work, ultrasound, the works," she says.

Sorry, baby. I know I promised we wouldn't be lab rats anymore, but unless you got a plan, we're stuck. Don't worry; I'm working on one. I just need time.

Settled into the wheelchair, she straps me in, but she doesn't blindfold me. Wherever they are taking me, it must be close or else they don't care what I see in this section of the facility. Outside my door, it's quiet. It's cold. My hospital garb does nothing to stop the chill. The only noise is the boots and flats on the tile behind me and the wheelchair's wheels turning. There are no other doors, only fluorescent lights overhead and infinite white walls. At the end of the hallway, there is another set of double doors that need a retinal ID to open.

The doors open slowly, revealing what looks like a nurse's station. I look down either side of the hallway and don't see a lot of doors. We cross the hall and continue straight until we stop at another black dome retinal ID and double doors.

Before me is a glass room with state-of-the art medical equipment. Polished machines that look unused gleam their virginity at me as if saying, *It's my first time. Be gentle.* I look at them in horror, knowing I'm the one about to be violated. Cabbage kicks me relentlessly, not wanting another test. All I want to do is put my hands on my stomach and try to comfort you, but they won't allow me. Not right now. I'm sorry, baby. I'm sorry I broke my promise. I tried to keep it.

The nurse wheels me alongside a table with feet stirrups and restraints. Just what every woman loves to see. The armed men hover over me as she unstraps my arms and ushers me onto the table. Once again, she straps me down, but not as restricted as when I arrived. At least the blood can still flow into my limbs and my hands aren't going numb.

Her eyes look haunted; like this isn't the first time she's done something that has broken her. They are sad. Abused-looking. She looks like the kind of woman you would find quivering in a corner instead of fighting. She is in a corner quivering and crying, but internally. How much longer can this woman take working here before she quits or kills herself? From the looks of it, I'd say within the next few months. Maybe while I'm here. Hopefully. Wouldn't that be karma?

"The doctor will be here soon. Just try to relax," she says, giving my shoulder a slight squeeze before leaving the table to go somewhere behind me.

Unable to move, I wait.

Maybe a minute passes before a short man wearing blue scrubs comes in. He's got a practiced friendly face that doctors display, part of their whole facade. "Hello. How are we feeling today?"

I stare, trying my best to not look terrified. It's not working.

"Is this really necessary?" the doctor asks the guards. "I think we'll be fine. Let's give this woman some privacy? Hmm?"

"Not everything is as innocent as it looks," mumbles a guard, stomping their boots on the floor, exiting the room.

"They are standing in the hallway, but it's better than having them hovering while being examined," the cheerful doctor says. "Nurse Jane, please get the vials ready. I want to draw blood before the ultrasound." The doctor turns to me like he would a child patient and says, "How are you with needles? I promise it won't hurt, but we need a few vials."

"Fine."

"Ah, the deadly f word," he says with a grin as if he's talking to his fucking wife. "Let me know if there is anything we can do to make your examination as comfortable as possible. We can't do much, but I can try to keep you comfortable."

It takes all of me not to scream.

He picks up the needle and delicately inserts it without even a pinch. He is pretty good. I can't even feel it. The way he holds the vial filling with blood makes me feel like there's no pressure on my arm. As much as I hate everything about this place, the doc isn't half bad. If he were my normal doctor, in a normal setting, I might have given him an A rating. But this isn't normal. If I weren't strapped down, I'd take the nearest sharpest tool and slice his neck open. Hell, I'd use my teeth.

The nurse lifts up my prisoner pajama shirt and lowers my pants, tucking paper in so they don't get any gel on them. How considerate. She squirts a warmed bottle of gel, which is actually nice since most have been ice cold. Why does this nightmarish place have the best doctors and staff? It's not fair.

Typing away, the doctor focuses on the monitor. The keyboard attached to the monitor has a regular typing board, plus switches and knobs I've never seen. There's even a black trackball to move around the screen. With a flick of a switch, the lights turn off and the glass walls tint so the room becomes dark.

He takes the wand and starts pressing it into my abdomen while watching the screen, eyes shifting left to right, watching my baby's movements. Every couple of moments, he clicks on something, the machine makes a beep, and then he moves the stick to another spot. From this angle, I can't see anything. I don't know what he's looking at, but even if I saw the screen, I'm not sure I'd know unless it was my baby's face.

"Would you like to say hi to the baby or know its sex?" the doctor asks as he glides the wand around my abdomen.

"I want a surprise." Why would I want to see my baby in this setting? In this place? The last time I saw cabbage, my baby didn't look completely human, but almost. Tears form in my eyes, but they strapped my hands down so I can't wipe them away as they slide down my cheeks. This moment... will it be one of the few memories I have of cabbage before... "Yes."

He turns the screen so I can see it and moves the wand around my belly. The tears won't stop. All want is to reach my stomach and touch you, but I can't. "I'm sorry," comes out as a whisper as I watch you do the kicks and somersaults I constantly feel.

The nurse gives me a tissue and releases my hand so I can dry my face. There's nothing within reach for me to grab, not the way they have me strapped down. I can barely reach my face. No, there's no way to escape right now, but I am getting them to trust me. Let the doctor and nurse think I'm passive and won't fight back in any capacity. I'm an innocent pregnant woman who is imprisoned against her will. I can use it against him when the time is right. Not when I have armed men pointing guns at my back. "Thank you. I haven't seen my baby yet. Not at this stage."

"When was your last appointment?" he asks, eyes glued to the screen.

"When I was fourteen weeks. I was too scared to go back."

"Why were you scared?" he asks, as if clueless.

"Because I thought something like this would happen."

He stops typing, gives me a nod, and turns the screen back around, returning to work. That's right, asshole. Let the guilt eat at you until it breaks you. No, I don't want it to break you. I want it to shatter you. Kill yourself because of what you have done and will do.

Cabbage bounces around, I assume agreeing. Don't worry, baby. I'll get them. They will be punished, just not today. We need to be smart.

The doctor jumps as I see a spark come out of the keyboard. He looks down at his hand, rubbing it and his whole arm. A few more flashes and pops come from the keyboard. Nurse Jane runs over and unplugs it from the computer. The sparks stop but the keyboard looks like garbage.

"Huh." The doctor stares at the malfunctioning keyboard. "I've never seen something like that before. Work on getting me a replacement," he says to the nurse.

She hurries out of the room while he goes to look at some paperwork. Both leave me on the table and don't give me a second thought.

The conversation with Crystal plays through my head. She had the audacity to call us friends last night. She should look up the definition of *friend* because I would never do this to Melisa. I'd kill anyone who would do this to her. That's what a friend is. Someone willing to rip out throats to protect the people they care about. Those are the kind of people who love. The kind of people who have souls.

Crystal is a sociopath with a degree in dissecting humans. I won't give her the respect of calling her a doctor or whatever she is. The only reason she is doing this is because she wants to tickle her curiosity. She wants to study those who don't wish to be analyzed under a magnifying glass. She lacks empathy and remorse.

She's pure evil. And evil spreads easily.

This whole damn place is infected. Baby, we need an exterminator.

28 Weeks - Who the fuck knows

I'm allowed to walk outside in the hot, sticky weather. My prison outfit sticks to my skin within minutes from the humidity. I get a fenced-in square of grass the size of forty-seven by sixty-three steps. Crystal called it a garden. It has a puny tree that doesn't give shade and three prickly bushes. Even the wimpy tree has thorns. No, not thorns. Angry barbs. I would even call them caltrops that prevent me from climbing the tree's measly branches.

Holding my belly, I walk around the box-shaped space like a pregnant lioness pacing around its cage, staking out its territory. It's only space. Not a safe space—those who are in cages don't get to be safe. Not ever. That's why I am vigilant. Problem is that now isn't really the time to be vigilant. It was before. Now I can't do anything but sit back, watch, wait, and plot.

I formulate harebrained schemes all day long that will only get me shot. At least I'm not insane enough to try them, not yet. Escape scenes and solutions from dumb action movies run through my head. Make an explosive out of the objects in my room and a weapon of some sort and blast my way out. Kill as many pieces of shit who work here until I reach the woods and run, dodging behind trees until I reach a tiny town miles away and find a police station, telling them the horror that I have been through, as long as this place doesn't own the local police. Then I'll be able to call Lucas and tell him to get me out of here, and he will sweep me up in his arms and fly me away.

It's then that I realize I never memorized his phone number and wake up from my fantasy.

This happens all day long, like some torturous game I like to play on myself.

The other problem is that I haven't factored in the hundreds of mercenaries armed to the teeth and strutting around the property. Or the fact I don't know a way out. I know how to get to my so-called garden, but the multiple fences topped with thick barbed wire set up around the perimeter is like a maze of metal before reaching a twenty-foot tall concrete barrier with multiple guard towers surrounding the entirety of the campus. At seven months pregnant, my ass isn't climbing up any fences. Plus, even if I managed to climb up one, I'd get stuck on the barbs, tearing apart my flesh while the guards in the towers pulverize me with their mounted machine guns.

But can the wall climbers escape once they reach where I am? Is that why I don't see anyone except for workers? Am I considered a nonthreat and the ones who can kill are locked up somewhere with the wall climbers? Is that why I'm allowed outside, but in my cage? Is it to protect me from everyone else here?

When I'm not thinking about everyone killing me or me killing everyone, I wonder about those people. I create stories about mutant people with superpowers who were captured and brought here so mad scientists can dissect them and sell their knowledge to the highest bidding military. I dream at night that we band together and figure out an escape plan. One of them will burn everything, the other will mess with the guards' minds, and they will set everyone who is here free. We escape and find other places as fucked-up as this and save those people too.

The only thing... I don't know what my power is. And I'm also not sure I want to find out.

"Come on. Time to go back inside," says one of the nicer guards. He talks to me like I'm a person, not cattle.

Three times they've threatened me. They've explained how easy it is to put me into an induced coma for the rest of my pregnancy. That it was only because they were being kind that they give me all these comforts. That my situation could get very uncomfortable, very fast.

I nod and do as I'm told. If I'm in a coma, I can't plan.

Most of the patrol who follow me everywhere won't look me in the eye. Maybe those men envision their mother, sister, or wife being locked up against their will while being heavily pregnant. I don't want to be alone around the few men who stare at me. They look like feral beasts on leashes. If left alone with one of them, I know they wouldn't give a second thought to raping or hurting me for their own sick delight. Men like them, people like them, don't have a conscience.

I think of murdering people like them all day. It's easy to say it's my main thought. Do I have a conscience anymore? Is it that easy to turn off?

The guard opens his eye wide and looks into the retinal scanner. It beeps, allowing us back inside. If I do formulate an actual plan, it will have to involve carrying around an eye. Good thing I'm not squeamish.

"Are you hungry for anything particular? Anything you would like me to request? How about chocolate chip cookies? I'm sure you would like that."

I stare at the man who acts like he's trying to reason with his own wife at the supermarket. He looks remorseful. Sad.

Maybe he wants to help but knows the consequence of helping me is that his own wife and family die. Maybe he needs me to request something since I haven't spoken to him yet. Maybe he needs reassurance that he is at least trying to be a good person. Maybe I shouldn't give in to him and let him suffer.

The motherfucker should have never applied for this job. "Soft serve vanilla ice cream. Salty potato chips—no fat-free nonsense or anything like that, Caesar dressing, pretzels, cheddar cheese popcorn, and a tub of chocolate frosting."

He blinks and looks at me as if I'm a statue who just gave him an order. "You've been thinking about it, huh?"

I give him a shrug.

"My wife had a thing for cheddar popcorn and white chocolate. She would make me get it for her at all times. Midnight gas station runs."

"Add vanilla frosting to the list too."

He smiles. "Will do."

He has a wife. He can sympathize. He might help. "What's your name?"

"Call me Bob."

"Thank you, Bob."

I have to guilt trip Bob first, before I kill him. Make them all feel guilty, at least the ones with consciences.

Nicknames are weird. I only go by my nickname because my actual name is horrible and no child should be called something so snooty. But the name Bobbie annoys me. No one names their son Bob on their birth certificate. It's always Robert. The name Robert can be shortened to Rob and Robbie, which sound normal, but Bob and Bobbie, where did the R go? Why not name the kid Bobert or Bobbie if that's what they want to call it.

Obviously all my security guards' names aren't Bob and Nurse Jane's last name isn't Doe, but a Bob got me double all the snacks I had listed, plus some things I think he added. Candy bars, cookies, and they brought in a larger fridge that has an assortment of drinks, yogurts, and Oreo cheesecake. There are also carrot sticks, celery, apples, oranges, and other healthy food that I'm not happy to see but promised to incorporate into my snacking along with the healthy meals they provide. I haven't gotten a menu or choice in meal, but neither have I refused to eat what they have brought me. It's all normal food. Pancakes, French toast, bacon, sausage, fruit, eggs, and cereal for breakfast. Lunch is soups, salads, and sandwiches—no deli meat. Dinner has been normal meals, nothing that I could downright snub. Chicken parmigiana, oven-roasted chicken, pork chops, meatloaf, spaghetti and meatballs, normal entrees that most meat eaters can agree on, and regular sides.

I should thank Bob tomorrow. But how should I make him feel guilty again? There are hundreds of ways. But which regret, which sin will keep him on my side? I push too much and he'll break before he can help me or will notice what I'm doing. Subtle is key.

Talking about his wife will be too direct and might make him feel threatened. I can't talk about anyone he knows; it has to be something else. Something personal but not. Religion maybe? No, he doesn't seem like the churchgoing type. He also doesn't seem like the type to go home and tell his wife all the crimes he's committed at work. No, he's the kind of man who bears all the weight and stress, striving to give her the carefree life she deserves.

This will take some time analyzing him to find a weakness that I can exploit. I'm going to be fishing and I have to be patient, as patient as possible, when there is a ticking clock. Baby, I don't know what you are this week. I don't know what to call you, but stay put. It's not time yet. I need you to wait as long as possible. Please. Mommy needs time. I might be the first mom to say this, but you can even give me an extra week or two.

Feeling fat and miserable, I close my eyes, terrified of the dreams I'll have. I've lost control of them. Some are good, some are depressing, but all of them involve Lucas. It's as if he's standing right in front of me. The warmth of his body makes my skin tingle. His breath on my neck makes me ache for him. In my dreams, I can normally have fantasy style sex with him, but since I've been imprisoned, all he wants to do is talk. Asking me where I am, how to get me out, as if he's actually in my dream, asking me these questions.

In my dreams, I don't want to talk about my nightmares. My nightmare is my life. All I want is to escape it and dream about the bliss I used to have, but he won't let me.

So now I'm scared to dream. Scared to be awake. Scared of this endless cycle that won't give me any peace.

What did I do to deserve this life? Was it something I did in a past life? Who was I, Bloody Queen Mary? The vampiress wannabe Elizabeth Bathory? Which horrible, sinister woman in history was I who needed to pay penance by living this horrible life? I'd really like to know. At least that would make more sense than everything else.

I wonder about the woman who sounded possessed when I was first brought here and if she's still alive. Part of me wishes I could have told Ken about her. The other half wants him to forget he ever met me. Now he'll have time to help all those possessed children. I hope he saves all of them. There has to be a way to help those kids and adults. I think about the woman singing in the airport, draining her blood, and hope Ken, along with his colleagues, can save as many as possible. None of them deserve to be in the passenger seat while a demon hijacks their body.

Before I know it, I'm asleep and in the room my dreams have been taking place in. The black room.

Lucas sits on the edge of the bed, looking like he was waiting for me. "Eve, what's wrong? What have they done?"

I'm still thinking about the woman in the airport bathroom. What were her dreams? Was she mother, wife? Who was she before becoming corrupted? "Nothing. Actually, they brought me all the snacks I requested." This is a dream. Our conversation doesn't exist. This room, this place, and everything in it are a figment of my imagination. It doesn't matter if I tell him here. It can be a practice run. "Lucas, promise me you won't call me crazy. Please."

"I would never. Come, talk to me," he says, patting the bed.

"I think, I think I'm giving birth to something celestial."

He straightens his back and tilts his head, considering the words I said carefully. "What would make you think that?"

I laugh. "Everything."

He didn't interrupt or laugh. He never smiled, but looked thoughtful. And not once did he call me crazy.

Sitting on the bed, I dry my eyes with a tissue from the box that never empties. I swear the box shouldn't have any left with how many I've used, but it feels full. Dreams are odd like that.

Lucas is lost in thought, stroking my arm. "I believe you, but I don't think you will understand or be able to. If celestial beings are at work, I'm not sure mortal minds could comprehend."

"Now you know everything. I'm sorry I've kept this from you. I didn't want you to think I was insane. Especially when I'm already questioning my sanity."

"My queen, I would never think that. Come." He lies down on his back, tugging on my arm to follow, then curls up around me. After a few moments, he asks, "Which celestial being do you think is the father? Does Ken have any ideas?"

"I don't know. I called him after the airport, but we haven't spoken since. He's been really busy with possession cases. But he said he had some people at the Vatican looking into it."

"But so far..." he asks, sounding hopeful.

"Nothing. Just a bunch of nonsense."

"I'm sorry you're going through all of this. I wish I was there going through it with you. Do you know where you are?"

"No," I say kind of forcefully.

"Eve, think. Where are you? How long was the flight?"

"I don't know." I move out of his arms and toward the edge of the bed. "I don't know. And even if I told you, it's not like it would matter. You're in my head. You're my dream."

He kneels behind me and rubs my shoulders. "How long was your flight? That would help narrow it down."

Chuckling, I say, "I don't know. Maybe two to three hours? Something like that."

"Okay, that's a start. What about outside? Have you seen anything?"

"I have a small patch of grass I can walk in. There's a tree and three plants. That's it. There are no other trees or anything to see except metal and concrete." I *humph*. "Even the fucking tree has thorns. I guess they really don't want me to climb it and try to jump over the fence."

"Thorns? How big?"

"Large. Each thorn is the size of my finger."

"That narrows it down. I should find you soon."

"Don't. Lucas, I know this is a dream and none of this information matters, but I beg the dream you not to come. They will kill you. I know it."

"Now, my queen, you are mistaken. That will never happen," he says, giving me a gentle kiss on the forehead. "Get some rest. I have work to do."

And for the first time in my dream, he walks out of the room through a door I have never seen. After he leaves, I open it, but find various clothes on hangers. With nothing else to do, I climb back into the large black bed, curl under the sheets, and close my eyes, pretending that he is still there.

Katie Zaber

29 Weeks - In a god forsaken place

What are you doing in there? Why won't you let me sleep? Are you nervous about the experiments they will perform on us in a couple of hours?

Me too.

I feel something inside. The only way to describe it is like a slow Morse code. A sluggish tapping from inside me that's different from the kicks and punches. My baby has stopped being gentle. The doctor said I'm supposed to count ten kicks after I eat, but there's no need to count. The little kicker is nonstop. But this feels different. It feels like my baby is trying out a tap language that it hopes I'll know. Sorry, little one. Momma's not fluent in that.

I turn on the stupid television with a remote that only has an up and down, side to side, start and pause buttons. The main screen flashes the time and weather, though I don't know why I get to see the weather. There's no state or town listed. It displays something as simple as sixty-eight and sunny with high humidity. It's not like I have a wardrobe and can pick what to wear each day like I'm going out on the town. I have ten identical outfits.

How much blood will they take as baby pummels me in protest? I wish I could protest more. I can't do anything big. Just small little protests. Nothing crazy. Nothing that would be punishable, just little inconveniences for my captors. My toilet seems to overflow and clog extremely easily. Watching them plunge my shit and piss is the only satisfaction I have. So I watch gleefully, because I won that small battle. I made you wade through my shit and clean it.

It's the small things that keep me sane… ish.

The familiar knock begins at the same time, six in the morning. Always. It's never five fifty-eight or two after six, it's always six o'clock on the dot. How do they do that? Do they have to wait until exactly six to get me? Is it a rule? It's creepy.

I'm still in bed when I could have gotten ready hours ago. No, I like to make them wait. It's the little inconveniences that make me smile. I take my time and slowly get out of bed and make my way to the bathroom to pee again.

They really gave me an impressive suite for a prison bathroom. The tub has jets, but I've never been a bath person. The rainfall shower has a bench to sit on. I like that. I can spend hours under the warm water falling down on me. It soothes my achy body, but it does nothing to ease my mind.

When I get back from the doctors, I'm going to hang in the shower until my walk. After breakfast, of course. I hope it's bacon, eggs, and waffles. Oh, I want it to be.

"Hurry, Everild. The doctor is very busy today," says Nurse Jane.

"Does he have a lot of appointments?" I ask.

"He's busy today," she says.

Hmm. I guess he is seeing a lot of patients. I nod and sit down in the wheelchair. For some reason, they insist on wheeling me back and forth to my examination, though they have gotten more lenient with the restraints. My legs are no longer strapped down, so that's a plus. My hands are still tied to the armrests, but that's it.

There's never anyone else in the hallway when they bring me to the doctor, the only other place I know how to get to besides the pathetic garden. Like the parade through the halls is timed. No one is allowed to be near me except for my handlers. Once I'm past the secured double doors and in the examination room, I wonder if people reappear from every doorway and go about their business as if paused while I'm rolling by. It's always quiet. Eerily quiet. Not like my first day here, when it had sounded like the corridors were busy with workers. I wonder what happened to that poor woman and how she's doing with the wall climbers, if she's even alive.

"Hello, Ms. Everild. How are we feeling today?" the doctor greets me as I'm wheeled into the room. The guards stay outside now and don't need to be told that I deserve a little privacy. I'm not sure if they are watching or not, but it's nice to not have them leering over me as I'm poked and prodded against my will.

"Bloated and hungry. The baby is doing something new; it feels like tapping."

"Hiccups. You can really feel it now since it's getting so big."

Hey, baby? I thought we had a no hiccupping agreement. It feels so weird.

"And how many kicks after you eat?"

"Countless."

"Excellent. Get onto the table. We have a busy day. Your last blood results show that you are doing well, limiting your snacking. All your blood levels were good, for how much you eat. Everything is perfect."

I nod.

Nurse Jane helps me onto the table and straps me down. For a second, I can see where the guards hang out while I'm examined. It's in an alcove across the hall with a couple of chairs, but close enough that they can barge in within seconds.

The nurse gets the warm bottle of gel ready, refusing to say a word. She doesn't like to talk to me or make eye contact. When I do get a glimpse of her face, she looks devastated. Good. I want this place to break its captors, not its prisoners. Since she won't look me in the eye, that's exactly where I stare relentlessly. I want her to feel uncomfortable enough to scream. Her skin should itch, her blood should boil—she should be in Hell for what she is part of.

She turns away, trembling. The guilt must be building to an unstable level. The question is will she explode or implode? Will she kill and help me escape, or will she give up and kill herself? She looks weak. Almost pathetic. My guess is she'll hang herself.

"Nurse, hand me the—if you can't handle this, leave. I have no time for the weak-minded," the doctor says in a tone that is empty of empathy. Wow. He is a great actor. For a moment, I thought he might feel guilt, but it's clear the man doesn't have emotions. He only knows how to feign bedside manner. He's a monster.

The nurse is caught in indecision. She releases a breath and begins to pant, turning her head toward me. For the first time, she looks me in the eye and holds my gaze. What are you planning to do? Can we help each other? She nods, then turns to face the doctor who has already dismissed her, returning to his paperwork.

"No."

Such a simple but strong word. Some people forget the power it has. The finality of the two-letter word. In the right hands, it can demolish anything. Even the walls you put up to protect yourself. The lies you tell yourself. One good *no* and they crumble into dust.

"Excuse me?" the doctor asks, adjusting his glasses. "Get out. Now."

"No," she whispers. Her mouth unhinges and she lunges at the doctor, shredding his throat with her teeth.

Blood squirts from her mouth and the gaping hole in his neck.

A tray table with plastic and metal tools crashes to the ground as the doctor reaches out for anything of use, something to fight back with before he falls onto his back with her clamping down on his jugular, spraying blood all over the glass room. From where I'm sitting, it looks like she's eating him, the way she chews on his flesh. Blood pools on the floor behind his head; he's still alive, gurgling and moving his hands. She releases him from her teeth, watching in satisfaction as he writhes. The expression on her face makes me think she has dreamed of this moment her whole life. The corners of her mouth lift, revealing a blood-drenched smile. Tilting her head back slightly, she goes for another bite on the other side of his neck, making the gashes match in size.

He gurgles on the floor, blood oozing out of him, looking up at me, pleading with his eyes for help. I look at the restraints and give him a *go fuck yourself* shrug. I watch the doctor bleed out. The light in his eyes dims as the nurse tries to bite his head off. The spine seems to be giving her a problem. Sitting on the table, where he violated me while wearing a physician's smile, I stare back silently and watch karma unfold in different shades of red.

Boots pound on the floor. Orders are yelled, but they sound muffled. The words are unclear over the whizzing coming from their oddly shaped guns as they unload a dozen bullets into Nurse Jane. Her body shudders back with each impact, adding to her manic movement, until it stops and lies still. The dead man under her still stares at me. I stare back.

The guards shout, I think even at me, but I don't hear the words. Plus, whatever they want me to do is impossible, since I'm physically unable to move.

Then I see movement on the floor. The nurse's bloody body jerks and leaps upright. The men have no response except to shoot. The standing corpse doesn't flinch as a hole appears in the center of her chest, widening until I can see clearly through the space where her heart should be, but it doesn't stop the demonic laughter escaping her lips as bullets zip through her.

Maybe if she didn't start laughing, they wouldn't have stopped shooting, but I think even these missionaries haven't dealt with possessions. Maybe other monsters, but the way they are staring at the nurse's reanimated corpse makes me believe they are used to killing monsters. Not facing ones who won't die.

One of them shouts about getting me out, another begins to unstrap me.

"He's coming. He isn't happy. Not at all." A disembodied voice booms out of the nurse, singing in a sick melody. The head bobs and twists unnaturally, giddy with excitement. "Oh, I wish I could be here when the fun starts. It would be so entertaining."

"Who's coming?" I ask.

She looks at me with soulless eyes. They are dark. Even if I didn't witness her death, I would still know the person in front of me was dead. A reanimated corpse. "You know. You've always known. But we don't like to be honest with ourselves, do we?"

"Which side are you on?"

"No sides. It's chaos. That's why you mortals are so confused. You always think it's black or white, but everything is gray. There are shades you can't even see. Nothing is purely evil and nothing is completely holy. Everything is damaged."

A loud click comes from my left along with a shout: "Cover her!"

The guard who was cutting my bonds turns to face me, grabs me by the head, and wraps his body around me.

The onslaught on my ears from the gunfire makes me dizzy. All I hear is ringing. The man who used his body to shield me lets go. He steps to the side, giving me a full view of the carnage. Nurse Jane no longer has a head. Searching the room, I can't find a skull or an ear, or any fragment that could be identified as part of a head. The fluorescent lights above are shaded red by the coat of blood already congealing on the glowing tubes. It adds to the sinister feeling in the room.

Everything is tinged red. It feels right.

The guard who helped me turns to get me off the table as another brings in a wheelchair.

"We need to get you out of here. Somewhere safe," says the young guard. I'd say he might be twenty-five.

"Can I go home? It's safe there," I whisper.

He doesn't say anything as he helps me into a chair and wheels me out of the massacre and back to my secured cell.

Five hours later, I'm still confined to my room. I think the whole place is on a lockdown. By now, I should have taken my daily garden walk.

I thought that watching them die would have made me happy. That it would have brought me some type of warped satisfaction. They weren't good people. They deserved nothing better. They violated me. But I don't feel happy.

I'm left troubled and in need of a priest.

Everywhere I go, possessions follow. The last three seemed demonic, I think.

Baby, is this my superpower or yours? Or is this a curse? I'm not sure how having possessed maniacs around me is beneficial; it's not like I can control them. It's not like I can help the people riding passenger inside their own bodies. I hope all their souls are freed and not dragged to Hell, unless that's where they deserve to go. It all seems really unfair.

It can't be that way. If God really cares about his children, he would at least let them go to heaven. If he let them go to Hell, would he really be a just God?

My mind replays every obscure conversation I've had. Every weird occurrence. The conclusion I've come up with isn't good. Not for me. Not for my baby. Those dark thoughts lead to others and more questions that I fear I know the answer to, but can't face.

I've never run from the truth. I've never dismissed concrete information. I'm a woman of science and facts, not emotions and whims. At least, I was. When did I change? How?

My door opens. No hard boots on the floor. Crystal is wearing comfortable flats and another ugly floral skater dress. I imagine her closet is full of them. "Hello, Everild. I've heard you had a very active day," she says in a soft, studious tone.

"Hmm. Those aren't the words I'd use to describe it. But sure," I say from my bed, not bothering to get up. She's not worth the effort.

"Nurse Jane was only twenty-six years old. So young. A life wasted. And your doctor, he had a family—"

"They got what they deserved."

She nods. "Tell me what happened."

"You have this entire building wired and under surveillance from every angle. You know."

She gives me a smile. "Ah, but, I want to hear it from you. Tell me about the conversation you had with Nurse Jane after she murdered your doctor."

"You mean after your guards shot a hole through her chest the size of my fist and she was still talking?"

"Yes."

"She said a bunch of mumbo jumbo crazy shit that didn't make any logical sense. I don't know what she was talking about."

"But you were trying to figure it out." She walks to the far wall and turns around. "I have a theory of my own. Of what is happening to you and those around you. It's difficult to run experiments to see if I'm correct, at least in your delicate state." She flashes a smile only a psychopath can muster. "But you won't stay that way forever. Neither will your child."

All I can do is grit my teeth. We're alone. I could lunge at her. Kill her right now.

Her eyes narrow as a smile spreads across her face. "You can try. I'd love to see you charge at me. Waddle"—she pauses. The glare in her eyes is sickening. She's enjoying this. This moment. This very moment. Torturing me—"As fast as you can. Let's see how comical you'll look. Afterward, you'll wake up in a few months and we'll start having some real fun."

No words can sum up the infinite amount of hate surging through my veins. My lips quiver. My stomach flips. Sweat builds up on my skin and drips down my brow. "And what do you have planned for us?"

"Well, if you tell me what you know," she says, shrugging, "and cooperate, we won't have to test as many theories."

"And if I know nothing?" The lights flicker.

She looks up at the ceiling, then slowly back to me. "I'm not stupid. You aren't either. Tell me about the possessions. Since you have been here, there have been two cases: when you first arrived and today. I can only hypothesize that there have been more." She clasps her hands in front of her flat stomach. She smiles, and I swear there is a tiny spark in her eyes. It's not love. It's not empathy. The bitch is curious.

The lights sputter out. For a brief moment, the room is pitch black. Emergency lights turn on, giving the room a green glow.

She stares at me. "How many?"

30 Weeks - God Only Knows, and He Doesn't Care

Some days, it's a tease to feel the breeze against my skin as I walk around my perimeter, knowing I'm outside but not free. Today, I needed to remember how sunlight feels on my skin.

"I'll be back in a moment. I'll be right on the other side of this door. You'll be good?" Bob, the friendliest of the Bobs on duty, asks me while eyeing the guard towers. He mumbles something into his walkie-talkie, which is strapped to his chest among the ammo and other lethal supplies, and with the new addition of Christian symbols. Crucifixes hang from his neck, but carefully, so they don't tangle with any of his gear.

No Bob, I'm not that stupid. How far do you think I would actually make it before you came back? I have the grace of a drunken hippo. It takes me forever to get anywhere. "I'll be good."

Like I have a choice.

Time for another lap. In a day, I usually get in about eight laps. I like to take my time and stroll. There's no need to rush my pacing. Today, I've done one so far. And the little bench they added looks comfortable. The rays of the sun warm my face and I decide I want my arms to enjoy the burning, tingling sensation it gives. With my eyes closed, I picture the beach, laying out with Lucas in the Florida Keys. Playing in the sand, ordering Michelin-star meals while feeling like the luckiest person in the world. I can still taste the lobster. The seared fish over lime rice. I can't stop craving those delectable dishes. Something tells me this landlocked area doesn't receive a steady supply of seafood.

In the distance, a beeping noise starts. It's only because there is a lack of noise that I can tell there is a new, quiet beep.

Doors from an entrance or exit that I've never seen used open, but no one exits. A blur moves toward my enclosure. Almost like seeing an outline of something, but I'm not sure what the outline is. It's like looking at a bubble person. I can see through them and if the sun doesn't hit what I'd call skin right, I wouldn't see the sheen at all. I watch the outline come closer into the shadow of the building, by my cage, and notice the blood trail on the grass.

Before my eyes, a slender but fit brunette wearing a neon green jumpsuit, which matches the color of her eyes, shimmers into sight on the other side of the fence, bracing it with a painful expression on her face. She's not completely visible and difficult to see. Like a ghost. The poor woman pants as she slowly lowers a hand to touch her abdomen. I can't tell if her injury is a bullet or stab wound, but she's in a lot of pain.

Her head raises bit by bit as she takes labored breaths.

At that second, I decide to start my pacing again. If this woman has escaped this far, she might actually make it, and I would never want to give her away by staring at her or bringing her any unwanted attention.

"How far along are you?" she asks, her voice ragged.

"Thirty weeks," I say, continuing my walk like I'm talking to myself.

"What are you? What's your name?" she asks between pants, trying to calm her breathing.

"Eve. Who are you? What are you?" I shoot back, wondering what kind of person can turn themselves invisible. "My guard will be back any second."

"Bell. Seriously, what are you? Why are they keeping a pregnant woman here? If I get out, I promise I'll send help."

From the inflection in her voice, I believe if this woman successfully gets out and has the resources and knows the right people, she would try to help. But I doubt she does.

I nod. I want to tell her to be careful, but that seems stupid in real life. What she's about to do will be painful and suicidal; it's the opposite of careful. I can't say good luck and jinx her. "I don't know. How many others are here, and what are they?"

She tilts her head as if she doesn't understand why I don't know. "Hundreds. Mostly adults, but there's a few teens and kids."

"How can you turn invisible? Are you a wall climber?"

At that moment, the door swings open. I jump a little but keep walking.

"Inside now!" Bob demands with a drawn gun and red face. "Hurry!"

I nod and hurry across the square and enter the building once more without looking back at the invisible woman.

Please don't make her enter this building again. Please let her be free. If you are listening, prove it. Free her. Free us. Don't pretend you're deaf, you motherfucker. I pray. Answer me.

Is it weird that I'm excited to go to bed so I can tell a figment of my imagination about the woman I met today? I knew there were other people here; they couldn't have built this fancy facility just for me. She looked mortified that they had captured a pregnant woman, like she hadn't seen that where she was being kept. However, she did say there were hundreds. So how big is this campus? How many floors up and down does this compound have?

If she gets out, will she actually send help? I hope the brave woman made it. Even if she didn't, I will dream she did. That's how I'll remember her.

I wake up in the ebony room, alone in the big bed. Lucas isn't here. I close my eyes and imagine him before me. He's wearing black silky boxer briefs and running his fingers through his shiny black hair. His midnight sky eyes glisten, then he gives me a sly smile. My imagination creates a perfect replica, but when I open my eyes, he is nowhere to be found.

"Come on, I need this. Where are you, Lucas?"

There's no response. Great. Now I've gone crazy in my dreams, too.

The room seems to shift, changing slightly every night. Sometimes, there is a wardrobe or a door to a closet. Other nights, there is no furniture except for the bed. I've also seen a black velvet chaise longue and a bench at the foot of the bed in that same material. There have been end tables with tissues and glasses of water. Other times, there has been nothing.

I never know how the room will be designed. Tonight, there is nothing but the bed in a circular room. The onyx walls are smooth and warm to the touch and seamless. Same with the floor. The normal rug under the bed is gone. The room feels different. Less used, maybe.

How much time passes here while I lie in bed sleeping? Will Lucas come once I wake up? Will we miss each other tonight? I really wanted to see him. Why can't I make him appear?

I curl up in the bed under the sheets and imagine his arms are wrapped around me the way I want. My eyes close as I fall back asleep inside my dream.

"Eve, I'm getting close," Lucas says, waking me up, giving me a kiss.

For a moment, I'm in shock. He found me? Is he really here? My eyes adjust to the room and I realize I'm still in the black room. How is it possible to fall asleep in a dream? "Lucas, come lay with me."

"How are you and cauliflower doing?"

"The baby is a little cauli this week?" My hands immediately cradle my stomach and think about my little one. You are getting so big, so fast. "I'm tired. I met someone today. Someone else who is being kept here. She can turn invisible. I think she may have escaped."

"Really? Invisible?"

"Well, more like a bubble person. If you looked closely, you could make out the outline of her body. We didn't have too much time to talk. But we were outside. There were only a few barbed wire fences and machine guns to get by. I hope she made it."

"Me too. Did she say anything else?"

"Only that many more people were being kept there."

"So it's a very big structure?"

"I'd say so. I haven't gotten a good look at the outside of the building, just my little area, but I'd call it a campus."

"What's the weather like?"

"Warmish. Seventies. Muggy."

"I'll see you soon. I'll find you," he says and gets off the bed to leave through a new door.

I grab his arm. "Stay, please. Just a little longer. I miss you so much."

He stands before the bed and engulfs me in a strong embrace. I close my eyes and rest my head against his moving chest.

I whisper, "I miss you. I miss you so much."

His chest heaves. "Eve, I can't wait to bring you home. I won't leave you again."

"Just be here with me now," I say, looking up, getting lost in his midnight eyes. They resemble the night sky from the famous painting. I cup his cheek and reach up to kiss him hard before pushing him onto the bed, flat on his back. He gives me a glance that says this isn't the time, but gives in. Maybe it's the look on my face. The look of desperation.

I need this. I need him.

Bang Bang

It must be six. Back in my prison, I feel cold under the bedsheets without Lucas wrapped around me. The new Nurse Jane rolls in a wheelchair embellished with religious symbols and newly added restraints. They all wear crucifixes around their necks and carry rosary beads in their pockets. I've even seen a few wear a brown necklace with two brown squares. I think they are called scapulars. Each square hangs over their chest and back. All the people who are around me wear their religious adornments like shields. Will these things actually protect them? I'd like to think that they don't.

Given how many cases of possession that occur daily, I don't think religion is a shield. Maybe the weak-minded are targeted because they can't think for themselves and are too mentally weak to withstand an attack. If you ask me, that paints a huge bull's-eye on all the ultra devotees' minds. When you stop critically thinking and leave God to decide, you weaken your own mind. Of course there is a happy medium, being a believer and also thinking for yourself, but with everything in life, there are extremists. I think moderation is key.

DNA – Demons N Angels

The new doctor doesn't talk to me. Neither does Nurse Jane. They do their jobs, refuse eye contact, and send me back to my room. But now I can't tell if it's from fear of me or because it's the way they handle their job.

My new doctor also didn't tell the guards to leave while he's examining me. So now I have an audience for every visit, which is daily. They don't tell me what they are looking for or what they want to check. They just poke and prod, draw blood, watch the ultrasound, insert devices I've never seen into me. It almost looks like a microphone with a long cord hooked up to a computer. When the doctor first used it on me, I asked what it was, but I was ignored. It didn't matter how much I yelled; they didn't answer. It was like they all wore earplugs.

He sticks the microphone object in me every other day. Each day, they take a little blood. They watch my little one do flips on the monitor for two hours, but won't give me a glimpse. Then they dump me back in my room.

I've tried to watch the guards. Their movements. Their schedules. But it's random. There is no set guard schedule. The only routine events are my trips to the doctor. Everything else—my garden walks, when they deliver my meals—is random. They supply me with only sporks and plastic knives to eat my food and check my trays to make sure I haven't kept the bendy knife that cuts nothing.

The spork might come in handy when I go to gouge out my unlucky victim's eye, though I imagine a metal spoon would get the job done faster, but the plastic cutlery will work. It will just take longer and be more painful, which makes me smile.

Katie Zaber

31 Weeks - Mad Scientist Laboratory

Done with my daily examination, my entourage escorts me to my room. Rolling down the halls, I search for anything that could be useful, a sign, a marker, a phone—anything that could be lifesaving if I could get my hands on it. There is nothing. The walls are always bare.

Six a.m., when I see the doctor, might be the best time to launch an escape. Nurse Jane's guards always stand a few feet apart from each other, no matter where they go. It must be some type of security protocol. It will be hard to knock out both of them. That will be the hardest part. Besides all the unknowns.

The other option is to wait until my garden walk. I'd be closer to the woods. Closer to escape. However, I don't know how I'll be able to scale the fences like that woman. It's been months since I've run or have done anything physical. My swollen body is going to be ten times harder to pull up a fence, over the razor-sharp wires, and carefully shimmy back down the other side. And since I'm not invisible, I'm going to be spotted before I even clear the first section of barbed wire. Maybe the guards will point and laugh instead of shooting.

So I think that plan will fail. I need another route out of here besides under the watchful eyes of the guard towers. There has to be a tunnel or something they use. I have never seen anyone outside my fence, so there must be multiple entrances and exits. This means more guards, more ammo, and a higher chance of getting lost.

It's not like I can steal a uniform and blend in with my stomach as huge as it is. Maybe if I were still in the second trimester, I could get away with it. There's no way I could now. I'd be spotted instantly. And once again, laughed at, hopefully.

Outside my room, I watch a Bob scan his eye into the black dome. That's a whole other problem, the retinal scan. I need to kill a guard and get their eye. The only time I'm alone with anyone is when I go to my garden. It would be much easier to take down a single nurse, but I have also never seen a nurse open a door. It's always a guard.

So that's going to be a struggle. Basically, I need a miracle.

That's your cue, oh great being in the clouds. Fucking do something, God! Save us. Save all of us. No? You aren't going to answer? Are you a coward?

"Home sweet home," a Bob says.

Your eye. I want to take your eye.

They wheel me into my room and wait for me to get out of the chair before following Nurse Jane back out.

I feel disgusting. I need a shower. I need to not leave the shower. Ever.

Alone again, I head to the walk-in shower and turn on the water and let it warm up. In the bedroom, I grab a fresh outfit and towels and hang them in the bathroom so I can change into them as soon as I get out. They could at least supply me with a bathrobe.

I am beginning to take off my shirt when I hear the radio on the television turn on. I peek my head out of the bathroom and see no one, and turn it off. Is it just me, or do weird things happen when we are around electronics? Is that another one of your powers, baby? Is it mine?

Really needing to relax in the shower for a little bit, I toss my clothes and sit down on the bench in the shower. The water falls down on me like warm rain, soothing and warming my aching body.

DNA – Demons N Angels

The radio turns back on.

"Don't be frightened. I'm here to help," says no one. Not anyone I can physically see.

How many invisible people are here? "Is the music and running water to cover your voice?"

"Yes. Turn your head to the left. The camera won't be able to see your lips moving."

"Who are you?"

"Name is Annabel. You met my daughter, Bell. She was recaptured, but told us that a pregnant woman was being kept close to the outside perimeter. That you are allowed outside. People like me are kept underground. Hmm, I can't wait to feel the sun on my skin again. What's your name?"

"Eve. How long have you been here?"

"Two years. You?"

Shit. And I'm over here complaining. "A month. What are you?"

"I'm a witch. And you? Your aura is like nothing I've ever seen. It's dark and beautiful. Almost like a canvas of black lava with molten red cracks and glowing stars painted on top of it."

"I don't know what I am. I thought I was normal until recently."

"How recent?"

"Weird stuff has been happening since I've become pregnant. And it keeps getting weirder."

"What kind of stuff?"

"You're going to think I'm crazy."

"Dear, you do realize you are talking to an invisible witch locked inside a prison for the occult?"

Damn, she's got me there. "Everyone keeps becoming possessed around me. It's happened more times than I'd like. Sometimes people die. The ones who survive don't have any recollection of what happened. I think, I think I might be

275

carrying something different. It's a baby, but also something more."

"No wonder they want to study you and your child," she says with a motherly tone. "I'm sorry, love."

"It's not just that." It doesn't matter if I tell this stranger. What damage can she do? "The baby doesn't have a father. Only me. Somehow, my body created it without any other DNA. Asexual reproduction. The doctor who was explaining this to me at fourteen weeks became possessed mid-conversation. I didn't go back to her."

"Dear child, it sounds like you are carrying something miraculous."

Tears run down my cheeks, blending in with the showers water. "What if it isn't a miracle? What if, what if my baby is the opposite?"

"Darling, do you plan on being a good mother?"

"Yes."

"Do you plan on teaching your child to be a good person, with a morally driven mind?"

"Of course."

"Then you have nothing to be afraid of. I'm a witch. I've passed on my knowledge to my foolhardy daughter. She's young, but she's learning. However, she knows right from wrong. They say power corrupts, but I've seen powerful people be the most generous and the poor act wicked. Also vice versa. The point I'm trying to make is that people are people. Just because they were given extra tools, handouts, doesn't change how they were raised. If you raise your child right, then you will have, eventually, a loving, normal adult. Fate can be changed."

"Do you believe in God?"

"I have to get my powers from some source. Something had to create everything. Something has to be that powerful. It only makes sense."

"So then you believe in the devil?"

"He walks among us daily, but I don't believe he is a bad guy. I believe he has a bad job. But, I could be wrong. I don't know everything and the little I know isn't worth much."

Just talking to this invisible stranger, telling her everything that has been weighing me down, is uplifting. She gives me comfort I didn't expect, in a dark place where I didn't think kindness would reach. Hot water blankets my body and I pretend the woman is engulfing me in a hug as I wipe away tears.

"My dear, if I succeed in escaping, I'll help you, in every way I can. But first, you need to help me."

"What do I need to do?"

"Just pretend I'm not here. Let me follow you and your guard to the garden. Once you're back inside, I'll scale the fences."

"You're going to get caught. The barbed wire will slice you to pieces. There will be a blood trail."

"Darling, I've taken care of that. Plus, I'm older and wiser than my daughter."

"How come you couldn't escape before?"

"There is a new energy here. It's strong, like a never-ending battery powerful enough that it trickles through the wards placed on the cells. They try to limit the amount of magic in the air, the amount that can be absorbed. Slowly over the last few weeks, it's been replenishing my power reserves and now, I think I'm strong enough to escape."

"How long can you stay invisible? Is it a spell? How many people are here? Are they all witches? Also, what about thermal imaging cameras? Even if you're invisible, they might still see you. They probably have new protocols for invisible people."

"For an hour or so hour. I also lower my body heat too. It's a complex spell. In order to keep doing it, I'm going to lie down under your bed and rest for a little bit until you go for your walk. Be a dear and make a mess. Leave the blankets on the floor, covering the gaps around the bed to give me some cover. As for how many are locked up here, hundreds. And no, dear, not everyone here is a witch. They collect anyone who isn't what they define as *normal*."

"Like what? Werewolves? Vampires?"

"Yes, and more. Things I don't even know or understand. All I know is none of us deserve to be caged. We have done nothing wrong."

"This battery you feel, can you tell where it's coming from?"

"No, just that it's nearby. Some others are able to sense it. Use it."

Am I the battery she's talking about? Is my baby the battery? Can we run out of fuel? "Where do you plan to go? Who is going to help you save all of us?"

"There are people gearing up for a war. We've been preparing. I have powerful allies and have made more since my capture. I will return with an army of what they call supernatural terrorists and show them the definition of pain. Treat them as they have been so kind to show us."

"Good. Hurry. We don't have much time. I don't know what they are going to do when my baby is born."

"How far along are you?"

"Thirty-one weeks."

"I will find help and bring them here as fast as possible. Just cross your legs until I'm back. I'm growing tired. I'll be under the bed. How long before you go on your walk?"

"They usually like to have me outside before lunch. Maybe an hour or two."

"What is your name, darling?"

"Eve. Rest up. I'm counting on you," I say, turning off the shower.

She doesn't respond. I assume she left the room so I could towel dry and dress.

There's no way to tell if she's under the bed but I toss the wet towel beside it, blocking the foot of the bed and flinging the comforter to one side. I hope I've rearranged the bed enough to give her adequate cover.

Baby, we have a chance. It's a shot in the dark, but we have a chance. Lying on the bed with my eyes closed, I think of Melisa. Have I made a new friend in this unlikely place? If Annabel makes it out and sends help, I'll name my child after her.

A Bob comes and knocks on my door, brandishing five crucifixes that I can see. I'd figure one would do the job, but what do I know? When he holds open the door, I take an awkward pregnant lady wobble and take up a ton of extra room getting through the doorway, making the guard take another step back. Hopefully I'm giving Annabel space to slide around. I don't have any idea how big she is and hope she made it out of the room. Guess I'll find out when I get back.

I take my time walking down the pristine hall. I wonder if the paint is called pristine, like the walls at Melisa's. What did Lucas tell her? I'm sure after so many calls and unanswered texts, she got in touch with him. Either that or she flew down to Orlando to track him down herself. All I want to do is give her a hug. Tonight, I'll dream of us going on an adventure together. Maybe a fun tropical vacation, like the one we went on. Lucas shouldn't be hogging all my dreams, even if I enjoy the time we have together in my mind. I miss him so much that I can't stop dreaming about him. Never did I think that after Jim, I would love again. Not this deeply.

A Bob stands in front of the dome, widens his eye, waits for the beep, and opens the door. It's warm and sunny. Very bright. There's not a cloud in the sky. Periwinkle blue stretches above the forest.

I roll up my sleeves so I can feel the heat on my arms and hope Annabel is feeling it, too. I begin my pacing; if I don't, it will make the guards curious. The grass is evenly worn from my constant trampling, making a path around my enclosure. After a few laps, I sit down on the bench they gave me and look at the scenery. The woods surrounding this place must be thick. It looks dark, very shaded from the trees. That should help give her cover if her spell doesn't last too long once she is away from the battery, who I suspect is me. It's only a guess, but the timing makes sense. With how much I eat and only gaining baby weight at a normal rate, I have to be burning the extra calories somehow. Maybe it's magic? Or it has something to do with power? Either way, with the amount of weird shit that's been happening, it only makes sense that my baby or I are supernatural batteries. What else would we be? Normal human beings? Hell no.

Annabel must be so much more skilled in her spellcraft than her daughter. I can't see any outline. There's no sheen or way to tell she is even outside. I really, really hope she made it outside.

A few minutes pass. There's a sudden weight on my hands, like someone put their hands on mine. I decide not to get up and continue pacing. That I'm tired and sitting here with a new friend, holding their hand before they attempt a suicidal escape is where I need to be. I need to give her my strength, my courage. It's the only thing I can give. Let her absorb all she needs for her fight out of here.

After twenty minutes, Bob tells me it's time to go in. I do so without looking back. She will escape. She will get me out. I have faith in her. I need to have faith in something.

Katie Zaber

32 Weeks - East Bumblefuck

Bang Bang

Right on time. I wish for one day, for one moment, that they would be late. Just to see if they could. Time for another poking and prodding by Doctor Asshole. Really, what can they possibly be learning from you daily?

Nurse Jane and the Bobs stomp into my room. They are always looking for hidden threats. Their eyes scan the room robotically, trained to find dangers lurking in the shadows, on the ceiling. Anywhere that would make a great hiding place, they look. All the smart hiding spots—the ceiling, behind doors—that's where they inspect first. It's as if they expect some veiled person to be bunking with me, waiting to ambush them from a secluded spot. I think the whole base has been on lockdown since Annabel attempted to escape. They haven't let me out to my garden. I've only had doctor visits. I hope she's free. The thought makes me smile.

If she made it out, she can tell our stories. Even if she can't come back or rally enough beings to fight, she can still warn others. She can still help. I hope she's alive and on the other side, feeling the sunlight on her skin, the breeze through her hair, breathing in free air. Not the recycled purified air pumped through the vents. Real air. The kind that has a fresh, faint, sweet smell as it fills the lungs.

"Hurry up. We don't have all day," Nurse Jane snarls.

"I have to pee." It's the little inconveniences. The tiny problems that make me smile, especially when I'm the culprit.

"Make it quick," she barks.

The guards stand there, discussing how I should be put into an induced coma until the baby is born. Or better yet, why don't they do a C-section and keep the baby in an incubator? At this many weeks, with the technology here, the baby should be strong enough to survive.

Tears slide down my face as I sit down on the cold toilet seat. The chill stops me from sobbing. "I'm sorry, baby. I'm sorry, sweetheart." A soft wriggling under my palm lets me know baby hears me. "I know. I know I promised, but unless she survives and creates an army, we won't get out," I whisper. "I wish we could. I wish I could show you the world and everything amazing in it. I wish I could teach you how to be a good person." Looking up at the ceiling, I whisper, "God, make my wishes come true, please. We need you. Or is this where you want us? Do you want us to die? Are you going to let us? Why? Why do any of this? Why do we need to suffer?"

It's funny how I find myself praying more and more. Between everything I've witnessed, like the possessions, I'd be stupid to not think something bigger was playing with its game pieces and we pawns are left in the dark, only able to move forward blindly before death. I may not know what's happening, but something is. Something I can't control.

A tirade of kicks lets me know baby isn't happy, and I let baby have a hissy fit.

I'm about to have one too.

It's weird how I miss the old, evil, dead doctor. At least he turned the monitor around so I could say hello. He treated me like a human to my face. I know it was all a charade, but it was nice to be spoken to, not at, or, even worse, like a science experiment.

"Subject B is active today," he says, staring at the monitor, watching you tumble and play in your womb playpen. You're outgrowing it too fast. Slow down. Stop.

Nurse Jane, with dead eyes, opens up a folder on the computer screen in her workspace. "Subject M's labs are optimal. She's in perfect health."

The doctor pushes the wand around my stomach, holding it in place, jabbing me uncomfortably. Complaining won't help, not with this man. He pretends I'm a science experiment, not a person. That's one way to handle the job. Detach oneself from humanity. Could he possibly have a normal life? A family and an average two-story home in a suburb. Or do people like him live alone, slaves to their work, the only companion in their life since no one would ever love a monster like him? I'd like to think he's alone, but the way he holds himself makes me think he has something to lose. Something that he loves. Maybe love is too strong of a word for a man like him, but there might be something that he claims that he doesn't want damaged or destroyed. An object or person he possesses.

Nurse Jane takes two long straps with wires connected to them and wraps them around my stomach. She positions the devices connected to the straps so they hear the heartbeat. They have done this a couple of times now. I think it's called a nonstress test. I think. Really, I don't know what they are doing or what they are looking or listening for. Maybe they are deciding when to remove my baby from me. They wouldn't let me give birth. That's not something they can control. No. They are going to cut my baby out of me, because that is what these people do. They are ruthless. They probably won't even let me hold my child. They are barbaric in the name of science. They are monsters. Every one of them.

Flashing lights in the hallway strobe. Both Bobs listen to commands barking at them from the walkie-talkies strapped to their chests as they jump into action. The order is simple and direct. *Secure the patient immediately.*

Nurse Jane's eyes grow large as she unstraps the device around my abdomen. "What's happening? What did you hear?"

"We need to get her to her room, now. You and the doctor report to your bunker. This isn't a drill," the older Bob states.

They don't wait for me to get off the examination table. It has wheels. Their radios are constantly shouting at them and any Bobs who will listen. The base is under attack, from what I can understand, but they use too many code words, words that make little sense. Tango, Foxtrot, numbers, and other nonsense words screamed through the radio that sound funny. Like a big joke.

As they run down the hallway, pushing my bed with speed, the warm gel on my stomach cools, even feels tingly as it dries. My arms and legs are still restrained—will they leave me like this?

Outside my room, a Bob with his weapon drawn does a retinal scan. The door opens. Neither looks like they are coming in.

"Untie me. You can't leave me tied up. Please," I beg. "Don't leave me like this, please!"

The younger guard looks at me and says, "You deserve nothing more, witch." He spits at me, just to make sure I understand how he feels.

The older Bob's eyebrows knit together as he chews on his lip. My eyes plead with him, but he shakes his head and closes the door, leaving me strapped to the gurney with spit and ultrasound gel cooling on my exposed belly.

It's quiet. No blaring alarms ringing. Someone has to be rescuing us or attempting. Is it possible Annabel could work this fast? Who else would attack? Whoever or whatever it is, they wouldn't attack the whole building for just one person and leave everyone else behind… would they?

Pop pop pop. I cringe, realizing the noise is guns being fired in the distance. I want to hide under the bed or in the bathroom. Under anything that can block wayward bullets. I consider rocking the table onto its side. It might give us more protection, but if I flip it over and land on you, I fear I'll go into labor or kill you.

Wiggling, I try to loosen the restraints. It's no use. The tight, thick bonds barely let my blood circulate. There's no way I can slide my hands out, even if I break my thumbs.

Sitting and waiting for something to happen is the worst feeling. Dread builds as the tension grows, weighing me down, suffocating me. The moment drags on for an immeasurable count of time as my heart threatens to break free from my chest. Cries come closer and closer.

"Please don't… eeerrrgh!" is the common cry from outside my door.

Crash. Fall. Gasp. Then silence.

Part of me doesn't know if I should call for help or if whoever is in the hallway will just kill us. Sweat pours down my face as I tremble in fear, unable to do a damn thing. A clicking noise comes from the door. Someone's unlocking it.

The doorknob moves. I hold my breath.

"Eve!"

What? How? How is he here? I should be happy. Relieved. But I'm confused, even if his voice is the only one I've wanted to hear. It's just unexpected. Like a dream or, no, a nightmare ending. "Lucas?"

He's standing on the threshold. Blood covers his right hand; an eye dangles from it. "Eve."

The eye makes a squish as he tosses it aside and darts across the room and begins unstrapping me as I sit in awe. As soon as my hands and legs are free, he draws my face to him. Brilliant dark blue eyes swallow me in their gaze as I slowly reach for his face. When my fingers touch his cheek and feel the warmth of his skin, I release air in my lungs that I didn't know I was holding. It's him. Somehow, some way, he found me.

A chill creeps over my body. Was he actually present in my dream? Was he actually there with me? How could he? "Lucas?"

"I'll explain once I get you safe. We need to leave, my queen." He helps me off the table and takes my hand in a way he never has. Almost possessive.

"Wait. We need to rescue the others. There are so many people here. We have to free them."

He gives me a look like he just got an instant migraine, then nods. "Fine. Do you know where they are being kept?"

"No. I think on the lower floors. Below ground."

He nods. "Can you walk?"

"Yes."

"Follow me," he says gripping my hand, stopping to pick up the eye he discarded. It still looks usable, not crushed.

Outside my room, a man lies on the ground. He's missing an eye and mumbling incoherently. It's one of the Bobs, the younger one who spit on me. The older Bob is crumpled on the tile with blood oozing from his head. Good. They deserve it. They all do.

Hand in hand, we walk down the once pristine hallway, now sticky red, him with a strut screaming self-confidence, making him look invincible, me covered in gel and wearing a patient gown, trembling, afraid this is only a nightmare.

Bobs and Nurse Janes sprawl on the ground, screaming in agony, holding their heads in their hands so tightly, it's like they are trying to prevent them from exploding. Some bash their heads into walls. Others discharge their guns or stab themselves in the chest. A few rock on their heels or lie on their side in the fetal position, whispering or screaming nonsense. None of them seem to notice us walking by.

"What happened to them?"

"Don't worry about it."

"Did you do this?" I ask, wanting to know but equally scared of the answer.

"Yes. It's what they deserve."

I won't argue with that, but how can he turn their minds into suicidal mush? How is he that strong? "Are you a witch?"

He smiles. "No, Eve. I'm not a witch. But you don't need to worry about that right now. I'll explain everything to you later. Once you are safe."

I nod. There's little more I can do right now as I watch full-grown adults writhe on the ground, screaming profanities while stabbing themselves. "Have you seen a woman wearing a floral print skater dress?"

"No, I haven't."

"Her name is Crystal. When we find her, I want to kill her myself."

This time, he nods and looks at me as if he's seeing me for the first time. He lifts the Bob's eye to the scanner outside the elevator. It beeps and the doors open, revealing a man and woman in lab coats dead on the floor with jagged, bloody glass sticking out of them. It might have been a water bottle or some type of lab equipment that they broke and either killed themselves or each other, but they died in each other's arms. How romantic, finding love while performing morbid science experiments. Sick assholes.

Lucas sweeps the glass with his thick Italian leather shoes, creating a path for me to walk. My hospital slippers aren't thick.

"My queen, how's our little cantaloupe?" he coos, kneeling down, kissing my belly as the elevator drops a few floors.

"Okay, I think. We'll be happier once we are out of here. Once everyone is out of here."

He wraps his arms around my waist and gives my belly another kiss before standing. "I've missed you, Eve. Rescuing you consumed my mind. You will never be in danger again, I swear." He reaches into his front pocket and pulls out my locket on a brand new chain and drapes it around my neck.

Normally, I would roll my eyes at him and think it was some romantic, even chauvinistic act, but after seeing everyone in his path crumble and fall as they clamp down on their skulls and kill themselves, I believe him. And I fear what that means as I feel the locket's weight rest against my chest. My fingers pry open the locket and find the cute picture of us together on the beach. What I wouldn't give to go back to that day and forget everything that has happened.

One fear at a time. Conquer one at a time, or at least understand them. First, get the fuck out of here. I shut the locket.

"My queen, stand here, to the side. It will only take a second to disarm them. I want to make sure the coast is clear," Lucas says, ushering me to the corner of the elevator, behind the buttons, giving me the most protection. He stands dead center of the doors with an eerie smile, different from any smile I've seen on his face. It's something dark, sinister… rapturous.

The doors open. From a side profile, I watch his eyes turn black, becoming an endless void. Bullets ricochet off an invisible force, leaving Lucas unscathed. All the while, he doesn't stop smiling like the Cheshire cat hunting a dozen blind mice.

The screams start. One by one, screams echo down the hallway, along with the clattering of guns. Some shots are still fired, but they don't sound like they are pointed in this direction. After fifteen seconds, the screams quiet down. All I hear is whimpers and mumbles.

"It's safe," Lucas says without turning, staring down the hallway, waiting for someone to ambush us. The hallway looks the same as the one outside my cell. Like a massacre took place.

Creeping out of the elevator, I walk up to what looks like a nurse's station with a control panel. Thirty numbered switches seem to correspond to the cells on this floor. My fingers grace over the red lights above the numbers, I assume meaning locked.

"Do you know what's behind these doors?"

"Who? These people don't deserve this because they are different. Did I?"

He *tsks* and shakes his head.

"Plus, if anyone attacks us, I'm sure you'll be able to handle it."

He gives me a smirk. "Already using me for your bidding."

I smile and flip the switch to the cell closest to us. No one comes out. Not at first. Then a brunette peeks out. "Hello?"

Twin teens follow her and step into the hallway. Both boys should be in high school. An elderly woman comes out. I flip the switch and the next and the next. Buzzing fills the air as the doors slide open. Questions mumble down the hall as the prisoners ask what happened and look around for answers.

Ten people in each cell? Ten. That's three hundred people just on this floor. The elevator had more levels. How many more are below ground?

"Did you do this?" a familiar voice calls out from a black-haired, olive-skinned woman. It's Bell.

Her face drops. I'm sure she was hoping for her mother. "He did."

Her eyes shift to him. She gives him one long nod. "Is it safe to escape?"

"The ground level is safe," he replies coolly.

"This will not be forgotten. I will open the lower cells and free the others." She walks toward me, Lucas steps forward, but I wave him back. Bell places her hands on my shoulder and says, "Rest now. Take care and protect yourself. I fear your life will continue to be complicated, that the madness will never cease. My name is Bell Belcan. Call my name six times when you are in need, and I will come to your aid, as will anyone here. Anyone who is part of my coven, who can help. We are in debt to you, Eve."

I want to correct her and tell her Lucas was the one who set everyone free, made it safe for them to leave. That he did all the dirty work. All I did was push a couple buttons. But something tells me she doesn't want to be indebted to him. I think she's smart. If she's wary of Lucas, what does that mean for me? For us? "Stay safe."

"You too," Bell says. She nods at me and smiles, turns to Lucas and says, with her head bowed slightly, "I am grateful." She then addresses everyone pouring out of their cells. Within moments, she has everyone organized and ready to infiltrate the lower level and free everyone else here.

Lucas says nothing back but watches Bell give orders while grabbing a Bob's eye and a gun. The other witches—I think that's what they are—grab guns as well. The older ones don't pick up any weapons. I assume they are as strong as Annabel, and now since they are free from their warded cells, they can absorb more… magic? I have no clue how it works. However, I notice a growing intensity of static electricity in the air.

"We must leave," Lucas says. "It's not safe for you to wander here while this pregnant. You need care and rest." I nod and follow him down a deserted hallway with an elevator at the end. "Outside, there's a chopper that will fly us to the local airport, where I have a jet waiting. I'll have you home soon. I think New York might be best right now."

Before I step into the elevator, I stop. I can't leave yet. I made a promise. "What about Crystal?"

"Is it that important to you that she dies? If she was in the vicinity, I probably killed her."

"I promised her that I would kill her."

He presses the elevator button. His jaw looks tight. His eyes are bloodshot. I don't think he's slept. "I killed everyone standing between you and me. She's probably among the dead."

"I need to know. I need to know she's dead and that she won't continue her work. I need to know she's gone." Tears soak my face as I tremble with rage. There's no way I can walk away from this without the knowledge that the bitch is dead.

"It's not important. Not right now. We'll make sure later. If she's still alive, we'll kill her together." He releases a sigh. "I thought I lost the both of you," he whispers. "If I couldn't find you, I don't know what I'd have done," he says, stepping onto the elevator.

What would he have destroyed if we were killed? What is he capable of? I follow, growing afraid of what he will do if I say no.

In the elevator, he turns to me. His face is covered in a fine mist of red, beading together with sweat as it drips down his face. His midnight blue eyes look ready to cry, but don't. "I won't let anything like that happen again. I swear it. Never."

"Thank you, Lucas. How? What are you?"

"I'll explain in time. We still need to get out of here safely."

"How?"

He sighs, "I'm an angel."

"What?" I ask and hug my baby. All I can think and pray is that he better not be a fallen angel, unless he's on our side, and if he is, does that mean we are evil? Does that mean my baby is born to raise Hell? It can't. I won't let that happen. Ever.

But can he help us? Has he known this whole time, and that's why he gave me the money and fed me at the diner? Does he actually care about me, or is he here to protect my baby? Whose baby am I carrying? Does he know? And if I ask, will he answer truthfully? How would I be able to tell if he was lying or not? "An angel? How are you on Earth? Were you sent to…"

"Meeting you was our fate, but I'm on Earth because of family problems. My story about being orphaned isn't a complete lie."

And I thought this day couldn't get stranger. "Isn't your father God?"

"Yes. He is the worst father you could imagine. He's abandoned everyone—mortal and immortal."

"Where did he go? Why would he leave?"

"No one knows. Some believe we aren't worthy and he's starting a new universe. Others think he gave up. Lost faith. No one knows for certain. All I know is that everything and everyone is in turmoil and it must be fixed."

None of this makes sense. God abandoning all his children. That wasn't something he was supposed to do. I laugh. I laugh and laugh, making Lucas stare at me, probably questioning my sanity.

"Are you okay, Eve?"

"Oh yeah. I was just thinking about all the devotees praying every day, dedicating themselves to someone who isn't even there. It's pretty funny."

He shakes his head and uses the eye one more time to open an elevator door. "Only you, Eve. Only you."

Wait, has he possessed some poor man this whole time? "Is this your angelic body?"

"Yes, this is my actual body."

No matter the scenario, I think I might be destined for Hell. Sleeping with an angel must be sacrilegious. It has to be.

Katie Zaber

33 Weeks - New York, New York

"Evie, come on. Talk to me. Tell me what's going on."

Everything is real. Everything that I thought was a story is reality. How do I explain that to Melisa? Is it even possible for her rational mind to accept the supernatural?

"Evie, you're so damn stubborn sometimes." Melisa stares at me on the tablet screen, waiting for a response. She's been video calling me daily since Lucas's jet—he now owns a jet, with his own personal, handpicked staff—flew us into LaGuardia, where a driver waited to take us back to his penthouse in New York.

Until today, Melisa hasn't pressed too hard about what happened. She's talked about work and her latest fling, which ended as fast as it began. The woman is going to die a bachelor, but I think she likes it that way. She's too independent to depend on someone or have someone depend solely on her for too long. It's just not her. We all have our things, our quirks. Mine just happens to be carrying a celestial child.

"I don't know what to say. It happened, and now it's over."

"You don't look like it's over."

We couldn't find any reports about Crystal's death. So that hangs over my head. I hope, pray that Lucas killed her. She needs to be dead. As much as I wanted to be the one to kill her, if Lucas was successful, then at least I'd sleep better at night knowing that one less evil soul walked the Earth. The fact that I don't know keeps me awake. Even though I'm beyond tired and normally a woman this far along would take naps all day if she could, I can't rest. It's impossible when I don't think Crystal died. Without confirmation, I won't sleep. It doesn't matter how strong, how invincible Lucas is. Nothing he can say or do will ease my anxiety until I see that bitch dead.

The organization who Crystal works for is a mystery. Lucas wasn't able to find much on them. They don't even have a name. The three buildings he searched when trying to find me had little to no paperwork. Everything was computerized and when he broke into them, all the files were erased, but he was able to get some information from a couple of employees who told him of other facilities and of a pregnant woman being kept somewhere in Missouri.

Another topic that makes me nervous: Lucas is an angel. Capital A, angel—which is better than being a demon, but still I'm uncertain how I feel about dating an immortal. He says he truly has feelings for me, but has never said love. However, he came to our rescue, but that only makes me more suspicious. Why did he come if he isn't in love with me? Is it his job to protect us? When I ask him questions, he dodges them and tells me not to worry. That he will always protect and care for us. For some reason, him saying that didn't comfort me.

"Evie. Don't make me travel to New York. Don't think for a second I don't already know the address and have mapped out how long of a drive it is. It's doable. I could be there in a couple of hours if you don't start talking for real—"

"—No. Don't come," I blurt out.

Melisa sits back. Her mouth hangs open. "Girl, what's going on? I'm worried about you."

"I'm fine. I'm just freaked out still. There's a lot to work out."

"You know, you can work through it faster if you talk about it. Not even with me. It could be with anyone. Even better yet, a trauma therapist."

"I can't see anyone."

"Why not?"

"More people are becoming possessed. I can't let anyone innocent or anyone I love be taken over. I can't let that happen to you."

"Oh, Evie, honey, I'm too strong to let something push me aside. Not inside this temple." She taps her head. "What aren't you telling me?"

"Nothing."

"Fine, I'm getting my purse—"

"Okay, okay. Where do you want me to start?"

"The beginning is always the best."

I told her everything and left nothing out. She didn't speak, she just sat back and listened as I cried and yelled about the fucked-up place that held me captive. About the Bobs and Nurse Janes. How crucifixes became a fashion statement in my presence after a very possible demonic possession left a nurse and doctor dead. I told her about the mother and daughter, Annabel and Bell. How a coven of witches owes me a favor and that I'm not sure if I should cash in.

"That's not everything, is it?" she asks after sitting in silence for a few minutes, digesting all the information. "How'd you get out?"

"Lucas."

"What did he do? Hire an army?"

"He doesn't need one. He is one."

"Is he an extremely powerful witch or something?"

"No, he's a, he's an angel." The words come out of my mouth in more of a choking noise. I think about the dream room and what Lucas told me. That it was a place in our minds, really his mind that he constructed to connect to me. Somehow, on my own, I was able to come back to it and even enter his mind without him knowing, giving him a surprise. Apparently, I must have some type of psychic powers that I've never used before, which is another thing I'm not ready to address.

"Huh." She shrugs. "I didn't take him for an angel. His more devilish, kind of an asshole, but the sexy, witty kind."

Tears pour down my face as I sob. My mind cannot handle any more insanity. I'm going to end up with a straightjacket on, testing out the cushions in a padded room. "You mean he is the devil?"

"What? No. No, honey. That was a joke. I was trying to make you laugh." Her face drops as she reaches for the screen, like she's trying to wipe my tears. "Lucas isn't the devil. It was a bad joke. That man is deeply in love with you."

"How are you sure? Lucas has never told me he loves me."

"Oh, honey, it's the way he looks at you. Like you're his miracle, the only thing he wants. It's easy to see it on his face."

"But if…"

"He loves you. Get all that other nonsense out of your head. I know shit is crazy. I'm still trying to swallow that there are witches, vampires, werewolves, and probably boogeymen—I'm getting myself a carry permit and sleeping with a gun under my pillow from now on—but Lucas is an angel sent to protect, love, and take care of you. At least that's how I see it. I'm still waiting for my sexy angel to fall into my arms, lucky bitch."

I give her a little smile. "I don't know. I just don't know about anything anymore."

"Have you talked to that priest friend, Ken? Tell him what's going on and ask him for help?"

"Not yet."

"Why do you like to hide away and sulk alone instead of getting the help and support you need? I swear, girl, I can't wait to see you in two weeks. We are going shopping and setting up that nursery. All baby stuff; all good things. We'll get you resettled into that house. Do all the finishing touches so it's perfect. And if there is anything else you want to talk about, vent about, or do, I'm here for you. Always will be."

"I love you, dude."

"All I want is to give you the world's biggest hug. I can't wait to do that in person."

"Me too."

"Eve, a special surprise lunch is here!" Lucas calls from down the hallway, his footsteps approaching the spare bedroom. "I ordered all of your favorites." His smile is sympathetic, patient, kind; maybe he does love me in his own way.

"You better eat. Evie, listen to Lucas. Sounds like he got you something special to snack on." Melisa winks. "Love you. I'll call you later and we can talk more about this. Every day, it will get better. Go eat!"

I roll my eyes at her and shrug. "Fine. If I must."

"Yes, you must," she says, laughing before hanging up.

Lucas gives me a hand and helps me up off the bed. I can get up; it's just not as easy anymore. He asks, "You two have a good chat?"

I don't know if he listens to what we are saying. Another reason I haven't told Melisa everything. Once I start talking, I'm afraid the venting won't end. "Yes. Just more daily nonsense. Told her a little about it."

"The more you talk about it, the easier it will get, and then eventually it will just be a bad experience in the past. Behind you. Not something to carry and stay afraid of."

Is it because he's an angel that he doesn't understand how long it might take for me to get over that traumatic experience? How my world has been flipped upside down and nothing will turn it right again? My mind is spinning. "I'm trying, but it's going to take time."

"And you have as much as you need. I just want you to know you are safe and nothing like that will ever happen again."

"I need time. Time to adjust and to feel normal again. I don't, not right now. How could I with everything that just happened? Everything I learned."

"Your eyes are open, but try not to focus on it or else it will overwhelm you. There's nothing you can do to change the universe, the world, the past. All you can do is move forward," he says, giving my hand a squeeze. "I will help you every way I know how, and if I'm ever lacking, please tell me. All I want is your happiness."

I look into his dark blue eyes and nod. "Thank you."

Out in the kitchen, spread across the island, is a smorgasbord of everything I love to eat. Everything. There's enough food to feed ten people, if not more. A huge selection of fried food, pizza with various toppings, cheeseburgers with bacon, a huge Caesar salad, a tub of homemade hand-churned vanilla ice cream, an assortment of breakfast foodies, even ravioli Alfredo, plus breadsticks, biscuits, and other goodies.

"Eat a little something. Try to eat a full meal this time. Butternut squash must be getting hungry in there," he says, rubbing my tummy.

I place my hand over his before walking to the takeout containers and consider having some bacon, but my stomach turns sour. "Thank you. Everything looks great. I just don't have an appetite. Maybe later."

He gives me a tight-lipped smile and nods. "Perhaps a meal outside of the apartment might make you feel better?"

I shake my head fast enough to give myself whiplash. My stomach growls quietly at the smells, and I decide to try a cheddar cheese biscuit. It tastes dry and salty. I can barely swallow the mouthful. I put the half-eaten biscuit on a plate and leave it on the table.

"Father Ken called again. He might have important news," Lucas says, even though he told me that after the first message. He's encouraged me to talk to him, but asked me not to say anything about him being an angel, which makes me nervous to say anything to the ex-priest.

"What would he know that you, an angel, don't?"

"I don't know everything. I'm not omniscient. More information is always useful, and he's left four urgent messages since you've been back."

I shrug and sigh.

"We also have to talk about other things," he says and looks away.

"What things?"

"Well, a doctor."

My blood turns cold. "No. No more doctors. I don't want to see anyone."

"You need one for when you deliver. There are a few birthing centers that we could go to. They are more like a hotel, not a hospital, and they have proper doctors who can help in case of an emergency."

"No. No people."

"Who's going to deliver your baby? Me? I don't know what to do. We need a professional, Eve."

"No. No people. No one," I cry as my eyes swell. "They all either want to study and kill us or they become possessed. I can't see anyone. I can't take that chance."

He gathers me in his arms. "Eve, oh Eve. I'm so sorry. Don't worry. Melisa isn't going to become possessed and the ex-priest? I wouldn't be afraid of him either. They are too strong-willed. Only the weak are at risk. Not them. But you need a doctor to take care of you, deliver butternut squash into this world."

"You don't know that. No one knows anything," I sob into his shoulder.

"Come here." He walks me to the sofa and cradles me in his arms. "I will protect you and I can protect them, but I don't think they need it. There are weaker people with a higher chance of possession than those two strong-minded individuals. Plus, being an angel, I can send the spirit back to where they belong with a single thought."

All I can do is cry more in his arms. As much as I'm equally terrified of him and what I've been sleeping with, his familiar embrace comforts me and I never want him to let go. He's right. There has never been a possession when he was by my side or in the direct vicinity. In the airport, we were too far apart. There were hundreds of people around us. Otherwise, it hasn't happened. Maybe he can protect us.

A little whine distracts me, coming from behind the sofa. "What's that?"

"Your other surprise. I guess the little guy woke up," he says with one of those *I'm up to something* grins, getting off the couch and picking up a large box with silver wrapping paper with large holes in it. The box wiggles and whimpers as he picks it up. "Whoa, this little guy is excited."

"Lucas?"

"Go ahead. Open it." He places the box gently on the ground in front of me and hands me a tissue to dry my eyes. His eyes glisten and his smile only gets bigger.

Eyes dry, I lift the lid slowly and find a little black puppy with golden splotches on his cheeks and above his eyebrows, staring up at me with chocolate brown eyes. A long, floppy tail wags from side to side as his little body trembles from excitement. "A puppy? Really? It's going to be hard training him with a newborn," I say but instantly know this little guy is mine forever. Paws and legs squirm as I pick him up and cradle him in my arms. His wet black nose sniffs my dress and a pink tongue comes out, licking my arms and hands—any skin he can slobber on. "Oh, Lucas. He's adorable. It's a boy, right?"

"Yes, the trainer he was working with was calling him Shuck. He's the runt of the litter."

"Oh, Shuck! You're so cute! I love him!"

"He's trained pretty well. He might have an accident or two getting used to his new home, but we shouldn't have too much trouble getting him potty trained. To make it easier, I have scheduled a new doggy door to be installed into the house in Florida. That way, he can go outside any time he wants."

"What kind of dog is he?" I ask, noticing how big his paws are. Shuck won't stay small for long.

"He's a Doberman-Boxer mix. They are great with children and protective of their family. He'll be our little guard puppy."

"Oh, Lucas, he's so cute! They will grow up together," I say and touch my belly. You're going to have a fur sibling, butternut squash. The little pup wiggles on my lap, not wanting to sit still but also too nervous to explore his new environment. I set him down on the floor and he instantly cowers by my feet. "Aww, baby. It's okay. This is your new home, Shuck."

He responds with a cute little whimper, pawing at my leg like he wants to get back up on my lap, but he's too small to reach.

"Seems like he has a little more growing to do before he's a strong, mighty guard dog," Lucas says, reaching down to scratch the dog behind his ears. "I bought a bed and food dishes, and some kibble for him. But we'll need to get everything else and get this little guy settled."

Chills creep up my arms and tears fill my eyes. "Are we a family? Do you really want to be with me, us, and be our family? Is that why you are here, on Earth?"

"Yes," he says, picking up the pup and placing him between us. Lucas sits on the couch and hugs me tight, looks me in the eye, and whispers, "I've always wanted a family of my own. I didn't think it was possible until you. You are everything I have ever dreamed of, and more. Maybe I don't say it enough, but you, Eve, my queen, are my wildest fantasy. My dream come true."

34 Weeks - Orlando, Florida

Shuck doesn't like flying. He's pacing around the jet, unable to sit still, no matter how much I try to get him to settle down and cuddle. He wants none of it. It's a good thing I decided not to feed him before we took off. He keeps dry heaving, and he's had two accidents already. I feel so bad for him. His tiny little body keeps shaking and his chocolate eyes bug out of his head as if asking, What's going on? What's happening? Why would you do this to me?

I feel helpless. There's still another hour and a half left in the flight. Part of me wants to tell the pilot to land and we'll drive the rest of the way. I want to tell them that my little guy is not handling this well and that I feel like I'm torturing poor Shuck. My stomach twists at the sight of him suffering; his eyes beg to make this stop. I know this won't kill him and he has to get used to flying, but when I see him crying and trembling beside me and I'm unable to console him, it makes me think, What if I can't comfort my little pineapple?

What if everything I do to help my baby is wrong and all I end up doing is hurting pineapple? If I can't calm down a dog, how am I going to be able to take care of a baby? Tears drip down my face as I stare at my little puppy, who is looking up at me, whimpering.

"Eve, what's wrong?" Lucas looks up from his phone.

I wonder who he talks to all the time since the work gig is up. He has done favors for the owners of the hotels and their properties, so he is allowed to stay at their establishments whenever he wants. What the favors are, I don't know and I honestly don't want to find out. It was the way he said *favors* that made me not want to know more. Nevertheless, he's constantly on his laptop or phone, working. His work is a mystery and I like it that way, for now. Angel business is not something I'm interested in, nor is it something I understand. As mortals, are we even capable of understanding something so foreign to our minds that we categorize mythology with fantasy? Most people have trouble accepting their neighbors' international customs. Is it possible to fathom celestial culture or politics? He's immortal. How could I begin to comprehend?

Right now, I'd rather revert to being blissfully ignorant about everything paranormal and read about it in fictional books, enjoying them as a story, not reality.

"Nothing, just nerves. Thinking about how I might not be a good mother. What if the baby doesn't stop crying and I can't help pineapple calm down? What will I do? How will I help pineapple? I can't be a mom," I cry.

He puts down his phone and scoots closer to me. "Eve, no. You are going to be the best mother in the world. Pineapple is going to be so lucky."

"I'm sorry, baby. I'm sorry, Shuck. I'm sorry. I can't."

"Eve, my queen, please calm down. You are going to make a wonderful mother. Poor Shuck is just a nervous first-time flier. You can't help that. But you can show him you're brave and strong and that there is nothing to be afraid of. Be a role model and maybe it will help him get over his fear," he says while wiping my cheeks. Lucas picks up Shuck, who doesn't enjoy being off the floor, but settles on my lap and starts licking my face like he's trying to lick away my tears.

"My brave little boy. Good boy," I tell him and feel his tail thump against my thigh as he showers me in kisses.

"See, he's already calming down and doing better. I'm sure after a couple more flights, he'll be a pro."

"I hope so. It hurts to see him so upset. It will kill me to see my child crying in any kind of pain."

"This child will never know real suffering," he says placing his hand on my stomach, just in time to feel a kick, which startles poor Shuck. "You are going to make an amazing mother. No more of that. No reason to cry." He wipes away any remaining tears, then wraps his arms around me. Shuck readjusts on my lap. It's a good thing he's so small or else he would have trouble fitting. "I think it's time for a little family nap."

I nod. I still haven't slept well since being rescued, no more than an hour or two. Down the hall is a separate room that has a bed and a little chair that will be nice if we travel after pineapple is born.

The upholstery on all the seats is a soft white leather, which I told Lucas was a mistake with a kid and dog, but he shrugged and said he would have them cleaned regularly or buy new seats. The carpet is black with white streaks that cleverly mark directions on the floor when the lights are off. There's a full galley kitchen with every appliance I could think of and a seat that folds out into a bed for Cleo, our flight crew. We could literally make a Thanksgiving dinner in the galley and not feel cramped; we'd just need to go on a long enough flight to cook the bird. The living room is nice, with a sofa seat that faces a big screen television, and there are four recliners surrounding a table. The jet can easily accommodate ten passengers, a flight attendant, a copilot, and a pilot.

"That sounds nice. A family nap. We won't get too many more of these." I wobble off the couch with Lucas's help. Shuck follows us down the hall, where I plop down on the ultra-soft bed that feels like a cloud.

"Of course we will. We will sleep whenever pineapple takes a nap. It might be the only way we'll get any rest."

Lucas climbs onto the bed and lies down, draping an arm over my belly. Shuck waits for us to get comfortable before jumping up and curling into a little ball at the foot of the bed.

As I sink into Lucas's embrace, part of me is still nervous of him, now that I know he's an angel. The other half has given up on being afraid and says screw it, I'm already in too deep. And in his arms, it just feels right.

The nap was over too soon, but felt amazing. Cleo, our flight attendant who I think Lucas poached from the private flight company she used to work for, knocked on our bedroom door fifteen minutes before landing with a cup of coffee and a cup of herbal tea. Apparently, she and the pilots are at our disposal whenever we need them. I asked about days off and holidays. Lucas said he took care of it. I'm sure they are all making a fortune.

As soon as the plane stops and the engines turn off, Shuck must know the flight is over and dashes to the door before it opens. He might have done well during the second half of the flight, but it still doesn't mean he liked it. I'll have to buy him motion sickness medicine the next time we travel.

A car waits for us as soon as we step off the plane. Within minutes, we are on our way home, but the driver is taking a different route, probably to avoid the grocery store where I was taken. From now on, I'll order groceries and have them delivered. I might even look into a personal grocery shopper. Lucas keeps saying I should do it, and it's not like money is an issue.

I look down at my phone and see two new text messages beside six phone calls from Ken. It's not that I haven't been interested in what he has to say. I'm more nervous about what I might confess. I feel safer talking to him at a distance. Seeing him in person would have been bad. For some reason, I have a feeling that if Ken and Lucas meet, Ken would not like Lucas. Even though he's an angel, I'm sure Ken would think our relationship wrong or alert some higher authorities and then they would try to hunt Lucas. Which would be a huge mistake on their part. Basically, I'm trying to prevent anyone else from dying. The power Lucas has makes him capable of creating an apocalypse. I really, really don't want to think what would have happened if they had killed me.

I still haven't asked him about his powers or if they are limited. Every time I attempt to ask him a question, I chicken out and decide I'd rather not know. It's a tug of war going on inside me. Overall, I feel like I can't leave him, hide from him, or avoid him, and honestly, he's done nothing but take care of us. The genuine moments we have shared are what I think about when I'm terrified of the strange, powerful man next to me. There's no denying the strong connection we have or my feelings for him.

So I'll protect him from the world and inadvertently protect the world from him. I look at my phone, swallow, and begin to type.

Hi, how's it going? Sorry I haven't responded. Been busy. Any news?

Seconds later, Ken texts back. He must have been waiting for me. *Where are you? Need to talk ASAP!*

In Florida. I can no longer travel back to the city. No more planes, not after that last flight.

It's important.

I can call you tonight around seven.

Can't say it over the phone.

Why not?

Three dots appear, then stop, then appear, then stop.

I look up from my phone and watch the driver hand the guard at the gate our pass ID to the neighborhood. Blocks away from home, I tuck my phone back inside my purse. If he doesn't respond, I'll still call him at seven and try to convince him to tell me the information he discovered.

"Home," Lucas says. "Are you excited to see your new backyard, Shuck?"

He wags his tail a little, still not happy about being in a moving vehicle. As soon as the car stops and Lucas opens the door, Shuck bolts out of the car onto the front yard grass. He stops and sniffs everything on the lawn and christens it.

It's hard coming back here.

The rental is parked in the garage next to the snazzy golf cart. The kitchen and living room aren't dusty. Lucas must have hired a cleaning agency to come in and dust the place before we came. There's so much to do before this really becomes a home for you, pineapple, before it feels like a home again for me. Sorry I'm so far behind, but you remember the little delay we had. Don't worry; everything will be ready for you. I place a hand on my belly as I walk down the hall into what will be your nursery. I stare at your room, its blank canvas. Fortunately, your Aunt Melisa will be here next week to help design it. I can't wait for you to meet her.

We order pizza from a local pizzeria and stuff ourselves. Afterward, Lucas excuses himself to the office to do some work. I mention who I am going to call and he just says to get information, don't give any. I reassure him I will tell no one, with an exception of Melisa, because we share everything. He agrees, gives me a kiss, and leaves Shuck and me alone in the backyard.

With my feet cooling in the pool, I stare at my phone. Ken never texted back. Fine.

The phone rings twice before he picks up.

"Eve, I've been looking at flights and I found a cheap one that leaves—"

"What? Can't you just tell me on the phone?"

"No, not everything. I'd rather tell you in person with your partner present. Some of it might… upset you."

"No. I'm afraid that will be hard to arrange. He's always traveling for work. Tell me what you can. I'd rather know now."

Ken sighs. "My contacts in Rome have discovered some older archives. A transcript from around twelve hundred A.D., documenting a woman being followed by demons everywhere she went while pregnant. It got so bad, she moved into a nunnery for protection, but the possessions didn't stop. Some nuns attacked the woman, so she fled to a monastery and stayed there until she died during childbirth, along with the babe. Seems everyone who was near her became possessed. It's the only occurrence they have found so far like your situation. They are still doing more work. For some reason, they wrote the records in some weird code. And from what they can decipher, some monks were also possessed, but it's written in a way to make it sound like the men were stronger than the nuns mentally, or something like that. The translation is very odd."

"She died, along with her baby?" Silent tears escape as I think of the terrified woman. Did she even have a chance to hold her baby? She tried so hard to deliver and save her child. Is that my fate? Maybe Lucas is right: We need professional help delivering you.

"Sorry. I'm also afraid that your partner might… or your neighbor will become possessed."

"I'm not worried about Lucas, but what about you?"

"Nothing can possess me. I made sure of that. Lucas? Are you sure you are safe with him?"

"Positive." I gulp as a bead of sweat drips down my forehead. "There haven't been any other possessions since that woman in the airport. Maybe it's just unlucky coincidences?"

"Huh. None?"

"Nope. Not that I know of." Crap. I just lied to a priest. It probably doesn't make it better that he's an ex-priest either. Fuck.

"Well, that's good news. Maybe I can hold off a few more days. As long as you feel safe."

"I'm fine. Really, I don't think you need to come down. What else were you going to tell me?"

"Nothing. There's just been a bigger uptick in possessions across the globe. Nobody knows why. I had thought for a minute that maybe there was a connection between you and them, but if it stopped happening, maybe I was wrong."

"I'll call you if anything else happens. Anything else?"

"Nope." He pauses like he wants to say something, but doesn't. After a few more seconds, I'm about to say goodnight but he says, "Stay safe. Be careful. I'm not sure this is over for you." The phone cuts off.

He knows I lied.

While having tea and coffee, Lucas told me about a new bakery that opened up, tempting me with chocolate croissants and cheese pastries with strawberries. It didn't take long to get me into the SUV.

At the store, I bought four. For myself. He of course got one plain croissant and a cappuccino. The tasty distraction worked until we pulled up to a building with the storks carrying pink and blue blankets in their beaks. Birthing Center. Something about that sounds cold. Enforced even.

The remodeled fancy ranch house is in a quiet development only three minutes away from the local hospital in case of emergencies, which might sound appealing to other women, but it only makes me nervous.

They set the backyard up to hang out and relax in. There's a dartboard on the fence and a tiki bar, hopefully without alcohol, even an ashtray with the remains of celebratory cigars. So this is the man's corner. Wonderful. I hate this place already. It's only missing a big screen television with sports.

A woman in her forties slides open the back door. She's wearing a sandy smock and matching pants. The clothing makes her look like the director of a yoga retreat. "Welcome, welcome. You must be Eve. Oh, you are so beautiful! Look at your bump! So precious. And you must be Lucas. I'm so happy to meet both of you. Please come inside. Can I get you anything: water, tea, coffee, a snack?"

"I'm fine, thank you. We just ate." We step into the house through the back sliding door and into a reception area that once was the living room. Cherry hardwood stained floors give the area a dark feel, but the yellow and orange couches and seats help brighten the room. Fresh tropical flowers in vases add a nice aroma to the air. A woman behind an open desk greets us and goes back to work.

The overly polite woman who I bet wants to talk about our energies and chakras shows us the pretty kitchen and the dining room that is free to use at any time during our stay. All topnotch appliances and sparkling clean counters.

Next, we check out the two identical examination rooms. They are comfortable rooms that kind of look like a doctor's office but have a laid-back feel. Down the hall, we enter the first birthing suite, the beach suite. It looks like a sterile hotel room with a beach theme. On the white washed plank walls are photographs of the beach and waves. The queen-sized bed looks comfortable and has a ton of fluffy blue and white pillows. There's a cushioned glider in the corner by the window and a large new couch. They stash away boxes of gloves and other medical supplies in unique hiding places that are just visible but not in your face. The bathroom is really nice. A huge walk-in shower with a bench, plus a large deep tub for water births or just to relax in. Double sinks and a separate toilet make the bathroom pretty luxurious.

It reminds me of the one they had where I was kept a prisoner.

The tour guide didn't want to let us leave without me making an appointment until I told her we were touring two other facilities and we'd let her know.

"You didn't like it," Lucas asks once the SUV's doors are closed.

"No. It was awful. Everything about it. Can't we just hire doctors to come to our home and have pineapple there?"

"It won't be as safe. What room would you give birth in?"

"The bedroom."

"What about a water birth?"

"Hell no. That sounds so gross. It's not a hot tub. The temperature is lukewarm, and it gets cold fast. I don't want to be all pruned if labor takes a while. Wading in the fluids and afterbirth sounds disgusting. No. Water births are not for me. I'd want to sit in the shower and rest. Let the warm water fall on me. That sounds relaxing."

"Fine, no water births. We could set up and hire a staff to be on call. If that's what you want, as long as we have a doctor and midwife present, I think you should be alright. The hospital isn't too far away either."

I think about the woman and child who supposedly died during childbirth. The more I think about it, the more I'm convinced the monks killed them, especially if they were also becoming possessed. If she had stayed home and never sought help from the church, she and her baby might have survived. "I don't think we'll need a hospital. It will take some organizing, but I think this is how I'll feel comfortable after everything. Do you think you can keep the staff from becoming possessed, just in case?"

Lucas nods as he drives down the highway, whizzing by the slow cars that appear to have nowhere to go. "Yes. You don't need to worry. As long as I'm by your side, no one will become possessed. I'll take care of everything."

When he says something like that, I worry, but at the same time, what's the point?

Katie Zaber

35 Weeks - Orlando, Florida

"So you're going to give birth here?" Melisa asks, shaking her head in disbelief. "Are you sure you won't want an epidural or real medical equipment in case of an emergency?"

"Positive. After what I went through, the last thing I want is to be at the hospital or anything that looks like a lab. I need to be comfortable and not have a panic attack while pushing this baby out," I say while rubbing my belly.

"I mean, I get it, but are you sure it's safe?" she asks while looking over the new hospital bed still wrapped in plastic and the little birthing area we have set up.

Tables, different-sized yoga balls for squats and stretching, a small ultrasound machine, oxygen tanks, IV stands, a portable shelf with different slots for gloves, gowns, alcohol wipes, tubes, and other medical equipment fill the corner of the master bedroom. There's also an inflatable tub that Lucas insisted on getting, just in case I change my mind. I argued that the water would get cold too fast, but he said he would take care of that, as always.

Everything is here; everyone is hired. If I went into labor right now, the room would spring into instant action. The doctor, doula, midwife, and nurse only live ten minutes away. I don't know exactly how much Lucas is paying them, but from the way they've been treating me, I'm going to guess it's a lot. It might be their yearly salary, if not more.

"Absolutely. Doctor Mitchell is fantastic. I feel safe with her. Plus, I'll have a midwife, doula, and a nurse to take care of me. There will be four highly trained people here to make sure everything goes well, and it will. I know it. I just need it to be here, in my home. Where I feel safe."

"Okay, Evie. As long as you have everything planned and thought out. Also, I was thinking I could come down. Give you a hand. I talked to my bosses, and they agreed I could start working remotely, if you want."

Tears swell in my eyes. I cried so much when we picked her up at the airport last night. My face was soaking wet by the time we got into the car, I was that overjoyed by the mere sight of her. She's always been closer to me than a best friend; she is the sister my parents never gave me. Without Melisa in my life, I don't think I would be as strong as I am. "Of course I want you here. I need you here." I say and hug her. "I never want you to leave."

"Good. It's going to be hard getting me to go. I won't want to leave. Especially since I have my own little house here and everything; it's perfect for me." She winks and steps away, looking at a bassinet. "We are supposed to shop together! You said you would wait!"

"I am, I am. We didn't buy that, I swear. My doula, Jill, gave that to me."

"What the hell is a doula, anyway? Like some birthing coach? Breathe! Breathe! Push! Push!" she says, laughing.

"They say it's good to have one, and Lucas wants me to be as safe as possible. I figure the more people taking care of me, the more relaxed he will be."

She cocks her head. "He's that nervous?"

"I think so. He's been a little anxious. Not as carefree as normal. I've never seen him snap at anyone before. I honestly wouldn't call what happened snapping, but he told the nurse, Elisa, that she was speaking too loud. It came out kind of harsh and out of nowhere. He apologized instantly and even bought her flowers. So I think he's nervous."

"Just as long as he isn't yelling at you."

"Never. He spoils me night and day."

"Good. He better treat you like a queen."

I laugh. "That's what he calls me: his queen."

"And is he your king?"

"Yes," I say, drawing out the s. "Eh, I'm still not one hundred percent comfortable with everything I know and what happened. I still have a ton of questions that I'm not ready to ask, mostly because I'm afraid of the answers, and I'm still working through everything else, but things are kind of back to normal between us."

"Have you been home alone yet?" Melisa knows how much I crave independence and personal freedom.

"Once. Lucas went to pick up bagels; he was gone for ten minutes before I had a panic attack. I got nervous and thought that every sound was someone trying to break in."

"You have Shuck now; he'll protect you, comfort you."

"He's a baby still." I reach down and pet my little shadow. The little guy never leaves my side. "Lucas had a security team come and install a bunch of additional features so if I press a button, everything locks. And I have a little panic room to hide in. It can fit four people. We converted a closet."

"A panic room. Lock yourself in until police come?"

"Until Lucas comes."

"Right," she draws it out and pauses. "Well, you're safe here. Plus, there are security gates and guards driving around. This place is pretty safe. Safer than other places. It's just going to take time. You'll get there."

Melisa hasn't treated Lucas differently since she's come to visit, but I can tell she's uneasy around him. She's monitoring him, just in case. I'm not sure what she's waiting or watching out for, but she won't turn her back on him. She has said nothing to me, but she hides her feelings, trying to protect me. I also think that's why she wants to move into the guest house. Either way, I love how brave she is to still be here beside me when all hell is breaking loose.

Ahem. "Ladies, your car awaits," Lucas says, poking his head into the room.

"You sure I should go without you?" I ask him, nervous about being taken or having someone become possessed around me. If he can prevent that from happening, I would like him to be with me constantly.

"I'm sure you will be fine for a couple hours together, with two personal shopping assistants and a personal bodyguard."

"You hired a bodyguard for me?"

"Yes. I thought Desmond might make you feel safer when you leave the house without me. He is the best, and I have worked with him before. He won't let anything happen to either of you."

The fact that Lucas knows this man makes me wary of who he is and what they worked on, but I decide not to ask. It's better that way. "What about possessions?"

"Desmond has dealt with those before as well. He is well-suited to protect you in my absence. I've made sure of it." Lucas looks so serious that I believe the man he hired isn't a normal man.

"What about everyone else?"

"Everything will be fine. I promise. Desmond has certain characteristics that will prevent that," he says without further explanation.

So Desmond isn't normal. "What will you be up to?"

"Working. Have fun. Shop for the baby, for yourselves, and buy everything and anything you want. Enjoy." He gives me a kiss before heading to his office.

I turn to Melisa. "You ready to go?"

She nods and watches the doorway where Lucas just stood. After a second, she smiles and wraps an arm around me. "So we have a no-limit credit card and were just told to buy everything and anything?"

"Yup."

A wicked grin spreads across her face. "This is going to be fun."

"How much do you think we spent?" Melisa asks as we sit down for lunch after spending the whole morning shopping for the nursery. In the distance, we can hear the jingle of Santa's bell as children line up to ask the big man for presents and take a picture with him. It's nice, but I don't like seeing it before Thanksgiving. The mall is decked in ornaments, twinkling lights, and Christmas whimsy. All the fall and Halloween decorations are down already. They need to stop rushing the holidays. Time moves fast; there's no need to rush it.

Desmond gives us space while we sit and eat, watching the area a couple seats away. I told our shopper assistants that we would be fine the rest of the day since all the big stuff was purchased. If we need any help carrying bags of clothes, we'll ask Desmond for a hand. He said nothing, but he did grunt. So I'm going to assume he agreed. The women have arranged for everything to be delivered tomorrow. The nursery is going to have every color of the rainbow. It will literally look like a splotch color palette. Happy and colorful. "Does it matter?" I ask and shrug.

"Nope. It doesn't." Melisa says in between slurping her milkshake and taking bites of her burger. "Do you wonder where it comes from? All his money?"

"Sometimes. And then I remind myself that I shouldn't tangle myself up in angelic affairs."

"You are in one."

I sigh, knowing I set myself up. "I don't know. I'm curious, but didn't that kill the cat?"

"Eh, you have nine lives." She shrugs and eats a French fry. "By my count, you've only used two. So you really didn't ask him anything?"

"Like what?" I ask her.

"I don't know. There are millions of questions. Like what's heaven like and how bad do you have to be in order to go to Hell?"

"Like sleeping with an angel bad?"

"I don't think that makes you bad. It just means you have good taste."

I put down my cheeseburger with extra bacon. "Taste? Part of me wants to run away. The other half wants to run into his arms. I've never been so conflicted."

She slurps her milkshake. "Then maybe you should find out more. It would help you decide."

"I don't think there's any decision for me to make. An angel wants me and I don't think he'd be so happy if I broke up with him. I'm kind of scared of what he would do if I ever did."

"What do you mean?" Melisa's forehead scrunches, her worry lines showing.

"He killed so many people with a single thought to rescue me. And it wasn't the only place where he went on a killing spree. He mentioned searching three other similar facilities. The thing that got to me was how simple, how easy it was for him. All the people, the staff, soldiers, they just started killing themselves or each other. They all deserved it, but if they killed me at that lab, I'm pretty certain Lucas would have gone mad. I'm not sure how many people would have died or if he would have stopped."

Leaning back in her chair, her face pales slightly. "Like he would have killed everyone?"

"It crossed my mind. Something cataclysmic. I honestly don't know how strong he is or what powers he has. He has endless wealth, is charming, charitable, respectful, and can kill a room of people with a thought. How many questions would you ask him?"

"So you do feel captive in the relationship."

"Kind of, but not. I don't know. I just wish none of this happened and that I never found out what he is or how dangerous." I take a bite of my burger and sip my vanilla milkshake. "What do you think? What would you do?"

"Get answers. That will at least stop some of those racing thoughts." She sighs. "Eve, you're not normal. You're different, and that's never scared me. So Lucas is different; why be scared of him? You shouldn't be scared of what's different; you should learn about it. And if you are both happy and he treats you well, that's all you need."

"You're right. I guess him being an angel isn't the worst thing. But I keep wondering, what if angels aren't what we think? Same with demons. What if we don't understand the dynamic or them at all? What if there is more to it than what we learned in church?"

"Like what?"

"I don't know. But now that I know witches, werewolves, vampires, and other things exist, it throws everything I knew out the window. Like, how does a witch cast spells? Where does that power come from? How did a bunch of witches grow stronger in my presence, as if a battery recharged their power and what's the connection... my child or me?"

"Have you asked Ken?" Melisa asks before taking the last two bites of her burger.

"I decided not to talk to him anymore. I'm certain if he found out about Lucas, things would turn sour fast. I don't know. I have a feeling that if the two of them meet, it would be bad."

"Why? If Lucas is an angel, wouldn't Ken want to meet him? Have some questions to ask?"

"He would probably see it as a bad thing. A bad omen. The fact that an angel wants to have a family on Earth..."

"Didn't you say there have been more possession cases that he's been dealing with?"

"Yeah, but I don't know if it's connected."

Melisa stares at something behind me, then smiles. "I know. We'll ask someone else."

"Huh?" I swallow my last bite of cheeseburger and crumple the wrapper.

"Come on; I have an idea." She gathers up all her trash and heads over to the garbage cans. I follow and carry my tray. "This way."

Immediately I see where she is taking me. "No. This is a waste of money."

"Excuse me? You have a pile of money to waste. Come on; this will be fun. Something to laugh about later. They are all phonies." She stops for a second and thinks. "Well, if this one is real, then maybe you will get some answers. Either way, it will be fun. And I've never had a psychic reading before. Let's see what she gets right."

Desmond gets up and follows us without saying a word. He's the strong silent type and looks lumpy. Like a tan pile of skin stuffed with knotty muscle. He's probably six foot seven, maybe an inch taller. He's a bald brute who probably terrifies everyone, but oddly makes me feel safer.

A woman with cinnamon-colored hair in a braid down to her knees sits next to the psychic sign that says twenty dollars for a five-minute reading. Filing her nails, she appears disinterested in the shoppers.

Melisa walks up to the woman. "Hi. We'd like two readings."

The mystic lifts her head slowly. Eerie green eyes stare at Melisa, then shift to me. "I've been expecting you. Follow me."

Melisa cocks her head to the side. "That's what she says to everyone. Get them freaked out before they even sit down. All theatrics."

Inside the woman's closet of a shop, there is a circular table with a white tablecloth and four folding chairs. There's no crystal ball. At least she's not that corny, but there are multiple tarot card decks, a teapot of steaming hot water, crushed herbs, and different symbols marked on the walls. The room feels odd. Like it's clean.

"My name is Lynn." Her eyes dart back and forth between the two of us, then settle on me. "I'll do your reading second. You're much louder. Pay first."

"Louder?" I ask, confused, taking out my credit card, hoping she can charge it.

"Your soul has much more to talk about. Don't worry; you'll have your turn." The psychic takes my card, swipes it, and passes it back. She then goes over to the pot of water and takes out two mugs. She puts some crushed leaves in the bottom of each cup before pouring the hot water over both of them. Then she brings the cups to the table, setting them in front of both of us.

I look down at the mystery tea. "What is this?"

"Caffeine-free Rooibos herbal tea. I do a tea leaf reading at the end. Drink the cup and I'll tell what your future holds by what is left behind."

"Rooibos tea? Is there anything else in it?" I ask and rub my belly, afraid the tea will make little spaghetti squash sick.

"Simple organic decaf tea. I get it from the tea shop a few doors down. It's packed with antioxidants. Plus it's good for the heart."

Melisa takes a sip and nods. "Tastes good. Not too hot. Did you put sugar in this?"

"Nope. It's naturally sweet."

I look behind me to see Desmond standing on the shop's threshold. He gives me one slight shake of the head before turning his back. What does he not like about this? If he thought my life was in danger, he would prevent anything bad from happening. Chills creep up my arms as I pick up my small cup of tea. The leaves stain the water deep reddish black. The tea is slightly sweet, with a hint of vanilla and cinnamon.

"What store sells this?" I ask, wanting to add it to my tea rotation. It's delicious.

"Just a few stores down, on the left. It's called Tea Time. Tell them Lynn sent you." She closes her eyes, takes a deep breath, mumbles a couple of words, and then opens her bright green eyes. "Give me your hands," she says to Melisa.

The woman looks at her palms and begins her reading. She tells Melisa that she will marry within the next four years and even adopt two children. We both snort and giggle. I really thought this woman was the real deal for a minute. Melisa married with two kids... that will never happen. She says that money will no longer be an issue and that she will experience happiness for a period before she knows true pain.

"What kind of pain?" Melisa asks.

"Loss. Extreme loss. I can't say who, but it will break you. However, you will heal with the support of your partner."

"Are you telling me a kid I adopt will die?" Melisa asks, a little too defensively.

"I can't say for certain. I just see a significant loss and grief in your future. Don't focus on that; we all experience tragedy at some point. This will just happen sooner, earlier than expected."

Melisa sits back and takes a sip of her tea, reminding me to do the same before it completely cools. "Anything about my kids or wife?"

"After the tragedy, your life becomes peaceful for another period before something happens. Not bad, but something impactful. A past will meet up with you. Someone you thought was dead will return. There's chaos, pain, and happiness for the rest of your life from that point on."

"So, you're telling me I only get brief moments of peace and happiness? That's all I have to look forward to? If you're going to give me a doom and gloom reading, at least give me advice, something to look out for." Melisa takes the last sip of her tea and gives the empty cup to the psychic.

She looks down into the cup, closes her eyes and says, "I have one bit of advice, but I don't think you will follow it."

"What's that?"

She opens her bright green eyes and points to me. "Stay away from her."

Goosebumps spread across my body. My eyes water. That is exactly what I was afraid of. That whatever I'm involved in is going to cause Melisa pain and suffering.

"No. Fuck, no! I'll never stop being there for Evie. Not for one second." Melisa stands and takes a step back, shaking her head. "No. She's my friend and you're crazy."

"I tell you what I see; it's up to you to decipher the information and decide what to do with it. Time for your reading," Lynn says, focusing her eerie eyes on me while extending her arms across the table and closing her eyes again. "Give me your hands."

I'm nervous, but I grasp hers.

"Your soul is dark and beautiful, unlike anything I've ever seen. Like lava covered with glitter. Sparkling and shimmering, but burning and smoldering. It's spectacular. You are something special, something unique. As well as your child." She gasps, as if in pain, takes in a deep breath, and screams, "Fire! Everything is burning! Everyone is burning! My skin, it blisters and peels. Your future, it's on fire!"

I reel away from the woman. Her breathing steadies. After a few moments, she looks up at me; her eyes become a softer color of green, almost normal-looking, but not quite.

"I'm sorry," Lynn says. "Sometimes when the vision is too intense, it makes me... intense."

All I can do is nod. I'm pretty sure she just glimpsed Hell, my future. The woman looks shaken, pale, and like she might pass out. At least she didn't become possessed, too.

I go to get up but Lynn picks up my empty teacup. She looks inside and drops the cup on the table, shattering the walls of the cup but somehow leaving the bottom fully intact. Clear as day, even after being dropped, there is a skull and crossbones symbol on the bottom of my cup.

The woman's face turns as white as the tablecloth. "I knew this was going to be a powerful reading. I just didn't know what it would entail. Be careful. Pray, if you're a woman of faith. Even if you're not, you may want a god on your side."

Melisa takes a step forward to see the leaves at the bottom of my cup. The blood in her face drains, leaving her face ashy. "What was on the bottom of mine?"

Lynn picks up Melisa's cup and tilts it for us to see.

It's a portrait of me.

36 Weeks - Orlando, Florida

Inside the fridge, there are a dozen assorted cupcakes on a crystal platter. Half chocolate tops with vanilla bottoms and vanilla tops with chocolate bottoms. The best of both worlds. I lick my lips and salivate at the decadent desserts covered in chocolate shavings. I'm supposed to grab a bottle of Champagne and glasses, not cupcakes, but they are tempting.

"Melisa!" I call out to her. "It's time for a toast."

She and her fiancé are in the den with Jim, watching the football game. Nobody expected her to propose and settle down. But to the surprise of all of us, she popped the question. I get to be her matron of honor. She wants Jim to be the officiant. Both of them want to wear wedding dresses. They want to surprise each other, but at the same time match or at least not clash. So I'm supposed to shop with both of them separately. This is going to be fun. There's so much to plan, so much to do, and they want to speed it up since they've been together for two years.

"Devil's puppet!" a raspy old voice shouts, startling me. The bottle and glasses crash to the floor. The Champagne cork pops off into the air, spraying alcohol everywhere. Shards of glass explode into glitter, then float away on an indoor breeze. I remember that voice. Jim's grandma. "Whore!"

Where is she?

"Brown to green, brighter and brighter," she says while cackling. "That's how I know the devil's in you."

She keeps yelling the same things over and over, her voice a booming weapon, echoing off the walls in ultrasonic bursts, blasting me with accusations, staggering me to the ground, disorienting me until I can't move.

"I'm not evil! I'm not! No!" I scream, holding my knees to my chest, rocking on my heels. Tears cascade down my face. "Stop! You're evil! You're the one who likes to torture people! Hypocrite!"

"Whore!" The word hits me in the back like an icy dagger, making me gasp for air. "Devil's in you!" It comes at me from the right and tries to break my ribs. "Imp! Devil's puppet!" The words slam into me at the same time, clobbering my head and pushing up from below my feet, trying to compress me, toppling me onto my side. More words fly at me from every direction, suffocating and squashing me. It feels like I'm being stoned to death with words.

Laughter roars through the structure with gale force winds, shaking the walls, blowing away the malicious slander tornado. The battering of violent words has stopped. But her words linger in my ears. Devil's puppet.

A stampede of children rattles the ceiling above.

Mischievous laughter followed by a loud crash comes from upstairs. Who's up there? I climb stairs that wind up and up, spiraling higher and higher, never ending. The landing keeps looking as far away as it did when I started to ascend. I feel like I'm running in place and there will never be an end.

Suddenly, an invisible force thrusts me up the stairs, landing in my house in Florida. Except all the walls are red and the floor and ceiling are black. The Caribbean charm is gone. All the colors, decorations, everything that made the place feel happy are missing. Vicious dogs bark outside, making me back away from the front door.

Giggles come from down the hall, from my little bunch of kale's nursery. Who could be playing in there?

Children's laughter gets louder and louder as I run down the hall. The walls are no longer red, but bleeding, oozing blood onto the floor. I try not to step on the thick, sticky fluid, but it's everywhere.

Amplified noises of children playing are the only thing I hear, drowning out all other sounds. Above, below, behind, in front of me, there's no telling where they are. They might be in the walls.

I reach the end of the hall and open the door to a room I've never seen. It's the nursery, but instead of a crib and rainbows, the walls, floor, and ceiling are black with thick veins running down them in a spiral design. Each surface appears to be breathing, billowing in and out as if alive.

A child sits on the floor, playing with dolls. Next to her is a baby in a swing. They are oblivious to what surrounds them. A little girl and baby boy with brown hair and blue-green eyes, clearly siblings, maybe two to three years apart. They look happy. Healthy. Beautiful. I want to hold them. Smell them. Kiss their beautiful faces. Brush their hair. Cradle them in my arms and never let them go.

Melisa shrieks from the other side of the house. Lucas lets out a blood-curdling cry. The girl holds up a doll, asking me to play with her, distracting me from the cries. Kneeling down, I pick up the doll, which is wearing a long blue dress and a black apron. It's almost like the dolls the Amish would sell with no face, but this has an X sewn in thick red thread for eyes. More screams come from down the hall. I don't want to leave the kids. A pain in my chest builds until it's unbearable. Tears run down my face as I kiss each child on the forehead and stand.

The screaming won't stop now. It's bloodcurdling. I have to make it stop.

I run down the long, bleeding hallway, screaming, "Melisa! Lucas!"

Smoke tendrils twirl in the air, slowly making their way down the red hall. I step into the empty kitchen, which is filling with smoke. No one is here. Where are the screams coming from? Are they in my head?

A burst of flames erupts. Hot white sears my eyes in a flash.

When I open them, everything is on fire. My clothes. My skin. My hair. Every part of me is on fire. I pat my arms, my legs, trying to smother the flames on my body, but they won't go out. It's as if I'm the fire.

The flames creep down the hall toward the room where the kids are playing. I try to stop the flames, stomp on them, suffocate them, but it's no use. They keep spreading up the walls, onto the ceiling and farther down the hallway. The children scream. They cry out for help. But it's too late.

The world is on fire and there's nothing I can do.

I wake up in a pool of sweat, in need of cold water. Getting out of bed is harder and harder to do, but I can do it when determined. Shuck lifts his head to see where I'm going. Realizing I'm only going to the bathroom, he puts his head back down.

The bathroom has nightlights, so I don't need to flick them on and blind myself. As soon as I start walking, the need to pee becomes urgent. The cold toilet seat on my butt feels great, besides the relief of peeing. I get up and wash my hands, then splash some cold water on my face. When I look in the mirror, my eyes are just as bright green as the psychic's, if not more. They look like glowing emeralds.

Floating in the pool relaxes my body. My legs and back are sore. All I feel is aches, but in the pool, all physical pains vanish and I don't have to fight gravity anymore.

I was sad to drop Melisa off at the airport, and also relieved. Inside her bag, I tucked a letter. In a couple of hours when she discovers it, I assume I'm going to get an angry text, but it might be in her best interest if I don't respond. Ever.

We talked about what the psychic said. Melisa keeps trying to convince me that the woman was a con artist and just tried to scare us out of our money. But I remember the grim look Lynn gave me when the teacup broke, the horror in her eyes. It was real. All of it was real. The poor woman had a vision and was sent to Hell, my hell. My future. So I'm going to assume everything she said about Melisa was true too.

In the letter, I told her not to come back. That this isn't a joke or some game. That the shit happening to me is real and I can't have her hurt by it. The fact that she keeps shrugging it off means she either can't mentally grasp it—which, in her defense, I'm having difficulties too—or she's trying to protect me by telling me it isn't real. Either way, it doesn't help. Keeping her miles away will at least ease my mind; she'll be one less person to worry about. I want her to be happy and if she's going to get married and have kids, as much as it would be cute for our kids to grow up together, I also want to keep her safe. Lynn warned her about me and she won't listen. After everything I've seen, I will.

Angels, demons, witches, werewolves, vampires, psychics, oh my. The list keeps growing and I'm one of them. Lucas mentioned I must have some psychic abilities. Who would I even talk to about them? There's no way I can tell Ken. I'm pretty sure the church is against psychics and witches. If he found out about me, he might burn me at the stake.

Ken has stopped texting all the time. He's only called once since the last time we talked and I sent him a text saying everything was fine. That there have been no possessions, and I was having family over for the next few weeks. He didn't respond. I know he knows I lied, and he's waiting for an apology or for me to say I was wrong and need help. But I have everything under control. And if I can learn how to control whatever power I have— which is something I don't think he would recommend—even better. He's probably a witch hunter in his spare time.

I keep thinking about Annabel and Bell and wonder if they found each other. Bell told me if I say her name six times, she will come to my aid. She didn't explain it, nor did I ask how. There wasn't time and my mind was spinning. Since being rescued, I've searched online for Bell or Annabel Belcan, but have found nothing. There's no information on a coven either, but I also don't know where they are from. The only people who might be able to help me are them. If only I could call them.

Saying Bell's name six times sounds silly. Like it would never work, but then again, I now know things like that do.

I look at Shuck, panting in the sun. The poor little guy wants to go in the pool, but is too scared. Even on the first step, the water is almost over his head. He looks thirsty. I need water too. I get out of the pool and he follows me to the outdoor kitchen, complete with a filtered water system. My water bottle keeps everything nice and cold, and so does his expensive water dish. I put his dish in the shade and tell him to sit. He won't stay. As soon as I walk away to float, he follows. Fine. I pick him up and carry him into the pool. When his paws touch the water, his legs start paddling like his life depends on it.

"Shuck, calm down. It's okay. I got you," I tell him while holding him close, but not so much that he scratches me. I bring him back to the stairs and he stands on the top step. His little head pokes out of the water. "At least you're cooler."

He looks so pissed.

"Fine." I pick him up and take him out. Thank god we don't have an actual grass backyard or else he'd be making a mess. There is some fake grass that he runs over to and rolls around on, attempting to dry off. The fake grass never gets hot and also feels nice on the feet. Bonus, we don't have to take care of it and that's one less person coming here to clean or do some type of maintenance.

I sink back into the pool. What do you think, kale? Should we say her name six times, just to see what happens? Will she appear in front of us instantly, transporting here, or will she arrive on a broom?

Bell Belcan, Bell Belcan, Bell Belcan, Bell Belcan, Bell Belcan, Bell—

"What's wrong?" Bell asks.

A voice pops into my head, making me splash. "Hello?"

"You don't need to talk aloud, just think it. Do you need me there right now?"

"No. No, I just didn't know how this worked. I'm sorry for bothering you." I think and try not to think of anything else, which is hard. When actively trying to not think of anything, a hundred random thoughts run through my head. What else can she hear or see? Can I see anything?

"I'm not busy. I'm home finally, with my mother."

"You found your mom? I'm so happy for the both of you."

"Yes. After we escaped, I found her preparing to attack north of Piedmont. Just an hour south from the base we were at. She was surprised to see me. Even more surprised when I told her how we all escaped. How are you? How is your little one?"

"Not done baking yet. I have questions that you might be able to answer."

"What kind?"

"The kind I'm terrified to ask."

"Where are you?"

"Florida."

"What part? We aren't too far. Our home is in northern Florida. Would you like us to come for a visit?"

"I live with the man you met, Lucas."

Bell stays quiet. *"I'll answer what I can now."*

She doesn't like him at all. I thought so. "Does this count as helping me?"

"No. I figured you'd end up calling my name out of curiosity."

"I don't know how any of this works. I'm sorry. I think I need training. I think I might be a psychic or maybe a witch."

"You're not a witch. It's possible you're a psychic. But why would you think that?"

"I've been having dreams. They feel so real. I think they might be my future or mean something. Like visions."

"When did the visions start?"

"I've always had vivid dreams. After my friend and I went to a psychic, they've only gotten more intense."

"Are you dreaming about what she told you?"

"Sometimes."

Laughter fills my head. *"It's your hormones, dear,"* Annabel says.

"Annabel? How, how are you able to talk to me too?"

"Connections that I have with my daughter, sitting next to her, spells, things you don't understand."

"So you think everything that the psychic said, the dreams I've had, are all hormones?"

"What did the psychic say?" Annabel asks. *"Most are cons."*

"What if her eyes turned bright green?"

"What did she say?" Bell asks, all the laughter stripped from her voice.

"She did a tea reading. On the bottom of my cup, there was a skull and crossbones. On my friend's, there was a picture of me in tea leaves."

"That doesn't mean death how we know it. Death isn't a bad thing. It can also symbolize new life," Annabel says, sounding motherly.

"From what the psychic said at the reading, I don't think so."

We spoke in my head for about fifteen minutes before my head started to throb. They said that the fact I could hold the connection between the three of us for that long means I am powerful. What I'm powerful in is a mystery to them. But they said it's hard to determine these things from a distance. They know that I at least have some type of psychic powers.

When I asked if they could come visit me, they said they would rather not enter *his* house. They wouldn't comment further, saying they know he's powerful, more powerful than anyone Bell has ever met and they want nothing to do with him.

But since we rescued everyone together, they felt they owed me a debt and would help guide me as much as they can. I'm curious, and it would be nice to see both of them without a metal fence or being completely invisible. We talked about getting together soon, most likely after the baby is born.

My phone rings, but it's too far away. I'm still floating in the pool. The weightless feeling really makes my back feel amazing. Maybe Lucas is right about water births.

Lucas strolls out and picks up my phone, walking it to me. "I don't recognize the number. It's coming up Nebraska."

"No." I splash my way to the pool stairs, dry off, and grab my phone. I haven't talked to them since we bought the house. It's been weeks, months. They don't even know I was gone. What could they possibly want?

Lucas gives me a puzzled look. "What's wrong?"

"I don't know why they are calling. They never call."

"Who?"

"My parents."

"Wonderful. Pick up and say hello; invite them down. They can stay in the guest house. It would be nice to meet them," he says with a wicked grin. I can't tell if he's trying to be nice or tormenting me. Maybe both.

I stare at the phone. They are the last people I want to deal with right now. A conversation with my mother is only going to make me want to hit my head into a wall until I black out, and my head already hurts. My dad won't be able to get in a single word. This is not what I want to do today.

"Hello."

"Bee," both of my parents say at the same time.

"We thought you weren't going to pick up. Your mom thought you were in labor."

"No, not yet. I've got a few weeks left."

"Well, I got nervous," my mom says. "I've been thinking about when you were born. How scared I was, how excited, how I didn't have my mother around, and that I secretly wished I did. I've also been thinking about the last time we saw you."

Nope, wasn't prepared for this today. Not a heartfelt conversation with my parents on a long-distance phone call. I refill my water and stretch out on the patio lounger next to Lucas. Shuck sees the both of us sitting down and decides he wants a lap to sit on and jumps up on Lucas, giving him a damp surprise. Lucas groans and moves the dog, but it's too late. His shorts have a wet spot in the shape of Shuck's body.

It's hard for me to hold back my laughter as my mom tries to have a heart-to-heart. "Oh yeah, about what?"

"Well, you're right," my mother says, almost knocking me over. She has never said those words to anyone. Thank god I'm sitting. "Your father's right. I've been an awful mother."

"We've been awful parents," my father cuts in.

"We haven't been there for you like we should have. But that's going to change. We wanted to come down before Christmas. Spend time with you, if you'll have us," my mother says with hope in her voice.

My stomach does a twist and I'm not certain ice cold water was the best thing to guzzle before hearing that. I fight back the urge to vomit. When the silence has gone on for too long, I finally respond. "Wait, when?"

"Your mom and I were thinking mid-month. Your due date, it's Christmas, right?"

"Yes."

"Well, we wanted to come down the week before the holiday. Spend some time with you before that little miracle is born, if the baby is on time. I'd love to pick out some cute clothes, go shopping with you. Meet your partner," Mom says, sounding curious.

"Ah, yeah, that sounds great. I'm just so surprised." I rub my temples; I'm going to need to lie down if I have any hope of getting rid of the headache before it turns into a migraine. "What day are you coming?"

Katie Zaber

37 Weeks - Orlando, Florida

The baby dropped yesterday and has stopped moving as much, making me slightly worried even though I know this can happen weeks before labor. It's weird how I miss the constant rolling waves under my skin as baby squirms inside; baby still does, but not as much. Now when I feel canary melon, it's a painful kick into my lungs that makes it hard to breathe. Sorry, baby. Your space is shrinking and Mom isn't going to get much bigger. Please be considerate of me.

Nevertheless, we wanted Doctor Mitchell to come by and do an examination. So far, she's done this twice at our home baby ward. Both times, she has said we are right on target and healthy. The gel she uses when she's looking at the baby is always warm. I made that a must when we bought the ultrasound machine. It's smaller than the ones in normal doctor offices, but it works just as well.

She takes the wand and moves it around my belly, smearing the warm gel while humming a tune. The doctor has delivered over a hundred and twenty-three babies this year alone. She had her own practice for eleven years before opening her own birthing center. She told me there has never been an issue she couldn't handle. Plus, she has worked with the midwife, Mary, and nurse, Elisa, for years. The doula, Jill, was highly recommended by her for at-home births. Really, the whole team has gone above and beyond to make me feel comfortable. They know I've experienced some trauma when it comes to doctors and are extra cheery but not corny, and also compassionate but not fake. Each person really seems to care. They all get an A++ rating.

"Looks like your little one is doing great. Baby is getting ready to make its debut. Say hi, Mommy!" Doctor Mitchell says while showing me the screen.

My baby is so beautiful. Everything is where it belongs. Little canary melon is even sucking its thumb. It's amazing how fast you've grown, from starting out the size of a seed to growing into a melon. "Do you think the baby will be coming out soon, like this week?"

"No. No, I don't think we'll be seeing this little one for a couple more weeks. Baby is still very comfortable, even if you aren't. No, I think you are fine to go about normally. Have you lost your mucous plug yet?"

"I don't think so. Nothing slimy has come out yet."

"Good. That means you have plenty of time."

"So a little road trip; do you think that would be okay?"

"How far?"

"A couple of hours."

She gives me a blank stare.

"Three hours. I'd be away for three nights. I'll be back in four days and can do another examination then."

"I think you should be fine. I don't see any signs that you will go into labor soon. Make sure you stop and stretch periodically. Set an alarm for every forty minutes. Get out of the car and move around for ten minutes. Do a lap or two around the car and stretch. Your hips will be hurting, but you should be fine. Remember to wear you back brace; it will help."

"Constant stretching and urinating. I think I can handle that."

"Be careful."

"I will." Don't worry, Doc. I'm only going to see a witch duo and test out my abilities at thirty-seven weeks. What can go wrong?

I've been speaking to Annabel and Bell. They agreed that I could spend a couple nights at their home, since they refuse to come here. They really don't like Lucas. I think they appreciate what he did, but he downright terrifies them. Honestly, I can sympathize. As much as I care for him, his power and capabilities terrify me. Anyone in their right mind would be petrified of what he could do.

Once the doctor is done, I clean up and tell Lucas my plan. Which he doesn't like in the slightest, but won't deny me my freedom. He's left the house a couple more times, and I was fine. Slightly nervous, but I felt calmer. Really, the dreams, the electrical glitches, and my eyes looking like emeralds make me more anxious. I've tried to remember the last time my eyes were brown. It might have been before I was pregnant.

The need to know more about myself outweighs the safety risks. Knowing my magical limits and strengths can potentially keep us safer. In most of the books I used to read, the only time the person with powers accidentally hurt the people they loved was when they didn't learn how to use them correctly. I won't do that to my baby. I won't be that reckless. Plus, I really want to know what I'm capable of and unfortunately, Lucas says he doesn't know anything about my powers. So he's no help on that subject.

To calm his mind and just in case, I checked out the route to their house. I pass by three hospitals, literally one an hour. There is also one only twenty-five minutes from their house in case of an emergency. I just won't tell him there is no labor and delivery department there. I should be fine, especially since I've been cleared by Dr. Mitchell. Yeah, I know I'll be uncomfortable, miserable, and achy the whole ride; however, if I learn anything about myself, it will be worth it.

The thing I'm worried about the most is a random possession. I don't think the Belcans are weak-minded and can be possessed, but I'm afraid if I need gas or if an emergency happens and I need help, someone will die. Right now, I think that's my biggest risk. Even though the women told me I have nothing to worry about with them, that they are too strong to succumb to that.

For extra caution—I don't know if this will work. It might be stupid— I bought a blessed cross to wear. Maybe it will protect others from us—if that's even what's happening. The pendant felt heavy when I put the chain around my neck this morning, but my skin didn't have an allergic reaction, so it must be real gold. It's tucked under my shirt while my locket is displayed proudly.

"Are you sure about this?" Lucas asks, helping me with my bag. He's upset that I won't bring Desmond. The mother and daughter told me to come alone. That they really don't trust anyone, especially after the ordeal they just went through. It's understandable. But they never said I couldn't bring my guard pup.

"I'm positive. Look how big Shuck has gotten," I say, holding up my puppy, who instantly starts licking my face, squirming and wagging his tail a mile a minute. We've gone on a car ride every day, going to parks and different fun places that he loves to go to and hates to leave. I think his fear of the car is finally over. The little pup has been gaining three pounds a week. Before we know it, tiny Shuck is going to be a big cuddly monster. I set him down on the passenger seat in his little doggy car seat and pat his head. "He's a big boy now; he'll protect me. It's a straight drive to their house. They will fill up the car with gas before I head home, to limit any interaction with people. It will only be three nights. I'll be home in four days. We'll go out to celebrate week thirty-eight over a nice dinner. I'll let you pick the place. But I'll have you know, I'm feeling something fancy and expensive."

He smiles for a second, then shakes his head. The remains of a smile fall from his lips. "Do you trust them? They are witches."

I tilt my head and give him a sideways glance. "How can I trust you? You're an angel who has lied to me, and I'm sure you still are."

He looks down but nods. The truth hurts. "If you ask questions, I'll answer them."

"We'll have that conversation when I come back. I think I might be ready to know more and talk. So you pick the place and make the reservation. Make it private dining." Lucas looks worried, equally nervous about the conversation, and maybe scared I'll never return. I grab his hand. "I will come back. This is my home and I feel safe here, in your arms, even if some things need to be cleared up."

He releases a sigh as a half smile creeps across his face. "Remember, any lies I've told you were only for your protection." He puts his hands on my shoulders, sees the locket, and touches it gently. "My queen, you make me so happy, I just want you safe and content."

"I am."

He nods but then makes a *tsk* noise. "I won't know where you are or how to find you. What if you don't come back? What if they do something to you? I don't like this."

He's got me there. I should give the address to someone just in case. "Fine. I'll text the address to Melisa. You have her phone number. If you don't hear from me or I don't come back, she'll give you the address. Not before."

She already knows about my trip and is pissed I'm doing it alone, but understands. She asked me to wait until she moves down and that we'd take the ride together, but that's closer to my due date, so it's even riskier. That letter I wrote, she said she never saw it and I'm crazy if I think she'd not just show up at my front door.

"That's better," he says, looking a little less worried. "I'll miss you."

"I'll miss you, too." I will miss him. Since he's rescued me, this will be our first night apart. Even though I'm weary of him being an angel, and what that means exactly, I will miss him.

He gives me a long and passionate kiss, tempting me to stay for a little longer, then kneels down and places a kiss on canary melon. "Be safe. Call me. Please check in with me and call me every hour while driving. Once you get there, call me again. I need to know you're safe."

"I will. I will call you whenever I stop to pee, which will be often. Before I go to bed, when I first wake up, when I leave; I'll call the whole time."

"Be careful. Keep the taser in hand's reach everywhere you go."

"It's on my key chain; I'll be holding it in my hand." The little thing looks like a USB stick with a button, but it packs a punch. If I shock a normal person with it, they would drop or at least flail around for a moment, giving me time to run away. I'm not stupid. I know that this little device won't do shit to a possessed person. If bullets could punch a hole through that nurse's chest and she could still speak, this little taser is just going to annoy them.

"I promise. Nothing will happen. I'll be fine." I reach up on my tiptoes and give him one last kiss before I climb into the SUV.

"See you soon. Drive safe," he says, leaning in one more time for another kiss, then closes the car door.

It's moments like this that make me think he genuinely cares for us. The look on his face, like what I'm doing is torturing him, but he still allows me to make the choice.

In return, I'll prevent him from doing anything catastrophic. I'll keep him happy. He's keeping me happy, safe, and wealthy. It's a fair exchange. Even if it isn't love, he called it fate. Maybe for him, it's the same thing.

For half the ride, I was on the turnpike before turning onto the county roads, heading deeper into the swamps bordering Georgia. Overall, it was an easy, scenic drive. Before leaving, I turned off all the other ways Lucas could, if he wanted to, track me. I really want to respect the Belcans. GPS said I would arrive in three hours and three minutes. Because of the pee and stretch breaks, it takes closer to four and a half hours.

I called Melisa, like I had promised, and gave her the address. She told me what items she packed and what is left on her to do list, getting ready for the temporary move. Lucas will fly the jet up there so she can load it up with everything she's bringing down. She is basically making the guest house her own—after my parents leave. There's no way my parents are staying in the same house as me when they visit. We need that buffer or else there will be a fight.

As much as I'm terrified for her and what the psychic said, I knew Melisa wasn't going to let me keep her safe. She's too stubborn. And even though I'm scared, I'm also happy she's by my side. I don't know if I can actually do all this without her support. It would be like losing a sister. My only sister.

Once I pull off onto another county road, I realize how rural the area has become. If they serve me alligator for dinner, I'm not sure how I'll react. I've heard it tastes like chicken, but I'm not certain baby will stomach that.

I make a turn down a wooded dirt road near Moccasin Swamp. Their house should be at the end. Really, it could be their driveway. I don't think there are any other houses. If there are, they are well hidden.

Along the dirt driveway, cypress trees block out most of the sun, allowing only small spots to penetrate the swamp grass. A sparkle in the trees catches my eye. It looks like a wind chime, made out of wood, glass, flowers, rocks, and shells.

It's not the only one. I slow the car and study the woods. They are everywhere. Tucked inside the Spanish moss, in tree crooks, and dangling from branches. No two are alike. I can't help the feeling that someone is watching me. Almost like the wind chimes are eyes.

A small raised log cabin with a freshly painted white porch and manicured garden is at the end of the street. Behind the house is the swamp, and what looks like a dock. A faded green Oldsmobile sits in the driveway, collecting rust. The front door opens. Two women who look like spitting images of each other, except one has more gray hair than black, step onto the porch.

Before I get out of the SUV, I put Shuck's leash on and gather my overnight bag, and the peach pie I brought for dessert. Shuck sniffs at everything as we walk past but sticks close to me. Maybe he smells the prehistoric predators swimming by and knows he would make a tasty snack. The smell of sweet vanilla, citrus, and spices hangs heavy in the air. Not too far away is a beautiful magnolia tree that must be gorgeous when in bloom.

"Hello! I'm so glad to properly meet the both of you. Thank you for inviting me."

"It's my pleasure, dear. Eve, you look fantastic." The older of the two, I assume Annabel, places a hand on my belly. "This one is strong. Almost ready to come out. Not yet, but by the end of the month, you will be holding this little one in your arms. Perchance on the winter solstices,"

Annabel says, then brushes a thick lock of smoky gray hair out of her face. She scrunches her face and looks at Shuck. "Who is this?"

"My guard pup, Shuck. Wow, you have a lovely property. Here, I brought this for dessert." I hand the pie to Bell who takes it, but steps away from Shuck.

"Thank you," Annabel says, kneeling down to pet the dog carefully. "Tell me Eve, do you feel anything different about this dog?"

The way they look at Shuck is how I'd look at a venomous snake. Annabel isn't as afraid as her daughter, Bell, who has taken a step back from my little furball. I look down at my little guy. His ears are floppy, his tongue is hanging out of his mouth, and his tail is wagging, excited to be outside with all the new smells. I scoop him up and inspect his wriggling body. "Nope. Looks like a normal puppy to me."

"You're not a witch," they say in unison.

"If you were," Annabel continues, "you'd know something was off. That there was something different about your dog."

"I don't sense anything. He just seems like a normal mutt."

"How 'bout Lucas? What do you sense about him?" Bell asks.

"Nothing."

"How 'bout us?"

I shrug. "I don't get any weird feelings."

Annabel shakes her head and folds her arms. "Normally, any ordinary person would sense something wrong when approaching your dog. You know that sensation when the hair stands up on the back of your neck? When your brain urges you to skedaddle? It's when normal humans are exposed to something taboo and it sends them running in the other direction. Think of it as a sixth sense sort of thing. That's what keeps us from venturing into bad places where the real evil hunts."

"Your sense doesn't seem to work," Bell says plainly. "Are your eyes always this shade?"

"No. Normally they are brown and only change when I'm moody. They haven't changed since I became pregnant, I think. Does everyone really get freaked out around you two?"

"Typically, when we are out in public, people avoid us. They will hurry past or cross the street to walk away from us."

Why don't I get that feeling? How is that beneficial? If I could sense something supernatural, wouldn't that help protect me? Is this my power, or is it my baby's?

"Interesting," Annabel says, eyeing me like some mystery. "Let's discover what else you can't sense."

"I'll show you your room," Bell says, opening the front door into their small cabin.

A small living room is big enough for a worn loveseat, two rocking chairs, and an end table. There's no television or any electronics, only a couple books and a battery-powered radio. Down the hall is my bedroom. A water basin sits on a table; I hope there is running water. Lace curtains cover the windows, allowing spots of light to shimmer in. The room doesn't have a musty smell like I had expected. Instead, it smells like the fresh-cut flowers in the vase on the nightstand.

I put down my bag. "Thank you. This is perfect."

"Glad we could oblige. We'll be in the kitchen, getting lunch together. Join us when you're ready."

"I'll be out in a minute." I send Lucas a text, letting him know I arrived and am about to eat lunch and that I'll call him later.

Shuck is still on his leash and that might be best, so he doesn't get into anything that he can destroy with his puppy teeth. He looks ready to explore the house and property, his tail wagging nonstop. Down the hall, I hear cabinets opening and closing. Their kitchen must be the biggest room in the house. It's almost as long as the whole structure. Different dried herbs bundled with twine hang from the rafters. There's a minifridge and oven with their electrical cords going out the window. They might be the only electrical appliances besides the blender on the counter. Some cabinets have doors, others don't, and hold rows of different spices, I think. There are a lot of jars filled with different colors.

"Sit down. I'm making fresh cornbread and we're reheating some Brunswick stew from last night," Annabel says as soon as I enter the kitchen.

"Thank you. That sounds great."

Above the stovetop, there is a shelf with candles and a little statue. Symbols in terra-cotta paint decorate the wall behind the shelf. Actually, now that I'm staring at it, the shelf could be an altar. "How long have you lived here?"

Without turning her head, Annabel says, "My whole life. This is my great-grandmother's home. My grandfather built it with his own hands. It hasn't changed much."

"Wow. Were they witches too?"

"It runs in the family," Bell says as she finishes stirring a pitcher of sweet tea. She grabs three glasses and the pitcher, bringing them to the table. "Most know from an early age that they are different, like the rest of their family. It's normal for parents and grandparents to teach the kids."

"I always felt different, but didn't know what was different about me," I say. "My parents don't speak about their parents. If I ask them questions, they change the subject."

"That's a shame you don't know them. I loved growing up with all my grandparents, aunts, and uncles," Annabel says as she takes a tray of hot cornbread out of the oven, filling the room with the delicious smell.

"Did they all live here?"

"Not in this house. But there are other houses on the property."

"How many acres is the property?"

Annabel carries a plate of steaming cornbread cut into pieces to the table. "Fifty."

The driveway, the space the house takes up, is a tiny fraction. I wonder how many people live on their property and in the other houses. "Fifty acres. Wow. That's a lot of land."

"We like the privacy it gives us." Annabel hovers over a pot on the stove. She gives it a stir and then swipes some of the juice off the ladle. She licks her finger. Happy with the way it tastes, she nods and takes a couple of bowls off the shelf and begins serving the stew.

While eating, they tell me a little more about their family. How they are all healers, but added that those who know how to heal the body know how to harm it, too. They like to grow their own food and rarely go to the supermarket. They go once every other month to pick up pantry staples. Otherwise, they trade with their neighbors. One of them raises pigs, another cows and goats. Bell takes care of a flock of chickens. There are also a few hunters that will sell rabbit, deer, alligator, and other meats and their skins. Their community is pretty self-reliant and they like it that way. As much as it sounds like a ton of work, it also sounds peaceful to live like that.

After lunch, Bell asked if I could help her in the garden. They need to gather up all the tomatoes and get ready to can them before the temperatures drop. Bell said a prayer in a language I've never heard before, spoken very softly before we started plucking vegetables. There were a few words I could pick out that sounded Latin, but I'm uncertain. When she finished, she explained it was to ask for permission to take what was ripe to sustain ourselves and not waste the plant's precious gift. I nod and keep to myself that God isn't listening and could care less. That I know from a semi-reliable resource that God is gone, which is part of some questions I plan on asking Lucas later.

As I pick plump tomatoes, a shimmer in the trees catches my eyes. "What are all the wind chimes in the trees for?"

"They are wards. They protect the property. Mom and I make them and repair them all the time."

"How many are there?"

"Over a hundred. We have been reinforcing them since our escape. Never know when you need some more protection. An extra set of eyes and ears."

"When you were taken, were you at home?"

"No. Fortunately, they didn't know where we live and attacked our coven while we were gathering for a weeklong summer solstice celebration."

"How many did they get?"

"Our twelve members and their families. We camp out together and make it a family event, to get the younger generations involved. But it wasn't just our coven. Over the years, Shade has been targeting others like us. Attacking, rounding up everyone that isn't vanilla."

"That's their name. The people who took us, Shade?"

"Not sure; it's the name we gave them. They are some division of the government, but if you ask the government about them, they say they don't exist. Shade changes their name and headquarters frequently. Their bases, like the one we were in, are usually hidden in odd corners of the country. Open land for miles, then suddenly an armed base."

"Why Shade?"

Bell puts down her basket of tomatoes. "They act like specters, ghosts. No one knows a thing about them. They come and take, then leave without a trace."

The day I was taken was a blurry nightmare. The woman and men in the van and on the plane that smelled freshly bleached. They moved fast and hard. Hopefully, they have been crippled and if not, I'll find out more information on them and tell Lucas to kill them all, except Crystal. I want to kill her myself.

"How long did it take to get back here?"

"It took us a long time to free everyone. We were afraid that the whole property would be bombed. You know how those sick people can think. Kill everyone they've been holding prisoner. We kept waiting for that to happen as we packed everyone off the base. The weres shifted as soon as they were out of the wards and took off into the woods. Everyone else needed transport out of Missouri."

I think back to that day and realize I don't remember the helicopter ride or getting off and onto the jet. From the moment I knew I was safe, my brain stopped processing. I don't remember any of it. It's more of a fuzzy memory than anything. Most of the time I was in shock, trying to put together everything I had learned. Between the prison, the prisoners, and Lucas coming to our rescue, there was a lot to digest. I should have been more aware. Helped more people escape. It's no wonder Lucas tried to whisk me away as fast as possible. He might have anticipated a bomb too, while I was stuck in a state of shock. "I'm sorry we didn't stay to help or do more."

"Don't be. Honestly, it probably was best that you guys left as fast as you did. We were all"—she thinks for a moment before continuing—"grateful for what he did. But the man makes me feel uneasy, along with every member of our coven. He gives me the feeling that tells me to run, haul ass the other direction and don't stop to ask why. Eve, I like you. I think you're a good person. I can't say what Lucas is, but he is not something to mess with. Like playing with an ancient, loaded weapon without instructions, someone is bound to get hurt."

"Do you know what he is?" I'll keep his secret, but why are they so afraid?

"Nope. Don't know and don't want to, either. I just know he is mighty and so is his destruction."

"Good day, sweet ladies!" An older man with dusky brown skin covered with freckles and frosty hair comes walking down a trail I didn't notice before. He's holding a couple of fish strung up on a line. "Your ma start cooking dinner? Thought I'd drop by with some extra catch."

Bell waves. "Nope. We just finished lunch. Those fish will make a tasty dinner."

Shuck starts barking frantically. His head swings from me to the man. His fur stands up on his back, making my mystery mutt look bigger. I've never seen my little guard pup actually try to guard. "Shuck. Stop that. It's okay," I say as I bend down to pet and reassure my little guy. "Calm down. He's a nice guy. It's okay. Stop barking."

After a few moments, he stops barking but doesn't calm down. A quiet, nonstop, throaty growl continues.

Bell brushes dirt from her hands onto the smock over her dress. "Mister Merrill, I'd like you to meet Ms. Eve Burns."

"Pleasure to meet you, Ms. Burns. Are you familiar with these parts?"

"Thank you, Mister Merrill. I am not. I just moved to central Florida. This area is lovely." Shuck growls at the man, but he doesn't come any closer, giving the dog his space. "Shuck, behave. I'm so sorry, Mister Merrill; I don't know what's gotten into my dog today."

"Some dogs just don't like me. It happens. Might be time to wash my socks again," he says with a cackle. "Perchance if there is time, I'll take you down some trails and show you some of the other local beauties besides these fine ladies," Merrill says, winking at Bell, his smile reaching from ear to ear. "I know where some of the prettiest and oldest gators live and where the ancient giants slumber. Now, I best be getting these fish to your ma so she can turn them into something delicious."

Even after he goes into the house, Shuck is still unhappy, glaring at the door. "I wonder what's gotten into Shuck? He's never acted this way before."

"His senses still work," Bell says, moving to the next tomato plant.

"But Shuck wasn't upset around you or your mother."

"Mister Merrill isn't a witch."

"What is he?"

"What could make your dog go nuts?"

I think for a second. "Is he a werewolf?"

"You know, I find it so odd that you couldn't sense him. Normally people get freaked and won't look at him or speak. They can't explain why they are afraid of him, but they instinctually know they are next to a predator and can't fight the urge to run away. You don't get those urges, huh?"

"No, I guess not. Why would that be helpful? Sounds more like it is going to get me killed."

"Something is bound to kill you one day. Powers are only useful if used correctly. You know nothing about yours. Soon you will. You are on the right path."

"So he's a werewolf? Are there more like him, but like werecats?"

"There are some different types. Mostly depends where in the world they are from. Wolf packs dominate most of North America and Canada; farther south, panthers. There are bears and wolverines that control some regions."

"Are there a lot of them?"

"Some are spread out and others live in clusters, but there are more than you know. They keep to themselves, very secretive. I'm not sure we will ever know their population numbers, just like they will never know how many witches or vampires there are. We will come together to fight a common cause, but normally we don't associate with one another."

"What about Merrill?"

"He's our neighbor. We treat all of our neighbors with respect and hospitality, just as they treat us. Plus," she says leaning in, "I think he has a crush on my mother. They think they are sneaky, but I've caught on."

"How long have they known each other?"

"Before being captured? About ten years."

"Was he captured?"

"No, he's been safe here. These woods are protected from outsiders. We also add our own forms of protection," she says, looking at the trees. "Merrill has been hunting these woods for decades. Most people, likes us, live on the fringes of society. You won't catch him anywhere near a city. This is where people like us are safest. Shade doesn't come here. They know better than to mess with witches at their homes. If we don't want someone on our property, they are as good as dead," she says while pulling out a weed that withers away into dust in her hand.

I look into the woods and stare at the closest ward. Something tells me it does more than just spy on the property.

Katie Zaber

38 Weeks – Moccasin Swamp, Florida

The next few days were peaceful. Warm days spent in the sun working with my hands, cool nights cuddling Shuck under blankets, sleeping soundly with no nightmares. Being in the old house without electricity, not being bombarded by the media, listening to the women talk at night around a bonfire, sipping homemade country wine with their various visitors, has been nice. It's a different way of living that I haven't experienced in a while. Chores, cleaning, gardening—I've really missed gardening the most. It has been rejuvenating. They were right. Keeping myself busy during the day helps me sleep better at night. Out here, working with my hands has given me the most restful sleep in months.

Annabel and Bell live off the land, like most of the people who live near them. Some of them have modern comforts; others like Merrill refuse to install electric or plumbing. He says that his little one-room hut doesn't need any upgrades. It hasn't changed since he was born in it along with his eight siblings, and it doesn't need to change today. At least the women have a solar-powered generator to charge and run small comforts. They both have a thing for margaritas and I can't wait to try their own homebrewed key lime pie wine.

Every night, they have people over and say it is a normal occurrence to have potlucks and bonfires with their neighbors. That doing so gives all the outcasts who live in the swamp a sense of community, a family, which most of them either lost or didn't get a chance to have.

Most of the people the mother and daughter have introduced to me aren't normal. Mostly witches and weres. Only one vampire, Maddie, who wasn't as scary as I thought. She was very nice and said that most vampires don't attack humans and like to be involved in society. It makes them still feel alive as the decades whiz by. Most vampires enjoy social clubs and don't want to do anything to jeopardize their source of nightly entertainment. Her partner, Nick, even stopped by and ate with us while Maddie sipped on a drink of red liquid from a glass like I would wine. Her eyes were glued to her partner, and she licked her lips every so often in a way that made her look hungry and horny.

All the people I met said they were too strong to become possessed and that I didn't need to worry. They were right. There have been no incidents. I listen to them as they talk and try not to ask too many questions. Although I really want to ask the weres to transform, I thought it would be offensive to ask and I honestly don't want to see the vampire's teeth. However, they are all kind enough to go into detail when I look confused. Mostly about their families and how one becomes a were, witch, or vampire. Witches are born from witch parents or grandparents. Someone in their family is a witch, but it can skip a generation, sometimes, which makes me think about my own estranged grandparents.

Weres can either be born into a family or bitten and transformed, though the transformation when bitten can be risky and lethal half the time. Vampires are always bitten. There are laws about who gets bitten and at what age, with a council that administers swift punishment to any vampire who either wantonly kills or attempts to transform people. Seventy percent of the victims die. Only a few wake up without a pulse and can never resume their normal lives as they had known them.

They all have self-governing elders who are elected to oversee their people, police, politics, and deal with any major events. They are much more unified and civilized than I had thought, and not as bloodthirsty. Every person I spoke with said there is always a bad were or vamp to give everyone else a bad name. Most of them just want to be left alone to live in peace with their families. That's why most of them live on the edge of town, away from normal humans who can sense that they are a were or vampire and need to flee. Odd how I don't get that feeling at all, not even the tiniest sense of dread around them. I still can't begin to understand how that can help me.

I'm no longer as frightened as I was about all the different beings out there. Meeting all of those people has helped my anxiety about what goes bump in the middle of the night. The only thing that we didn't figure out is what I am. The only thing Annabel and Bell picked up was that I have some strength in gardening and growing, but they said that could also because I was pregnant and in a nurturing state.

No one else could give me any real insight into what I am or why I don't have that sense. Not even the extremely old, blind witch, Agatha, who walked across the swamp by herself. I don't know how she didn't walk into an alligator's mouth, but apparently she lives on her own and explores the woods every day, foraging for herbs and berries and checking her game traps. Agatha said she didn't know what any of it meant concerning me, but to her, it meant something interesting was about to take place. She also thinks the baby is the battery, not me, but that was the only thing she said that was any bit informative and also speculative. As for the electronics going haywire when I'm around, they don't know what that's about. But maybe the battery needs to discharge some energy? No one can give me any real answers, but at least I have people to talk to who don't think I'm crazy.

It's been a peaceful couple of days and I'm sad to go, but I'll be happy to take a long shower and float in my pool. "Thank you for getting gas. I'm still nervous of infecting people with possessions."

Annabel gives me one last hug before I get into the SUV. "I'm sorry, darling, that we weren't able to help you more. At least we know some things you can't do. We still learned, even if it isn't much."

"Thank you for everything. It was so nice just to be here. A nice change."

Bell cuts in to give me a hug. "I'm positive more odd things will happen. Take note and stay in touch. We are always here to give advice. And remember, when the time comes to ask for our aid, we will come. Do your best to try to not involve him though."

Bell means Lucas. She won't say his name and even said something along the lines of how that simple name wasn't part of his true identity. That who he is isn't what I see. I have a list of questions to ask him over dinner, which I am excited about. I want to learn more. This time away from technology and constant entertainment has left me with time to think and not panic.

"I will. I'll let you know when I get home. I wish I could communicate with everyone this way," I say and tap my temple. It's so much easier.

"It's interesting that you can. Eventually we'll figure you out," Annabel says, picking Shuck up and putting him in his doggy seat. It only took him a couple of hours to win Annabel and Bell over. They still think something is weird about him, but they also think he's a cute puppy. "Until then, we will have to wait patiently for hints."

"That's all we can do," I say before closing the door and rolling down the window. "Take care."

They say goodbye and wish me a safe drive. Somehow the drive feels longer than it did on the way up. Guess that's part of me not wanting to leave. It felt so right being there. Like it was where I belong. The swamp was beginning to grow on me.

Yikes, mini-watermelon, that last one hurt. You need to stop punting Mommy from the inside. It's like you're actually trying to kick your way out. Be patient; you'll come out soon. You're not done baking yet. And don't do that while I'm driving. You're going to get us killed.

Also, a little advice. I know we've talked about this before, but maybe switch up your arrival date. Trust Mommy on this: You don't want your birthday on Christmas. Your birthday parties are going to be in between holidays and you're not going to like it. Mommy knows. It's okay if you come next week. I think you should.

Pop!

My back passenger tire bursts. The SUV skids toward the right side of the road, threatening to spin. I bounce in the driver's seat as I pull to the left, attempting to keep the vehicle straight. It doesn't just feel like the SUV wants to spin; at this speed, it feels like it has enough momentum to flip. I fight the urge to jam on the brakes. My father taught me that touching the brake pedal is the last thing I want to do during a tire blowout. Staying straight is key. Eventually, it will begin to slow down on its own without my foot on the gas. There are no other vehicles on the road, no one to crash into. I just have to guide the SUV until it stops.

All the jostling makes my stomach feel weird, giving me a cramp in my lower back that feels like it wraps around to my belly button. Then it twists and twists. My muscles feel like they are being torn apart. A scream explodes from my chest. Tears slide down my face. My back tenses as another strong and violent spasm erupts through my body, leaving me gasping, making it even harder to hold on to the wheel as I'm being bucked around. I tighten my grip and growl at the pain flooding my senses. I have to hold on.

It feels like forever, stuck in a limbo of pain, before I can slow the SUV down enough to ease the brake, gradually bringing it to a stop. I put the car in park and wrap my arms around my belly.

Watermelon? Are you okay? Please be okay. I hope that didn't make you want to come now. Stay put. I massage my belly. This is not the place or time. Please don't do anything. Come on; stay in there. The longer you stay in there, the healthier you will be, sweetheart. And right now, out in the middle of nowhere isn't where you want to be born. I promise.

Gradually, the pain subsides. Was that one of those practice contractions? I have never felt anything like that. It took my breath away.

Hearing whines, I look over. "Shuck, you okay?"

I lift the flap to his doggy crate. He whimpers and trembles but sniffs my hand to greet me. I carefully lift him out and inspect his little body. His car seat might have just saved his life. That was a great buy. My little guy looks startled; he might have a little whiplash, but overall he looks okay. Even his tail is starting to wag again.

"Alright, let's see how bad the damage is," I tell Shuck and place his shaking body back into his seat. This will definitely make him afraid of cars again, just when we were making progress.

I look in the rearview mirror. Shreds of the tire lay scattered all over the road. I'm about a half hour away from the Belcans. I've changed a popped tire before, except I wasn't pregnant. Maybe I can fix this.

"Okay, baby, bear with me," I say while opening the door and getting out carefully. "We have to do this. We can't ask for help. We must keep moving."

I feel some waves rolling under my skin, a gentle, loving kick. I hope that's your way of agreeing with me.

The whole vehicle tilts at an odd angle. Torn pieces of the tire still remain attached, which was probably why it was such a bumpy stop. There should be a spare tire in the trunk. Maybe there isn't too much damage and I can drive it back, real slow. Now, the ultimate question: Can I lift the jack, and should I? They can sometimes be heavy, and I might need a hefty one to prop up the SUV. I lift the fake carpet, hiding the donut and jack. The spare tire is bulky, but easy to roll out of the trunk. The shiny black jack looks heavier. Next to it is a patch kit. Not like that would do anything to help me right now, but it looks lighter. Wrapping my hands around the jack, I bend from my knees and try to not strain myself as I straighten my legs.

"Oh, fuck." I drop the jack. The car bounces as I reel forward, hovering over the bumper. I brace myself with my arms. The pain in my back. It's bad. "Motherfucker."

My lower back feels like it just twisted and straightened. The motion continues across my stomach, like a violent seizure starting at either side of my spine and moving like a tidal wave around my body. Shuck whines from the passenger seat, yipping. Sweat trickles down my face as I'm finally able to take a breath.

Don't come out, baby. Not now. Please, not now. Please. I can't go back to a hospital. I would rather give birth at the Belcans' house without electricity. Just wait a little longer. Only a couple more hours and then you can come out if you need to. But not now. Not here.

Hobbling back to the driver's seat, I leave the trunk open and collapse. Shuck leaps out of his car seat and onto the center console, sniffing my belly. Thankfully, that contraction stopped. How far apart was that? My water didn't break, so I should be okay… right?

Let's make a deal. I promise not to lift anything if you promise not to do that again until we are home. Deal?

As much as I don't want to bother them, I really only have two choices. If I call Lucas, he'll send a helicopter to scoop me up, and I don't want to deal with all that fuss. It would be much easier to call a tow and ask Annabel and Bell to give me a ride closer to Orlando, where Lucas or Desmond can pick me up and bring me home. A helicopter ride sounds nauseating, and I'd rather give the Belcans money for their troubles.

"Hey, Bell," I think. *"I need some help. My back tire blew out on Route 121. I hate to ask, but could you give me a hand? We might be able to change it, but I might need a tow."*

"Absolutely. We're on our way," Bell says. *"Are you alright? How's the baby?"*

"Baby is fine. I just had a couple of contractions. My water didn't break or anything, so I think I'm alright. Sitting down now. I tried to lift the jack—that was a mistake."

"Darling! Don't lift anything! Don't do anything! We will be there in a half hour! Rest. Don't talk to anyone. Wave them on. If you need a tow, we'll arrange it. If you have any more contractions, tell me."

"I will. Thank you," I think.

My little furball of mystery stands up on his back legs to give my face a lick. "Oh, Shuck, what are you? Hmm? Why am I not afraid of you?"

The little dog responds by licking my hands and arms, then settles down on the tiny space left of my lap, squeezing between the steering wheel and my baby bump, half his body hanging off me. He's so cute and cuddly. How could he be anything else but a loyal dog?

No cars drive past on the lonesome road, which I'm incredibly grateful for. I just have to sit and wait patiently. Breathing in and out is all I try to concentrate on for a few minutes as I rub my belly. There hasn't been any sudden back pain since and my body wants to stretch, so I disturb Shuck, wiggle my body out, and close the trunk. Standing up only makes me want to pee; honestly, everything makes me want to pee. Peeing makes me want to pee. I put the leash on Shuck and walk over to the side of the road; he might need to go, too.

There's a slope into the woods that is slightly private. There are no bodies of water or gators hiding that I can see. And Shuck isn't barking like a lunatic in any direction. When Merrill took us for a walk in the swamp and Shuck saw the gators sunning, he went nuts. I'm pretty sure he'd let me know if he smelled one nearby. I wore a sundress today so I could easily squat wherever I need to. Better to go outside real fast than chance running into someone at a store restroom. No one is going to say anything to a pregnant woman peeing on the side of the road because her baby thinks her bladder is its own personal pillow. Plus, it's not like there are many gas stations or convenience stores around.

Thirty minutes later, an Oldsmobile pulls up.

"Darling," Annabel says, her mouth hanging open. "This is going to have to get towed. See how when it blew out, it destroyed all this stuff. I don't know what this is, but I know I can't just put the donut on and let you drive away."

"Damn. All I want is to go home."

"We'll give you a lift. Drop you off near your house," Bell says.

"Thank you. I'm so sorry to ask and I'll pay for gas and a hotel stay. You were closer than Lucas and I didn't want him to know the area where you live."

Annabel nods. "And we appreciate that. My oh my, this could have been a whole lot worse."

I look at the damage done and think about how lucky we are the SUV didn't flip.

A black Ford pickup, the first vehicle I've seen besides Annabel and Bell's, pulls up in front of mine.

I start backing away, heading toward their Oldsmobile. "You have to tell him we are fine and don't need help."

Annabel pats my hand. "We have this. Don't you worry. Nothing bad is going to happen, dear. I'll get Shuck for you; sit down and rest."

A fit, gray-haired man with a clean-shaven face walks up. He's wearing a flannel and blue jeans. "Tire trouble? I'll get you going in just a few minutes. No need for any fancy AAA."

"Thank you, sir, but the damage is extensive and we'll need a tow. We've already called. Thank you. Have a great day," Bell says.

"Nonsense, sweetheart. There isn't a blowout I can't fix," he says, approaching the SUV's trunk. "I'll have it back together in a few minutes, Lord providing."

Shuck starts to whimper from the front seat of my SUV. His whines slowly become puppy growls. Annabel walks over to his side of the SUV to let him out.

I open up their car door, trying to keep a distance between us. "Please. I'll be alright. You should go. Leave now. Please," I beg the man. "Go. I don't need your help! We're fine!"

The man opens my trunk and clears his throat. "You heathens," comes out raspy and harsh, "probably have never heard of the Good Samaritan." He turns around, lifts the shiny black, fifty-pound jack and hurls it at the Oldsmobile, smashing it through the windshield and into the driver's seat, ripping the steering wheel out of its place.

"Run!" I yell at the mother and daughter. "Go!" I know what someone like this is capable of, the amount of carnage. I should have never involved them. I'm so stupid.

"You're not going anywhere this time," the old man says, smiling wickedly as he picks up the tire iron. "You've had plenty of opportunities to repent. But still you continue down the wrong path."

"Get away from me! Leave me alone!" I scream and sob.

"This is His will."

Annabel stands by the passenger side, Bell a few feet away, both mumbling something over and over, their brown eyes now bright green.

He cocks his head at the mother and daughter. "You side with the nefarious. You all belong in Hell," he says in a voice that doesn't come out of a normal old man.

It sounds eerily similar to the one I heard in St. Patrick's Cathedral. With a swipe of his hand, the women fall to their knees, gasping for air. Their hands grab at their throats as if they are trying to rip an invisible hand away.

"Stop," I cry as tears run down my face. "Please. Don't hurt them!"

His voice booms. "Their insolence towards my lord must end, like your abomination."

They gag on the ground, unable to make a sound. Shuck jumps out of his doggy seat, leaps across the back seat, and jumps out of the trunk. His jaws widen, aiming for the jugular, but his tiny body doesn't make it and he clamps down on the man's shoulder. The possessed thrashes his arms, trying to get my dog off him as blood drips from his wound. A sharp pain shoots from my back and wraps around my stomach, almost bringing me to my knees, closing my eyes, sucking a breath out of me. I hear a yelp, open my eyes, and see my dog hanging in the man's grip.

"Is this your pet? This creature?"

My brave Shuck tries to bite at his fingers, clawing at the asshole, holding him by the scruff. But his little body can't do much and he begins to whimper and looks at me with those big puppy dog eyes. I'm sorry, baby. I'm sorry, babies. I don't think I can do this.

Maybe this is my horrible destiny.

No. No. No. This isn't how we end.

I refuse.

I'm not going to be part of this anymore. No one ever asked me if I wanted to be involved in some celestial bullshit. It's my life. I'm in control. I make the decisions. I allow things to happen. It's me. Not anyone else. Me.

"*No! Stop!*" A commanding voice explodes from my chest. The man stops what he is doing and blankly stares. Beside me, I hear Annabel and Bell gulping air. "*Put down my dog, then put your hands up!*"

His face twitches as he places Shuck on the ground; his hands shoot up into the air, even though he fights the impulse. My brave pup runs behind me, cowering.

Huh. That's interesting and new.

"*Do jumping jacks.*"

"No, this cannot happen. Why would he give you such a power?" the elderly man says as he jumps up and down.

"*Touch your toes.*"

He stops doing jumping jacks and touches his toes. "This doesn't—"

"*Shut up. Only talk when asked a question.*" How am I doing this? How am I controlling this possessed person? Have I always had control? I turn to Annabel and Bell. "Are you two alright?"

They are no longer gasping and the color is returning to their faces. They nod and I turn my attention back to the possessed being.

"Let's be clear! This child," I yell, clutching my stomach, "is mine. You will never, ever take watermelon from me! You hear? You will fail every time. You will never kill me or my child. And if you ever come near us again, I will make it my personal obsession to discover a permanent way to kill whatever the fuck you are." I growl, "Leave us alone!"

The man's mouth tries to move but is unable.

"Speak."

"This child will—"

"*Shut up.*" Ahem. Every time I reach inside, to that powerful voice that's in there, it makes my throat dry and head hurt, but it's very useful. "My child, this baby, will be exactly how I raise it to be. I will mold this child into a wonderful, fully functioning adult who will respect everyone and know how to love. Watermelon's fate isn't decided. Not yet. And you, you don't have any power over my child's future. Not for a second. So don't fool yourself into thinking you have any power or control. I have the power. I have the control. Not you. Never again."

The man blinks.

"Don't come near me ever. Every time you think of me and my child, I want it to hurt. I want it to feel like a spike is being driven through your skull. Nod if you understand everything I've said."

He nods.

"Free this man and let him return to his body unharmed."

The man's eyes roll to the back of his head as he drops to the ground, narrowly missing my SUV's bumper.

"Well, that's something you don't see every day." Bell stands up and gives her mother a hand. She rubs her throat and walks toward the poor old man. He might need to go to the hospital. Hopefully, he didn't break anything.

"Be careful. I think it's gone, but I can't be sure."

Annabel clears her throat. "I can feel the absence of its presence."

Bell looks the man over. He's moaning on the pavement. "Why didn't you ask more questions? Was it hard to control?"

"It felt weird. My head was pounding. It was getting hard to think. Like holding my breath underwater."

Annabel is suddenly bracing me. "Darling, you need to sit down right this second. I'm going to get in touch with some friends. They'll help us sort out this mess."

Bell looks down at me like that's my excuse? Like she would have kept pushing past the pain and mental fatigue, which I'm sure she's trained to do. But I'm new to this kind of stuff and proud that I was able to do what I did for the first time without injuring anyone.

What did I just do? "I just wanted it gone. I've seen so many people die while possessed. That kind man doesn't deserve it. Plus, anything it had to say, I don't care about. I just want a normal life."

"You were ordering it what to do. You could have commanded him to tell you the truth." She looks angry as her eyes slowly change back to their rich, dark brown color.

"His version. What he believes is the future and truth. Perspective can warp one's reality. If he believes it's real, it's real to him, so it becomes the truth. But his faith doesn't control me or my child. No one does. No one. I have the power to bring this baby into this world, raise it to be a good person. That's my power."

Annabel pats my arm and sits me down on the driver's seat of the SUV. "No, honey. That's only one of them."

Thirty minutes after the possession ended, Nick, Maddie the vampire's partner, picked us up in his shiny four-door pickup truck. Bell stayed with the cars and the old man while she waited for tow trucks and an ambulance for his back and bitten shoulder. She reported no car accident but said that there was a mishap with the jack, which was left exactly where the confused man heaved it. He couldn't recall what had happened. The only thing he knew was that he stopped to give us a hand. He thinks when he reached down to pick up the jack, he blacked out from the sudden pain. What he couldn't explain is how the jack ended up in the front seat of the other car or what bit him. I'm sure the tow truck drivers had questions, and so did the paramedics. But Bell said she would take care of everything. Her hazel eyes were turning green again when Annabel and I left.

Nick brought us back to his modern ranch-style home. There was no sight of Maddie, but then again, it was half past noon, so she must have been asleep. Even though I wanted to ask if she sleeps in a coffin, I decided it would be rude and I shouldn't stereotype.

As soon as I got back to Nick's, I called Lucas and told him in brief what had happened and that I would need a ride. And how we need to repair the Belcans' car or, better yet, buy them a new one. He panicked at first but calmed down when I told him we were fine. After a few minutes of arguing, he finally agreed that he would come to pick me up in a normal car, not in the jet or a helicopter. To my relief, I haven't had a single contraction since the incident. Still, once we get home, I'll call Dr. Mitchell over to double-check.

Lucas arrived at the park down the street from Nick's in less than two hours, driving a newly leased Escalade. I had asked him to come alone so we could drive back together. No matter how many times we've had a driver, it always feels odd and I would rather it just be us.

Annabel and Nick said hello from a distance. They were friendly but stood apart. Lucas, as soon as he parked the car, ran to me, kneeled, placed his head on my belly, and wrapped his arms tight around me. When he finally stood, he kissed me repeatedly and wouldn't let me go. He looked paler than usual but visibly relieved.

Annabel looked slightly more relaxed after Lucas showered me with kisses. I think seeing his compassionate side made him appear more normal and not as cataclysmic. Within five minutes of meeting at the park, we were back on the road again, this time with Lucas driving and miserable Shuck in the back seat, trembling in his doggy seat. Lucas isn't a bad driver, even though he normally has a lead foot, but right now, he's driving like a grandpa. The speedometer won't go a mile over the speed limit and I think the cars zooming past on the highway are making the angel nervous.

"Why don't we explore and take the back roads?"

"It will take longer. Don't you want to get home and rest?"

"I'm resting in the car. I still need to get up and stretch every forty minutes and pee every fifteen. It's easier if we don't have to get on and off the turnpike. Plus, watermelon and I are getting hungry. I'm getting a headache too. There's bound to be a good local diner."

"Like the one where we first met," he says with a grin, taking the exit ramp. "Do you want a breakfast buffet, my queen?" The built-in GPS reroutes, trying to bring us back to the turnpike.

I hit the *no toll road* button and say, "No, I'm thinking lunch. Something savory. But since we had to cancel our dinner reservation, are you ready for my first question?"

He shifts in his seat. "Go ahead."

"The whole thing at the diner and the hotel, was it planned?"

His eyes focus on the road. "I knew of you. Knew I wanted to meet you. Where that ended, I didn't know, but I knew you were, in some way, part of my destiny—if that makes any sense. I knew you would be at the diner and I used the opportunity to help you and introduce myself. When you called me weeks later, you surprised me. I wasn't sure if I would see or hear from you again, but I had hoped."

"Something kept urging me to call or think about you. Every few days, I would find your business card in my hand and forget taking it out. How did you know I would be there?"

"Are you sure you want to have this conversation in the car or in public? Where this leads might upset you."

"I'm ready to hear it. And then I'll tell you everything about my day. The long version."

"I had heard from my immortal connections of a woman carrying one of my brother's children and that she was thriving. The woman doesn't always survive copulation, let alone carry, so I was intrigued. When I discovered you were being hunted and traveling alone, I wanted to help. Especially after I met you. There is a spark in you. Something special, unique. You know the story of the Virgin Mary and how she became pregnant?"

"Yes. The angel Gabriel came in the night with the message about the birth of Jesus. Wait, did he rape her?"

"Yes. For her, it was more of a fanciful dream. In reality, she was still technically a virgin, but in her dreams, not so much. It's hard to explain how it's done, but she was told she was conceiving God's son. You know the rest. It worked out for her, but it doesn't always. Some never wake up."

Dread fills my chest. An angel raped Mary. That poor girl was probably no older than sixteen, and told a lie. The woman in Italy, running from possessed nuns into the arms of murderous monks, all because she was trying to protect herself and her child. Were they both taken to a bedroom, similar to how I spoke to Lucas in my dreams? He looks nervous, afraid of my next question, knowing where all this will lead. "Was that what happened to me? An angel came to me in a dream?"

"Yes."

"So, I'm going to give birth to a nephilim?"

"Yes."

Part of me wants to scream, the other half wants to jump out of the car. My fear is true. That I was raped in a way I can't explain. Would I remember such a dream? Would I remember the angel's face? Is he sitting next to me? "Are you my baby's father?"

"I believe your child's father is Gabriel. He's known for impregnating mortal women and leaving them to fend for themselves. He's done it multiple times."

My hands rest on my bump, thumbs making small circles. Watermelon communicates by sending back soothing waves of motion below my skin. Listen to me, baby; you are nothing like your sperm donor father. You're not going to be like the asshole who raped me and took my life. He is not your future or part of it. Don't take it personally, but if it wasn't for him, Jim and I would still be happily married. My life wouldn't have spiraled out of control. None of this insanity would have happened.

A single tear runs down my cheek.

I'm not upset with you, baby, but I'll be honest, if I ever find your father, I will kill him. I will find a way.

Wait... the angelic possession. The spirit possessing those people, ready to kill us... could that have been your father?

My head floods with questions. I have to tell Lucas everything. Part of me was hiding so much because I was too scared, too afraid, and too mad that I didn't know he was an angel. But now, maybe he can help me find some type of peace. Help me raise something I might not be able to on my own. It's hard being a single mother and trying to raise a normal kid, but a nephilim? Will my baby grow wings? Will it have any powers? Does it already? Will those powers manifest right after birth or is it a maturity thing? What am I in for?

Maybe Lucas knows.

And maybe he can do me a solid and kill that motherfucker, Gabriel.

Or better yet, I want to try out my new power on the asshole. See if I can kill an angel. Where do angels go when they die? Can they die? Can my powers actually work on an angel or is it only the possessed, and how bad of a person would I be to try my power on Lucas?

The sign ahead says *homemade BBQ coming up*. Even though I feel like I'm going to be sick, I also need something in my stomach to become sick, and I won't punish innocent watermelon by starving ourselves. My head is pounding. Breakfast was at daybreak; it's been hours. There are picnic tables outside under a couple of big, shady trees. There's no line at the walk-up counter. We can just grab something simple and go.

Now, how to make that voice work? I don't know exactly what I did. It just happened when I thought everyone was going to die. My emotions are pretty high right now. I look in the mirror; my eyes are the color of shamrocks. "I want to try something."

"What?"

I try to remember the feeling I had earlier today and draw energy from a place deep inside, focusing my will into the words, *"Pull over at that BBQ restaurant."*

The SUV veers to the right and slows down. Lucas shakes his head like he was just slapped in the face. He fights himself to regain control of the vehicle, and does after a second of struggle. "Did you, did you do that? How?"

Oh wow. My powers don't just work on the possessed, they work on angels. Though not well. He seems to be able to resist. It might have to do with this being his real angelic body. *"Pull into the parking lot."*

He hits the gas and drives the last hundred feet to the BBQ parking lot and parks. His mouth hangs open, astonished.

"I'm sorry. I wanted to see if that actually worked. I have so much to tell you."

He pulls into a parking spot and shifts the gear into park. His hands shake slightly. The angel next to me pales. He looks, utterly horrified, at me.

39 Weeks - Orlando, Florida

I promised him I would never do that again. That I would never take away his free will as long as he never took mine. He agreed and said there was nothing more important than freedom. Ever since, he's been slightly on edge. He says that's because there has never been anyone like me, a mortal who can command angels, and he doesn't know what that means. We aren't sure, but it's possible I can do the same with demons. It crossed my mind, using my voice on him and commanding him to tell me the truth, but I decided that after hours of talking and everything he's done, I trust him. It's what he does that makes me trust him.

For hours, we talked about weird things and I think we finally got to know each other on a whole other level. So many things we never talked about. Like how mundane Heaven is and that it's not as magical as humans believe. Also, he emphasized how much he hates his father, God. All the angels are in dismay because he isn't there to reign over them. Heaven is in shambles. Everything above and below is in chaos. The rules are gone and so is God.

Apparently, He left before Jesus was born, and he may not know that devout Christians worship Jesus. Gabriel had claimed to start Christianity in his father's honor, trying to convince him to come back from the depths of the universe he retreated to. It didn't appease his father, and he hasn't returned.

So raping those women in the name of God, it was all for nothing. Why was I raped? What was the goal? What was I, just a one-night stand? Or is there something more and I'm just beginning to unravel the truth? Is this baby supposed to be the next messiah?

Oh, what are we going to do, honeydew? Really, let me know if you have a better plan, because I'm not sure I know what I'm doing. Honestly, I'm winging it.

I know what I'm avoiding at the moment, though.

Or I should say who. I'm pretending to nap. Last night, eating dinner with my parents was fine. Nothing crazy happened. They didn't bring up any weird topics or start talking about some outlandish conspiracy theories. They were on their best behavior.

Right now, Lucas is distracting them by driving them around the area, showing them how close we are to the theme parks, but also far enough. They enjoyed the fireworks in the backyard last night and didn't comment about big business or say anything argumentative. We had dinner delivered and ate under the stars. I haven't been feeling like going out. All I want to do is nap, organize, and clean. My mother said that's normal and she's just glad to be here, even if it's just for a short visit. After they saw the guest house, they commented how they can't wait to come back and meet their grandbaby.

There is only one word I can use to describe how I feel: swollen. Honeydew, I'm ready. How about you? I think today would be a great day to come. Or tomorrow, even. Please don't drag this out any longer. I can't see my puffy feet. You keep using my bladder as a pillow and I really want to stop peeing. Like right now, how I'm peeing again instead of napping, which is all I really want to do.

Oh, that's new. On the toilet paper, it looks like egg whites with little specks of brown and red. Is that the mucous plug? There's nothing else weird in the toilet. I'll have to call my doctor and tell her.

My phone is still on my night stand, charging. It's odd how often I've been looking at it, checking it to see if Ken has called me back. After avoiding and lying to him, I'm now trying to get in touch and he's not responding. I'm beginning to worry. Hopefully he's just mad at me. In my last message, I told him I was sorry I had been hiding information and that we really need to talk. I'll never tell him about Lucas, though. Only about myself. I also want to know if there is any more information on that woman the monks killed.

But really, I'm curious. What if I can exercise demonic possessions and can help him? I'd like to test that out. That's why I want to talk to him. At least I can take care of possessions down in Florida and help the cause. As much as I'm nervous he's going to call me a witch, I think it would be beneficial for him.

All this is after little honeydew is done breastfeeding and I'm in fit shape. I might be able to hurt them with my words, but physically, I'm feeble. However, I figured it would be good to talk to Ken and apologize.

I text the doctor. I'm sure everything is fine and that this is normal, along with the Braxton Hicks. It's just another sign that my body is preparing to have a baby. All I want is for this baby to come out normal. And soon.

Now that I know it's a nephilim, I keep having nightmares of the baby coming out with wings, or bursting through my stomach because I wasn't pushing hard or fast enough. Every time Dr. Mitchell does an ultrasound, I ask her if I can see the baby's back and shoulders. Thankfully, there are no signs of wings or bumps. The woman must think I'm crazy, but she's always kind and explains everything, fully answering every question I have. I'm really glad we found her and the team. After everything I went through with the Shades at their facility, I didn't think I'd trust anyone in scrubs or in a uniform again.

As much as I want to sleep, the nightmares are nonstop. Some nights, I dream that I'm back in that prison, giving birth. Other nights, it's nephilim nightmares. If I'm not tossing and turning from those two horrors, it's an *I can't push anymore because the pain is too intense and why didn't I get an epidural* nightmare where I'm screaming in pain and unable to move because honeydew is coming out, but I can't push any harder. The baby is stuck halfway out of me and I can't finish pushing. In these dreams, I'm alone. The birthing team isn't with me for some unexplainable reason, and neither is Lucas.

A couple of the times, I've woken Lucas and Shuck. Poor dog. He's now traumatized of any moving vehicles. I've found him chewing on the golf cart's tire like it was part of his revenge plan, and now he's getting scared of sleeping with us because I keep kicking him during my nightmares. One night, I'll wake up to him, nipping my toes.

My doula, Jill, said that I should start doing hypnobirthing classes in order to prepare. She said it might also help calm my mind because it's meditation. I asked her how hard is it to meditate while pushing out a baby; she said some women can become so Zenlike that they say it's painless. That made me laugh really hard. Those women are liars. Even these practice contractions I've been getting can be a little intense. Sometimes it feels like a little twitch; other times, I think, is this the beginning of labor?

But then nothing happens for hours.

Baby, come on. Please, come out soon. Mommy needs a break from this.

I turn on my television and start my breathing exercises while sitting on my yoga ball, which is the most comfortable thing to sit on. The way it stretches everything out feels amazing. If I ever conceive again, I'm going to use a birthing ball the whole time. It's great exercise and I think it really helps. But it's not like we could have a normal pregnancy, huh, honeydew?

Maybe next time, if I'm crazy enough to do this again, I'll have a normal, relaxed nine months. Filled with yoga, Lamaze classes, a gender reveal party, a baby shower, maybe even a photo shoot with me holding my belly in cute and sexy ways.

But right now, this late in the game, all I want is for the baby to come out. Doctor Mitchell texted back, asking how I was feeling or if there were any cramps, bleeding, or anything else different? I told her that everything has been fine. She replied that it most certainly was part of my mucous plug coming out and there should be more soon. However, it doesn't mean that the baby will be here today, tomorrow, or even this week. It's just another indicator that my body is getting ready.

Damn. I was hoping it meant you would come out today. Come on, baby. Today is a nice day to enter the world. Why not?

While wobbling back and forth on my ball, I hear the garage door beep open. Shuck jumps off the bed and runs to the kitchen, then comes zooming down the hallway, then zooms back to the kitchen, excited people are home. As I get off the ball, I realize I need to pee again. I think it's only been ten minutes. Not even. Augh. Baby, get out.

More egg whites when I wipe, which only makes me think of scrambled eggs, which makes me want to puke. I might not be able to eat eggs again after that connection. Gagging, I flush, wash, and waddle to the kitchen, where all the commotion is coming from.

Lucas comes over and wraps his arms around me, planting a kiss on my forehead. "How was your nap, my queen?"

I thought my mother would mention how calling me his queen is showing possession of me, or that she would give me some type of feminist speech about how it's wrong, but I know my father has a nickname for her. It's a secret and only between the two of them, but he still calls her it in private. If Lucas wants to worship me, so be it. I won't complain. "I peed a lot."

"That is something you do frequently," he says with a grin.

"I need a cup of tea," my mother announces. "Would you like one, Bee?"

"Yes, please, and food."

"I knew you'd be hungry. Do you want to go out or stay in?" Lucas asks.

"In," I say while nuzzling my head into his shoulder. "I'm so exhausted."

My mom fills up the electric kettle and turns it on. "It's a lot of work growing a baby. People don't realize how much a mother gives," she says while getting out tea bags. "It's the most exhausting point of your life—up until the baby doesn't sleep and wants to be held day and night. Then you forget what sleep feels like."

"I wasn't that bad of a baby, was I?"

"Ah, your mother is exaggerating. You slept alright most nights, though there were a few when you just wouldn't tire out. Long car rides and warm whole milk. That helped."

"Oh, remember that couple who would sell us fresh cow's milk after I was done nursing? That farm was beautiful. Plenty of fresh cow and goat's milk. Every day, we'd take a stroll with you in your stroller. It was our family outing. They also sold eggs and meats when she slaughtered. It was a nice ranch."

"What state was that in?" I ask while I rock back and forth on my heels. I imagine it looks like I'm riding an invisible pony. My legs are spread apart, with a slight gap in between them. Shifting back and forth feels so much better than sitting.

She takes a moment to respond. "I think it was Wisconsin."

"Is that where your mother lives?"

My father walks across the room and pats my shoulder. "Think I'll let you drink tea by yourselves. I'm going to take a nap."

"I'll look over some menus and order a nice dinner for delivery. Something special," Lucas says, also retreating.

He knows I want to ask some question about my grandparents. Between my father and mother, I would suspect my mother's parents to be witches rather than my father's. It's the way my mother talks about her parents. My father is just distant with his and never says anything about them. My mother always said her parents were awful people, but never explained why.

"Why have you never talked about your parents?"

"Because it's safer," my mother says, her voice cracking. "All these years, after thinking about how to say it, rehearsing the conversation, how to tell you about everything, you'd think I'd have an easier time." The kettle screams and she pours us a cup of berry tea. She takes a sip of piping hot tea, which, just watching, makes my mouth burn. She sighs. "We kept you from your grandparents because they weren't good people. The cult they are part of is terrifying. They are from upper Michigan. We lived northwest of Marquette."

"A cult? Are they witches?"

Tea spills as her cup crashes onto the counter. She doesn't even look down at the hot water burning her hands. "How did you know?"

I ignore the mess. "Tell me everything."

She grabs a kitchen towel and starts sopping up the tea, staring at the puddle. "It skipped a generation, with me. My parents thought I was going to be something great. Something powerful. Something unreal. I remember dancing under the moonlight as a child with the other women. The beating drums, the chants, the sense of community, family. But all I was was me. Nothing more. Nothing powerful. They waited until I was sixteen. They kept thinking that I matured slower, that my power would emerge as I got older, but it never happened. You should have seen how disappointed they were. Even disgraced. They excluded me from any coven activities after my sixteenth birthday. They started their own cult shortly after. When your father and I told them we were pregnant with you, they started talking to me again. And for a moment, it felt like they loved me. That they cared about me, but it was a lie." My mother wipes a tear from her face. "When you were born, it was an odd day."

"What do you mean?" Please don't say anything biblical. Please don't say anything biblical.

"There was an earthquake that morning. All around the world, people reported seismic activity. That night, shooting stars flew across the sky. When I looked into both events, years later, scientists couldn't explain the tremor felt around the world or the shooting stars that weren't seen until the moment you were born."

That's not what I want to hear. "What did your parents do?"

"They rejoiced. They said you were the baby that they had hoped for. That the child they tried to bring into this world had finally arrived."

I suck in a breath. This is why she always resented me on some level. Her parents didn't want her; they wanted me. I can't even fathom how a new mother would feel, tossed aside by her own parents for her daughter.

"They came to the hospital, just like Keith's. They said they had wanted to see you. They even brought a teddy bear, a card, and balloons." Tears pour out of my mother's eyes. I grab her hand and give it a squeeze. With her free hand, she wipes away the streaks on her face. "His parents held you first while mine asked me about the delivery. Asking me questions, pretending to care. Then they got their chance to hold you. They became hysterical. They tried to take you from us, leave the hospital. Security had to get involved and they were escorted out of the building. But they saw your eyes and knew. Bee, you were born with bright green, glowing eyes."

I snap my hand back. So they knew the whole time that I was a witch or something. "Wait. Is that why you wouldn't let me go to school? Be around other people?"

"The day we left the hospital to bring you home, my parents were waiting outside our house. They ambushed us and said that they needed you. Police were called, a fight broke out. We escaped. We've never gone back to Michigan. We kept you out of school because we didn't want anyone to find you. We changed our names. I know how much you hated your name. I'm sorry. We had to choose names that wouldn't give us away."

All I can do is blink. I was ready to hear that my grandmother is a witch and she got into a fight with my mother over something stupid. Maybe my grandparents didn't approve of my father sort of thing. Not something like this.

"Bee, all I ever wanted was to protect you from them and give you a good life. A normal life. We didn't have a lot of choices and soon found out how much harder it would be keeping you away from them."

"What were they going to do with me?"

"I don't know. We didn't ask. They are secretive, powerful maniacs. Every time they tried to take you from us, we escaped, barely. Sometimes we'd lose everything we'd worked for."

"So it wasn't the DEA after us?"

My mother laughs. "A couple times, they came sniffing around. But mostly it was my parents and their cult. We tried so hard to protect you from them. So hard."

"The security guards?"

"Some were witches we hired to protect us. Your father and I aren't strong. We wouldn't survive a fight with my parents. We needed the help."

Everything I thought about my childhood was wrong. "So you always knew I was different?"

"Honestly, we didn't know what you are. When you were little, we would put different talismans in front of you to see if you reacted or liked a particular one. I never felt anything, but I knew witches could feel things that normal people can't. Like they can sense energy and manipulate it. However, you didn't care about any of the charms. It was like none of it gave you a reaction. So we didn't think you were a witch, but we also didn't have anyone to ask. No one we trusted. I had been around psychics and witches my whole life. I didn't think you were one of those; I just didn't know what you are, except special. Unique."

I try to stifle back a sob, but all the pain is too much. Everything my mother and father went through, trying to keep me safe from the unknown. My heart aches for them. I'm still pissed, but now I understand. As obscure as it all is, it makes sense.

My mother comes to my side and gives me a hug. "Honey, I'm so sorry about everything. I wish there was a way that I could have taken this away from you and given you the life you deserved. The life we wanted you to have. That's all we ever wanted." She holds me tight, stroking my hair. "Bee, when did you find out that you were different?"

"Mommy," I cry. "I've had really hard and weird pregnancy," I say, weeping in my mother's arms.

My mother and I talked for hours about her evil parents. The corpses of animals and blood trails she would find in the woods behind their house after they started their own cult. At least, she always hoped it was a wild animal. The times she didn't find a carcass, but a ton of blood that always made her vomit. When she turned eighteen, she moved out and lived with a friend until she met my father. Her childhood was horrible, and I thought I had it bad. The pressure her parents put on her. No wonder they never forced me to do anything. The way they raised me makes sense. She didn't want to repeat any of her parents' mistakes. It would have messed me up even more if I had been told, from an early age, that I was powerful and that I'd have huge responsibilities. They never told her what they were, but her parents said she would change the world.

I'd be terrified if I was told that as a kid.

I'm terrified as an adult. Especially since I'm supposed to be the powerful person her parents have been waiting for. What kind of power do I really have? Do I want to know? Can I pretend that I'm normal and maybe my life will be too? I'm going to have to talk to Annabel and Bell, to see if they know of any covens from Michigan and possibly what they were up to.

My mom cried with me after I told her everything that has happened since the clerk at the pharmacy and my first doctor's appointment with the junkie outside, up until I sent a possessing angel back to wherever it came from. I didn't tell her about Lucas, but I told her everything else. Everything I told her, she said, was exactly what she had tried to prevent. All she wanted was for me to have a regular life. She wept just as much as I did. When I told her about the prison, she went ballistic.

Since that conversation, it feels like the air has lifted. It's been a nice couple of days with my parents. We did something that I haven't done since I was very little. Something special. We decorated a Christmas tree as a family. Of course my parents bought us a baby's first Christmas ornament in the shape of a little rattle. We had a glazed ham dinner, ordered from some place Lucas picked, and had a pre-Christmas dinner, since I don't want to do anything next week.

It was sad dropping them off at the airport, but I was happy to pick up Melisa. Who, even though she's here, is very, very busy with work. She works with sales and because it's the holiday season, she's working sixty hours a week, if not more. I honestly don't know how she even packed to move or anything. Right now, she's typing away and is supposed to have a conference call. Afterward, we'll have lunch together. I love having her nearby and the fact that she likes to give us privacy and have her own. It's like we're roommates again, which I love.

My phone rings. It's the bell chimes that remind me of a church.

"Hello." Finally, Ken is returning my phone calls.

"Sorry, Eve. I've been busy. Everything okay?"

"Kind of. I need to tell you some things. Actually, a lot. I've learned so much."

The phone is silent for a couple of seconds. "Have there been any more possessions?"

"Yes."

"What happened?"

"I was able to exorcise what I think was an angel." There is silence on the other end of the phone. It stretches out until I'm not sure if he's still on the line. "Ken?"

"Sorry. I'm just trying to comprehend what you just said. You were able to exorcise what you think was an angel possessing someone?"

"Yeah. It's been a really weird couple of weeks. Months. This whole pregnancy—no—my whole life is messed up."

"Don't you have a house in Florida? I'm in Tampa. There seems to be more and more cases down here than in New York at the moment. They keep popping up left and right."

"All the possessions, this uptick, it might have do with me."

He sighs. "Damn. That's what I was afraid you might say. I'm about to arrive at my next case with possessed twins. Hopefully, if all goes well, I'll be done in a couple hours."

"Twins? How old?"

"Double trouble ten-year-old boys."

"Can I help?"

"I don't think so. I've got this under control."

"I might be able to help them. Maybe do what I did the other day."

"I don't know what *you* did the other day, but my associate and I have this under control."

"Will the boys be okay?"

"They should be fine. They are in good hands. Text me your address and I'll stop by when I have a moment."

We hang up. For a few minutes, I stare at the screen, unable to hit the send button. As much as I'm terrified for Lucas and Ken to meet, against my gut instinct, I send him the address.

I had to give the security guard at the gate Ken's information in order for him to be allowed onto the property. When I told Lucas about Ken coming over, he was nervous, but I told him I needed to talk to someone and find a way, with my power, to help others. I added that I wanted to apologize to Ken for lying. We both decided that Lucas should stay in his office the whole time and not meet Ken. If he can sense angels and demons, it might be better for my angel to stay away. At least until after Ken and I talk.

He texted me this morning and said he had a couple of free hours and could be in my area around noon. I made sure to have a pot of coffee for him, tea for me, and a box of pastries—mostly for me, but I decided to share.

Melisa is busy with work, and I told her I wanted a private conversation. She said fine, that she knows I'm going to tell her everything anyway. At this point, she does know everything. I filled her in about my birth, my parents, everything I know. And she's handling it pretty well. I'm not sure if she's crying herself to sleep at night, and I haven't inquired about that handgun she wanted to buy, but overall she isn't on meds and in a padded room, which is where I thought I'd be going—and still might be.

There's a knock on the front door. It's almost one o'clock. I find it odd going to the front door. This might be the first time I'm opening it for anyone. Normally, everyone pulls into the garage or knocks on the side entrance.

Ken is holding an extra large cup of coffee. He's wearing a wrinkled black buttoned-up t-shirt and a pair of blue jeans. The collared t-shirt looks odd but somehow still religious. Maybe it's his muscles peeking out from under the sleeves. Most priests I've met are pretty scrawny. I know he's been in a few fights, sending demons back to Hell, but I've never seen a priest with huge biceps. His clothes look slept in. It doesn't look like he has showered, either, from the amount of crust in the corners of his eyes. He reeks of cheap liquor and cigarettes.

I look around. "Hi, Ken. Thanks for coming. I thought your associate might be with you."

"No, he got called into work. I don't know how much time I have, honestly. It's been a rough couple of months." He looks like he has aged. There's more gray hair hiding in his ginger curls and in his unkempt beard.

"Come on in. I have more coffee and some breakfast if you're hungry."

"I could always use a refill," he says, shaking his almost-empty-sounding cup. From the stains all over the outside, it looks like he's refilled it multiple times. "Nice home. When you said it's near the theme parks, I didn't realize how close."

"No one does."

He steps inside and looks around. "You look good, Eve. How close are you to your due date?"

"Close. I can go into labor at any minute."

"Let's hope it's not now," he says, both joking but also looking serious.

Shuck barks like crazy from outside, jumping on the sliding door, upset I didn't let him greet Ken at the door. Since I know something is different about Shuck, but not exactly what, I figure it might be better to introduce Ken to the pup slowly in case he tries to exorcise my little guy.

Instantly, Ken notices the dog and starts walking toward him. "What kind of dog is he?"

"That's Shuck. What kind of dog do you think he is?" So he does sense something that I can't.

"He looks like a mutt. Where did you get him?"

"We adopted him from a place in New York."

"Has he ever done anything… weird?" Ken asks, kneeling on the floor, looking at the dog through the window.

"Nope. Just wags his tail and barks whenever someone comes home. Normal puppy stuff." I decide to open the slider and let him pet Shuck, since he doesn't look hostile. It will calm the dog down, and maybe if Ken sees he's a regular puppy, he might be less concerned.

Shuck scrambles into the house and sniffs Ken's hand, licks it, then flips over onto his back, waiting for a belly rub. His tongue hangs out of his mouth as he pants, paws waving in the air, tail swinging, happy to make a new friend.

"Huh. I've never met a dog like him before."

"What makes you say that?"

"He feels different. Like he's not part of our world. I wouldn't call him possessed, but different. Eve, you are a woman full of mystery and puzzles. Let's figure out one before moving on to others," he says, indulging the pup with a belly rub.

"Enough for now, little guy." He pats Shuck on the head and stands. "Let's get to business. Tell me everything. And this time, don't waste my time and lie."

"I won't," I say to Ken, leading him outside to the patio. Did I just lie to a priest again since I won't tell him about Lucas? Does it matter that I'm omitting the truth because, really, there is no God. Maybe I should leave that out too.

DNA – Demons N Angels

※

Ken's been busy dealing with what some people are calling the end times. Biblical phenomena that signal the beginning of the end of the world. Blood pouring down from the sky in Northern India, infestations eating acres of crops a day in Africa, cattle dropping dead across the United States, weird plagues that have been eradicated in the Pacific Islands are sprouting back up, stuff that doesn't happen and when it does, it means bad news. Ken is still focusing on possessions, but others he works with are busy around the globe.

"So you're telling me that you're pregnant with a nephilim." He reaches into his pocket for the first time in the conversation, takes out a flask, and takes a long swig. "I'd offer you some, but I think I need all of this and, well…" He takes another swig. "A nephilim? Here?" He gets up, paces back and forth, takes a third pull, lights a cigarette, and starts laughing. "Bloody hell. How are you calm?"

"I've had a few more minutes to work through the news, but I assure you, between everything that has happened, I've been freaking out."

He paces. Shuck tries to walk with him, thinking he's going somewhere but then decides he's done with that game and pounces on a chew toy. Ken faces me and asks, "Are you sure?"

"As much as I don't want this to happen, I'm pretty certain. It makes sense. Everything."

"I mean, I don't doubt what you've been through. I've known about witches and all the other types, but angels and demons? A nephilim? This is different. I don't even know what to do with this information. Do you know who, which angel did this?"

"I suspect Gabriel, but I don't know for sure."

"Then how do you know it's a nephilim?"

"The signs. Everything that has happened."

He smokes the cigarette to the filter and lights another one with it before tossing the remains of it in the bottom of his empty coffee cup, where it sizzles out.

"Tell me more about the archives," I say. "Have they found anything else out?"

He turns his head, lost in his thoughts. His eyes aren't focused. "In Rome? Yeah, they've been peeling through some records that haven't seen light in centuries. Needed special permission. They just started to decipher the pages. But they think they have found more cases. More odd births concerning possessions. They won't know what they are looking at for another week or so. Let's hope they have some more information on what to do next," he says, looking at my belly.

I hug my baby. "I know what I'm doing, raising this baby." He looks away, doesn't say anything like *we should kill it*, nothing horrible like that, but I'm sure it's going through his mind. Time to change subjects. "Do you think I could help? With the possessions? Do you think after this little one is out of the oven that I could try to exorcise a demon?"

"Ah, I mean, I don't see why not. If it doesn't work, I'll just take over. It's not like you haven't dealt with this kind of stuff, so it shouldn't scare you too much. But Eve, are you sure you want to continue down this path? The more you get involved, the deeper this goes, the more you'll never have a normal life. Nor will you want to."

The ex-priest looks sad. I wonder what kind of life he wanted, what life he could have hoped for if his brother was never possessed, if he never learned about the occult. Would he have been a dentist or a veterinarian with a big family?

I look down at my bump and feel honeydew stretching and rolling. "Ken, I think it's already too late."

Katie Zaber

40 Weeks - Orlando, Florida

Christmas music plays in the background from some movie on the television. Twinkling bells. They are supposed to sound pretty, magical, angelic, but they don't. They sound forced. Like each beat of the bell from the bell ringer is laborious, painful. The swinging of bells makes me think of contractions, back and forth. Relentless. They keep coming every five to seven minutes, but you, little pumpkin, just don't want to come out yet. Do you?

Can I tell you a secret? Mommy's done. Very done right now. It's time, honey. Please? I'm begging you. Come out now. Not only am I beyond exhausted, but I feel gross. Everything feels gross. It feels like I have menstrual cramps again, which I thought you would give me a break from, but no, it feels like I should be getting my period. Every time I go to the bathroom, something else comes out too and I have to wear a panty liner. Have I told you, baby, that you are gross? I love you, but really, you're making a mess down there.

Lucas called Dr. Mitchell this morning to have her check me out. I really don't want to keep having her come over after every contraction. But he's worried. Anxious. He said a lot of women don't survive conception. I'm not certain how many were actually able to give birth and survive. I only know of one other woman in history who was successful. And I'm thankful I have a home to give birth in, not a manger. This is a complete medical upgrade and everything will be fine. That's what I keep telling myself.

"Nope. Not yet. Not even close," says the doctor. "Only four centimeters. You still have plenty of time. Your water hasn't even broken yet. You haven't had your blood show. Once that happens, then we're looking at twenty-four hours. This might go on for a couple days."

"No, Doctor. I can't do this anymore," I cry.

"Nonsense. I said might. This little one might surprise us and come tonight. We don't know. But what I do know is that you can do this. Take more showers and baths. The warm water will soothe you. Relax. Your baby isn't ready yet. I find it's best not to rush or induce labor. But if you want, eat spicy foods. Kiwis, eggplant, pineapples, and dates; there are even recipes online of pizza that is supposed to help induce."

"Will any of it actually work?" I ask hopefully. I hate spicy food, but right now I'll chug a bottle of hot sauce.

"Wives' tales. Spicy foods and fruit maybe, but I don't think there is any scientific proof," she says, taking off her gloves and throwing them away. "Walk around and if you still feel comfortable, have sex. Do some nipple stimulation; that helps. But until your contractions are closer, five minutes apart, there's nothing to do but wait. Huh, today is the twenty-third. This kid might actually come on its due date. Doesn't happen often but, right now I'd guess the baby will be born in the next three days. If not, we'll discuss stripping the membrane and other options to help you along."

I look at Lucas. "Order me everything she said. I'm eating all of it." I almost say out loud, *while we have sex* but decide against saying that in front of the doctor.

"Give me a call if you have any questions or if anything happens. Anything at all."

"Thank you," I tell the doctor.

Lucas walks her out while I go back to ball bouncing. It feels so good to stretch out everything and keep moving. Plus, if it helps evict pumpkin faster, all the better. That's right, baby. You are getting an eviction notice today. It's happening. Get ready for a big glass of hot sauce.

"Are you sure you want to eat that?" Lucas asks, eyes watering.

My eyes are wet too from the heat coming off the wings. Just the smell of them makes my eyes melt. You feel anything yet, baby? No? "Yes. Keep them coming."

"You are going to make yourself sick with all the spices," he says, shaking his head.

"Are you kidding? I think this smells yummy. The hotter, the better," Melisa says, sweat pouring off the top of her head. "If you don't need to take a cold shower after eating a plate of hot wings, it wasn't spicy enough."

Lucas looks at her and says, "You're crazy."

"Give me that hot sauce. Maybe if I put a little more on this wing, I'll get another contraction."

Lucas makes a *tsk* noise and sighs. "Don't give any of that to Shuck. He's going to breathe fire."

I look down at my little guy begging at my feet. "Shuck, do you want to be a little dragon?" I break a piece of chicken meat with no sauce off a wing and bring it to his nose. He takes one sniff, then backs away.

"See," Lucas says, crossing his arms.

I laugh. The dog will normally devour anything I put in front of him. A small, quick ten-second contraction ripples through my muscles; it's one that I can ignore. "If this buffet doesn't get pumpkin moving, I'm going to go crazy."

Melisa takes finishes another wing. "I think pumpkin is doing this on purpose. That baby is going to be one stubborn kid. Still haven't thought of any names yet?"

"Nope. I'll know what to call little pumpkin when we meet."

"You haven't even thought of a couple? You could always name the baby after someone. Like if it's a girl, you could always go with... Melisa. It's a great name." She bites into another wing. The bone plate is starting to pile up between the both of us. Even if she can tolerate the spice more than me, I'm still hungry and I've just polished off a dozen. She's only eaten eight.

"Nah, it will be something different. I don't know. I honestly haven't thought about a single name. Any of the names I've looked at don't sound right. I'll know soon," I say and rub my belly.

There's smoke. A lot of smoke. And heat. Not like when you sit outside and get a tan, but like the heat from an oven when you open it and it blasts you in the face at four hundred degrees. The kind of heat that feels like your eyebrows have singed off.

Children's laughter fills the hallway. Giggles and playful banter that become shrieks of terror come from behind a locked door. Banging on the doors, I try to rescue the kids, but there's too much smoke and I don't know what room they are in. Every time I think I'm smashing into the right door, their cries sound like they are coming from a different room. I keep pounding, but it's too late. Everything is on fire. Including me.

"Eve, Eve. Wake up," a distant voice calls out. "Eve, Eve, wake up. The bed is wet."

Somehow, I fell asleep. My underwear is damp and warm. The mattress under me is also wet, not soaked but damp, like I might have accidentally peed in my sleep, which, from the nightmares, has happened a couple times. Thank god for the mattress protector.

"Augh. I need to go to the bathroom." I roll out of bed and stand, only to feel a warm, constant trickle going down my leg. I clench my muscles, trying not to pee all over the floor, but I can't stop the flow. "Ah, Lucas?"

He is sitting up, getting ready to change the sheets. "Did you pee or…"

"I think you might want to call the doctor," I say just in time before a contraction starts. A big one. It crawls slowly from my back around my stomach, sucking my breath out, leaving me in a hunched position for thirty seconds. "Now. Call now. I have to pee, but I can't tell what's coming out of me anymore."

He already has the phone to his ear with one hand as he helps me to the bathroom with the other. On the way to the toilet, I notice the clock: six-thirty a.m. on Christmas Eve. Really, baby, you couldn't have come yesterday? You really needed to be a Christmas baby?

"Doctor will be here in fifteen minutes. The rest of the team should be here around the same time too. Do you want me to wake Melisa?"

"No, let her sleep in for a little longer. The contractions aren't close enough yet," I say while I pee and other fluids come out. It's a weird sensation. Another contraction begins. My body tenses as I feel the muscles pull together, then release like an accordion. This one isn't as bad as the last. "That was close. I don't know how far apart that was," I groan, "but it hurts."

"That was only a few minutes. Doctor Mitchell will be here soon."

He gives me a kiss on the forehead and rubs my back. I'm still sitting on the toilet. It still feels like I'm dripping. Like a warm, leaky faucet that won't stop.

"Let's get you in the shower. Relax under the water while I make you a cup of tea, my queen."

"That sounds good."

He helps me out of my clothes and into the shower, comfortably seated on the bench. I get a few minutes of peace before I feel another cramp tighten in my belly. It's not as bad as the last one and doesn't make me bend over. The warm water is soothing, and as much as I wasn't a fan of the birthing pool, I might actually get in it.

"Girl, hey, how are you doing?" Melisa comes into the bathroom wearing a fuzzy purple bathrobe. She almost looks like Barney.

"Okay. Why aren't you sleeping?"

"Had the windows open and I heard a moan. Saw the lights come on in the kitchen and thought that it might be time."

"My water broke. I don't know if it's now or later. The last two contractions weren't too big, but they were closer. I haven't timed them, but I'd estimate three to four minutes apart."

"Damn. When is your team coming?"

"They are on the way. Can you hand me that towel? I want to get out and walk."

"Sure, Evie. Whatever you need, I'm here."

"I love you, dude."

She opens the shower door and turns off the water for me, passing me the towel. "Here we go," she says, helping me off the shower bench. "Let's get you out of the slippery bathroom. Just being in here is making me anxious."

She holds my arm as we walk over to my bed and, with Melisa's help, I pull a nightgown over my head. I don't bother with underwear. No bra, nothing. I just want to be naked. It's too hot. The temperature on the wall says sixty-four. I don't believe it.

"Hello, Mommy," Jill says, coming into the bedroom. She lives the closest. Her hair is up in a tight bun and she's wearing green leggings with a red shirt. "I hear today is the big day. Oh, you are so beautiful," she says, cupping my cheek, and then places a hand on my belly. "A little present for the world. Such a happy day."

I think of my doula as a coach. An extra support member who stands beside me while giving birth. Even if she isn't medically trained, she has experience. Most of the time when I see her, she tells me how strong I am, how beautiful, and is always trying to empower me. I've never been to her house, but I'd guess there are crystals and geodes all over the place. She's all about positive energy.

Five minutes later, Doctor Mitchell comes in wearing yellow scrubs and a backpack, with a cup of coffee in one hand and briefcase in the other. "I've spoken with Mary and Elisa; they should be here in the next couple of minutes. How are you feeling, Eve?"

"I want pumpkin out."

"I know, I know. Soon. Jill, if you would help her onto the table so I can take a peek, see how far along she is."

I walk to the table and Jill helps me up onto it and slides my gown up. Yeah, no underwear was a safe bet. After this, I'll put on a disposable panty. I'm sure it will be a mess from this point out.

"Breakfast should be here within an hour," Lucas says, carrying a mug. "I have tea and coffee in the kitchen until it arrives. Here you are, my queen." The tea smells inviting, exactly how I like it, decaf black tea with milk and sugar.

Mary and Elisa follow Lucas into the room, putting down their gear and getting organized. Everyone around us moves into action, putting on gloves, straightening out this, getting out that—it's a whirlwind. Doctor Mitchell comes over to the table with her purple gloves on. I give the cup back to Lucas and prepare for her to examine me.

"Time to find out how dilated you are." She sticks her fingers inside, spreading her two fingers apart. "You're about five centimeters. Closer. In a few hours, this little one will be making a debut."

"Not now?" I ask, hoping that maybe she can do something, anything.

Doctor Mitchell peels off her gloves and says, "I'm afraid not. This takes time. You have to wear this. It monitors both of your heart rates." She straps a belt with a device the size of a cell phone around my belly. When it touches my skin, it beeps in two different tones. "That fast heartbeat is the baby, the slower one is yours."

"How fast is too fast?" I ask, hearing the beats pick up pace more than during the nonstress test.

"I'll let you know. Don't worry about that. All of this is normal. It's just another way to keep you both healthy. Start walking around. That helps. Sometimes the movement speeds everything along."

Jill nods. "Yup, walking helps. Why don't you, Lucas, and Shuck go for a little walk in the backyard? Get some fresh air. We'll straighten up this area, I'll light some candles, we'll put on some nice soothing music, make this room a calm space."

Lucas helps me off the table and the women go to work. The bed is still a mess, but Melisa is working on changing the sheets. Jill is cleaning the floor and the trail to the bathroom. Elisa is unraveling a hose from the bathroom sink to the inflatable pool. The thought of sitting in a pool with everything that's coming out of me is gross, but floating in general sounds nice. It's really been relaxing to float in the pool; it takes pressure off my back.

"We'll walk around the backyard. Do laps with Shuck. He's been worried," Lucas says, distracting me from all the movement.

Shuck is a step behind, following me diligently. Outside, the dawn air is cooler than inside, allowing me to relax in the early morning sun. We take a few steps onto the patio. Lucas hands me my tea mug and I take a sip. Reaching forward to put my cup down, I feel muscles tighten in my back, flowing like a wave over my stomach. The cramps intensify, making me moan, and I curl over the patio table. One hand grabs Lucas's arm, the other the table. His free hand rubs my lower back, massaging it gently.

Squatting in this awkward position feels good. It used to be when I would start feeling these contractions that moving would help make them less painful. That's not helping anymore. I must be getting closer. That one had to have been close to a minute long.

"Do you want to go back inside?" he asks, stroking my back.

"No. Keep walking. Maybe a couple more of those and then I'll be ready to push."

If only it were that easy.

Walking. Floating. Squatting on my yoga ball. Pacing back and forth. Getting in and out of the shower. Stretching out on all fours like a dog. This is all I can do right now. When I have a moment of rest, I guzzle water and close my eyes. As much as I would love to eat, I don't have an appetite. It might be from all the pain. I almost feel nauseous, but not. It also might be from the cramps that just won't stop. The smell of the dinner buffet from the kitchen is appealing, until a contraction hits and I think if I ate, I'd throw up.

"Never again," I tell Melisa. "Never again will I do this."

She sits back and smiles.

"No, really. If I ever tell you I'm thinking of having another kid, I want you to punch me in the stomach. Like super hard to remind me of the pain."

"Ooh, I think I'll take you up on that offer at least once," she says, passing me my water bottle while I lean forward on my birthing ball.

Hunched over feels good. Plus, the constant movement helps distract me from the pain, and I'm not certain I could stay still if I tried. Making *oh* noises and moans with long breaths also is what I'm focusing on. Any information that I learned from watching those videos is out the window. All I'm doing is listening to my body. If I feel the need to get on all fours and moan, I do it. If my body wants to feel less gravity, I step into the pool and float, letting the buoyancy ease the contractions. If I want to sit in the shower, I sit on the bench and let the water flow over me.

"Oh!" A contraction hits my back harder than any previous ones, stretching and pulling apart my muscles before squeezing them together in a gradual movement of agony. "Oh, no!" The spasm makes me grit my teeth. I wish I was back in the pool for that one.

"I think it's time to check how dilated you are. If you are comfortable, you don't need to move." Doctor Mitchell comes over and lifts my gown while I'm leaning over my ball.

"I'm not comfortable and I'm not moving."

"That's perfectly fine," the doctor says while sliding her fingers in. "Nine centimeters. A few more strong contractions and you'll be ready to push."

"More? I don't want to anymore! Rggh!" Another violent one hits me. My body trembles as I try to control the movement. My hands clench into tight balls, making my knuckles turn white as I cry in pain. "I want to go back in the pool!"

It felt better in there, floating. The weightless feeling in my belly made the contractions less severe. Lucas and Melisa brace me and help me stand. A small contraction begins. I wrap my arms around Lucas and sway my hips. He swings with me and it feels for a moment like we are dancing as I wiggle out the pain. His midnight sky eyes shimmer. I lean my head against his chest and rock back and forth in his arms.

"We haven't danced together in a long time," he says, caressing and bracing my arms.

"We'll have to do that more often after pumpkin comes," I tell him with a heavy breath.

Now that I can walk, I get back into the pool. Lucas bought a little bucket water heater that looks like a curling iron. Jill sticks it into a pot of water, heats it up, and dumps it in. She monitors the pool temperature, making sure it doesn't go above a hundred degrees or below ninety-seven. Her other job is making sure the pool is clean by fishing out any clumps of I-don't-want-to-know. It keeps the pool almost clean. Inside, I lean against the inflatable edge and grip it with both hands as another contraction builds and builds, threatening to never stop.

Shuck runs in and out of the room when I start to cry. I think he doesn't know what to do, but he wants to help. So instead he runs around like a crazy dog having a panic attack. My poor pup.

"You're doing great, Eve. Just keep breathing," Jill says while she adds more hot water.

Melisa brings my water bottle, refilled with a straw in it, and holds it in front of me so I can just sip.

Mary takes a cool washcloth and passes it to Lucas to dab my brow. They really all work together well. I thought having four people besides Melisa and Lucas was going to be too many in the house, but it's the perfect amount. Even if most of the time they sit and look bored at me, waiting for the show to start. For their jobs to begin.

The doctor and Mary the midwife are the ones working the most; Jill my doula and Elisa are here to assist and take care of the baby while Mary and Dr. Mitchell take care of me. So until pumpkin joins us, they aren't too busy at the moment. In the meantime, they work on keeping me comfortable, which, unless they can get this baby out faster, there's no way to make that happen.

Thunder rumbles in the distance, coming closer. Melisa looks out the window. "It doesn't look like rain." The lights flicker. "Maybe that was a car accident or something. Someone must have hit a pole."

I howl as pain floods my senses. On my knees in the pool, I scream.

"Soon," Doctor Mitchell says. I hate that word.

Everyone gets into place. Outside the pool, directly in front of me, Melisa and Lucas sit ready to help with whatever I need. Lucas cools my brow and holds my hand. Melisa offers me water when I need it. Behind me, Mary waits so she can easily catch the baby. Elisa stands next to her. Both women look ready to dive into the pool in case of an emergency.

The lights keep fluttering. And then, the power goes out. "Thankfully I brought candles, but do you have more?" Jill asks as everyone takes out their phones and turns on their flashlights.

Melisa gets up, "I think I saw some in the hallway closet." She runs out of the room.

The house sounds still. There is an eerie lack of nose, in between all the grunts I make. Like dead air. No fans. No motors running. No currents sending energy to the various devices in the house. Just silence.

Another contraction rips through me. I yell, as it feels like I'm splitting apart.

Melisa runs back into the room with a couple scented candles. She and Jill light them, placing them to help us see.

Tears fill my eyes. This is the most pain I've ever been in. Nothing compares to this. Nothing.

"Eve, look at me. Listen to my words. When I say push, I want you to push," Doctor Mitchell says in a steady tone.

A hand rubs my back. "You're doing great, Mommy. Just stay focused," Jill says.

I gasp for a breath and feel the next wave of pain strike. "Oh!"

"Push!" the doctor yells.

"Rggh!" I push. Tears stream down my face. Shaking, I push and push until there is no air left in my lungs. My body trembles. Sweat drenches my hair, runs down my neck and chest.

"Just a couple more," Dr. Mitchell says.

A couple more. I don't know if I can. This is almost unbearable. I should have gotten an epidural.

"Push!" Dr. Mitchell says.

I do. I listen to my body and push, screaming the whole time.

"I can see hair!" Mary says.

The pain... it's unlike anything I've ever felt. I don't know if I can do this. I open my eyes and take a deep breath in. Lucas flashes one of his genuine smiles, making the stars in his eyes sparkle. His hand clamps onto mine.

Melisa rubs my arm and offers me a sip of water. "You got this. You are stronger than you know. Girl, get this baby out."

I nod and brace myself. Teeth grinding, I feel the next spasm and hear the word *push* and give everything I can. Someone says slows down. I try to control the force and stop. It's like trying to stop a tsunami. I take a long inhale, expanding my lungs as far as they will inflate.

"One more. Go!"

I push. I scream. I sweat. I cry. I curse. I feel.

Shuck howls with me from the other room.

Then it happens. A slip and whoosh as my child slides out and into the world. I gasp and watch Mary carefully bring my baby out of the water and place the wailing newborn in my arms.

Pumpkin screams. I behold my little creation in the soft candlelight. "Hi. Hi, honey. I love you. Hi."

I laugh and cry, looking at my sweet baby. The child in my arms is perfect. Rosy cheeks. Green-blue eyes. Wisps of brown hair. Chubby arms. Five fingers. Plump belly. No wings. No halo. Just perfection. "It's a girl."

Everyone oohs and awws, giving me their congratulations, telling me how cute she is, and how beautiful. Someone mentions the time, nine thirty-six. The electricity turns on. The lights flicker, illuminating her lovely face.

Lucas leans in and touches her little cheek. "She's precious."

"Hi. This is your daddy," I tell my baby.

"Daddy, would you like to do the honors?" Mary asks, handing him scissors for the umbilical cord. She takes two clamps and puts them close to the baby's belly button.

"Yes." He takes the scissors. "Right here?"

"Yup. They don't feel anything. The cord is tough to cut; keep cutting until you're through," Mary says.

He cuts carefully and slowly, severing the cord that has kept us connected this whole time. Tears fill my eyes as I realize we will no longer be attached to one another.

She stops crying and moves her lips together in search of a nipple. I bring her to my breast and I watch her take her first sip. The feeling is weird as she pulls and sucks.

"Hi, Seraphina. Seraphina Ann Burns, welcome to the world."

"That's a beautiful name," Melisa says, peering over my shoulder to get a glimpse.

"You like her name?" I ask Lucas.

"I think it's perfect for her," he says, giving her a kiss on the head. "She's beautiful. Gorgeous like her mother."

It pains me to hand her over to be weighed and examined, but Mary and Elisa are pros and I need this moment to freshen up. Once we get into bed, I don't think the two of us are getting out. I plan on snuggling that little body all night and day. Daddy can get diapers and anything else we need while we camp out in bed. He'll be our butler.

When I was sitting in the pool, I didn't think about what I was sitting in. In the shower, I cringe, watching blood drip off me. Overall, I was lucky. Only two stitches. At seven pounds, one ounce and seventeen inches long, she's tiny. A petite little girl.

It doesn't take long to get changed into fresh clothes, into bed, and snuggling with my daughter against my chest. Jill and Melisa started to clean up the pool so that by the time I got out of the bathroom, everything was almost dismantled and cleaned up.

A half hour after my shower, I've eaten a chicken parmesan sandwich and called my parents to tell them the news and sent them a picture of her cute little face. Within that time, the team had the pool fully taken down, the area sterilized, and the room put back together like labor and delivery didn't take place in that corner of the bedroom.

Alone—well, just the two of us and Shuck—I climb into bed and arrange my pillows at an angle so it's comfortable to sit. Since she suckled from my left, I get her settled onto my right. Even though she's cleaned up, she has this new baby smell. A smell that I could sniff all day and night. It's soothing.

Melisa went to her guest house to take a shower and get some sleep. Lucas is showing the delivery team out, I'm sure giving each one a large tip for all their incredible work.

My phone on the nightstand does a bell chime. I reach to get it, gazing at my beautiful girl, when something catches my eye. I lift her tiny head up to mine. Milk dribbles from my breast and her lips as she whines in protest.

She whimpers, wanting to reattach to my boob, but I tilt her head. I look into her right ear. There, on the edge of her ear canal, is a tiny little birthmark. I spent well over twenty minutes looking over every inch of her tiny frame and saw nothing before. The closer I look, the more I know what it is.

Bells ring on my phone again, a reminder of the message I haven't looked at. It's hard to look away from the cooing baby in my lap. It's hard to take my eyes away from the truth. What I've known the whole time.

She looks up at me with helpless, big teal eyes. Her lips keep trying to suckle. Her arms keep trying to wriggle inside the swaddled blanket, but it's snug tight. A smile glides across her milky lips as she stares up at me. Her mommy.

She's mine.

Mine to mold. Mine to teach. Mine to guide. Mine to love.

I will make her into a good person. Maybe that's part of my power.

I look at my phone and see a simple message from Ken. A single word warning.

Antichrist.

I pick up my daughter and snuggle her against my chest. She goes back to suckling and closes her eyes. Her tiny fingers curl against my skin as she drifts into a peaceful slumber.

I look back down at my phone and type a simple response.

I know.

The end.

Katie Zaber

Acknowledgements

As always, I want to thank Susan Gottfried for correcting my horrible grammar, Agata Bukovero for her beautiful artwork, and Mira Singer for formatting. Thank you.

I want to thank my boyfriend who keeps me fed and laundry clean. I couldn't do any of this without your constant support, guidance, and love.

Parents, my crazy imagination came from somewhere—I blame you!

My family and friends are amazing. I couldn't ask for a better support group.

I need to thank my hard working beta readers. Their insight has been invaluable.

This has been another wacky year, but I'm grateful for many things, including the people in my life and my readers.

Thank you.

Katie Zaber

Katie Zaber knows the best way to decide who is cooking dinner is with a Nerf gun fight in the living room. Her boyfriend is an exceptional cook. When she isn't baking, going to wine tastings, or reading, she's busy planning her next trip to Six Flags Great Adventure or Long Beach Island, New Jersey. As a child, her mother would read stories about Atlantis and other fictional places that she dreamed of exploring, fueling her love of history, adventure, and fantasy. These days, she's busy with her many projects and endless ideas.

https://zaberbooks.com/
https://www.facebook.com/dalyaseries
https://twitter.com/Zaberbooks

Printed in Great Britain
by Amazon